S0-ARY-485

Praise for *Such a Pretty Face*

"This is a very enjoyable anthology based on the premise that not all heroes have marvelous pecs and abs and the heroine is not always a beautiful, blonde size three. Here the characters may be of a larger than normal size, but their heroic actions are just as big as they are."

"Elizabeth Ann Scarborough tells the story of a normal princess who is cursed and turns into a plump princess who ultimately finds herself in "Worse Than the Curse". "A Hero, Plain and Simple" by Ralph Gamelli tells of a reporter who get a new slant on a story from the janitor. "The Blood Orange Tree" by Marian Crane is the story of a youth out of place in Phoenix looking for the seedlings needed to save his people. Jon Hansen's tale of the "Eater" is one of genetic advancement to help during toxic spills. Casilla turned dangerously thin after calling up "Demon Bone" in a tale by Teresa Noelle Roberts. Catherine Lundoff's tale of "Vadija" is the story of one woman's search to find out how she lost her laugh. A seven foot three hundred pound warrior woman dresses as the Queen of the Amazons to affect "Lady Emerdirael's Rescue" by Lisa Deason."

"Other tales by Gene Wolfe, KD Wentworth, Jody Lynn Nye, and many others make this one of the most unusual and rewarding volumes of the year so far. This is a book filled with pleasant surprises that should be enjoyed by all. It also goes a long way into showing that everyone can be a hero regardless of stature or girth. Be on the look out for this."—*Baryon Magazine* #77

"Some of you may already know Lee Martindale from her appearances in *MZB's Fantasy Magazine* or from her own magazine *Rump Parliament*, a size-acceptance magazine that has featured some awesome speculative fiction stories over the years. *Such a Pretty Face* offers a smorgasbord of stories populated with hefty heroines and heroes. Some are sweet, some are spicy, some are bitter…all will stick to your ribs. My favorites include Jane Yolen's poem "Fat Is Not a Fairy Tale," the spooky "Demon Bone" by Teresa Noelle Roberts which explores Elemental magic, "The Fat Cats' Tale" by Martha A. Compton which explains why cats dash madly about at times, Laura J. Underwood's mythic "The Wife of Ben-Y-Ghloe" which reminds me of certain Celtic and Native American legends, and "A Taste of Song" by K.D. Wentworth which takes shows how the difference between a blessing and a curse lies in the ear of the beholder."

"Only rarely can I pick a single favorite story out of an entire anthology, but this time the prize goes to "The Search for a Sipping House" by Joette M. Rozanski. For vampire fans, this story alone justifies the cost of the book. The author begins with the fascinating premise that vampires can shapeshift into either animal or—go ahead, laugh, it's hilarious—*furniture* forms. The "Animates" and "Inanimates" do not get along at all well. This story concerns a Brood of vampires who take form as a lamp, a marble sculpture, an end table, even a rocking chair. They need to find a place to stay, but that's not easy for a set of mismatched furniture that has a tendency to bite! This is the most original motif, and the funniest vampire story, that I've read in ages. But it's also got some heart-wrenching drama to it. I would just love to see this developed into a novel; it would really stand out in today's deluge of blood-drenched bodice-rippers."

"Overall, I found this anthology immensely satisfying. You can practically dance to the music of shattering stereotypes. In these pages, fat people are beautiful, desirable, sexy, competent, intelligent, whimsical, resourceful, confident…powerful. These are people who can make a difference. Lee Martindale has put together a splendid set of stories that demonstrate the worthiness of fat characters; hopefully now more editors will follow in her footsteps, so we can see more of this quality fiction on the market. Check out the publisher's Website at: **http://www.MeishaMerlin.com"**

"*Such a Pretty Face* covers a wide range of fantasy, science fiction, and horror; fans of any type of speculative fiction will love it. But it's an absolute essential for anyone of size...particularly those who have personally heard the horrible comment on which the title is based: "You have such a pretty face, dear; you'd be gorgeous if only you lost some weight." Give the critics a poke in the eye and read this book; it will prove beyond all shadow of a doubt that heroic potential is not something you can measure with a bathroom scale."

Uncommon Sense Award

"This award goes to Lee Martindale and Meisha Merlin Publishing, Inc. for their commitment to honing the cutting edge of speculative fiction by identifying—and then smashing through—one of the few remaining barriers in the genre. In today's more liberal atmosphere, you rarely find a consistent pattern in editorial prejudice, but there has indeed remained a tendency to reject stories that feature fat characters in prominent, positive roles. It's hard to find even a well-rounded fat villain, for that matter. Yet, supported by the editor and publisher, the authors in this book rose to the challenge. *Such a Pretty Face* proves once and for all that girth is no measure for greatness. These plus-size protagonists will really steal your heart. I hope this anthology raises awareness among editors, authors, and readers so that we can see more stories like these in other venues. Take a bow, ladies and gentlemen: you did a fabulous job."—*Spicy Green Iguana*, May 2000

"Fat is a fantasy (and SF) issue in this anthology, which provides 23 stories with well-padded characters... The rather inspiring forword and introduction discuss the challenge of writing fat-positive stories. In Practice, while some of the authors tackle the issue head-on, others simply portray chatacters who happen to be hefty. My favorite stories took a humorous angle, playing off of expectations, often in more ways than one."—*Locus,* June2000

Such a Pretty Face

edited by

Lee Martindale

Meisha Merlin Publishing, Inc
Atlanta, GA

This is a work of fiction. All the characters and events portrayed in this book are fictitious. Any resemblance to real people or events is purely coincidental.

SUCH A PRETTY FACE

An MM Publishing Book
Published by Meisha Merlin Publishing, Inc.
PO Box 7
Decatur, GA 30031

Editing & interior layout by Stephen Pagel
Copyediting & proofreading by Teddi Stransky
Cover art by Doug Beekman

ISBN: Hard cover 1-892065-27-4
Soft cover 1-892065-28-2

http://www.MeishaMerlin.com

First MM Publishing edition: May 2000

Printed in the United States of America
0 9 8 7 6 5 4 3 2 1

Table of Contents

Dedication 10
Foreword by Judy Sullivan 11
Introduction by Lee Martindale 15
Fat Is Not A Fairy Tale by Jane Yolen 19
Worse Than The Curse by Elizabeth Ann Scarborough 21
A Hero, Plain and Simple by Ralph Gamelli 45
Seliki by Cynthia McQuillin 53
The Blood Orange Tree by Marian Crane 59
Eater by Jon Hansen 73
Demon Bone by Teresa Noelle Roberts 85
The Fat Cats' Tale by Martha A. Compton 99
Vadija by Catherine Lundoff 109
Lady Emerdirael's Rescue by Lisa Deason 119
The Wife of Ben-Y-Ghloe by Laura J. Underwood 135
Chance Hospitality by Carol Y. Huber & Mike C. Baker 151
The Fat Magician by Gene Wolfe 157
The Search For A Sipping House by Joette M. Rozanski 169
A Taste of Song by K. D. Wentworth 183
Casting Against Type by Jody Lynn Nye 199
Meluse's Counsel by Connie Wilkins 215
Polyformus Perfectus by Paula L. Fleming 225
Eleven To Seven by Bradley H. Sinor 241
Last Chance Gravity Fill Station by Celeste Allen 249
Nuclear Winter by Selina Rosen 261
The Djinn Game by Patrice E. Sarath 265
Stoop Ladies by Barbara Krasnoff 279
Naratha's Shadow by Sharon Lee & Steve Miller 289
About the Editor 307
About the Authors 309

Dedications

In bright memory of Avalon's Lady,
because some debts can never be paid,

and

For Judy, who set the challenge,
Cynthia, who set the path,
Bob, who set the tune,
And, most especially,
For George, who sets the universe aright.

Foreword

Speculative fiction writers dream up worlds and situations beyond the realm of our reality, but most still seem unable to break the mind-set regarding size. Reflecting the bias and prejudice of their culture, they devise heroes who are strong, clever, handsome, human, alien, mechanical, pointy-eared, blue, green and/or hairy, but almost never fat. In a genre where humans (and others) of virtually every description are sculpted to capture our minds and challenge our views of reality, they are almost, unless background characters, never fleshed out as fat.

There are, of course, some central, positively-portrayed characters of size populating speculative fiction. Robert A. Heinlein has given us several, including Jubal Harshaw and Anne The Fair Witness in *Stranger In A Strange Land.* Heinlein also wrote a man into *The Man Who Sold the Moon* who was described as being too old and too fat to go to the moon but who did it regardless. Other stories which give fat characters a fair shake include *Two To Conquer* by Marion Zimmer Bradley and Rosemary Edghill's *Sword of Maiden's Tears.* But these characters and stories are certainly the exception, rather than the rule.

When science fiction and fantasy characters are described as being fat, they are almost always based solely on negative stereotypes. *Star Wars'* Jabba the Hutt is slovenly, greedy and evil, the epitome of wantonness taken to excess. The infamous Dune character, Baron Vladimir Harkonnen, is a thoroughly disgusting creature—diseased, ugly, brutal, cruel and crass to the extreme. Neither has any redeeming qualities.

At Diversicon (SF Minnesota) in 1999, a panel headed by Paula Fleming addressed the question "Do You Have to Look Good in Skintight Spandex to Explore the Universe?" Panelists Terry Garey, Phyllis Ann Karr, Harry LeBlanc and

Lois McMaster Bujold headed up a lively discussion that addressed many issues pertaining to writing fat characters: the definition of "overweight"; why fat people are the target of bias; stereotypes regarding sex; other stereotypes, including lack of self-control, laziness, etc.; and the practical aspects for a fat space-traveler. Paula believes the participants came away feeling validated in writing fat characters and more aware of the stereotypes. She anticipates seeing more fat characters in speculative fiction in the future.

Lee Martindale, size-activist, writer and editor, has called on her experience in these related fields to create this exciting anthology of size-positive stories. She has sought out and brought together an innovative collection of science fiction and fantasy short stories populated with interesting men and women of abundance. These are characters and situations we can not only enjoy but identify with.

Donella of "The Wife of Ben-Y-Ghloe," is calm, loyal, strong, and quick to take action. Laura Underwood, the writer who brought her to life, says, "If we fail to look at what is inside a person, the real person beneath the exterior, I think we do a discredit to ourselves and others. I hope that by creating characters like Donella, I will be adding to literature a character who will just be remembered as a wonderful person to know."

Paula Fleming gifts us with Ruby Chandel in her story "Polyformus Perfectus." Ruby is a 5'5", 200-pound black woman with a B.S. in xenobiology and a Master's in sports physiology. She teaches fitness classes at gyms on space colonies, with clientele of all shapes and abilities, including those with tentacles and five legs. She is brassy, tough, caring and definitely not stereotypical.

These are just two of the innovative, size-positive characters the reader will get to know and love. They will challenge other writers to add size diversity to their own work.

Lee Martindale is an accomplished writer with her own list of genre fiction, including "Yearbride" from Marion

Zimmer Bradley's *Snows of Darkover* anthology, "Mrs. Bailey's Harp" from John Peyton's *Zone 9* Magazine, "The Impression of Power" from Marion Zimmer Bradley and Rachel Holmen's *Sword and Sorceress #14,* "Hell Hath No Fury..." from *Sword and Sorceress #17*, "Neighborhood Watch" from Issue #40 of *Marion Zimmer Bradley's Fantasy Magazine*, "The Folly of Assumption" in *Pulp Eternity*—the *Alternatives I* Issue, and "No Warranties Expressed" in *XOddity Magazine.* In "Neighborhood Watch" and "The Folly of Assumption," Lee added fat characters whose size was an important—and positive—element of the stories to the body of fantasy literature.

Lee's feisty magazine *Rump Parliament* has been the number one source for information for size activists in the world since its inception in 1992. Not only does she keep close tabs on size discrimination and prejudice in every aspect of the fat person's life, she reports with a no-holds-barred flair, boldly calling absolutely anyone to task for bad behavior and praising those who *get it* and *live it.*

This anthology is a natural progression for her work to take. *Such A Pretty Face* will open the minds of publishers, writers and readers to strong, well-crafted characters who reflect the range of sizes in the *real* world.

Open your mind and enjoy!

Judy Sullivan
Author, *Size Wise*
September 1999

Introduction

It's been over thirty years since a friend in college introduced me to science fiction, and only a little less than that since another put me on the path to Faery. As these things go, I was a latecomer to both. And while the frenzy of the newly-converted long ago mellowed to comfortable enthusiasm not unlike a years-old, well-established domestic partnership, the reasons I read SF&F happily remain the same.

I am, without apologies, an imagination junkie. I crave new ideas, the presentation of new concepts, and having my chocks knocked out from under me with a new slant on the conventional. Speculative fiction feeds that craving better than any other genre I know, with the happy side benefit of being just plain good storytelling.

It does something else better, too. It often takes old ideas and concepts that have fallen out of societal fashion and reintroduces them to readers with enough imagination to appreciate them. I'm thinking here of ideas such as *loyalty, honor* and *courage*, and concepts like *the hero*. I've even heard it suggested that the reason people read science fiction and fantasy is because there are few heroes in *real life*.

Which brings me to another theory I once heard advanced by an individual who looked my Venus of Willendorf body up and down and didn't even *try* to hide her look of disgust: that the reason so many fat people read SF&F is because there are no fat heroes in *real life*. "Fat people," she pontificated, "simply *cannot* be heroic."

I disagree; I grew up with fat heroes. Among them, the grandfather who raised me and to whom I give a good portion of the credit for the fighter I grew up to be. He was fat, a bear of a man, and a hero every day of his life. And my high school Latin teacher who was very short, very round, more than a bit dotty and who maintained the shelter where sparks of independent thought, creativity and love of learning could survive the educational system.

I still meet fat heroes on a daily basis. The people who refuse to take "you're too fat to work here" for an answer. The size issues activists working to change societal attitudes, medical disinformation and the silly notion that body bigotry is "for our own good." The writers who refuse to grab the cheap and easy laugh of "fat jokes" or use the shorthand of stereotypes. And the thousands upon thousands of fat people who refuse to measure down to the rubber ruler of height/weight charts (or whatever they're being called this week), who pointedly ask "over WHOSE weight?", who reject societal pressure to be less than they are, and who opt for being strong, healthy and fully involved with life.

This anthology began with a premise—that heroes come in all sizes, and the conviction that it was time, and long past time, to tell the tales of those on the upper end of the size diversity spectrum. It took form thanks to the courage and unstinting support of Stephen Pagel and Meisha Merlin Publishing. But without the writers, who turned their talents to the telling of tales it was time to tell, it would never have come about. To them go my deepest thanks and my profound appreciation.

And now to you, good reader, comes the most important part. Do you have the imagination to consider something besides the current conventions of *ideal*? Can you handle the idea of heroes who look like more than half of the population? Are you ready to encounter one who just might look like you? Be warned: it's a rather heady experience, and more than a little fun.

Enjoy!

Lee Martindale, Editor
HarpHaven, Plano, Texas
October 1999

Such a Pretty Face

Fat Is Not A Fairy Tale
by Jane Yolen

I am thinking of a fairy tale,
Cinder Elephant,
Sleeping Tubby,
Snow Weight,
where the princess is not
anorexic, wasp-waisted,
flinging herself down the stairs.

I am thinking of a fairy tale,
Hansel and Great,
Repoundsel,
Bounty and the Beast,
where the beauty
has a pillowed breast,
and fingers plump as sausage.

I am thinking of a fairy tale
that is not yet written,
for a teller not yet born,
for a listener not yet conceived,
for a world not yet won,
where everything round is good:
the sun, wheels, cookies, and the princess.

Call it backlash from a warped childhood ("Mommy, did the Princess look like me?" "No, dear…she was thin and pretty"), but I've always wanted to see a fairy tale that turned that particular convention on its shell-like ear. Either someone let slip my secret, or Elizabeth Ann Scarborough is similarly warped. Either way, the result is a treat.

Worse Than The Curse
by Elizabeth Ann Scarborough

In the old days, the crowd of suitors at the palace gate had been downright unmanageable. Knights and princes and even a king or two, each trying to pull rank on the other, had clamored for a glimpse of, a word from, a moment with the beautiful Princess Babette. Princess Babette was, as was *de rigueur* for one of her station, the fairest of the fair. The gold of her hair was as lustrous as all of that in the royal treasury, the blue of her eyes was as guilelessly clear and deep as a cloudless spring sky, the rose of her cheeks and lips put the sunsets and dawns to shame, and her complexion was dewy and creamy.

As if the fine coloring wasn't enough, her very bones were beautiful: high cheeks, a firm chin and a wingcurve of jawline sweeping above a swanlike neck. Her figure was a symphony of slender, willowy grace, amply but not over-generously curved at breast and hip.

And all of that beauty went to he who won her hand in marriage, along with the aforementioned treasury (which was far more abundant, if no more lustrous, than Babette's tresses), a great deal of fertile land, and a large and competent army. In short, a kingdom for which many of the noble suitors would have been happy to marry a far less beauteous princess.

Every day the royal audience chamber was choked with petitioners for the hand of the princess. Babette's royal mum and dad lay awake nights thinking of impossible tasks for the fellows to do, impossible things for them to fetch, to prove themselves worthy of the princess. Babette herself loved dreaming up and suggesting little embellishments—the mountain to be scaled by the king with the unfortunate wart on his nose should be made of glass, for instance. That would keep him busy. He'd have to find the thing first. She herself would have given less difficult tasks to the younger, better-looking princes, but often these did not have fortunes that matched her own, and the King her father sent the poor dears off to claim the single eyes of fire-breathing dragons or clean the stables of giants.

Fortunately, unlike the impractical suitors of princesses in stories, most of the kings and princes and knights understood such tasks for what they were—a way of being told they were basically unacceptable unless they proved to be more than human. They were gently-born humans, it was true. Noble, even royal humans. But when it came to fire-breathing dragons, again unlike the hapless princes in storybooks, the suitors showed a streak of self-preservation and common sense that, had Babette's father and mother thought about it, were quite desirable characteristics in a son-in-law. Though they sighed and pined and cast many a backward look at the beautiful Babette as they slunk away, most of the suitors declined to die for her and decided instead to fall in love with someone a bit more accessible.

Not so with one candidate, however. King Vladimirror I was very tenacious. He was actually a wizard, the former Grand Vizier of a mighty kingdom, and by his wizardry he had overthrown the rightful monarch. He had no scruples about using that same magic to climb glass mountains, clean giants' stables, quench fire-breathing dragons, and whatever else was required.

Babette's problem in this case was simple. She didn't like him. Didn't trust him. As he crawled up one side of the glass mountain atop which she perched, she could feel her skin wanting to crawl down the other side.

"Now!" he announced, when he stood on the pinnacle with her. "I am ready to claim my prize."

"Not so fast," she said, hastily dreaming up another

embellishment. "You've only passed the first part of the test."

"What do you mean the first part?" he demanded. "I've done more than any of the other candidates."

"Yes," she said, "but *they* didn't even finish the first part. There's more."

"Very well," he said. "I will do anything to win you."

"Why?" she asked.

"I beg your pardon?"

"Why will you do anything to win me? The obvious answer is my dowry, but I'm told you live too far away for us to consolidate our lands, and that your kingdom is far wealthier than ours. Are you a very greedy king, that you want the little wealth I could bring with me?"

He *was* actually a very greedy man indeed, but his greed had never been confined to gold. His eyes roamed over the territory he currently desired and he thought of the pleasure of owning something—someone—other men had coveted, of the power he would have over her to do his bidding. "The answer should be obvious every time you look into your glass, madame. You are very beautiful."

"True. But you're not. So my next question is, why should I be won by you?"

"I have braved the dangers set before your suitors and I alone have prevailed."

"Yes, but you used trickery."

"Magic, madame. I am wise in the ways of magic."

"Wise? That is not the same thing. And I have never heard that a tricky husband was necessarily the best one. No, I think you have used an unfair advantage and besides, I don't wish to travel so far from home. So sorry. Wrong answers, but thanks for playing. Next!"

Vladimirror was angry. Vladimirror was wrothy, in fact. Foaming at the mouth, in fact. No upstart princess, be she more beautiful than the dawn, was going to humiliate him in that fashion. Or any other fashion, for that matter. "If I can't have you, my proud beauty, no one will," he fumed.

Even to him, that sounded a little trite but then, he was a wizard with spells, not a wizard with words. Nonetheless, he added, "Not even yourself."

"Fine," she said. "Do you mind? It's getting hot up here and I want to get down," and with that she slid down the mountain on her shapely satin-clad rump.

Vladimirror was very unhappy about all of this, but he had not overthrown a monarch because he wore his heart on his sleeve or said what was on his mind. He had cast a curse upon her, though she hadn't noticed, and he left the kingdom smiling, anxious to return to his own kingdom and watch in his scrying glass as his revenge against the haughty princess manifested itself.

"You put the wind up that last one, m'dear," the King said, as he and the Queen joined their daughter and a few hundred of their closest courtiers in sampling the sweetmeats and candies the various suitors had brought in tribute to the princess.

She didn't answer. She was concentrating on the sweetness of the marzipan she had just slipped between her lips. Sweet somethings on the tongue were ever so much nicer than sweet nothings in the ear, she mused.

Unbeknownst to her, the wizard's spell had the result of multiplying the effect of the food she put to her lips. Every morsel added girth to her lissome body. She didn't notice that night, when she slipped under her velvet counterpane and pulled the jeweled midnight-blue draperies surrounding her bed. But the next morning, when her handmaidens tried to help her into her gown of white samite trimmed with little seed pearls and white diamonds, the gown did not fit. She could not even pull it on. Fortunately, all of the handmaidens for fashion-conscious princesses had to be expert dressmakers and designers, and they were able to slit the seams and piece in new fabric. Still, the effect in the mirror was less pleasing to the princess than it had formerly been.

Babette decided white was maybe not her best color. But laborious changes of garment revealed that blue was no better, nor red, green, yellow, violet, lavender, fuchsia, cloth of gold, or silver. Black, the handmaidens informed her, was slimming, but it made Babette feel like a widow.

Oh dear. And she hadn't even married yet. She supposed she had better look at some of the young men more closely.

She didn't get a chance. As soon as the next lot of princes saw her, most of them made their apologies and left. The rest waited until they heard the tests, then they left, too.

Babette felt strangely light, despite her increased weight. She was suddenly left alone—relatively speaking. No suitors waiting. No glass mountains to perch on. No one seemed to care what she was wearing or how she wore her hair. In fact, everyone, including her parents, seemed to be looking the other way when she approached. It made her feel invisible. That was annoying, but also something of a relief. The truth was, no one seemed to recognize her for herself. It was as if Princess Babette was someone else entirely and she was just…this largish girl, who was actually rather hungry.

This proved to be a bit of a problem for everyone else. Now, when Babette reached for the sweetmeats the princes had left behind, her father sighed and her mother gave her A Look. The closest lady-in-waiting said, "Your Highness, perhaps you would like to wait until we can order more rare and lustrous fabric from the importers?" And though she took no more at meal times than she was accustomed to taking, she felt eyes watching each morsel she put to her lips, and found she had quite lost her appetite until she was alone, back in her rooms again.

She was, as one wit put it, "The mock of the town." From being a proud and beautiful princess surrounded by suitors, she had gone almost overnight into being plump and ignored, even by those whom she was quite sure loved her.

It was as if she were a ghost in her own castle. Her own servants snubbed her and when she reacted angrily, her mother, passing by, overheard and took her aside. The Queen searched her daughter's face, her eyes full of pain, and said, "You must not blame your maidens, daughter, or anyone else if you are not as well-treated now as in your slimmer days. Wrath will not restore your beauty nor the power it lent you. With your slenderness, you have lost something of your character."

"But, Mama, that's ridiculous!" Babette stormed. "I haven't lost my character at all. I'm still a virgin!"

"Of course you are. And likely to remain that way unless you take yourself in hand." The sad thing was, Babette could see that the Queen thought she was being kind and giving wise advice. Part of it was wise. Babette never again took out her own frustration on her handmaidens or other people. She learned to get what she needed from them by looking them in the eye and getting them to stick to their jobs. If she saw in their expressions some pain or worry unrelated to herself, she got them to tell her of it, and relieved it if she could. Otherwise she would never have gotten anything done.

But still, without hours to fill dressing and dancing and entertaining suitors, she had a great deal of time on her hands. She drifted, quite by accident, into the great hall where her father was teaching her elder brother, the Crown Prince, about ruling and making good decisions and passing judgments. She sat on the sidelines and listened, day after day, as her father heard each case and spoke to his advisors and listened to them. Then he and her brother weighed each fact until they came to a verdict, issued a decree, upheld or struck down a law, granted an exemption, or a punishment, as the case required. Her father, she realized suddenly, was a very good king. Her brother would be a good king, too, she could tell. They were both fair, listened well, and truly cared about the fate of the people in front of them. They understood how other problems within the kingdom would affect the welfare of those same people.

She came to feel extremely humble and saddened. With such an example she could have been a good ruler too, at the side of one of those princes. Even one of the ones who wasn't really handsome or daring might have been good at kinging, with her help.

Vladimirror watched her from afar and saw her bursting and bulging in her dresses, looking bewildered and shocked at how people treated her, and then sad and whipped, sitting alone in her chambers. He sent a message by carrier crow and it flew in the face of the chambermaid and frightened her.

"What does it say?" the chambermaid asked when the princess had quieted the servant's shrieks, caught the crow, taken the message vial from its leg and was reading.

"It's from that wily wizard of the East," Babette said, frowning. "He's taking responsibility for my current...condition, and offers to give me back my figure if I pass three of *his* tests. It requires me to travel incognito, I'm afraid. You'll have to change clothes with me."

"*How* incognito?" the chambermaid asked. "You may need to travel in something a little rougher than the gown I'm wearing. It used to be yours, remember?"

Babette eyed the pink samite gown with the little ruby insets thoughtfully. "You might have a point there. If you would be so kind as to go to the kitchen and fetch the cook. Her gown should fit me. And I will need some food for the journey as well."

The chambermaid rolled her eyes, as if her plump princess *would* be thinking of food and cooks even at such a time, but obeyed. The cook took a long time coming and when she came, she carried a coarsely woven frock that matched the one she wore. Babette cocked an eyebrow and the cook said, "I brought you me other gown, 'ighness. It wouldn't do, me cookin' in your finery, and it'll bring a good price at the market if I don't get it all stained with grease and such. That silky stuff stains right through the apron, it does. So you can 'ave this 'un and I'll keep yours nice and clean. Might be I can wear it to me daughter's wedding before I sells it."

Babette nodded, thanked her, slipped out of her dress and handed it over. When the cook departed, the chambermaid tried to help her mistress on with the old rough brown garment, splattered with gravy stains across the bosom. Babette shook her head. "I'll have to get used to dressing and undressing myself if I'm going to be incognito." The princess was appalled to find that the cook's frock fit her perfectly, and without too much room to spare. The cook had always been the largest woman in the palace.

The chambermaid clucked her tongue. "I wish Your Highness could find it in you to go incognito with two or three of the palace guard. It's as much as my job's worth to let you go haring off like this."

Babette spoke with the haughtiness of her thinner days, "You forget your place, Madeline. I am still the princess, gravy-stained gown or no, and you are still the chambermaid. You have no authority to stop me. Besides, I very much doubt anyone will notice or care all that much," she added with a tear of self-pity rolling down her cheek and chins.

Rather to her surprise, Madeline patted her hand consolingly. "Here now, ducks—I mean Your Highness—don't take on so. That's not true, though you may think so. Your people will come around once they gets used to you. Same thing happened to my sister Sophie after the twins was born. She was afraid her man was going to leave her but he got used to her, didn't he? Now he just says there's more of her to love and meanwhile Soph's had our Wat and our Alice born, hasn't she?"

"Kind of you to say so, Madeline," Babette said, though actually it didn't give her, still a virgin, much comfort to think that she had the same weight problem as a mother of at least four.

"Here's your food now, ma'am. But Cook says as how if you should come back after supper, she'll leave the makings of a cold meal for me to fetch for you in the kitchen."

"You and Cook are both very thoughtful, Madeline," Babette said. She had never noticed that before but then, servants were expected to be thoughtful, weren't they? It was their job. "I'll just be off now."

"Aren't you going to take off your crown and bind up your hair, ma'am?" Madeline asked. "I mean, if you want to disguise yourself as a common woman. Just a suggestion."

"Oh, silly me," Babette said, "of course," and put the crown in her jewelry box and allowed Madeline to braid her hair into two long braids, then loop each of them up and tie her own kerchief around it. "How do I look now?" Babette asked.

"We-ell," Madeline giggled. "I reckon it's not that easy to make a sow's ear from a silken purse either, if you don't mind my saying so, but them little embroidered shoes don't seem like the right accessories to me."

"Oh dear. I can't go barefoot! I'd be lame in no time!"

"Be back in a tic, ma'am," Madeline said, and returned with some wooden clogs. "These will protect your feet and help you look your part as well."

They were not, however, very comfortable; they were, in fact, inflexible and clunky. Babette had to remember to pick her feet up off the floor and put them down again, rather than gliding heel and toe as she was accustomed.

But Madeline was satisfied with the disguise at last and saw her to the castle gate, handing over her cloth-wrapped parcel of food at the last minute before waving goodbye.

Now then, Babette thought, what tests are these that the wizard had for her before she could resume her rightful shape and place in life?

In his palace tower, the wizard looked into his scrying glass and saw the humbly-dressed princess, her wealth of golden hair braided up like a goose girl's, and chuckled happily to himself before releasing a carrier crow.

The crow dive-bombed the unsuspecting princess, who ducked and swung her arms, frightening a horse pulling a wagonload of dung. The horse reared and the cart upset and Babette slipped on some of the contents and fell onto her backside in the ordure.

She said something very unprincesslike as the message tube dropped into her newly-fragrant lap. "You must walk seven times seven leagues in seven times seven months. You must climb seven mountains, ford seven rivers, and swim seven seas."

"Right," she said, though she couldn't help wondering why wizards were always so preoccupied with sevens. He would have been very tedious to be married to, she thought. No wonder she had disliked him on sight. But she set off briskly, avoiding the curses of the dung-wagon driver. A swim in one of seven rivers sounded well worth walking seven leagues for at this point. In fact, she thought of turning back to the palace to have a wash before she started. But she doubted the guards would recognize her, which was rather the point, even if they let her get close enough, stinking as she was, to see her properly. Oh well, the sooner she started, the sooner she'd be there.

Walking in clogs had very little in common with walking in seven-league boots, she realized after half of the first league. The clogs did not offer much in the way of striding ability. Finally, once she was walking on the road that wound through meadows, she removed the offending footwear and walked barefoot in the grass, which was quite nice except for the occasional sticker patch.

She was also plagued by insects drawn to her new perfume. She swatted them with her food bundle and used some very ignoble language in her attempts to discourage them. Unfortunately, the mountain she had to climb that day was not high enough to be sufficiently cold for the insects to fall away from her. When at last she reached bottom of the mountain she found a stream and, carrying her food packet and her clogs above her head, began to wade.

At which point she became the object of aerial attack by seven crows, who tore the food packet from her hands and knocked away the clogs. They scattered what food they did not steal into the water, though she was left holding half of one of Cook's best roast swan sandwiches.

When she bit down on it, she almost broke one of her teeth on another message tube. "You must travel through seven forests, sleeping on the ground among the beasts, finding bee pollen, chickweed," and a long list of herbs which she wouldn't know from ornamental ivy. Contemplating the soggy half of her sandwich, she wondered how these herbs tasted, preferably fried.

"Share your food with a poor old woman, dearie?" a shaky voice asked.

"All I have left is half a roast swan sandwich," the princess replied. She was hungry—very hungry really, but the sandwich didn't look like much. "It's rather soggy."

The old woman, who was very ugly indeed, looked anxiously from the sandwich to Babette's face and back again, licking her chops.

"Oh, all right," the Princess said. "I'll split it with you, how's that?" She tried not to sound as reluctant as she was. After all, she may have until recently been a beautiful blonde, but that didn't mean she was stupid. She knew the fairy tales. She knew the score. You didn't ever, ever, refuse food or help to little old ladies you met on the road, because they would either A) turn you into a frog (though that was usually for arrogant princes rather than hungry princesses), B) make something nasty fall from your mouth eternally, or C) refuse to share with you the knowledge of herbs and simples all old biddies supposedly had.

She was a little surprised when the old lady did none of the above. Instead, she snatched the entire half a sandwich from the princess's hand and threw it in the stream where it was carried off.

"Wh-" the princess began. But the old woman was flinging off her rags and lifting her ugly mask to reveal the face and robes of the wizard Vladimirror, who giggled evilly at her.

"No roast swan for you, little glutton. In fact, no sugar, salt, wheat, corn, fruit, bread of any kind for the duration if you ever want to look like a proper princess again."

"But that's everything!" she wailed. "What will I eat?"

"Crow, Your Highness. You can eat crow. That is, if you can catch one. You are truly pathetic away from your parents, you know. By the time you slim down again, you're going to be wanting a spell to get your youth back along with your recovered waistline."

"If I do, it certainly won't be so the likes of you will want to marry me," she snapped. "You are a horrid, beastly man."

"And *you* are a thoroughly lost and very fat princess and will remain that way if you don't start moving," the wizard told her. Then he turned into a crow and flew away. She was mad enough that she thought if she could catch him she *would* have surely eaten one crow.

Still hungry, she kept wandering, and frankly had no idea how many leagues she had gone, though she did have to cross a river. By the time she got across, it was night. And cold. The leaves were turning. Actually, she hadn't seen that too many times. Where she lived it was mostly good farming country, and beyond the castle was the village and beyond the village the fields. Not a great many trees any longer. The leaves were quite pretty and piled up nicely for her to lie down on, once she realized she was going to have to actually sleep in the forest on the ground with no blanket and nothing but what she was wearing. Very shortly she discovered that, if she burrowed into the leaves and covered herself with them, they added a little warmth. Picking leaves beside a very large tree was helpful as a windbreak too. But when night fell and she heard footsteps, snuffles, and cries all around her and when she dared peek out, saw eyes glowing in the darkness…

Well, needless to say, she didn't sleep late that morning, lest she wake up just in time to find herself breakfast in bed for some bear or lion, dragon, boar, or goodness only knew what else. She walked much faster the next day but did not leave the forest, and after another night in the leaves, crossed another river and climbed another mountain without leaving the trees. This went on for a week. Seven days, actually, when she had nothing much to eat and felt in grave danger of being eaten.

So she was understandably very hungry, footsore and weary when she saw smoke rising from a chimney and came upon what looked like a woodcutter's hut. Woodcutters were always very handy in fairytales, too. Except this one wasn't home. There was, however, another ugly old lady there, along with a calico cat.

Seeing the old woman sweeping at the door, Babette very nearly turned and ran, but the old woman called out to her. "Who's there? Whoever you are, could you help me a moment, please?"

"Oh no, you don't," Babette muttered. But since she was still only a fat young princess and not a toad, she figured she still had something to lose, so she cautiously turned back to the hut.

"Excuse me, beldame," she said with all the courtesy she could muster, "but I haven't had very good luck with pathetic old ladies lately. Would you mind taking off that shawl and tugging at your face so I can see whether or not you're this evil wizard who tricked me before?"

The old lady gave a reassuringly elderly cackle not a bit like the wizard's giggle. "Certainly, my pretty," she said and accommodatingly made faces with her face and whirled her shawl in the air like a flag.

"My pretty" eh? Babette decided she liked this old girl, who was evidently not the wizard. "So what can I do for you? If it's food, I'm sorry, but that wizard I mentioned tricked me out of my last morsel."

"Oh no, my pretty, nothing like that. In fact, I was about to invite you in for some nice crow stew I've made up fresh today. But first, I wanted you to see if you can reach behind the stove. My cat brought a mouse in, and the wicked thing hid behind the stove and died. Can you fetch it out? It's stinking up the house."

"Ewwww," Babette said.

"I wouldn't ask it of you except I'm blind, which as you probably know from the stories makes all of my other senses extra keen, so the smell is driving me mad."

Blind, huh? Hence the "my pretty." Oh well. She seemed nice enough. And though the house smelled ripe with dead mouse, it still didn't smell as bad as Babette herself had smelled until recently.

Whipping off her kerchief, Babette put it over her hand and groped until her kerchief-shielded fingers squished into ripe mouse, which she pulled out, without looking, and flung into the woods, along with the kerchief.

The crow stew was a little bitter. "It's better with extra salt," the old woman said. "I don't normally have it, but there was a whole flock of crows in front of the house today, and my cat here is very, very fast."

The cat licked her front paws, one red and one white.

Babette looked longingly at the little dish of salt but shook her head. After all she'd been through, she supposed she could do without. "I'm not allowed salt."

"What? Whyever not?" the old woman asked.

"I'm having a curse cured, you see, and it's one of the magical formulas for curing it." She dug into a pocket and read her the wizard's message. "Have you any idea where these herbs and simples can be found, beldame?"

"I wish you'd stop calling me that," the old woman said. "My name is Fifi. Fifi La Fey."

"Sorry, Mistress Fifi. I'm Pr-uh precisely who you think I am, a young woman from town who got lost in these woods trying to fulfill these idiotic instructions from a wizard. My name is Barbara," she said. The old woman was an unlikely "Fifi" and the princess suspected she was an even more implausible "Babette" at this point. "Barbara…er…Cook."

"Well, Barbara, as I've mentioned, I'm blind, but my adopted son Pr-presently will be home. I call him Burl. Because he works with wood. Get it?"

Babette laughed. Now that she was comfortable, she found relief made her easily amused. "And does he know more about herbs and simples than you do?"

"No, of course not. I know all about them. I just can't see them any longer. But when he gets back, I can tell him where they may be found and he can help you find them. He's gone off to fetch Hamlet to us."

"Who is Hamlet?" Babette asked.

"The minstrel who comes by now and then. Specializes in long gloomy battles and dirges and laments. But being a traveling man, he is also very up on current events. Can you write that down? Laments? Events? He might want to use those lines in one of his songs."

"I'll try to remember," Babette promised.

"Would you be kind enough to fetch some water from the stream?"

Babette did. The pail was very heavy and she was very tired. Worst of all, there was a quiet little pool off to one side of the stream and when she looked into it, a fat girl with disheveled blond braids, a dirty face and dimples looked back at her. All that hunger and walking and crow-eating, and she was just as heavy as ever!

She hauled the water back and was going to ask if there was a place where she could sleep. But Fifi started to heat the water, at which time they discovered the fire had gone out and the last of the kindling was gone. So Babette had to quickly take verbal instructions on how to chop wood without chopping off her feet or hands. Then she learned to build a fire, after filling the room with smoke. When the water was heated, Fifi started to load a basin with dishes but missed and dropped their plates to the floor.

"Oh, dear," Fifi said. "And these few are the last ones I made before my eyesight went. I don't suppose you're a potter by any chance, are you?"

"No," said Babette, yawning. "And I don't think I have time to learn before I completely fall asleep. Why don't I finish the washing up?"

Babette stayed with Fifi for seven days. Babette did all the fetching and carrying and cleaning under Fifi's direction.

It was hard work, but then Fifi was good company, and Babette was fed regularly, even if it was only crow stew. She was most grateful not to have to sleep by herself out in the freezing nighttime forest waiting to be gobbled. She never in all her royal life would have imagined it, but she actually was enjoying herself a little. It was nice having one person to talk to who wouldn't go right behind your back and start some nasty story about you and who couldn't see you and didn't care what you looked like.

Then one day, as she was peeling potatoes for the crow stew, Fifi asked, "Tell me something, Barbara. Why you?"

"Excuse me?"

"Why did the wizard put the curse on you that you must wander around eating crows and doing all of these strenuous things?"

"Well, he wanted to marry me," Babette said. "And he *did* pass all the tests and things, but I just didn't *like* him and when I asked him questions, the answers he gave made me feel...well...let's just say I didn't want to marry him, tests or no tests. So he left and then all at once everything I ate started making me bigger. And then *he* sent a message telling me he was the one making my food do that to me, and if I would follow his instructions and pass *his* tests, he'd reverse the curse."

Fifi's expression grew shrewd and calculating, but her voice was light as she asked, "Do you think he will? I mean, is crow particularly unfattening or is it just that he wants you to eat it because it, of all birds, doesn't taste much like chicken and he wants to avenge himself on you?"

"That had crossed my mind," Babette admitted. "Almost as often as I crossed my own path while I was getting lost. The truth is, I don't know. But I had to try. I'll never get a husband looking this way, and my parents and all the courtiers act like I've become invisible because they don't want their disgust to show in their faces." She realized she shouldn't have said anything about the courtiers but Fifi didn't seem to notice.

"Disgust?" she asked instead. "Are you very ugly?"

"I don't think so," Babette answered honestly. "Just very heavy and...well, very...ordinary. Whereas, before, I was beautiful. It makes a big difference."

Before Fifi could comment, a voice called from the outside, "Mother, I'm home! Sorry it took so long. You must have had warm weather here, the wood seems to have lasted..." the voice broke off as a large, solid man blocked out the sunlight coming through the doorway. His face was in shadow.

"Burl! You're home! You were such a long time, I thought you'd found yourself a nice girl out there, settled down, and would bring grandchildren with you when you came. No, the wood didn't last that long," she said. She had risen and given the big man a hug, warmly returned, before he followed her inside the hut. "But my new friend Barbara here has been a big help."

"Much obliged, Mistress Barbara," Burl said, ducking his head so that she *still* couldn't see his face.

"Where's Hamlet?" Fifi asked.

"That's what took me so long, Mother. He got a gig and he thought it would be over with the first day, but then one disaster happened after another, and he has to make it into an epic ballad, and then he'll have to sing it throughout all the local districts. After all, someone might have spotted her."

"Spotted who?" Fifi asked.

"The missing princess. Of course, you don't know but...say, is that crow stew ready yet?"

"Barbara was just adding the potatoes. I imagine the bread should be coming out of the oven now, don't you think, Barbara?"

But before she could turn, Burl was pulling the loaf from the oven and putting it on the table to cool.

"What missing princess?" Fifi asked.

"Oh, well, it's a long story. But the royal house, as this kingdom has known it, is not in power at present."

"What?" Princess Babette asked.

"Yes, shocking isn't it?" Burl asked. "First, the Princess was said by the palace to have some kind of health problem and, the next thing everybody heard, she had disappeared. The cook was found with one of her gowns, and the king had the cook and one of the chambermaids, who was supposedly an accomplice, locked in the dungeon. They had some strange story of crows carrying poor Princess Babette away, I guess. The King and the Prince immediately got on their horses and went looking for her high and low but, according to the lords who were with them, as they were crossing a particularly tricky bit of stream, all of a sudden thousands of crows flew out of nowhere and dived at the heads of the King and Prince. The Prince fell off his horse and would have been swept downstream and drowned, but the King plunged in after him. They both went over a slight cataract. Their attendants were able to drag them out at the bottom, but both were unconscious and have remained so. Meanwhile, the cook's replacement was not a very good one, and the Queen is ill unto death with food poisoning."

"Oh, poor Mother!" Babette cried. Then covered by saying, "My mother would never do anything wrong on purpose."

"Oh, that's *right*!" Fifi said. "Your name is Cook. So your mother is the palace cook who's in the dungeon? Oh dear."

"Yes, I must get back to the palace at once and see what can be done!" Babette said. "Oh, Fifi, you've been so kind. And I have no idea how I'm going to find my way back there but I just have to. Poor F…poor King and Prince, too. And the whole government must be a shambles with everyone so ill."

"Oh, it is, Mistress Barbara," Burl said. "And the poor princess missing and no one in her family to organize the search either. If she is still alive, she must be beside herself."

"She was…is, I suppose she must be, I mean," Babette said.

"We can't let you go alone, child," Fifi said. To Burl she confided, "Barbara had been wandering in the woods for days when she found the hut. She needs help getting back to the palace so she can see about her mother."

"I'll just chop some more wood and haul some more water for you before we go, then I'll take her back, Mother."

"No, I think I'll go, too. It sounds as if the capital is in turmoil just now. I could do with a bit of excitement."

And so, once they had filled themselves with more crow stew, the three of them set out through the forest. They didn't take any food, because Burl was a very good hunter and trapper and could always find more crows; the birds flew in circles around them, but never once approached Babette, which was fine with her.

They brought extra blankets and all slept close together, Babette feeling safer than she'd ever felt in her palace bed, smelling the woody scent of Burl's skin and feeling the warmth his big body generated. His mother slept between them, very snug indeed with a substantial person on either side of her.

By the time they were within sight of the palace and the village, Babette had come to a decision. "You are the dearest friends I've ever had and good people," she said. "So I cannot lie to you. I am Princess Babette."

"Of course you are," Fifi said. "I knew it all along."

"You did?"

"Yes, and so did Burl. He's met you before."

Babette lowered her eyes and felt warm and fluttery all over. "He did? I can't believe I didn't remember."

"There were a great many folk about then, Your Highness, and I couldn't get right up close."

"No, probably not, but you will now, and you too, Fifi. I will need your assistance getting into the palace so I can help my family, release Cook and Madeline from the dungeon, and return the Kingdom to some semblance of order. But the guards will never recognize me."

Burl nodded. "You've changed a lot since I saw you last."

"I know," Babette said, remembering for a moment her misery at her once girlish figure and all of the admiring attention she had lost, especially from males. Knowing that Burl had seen both her before self and her after self made her feel strangely awkward and sad. She didn't mind it so much with Fifi, but for Burl to think that she was less than she had been by being more than she had been embarrassed her.

"You're more like a real person now," Burl continued. "You've got cute dimples and you laugh a lot and worry over people who've been hurt and you're…well, I don't know how to put it, and maybe it was because of the stress you were under before but, frankly, I left without—uh—doing what I came to do after I saw the princess—I mean you—ordering all those princes around and picking through their gifts and pouting. You don't seem like that princess. You're a much pleasanter person than she was."

Suspicion began to grow in Babette's mind. Burl was very well-spoken indeed for a humble woodcutter, and his features had a noble cast to them. He was, in fact, very handsome in a rugged, honest sort of way. He looked just the way she thought a real man ought to look. But all of that had to be set aside while she convinced the guards to let her to the palace.

"We're here to help you, my dear," Fifi said. And they did too, more than Babette anticipated.

Help came from another unexpected and unintentional source as well. When the three of them were near the palace gates, they were once more suddenly surrounded by crows. "Look," Babette said, glaring into each and every pair of beady black eyes as if thinking to confront the wizard, "You birds tell your master he can do whatever he likes, but his cure is worse than his curse, at least so far, and I have a family emergency here and a kingdom to run. Now scat before we cook you!" she said, flinging her hands up and scattering crows.

As she brought her hands back down again, she saw that they were A) clean, B) bejeweled, and C) sleeved with white samite which matched the rest of the gown she now wore. "What in the world?" she asked, groping at her long and perfectly coiffed golden hair to find her royal circlet in place.

Fifi, no longer an ugly old woman but a very lovely and stately silver-haired, well dressed lady of indeterminate age, fixed keen eyes (no longer blind) on the palace guards and asked, "What are you waiting for? Prince Beauregard Burlingame the 54th and I have come to see Her Royal Highness Princess Babette home to the sickbeds of her family. Please open the gates."

They did. Fairytales were supposed to have happened "Once Upon a Time", but that time was recent enough that even palace guards knew an honest-to-goodness fairy godmother when they saw one and they weren't about to risk her wrath. If she turned princes into toads, think what she would do to a common soldier for disobeying her! Besides, that was most certainly Princess Babette—at least the most recent, chubby version of the princess. And she wasn't whining or pouting either, like they remembered. She was not only large, she was definitely in charge.

And so she was. She immediately had Cook and Madeline released from the dungeons, whereupon Cook immediately whipped up, under Fifi's direction, some healing broths that she and Madeline helped the other servants administer to the ailing royals. Meanwhile, Babette strode into the audience chamber just in time to keep the ministers from surrendering to the neighboring kingdom of Heinzland, which was threatening war. Further investigation by Burl, who questioned the messenger delivering the surrender terms, revealed that King (formerly Grand Vizier) Vladimirror of distant Corristan had offered to trade lands he held to them in exchange for hegemony over Babette's father's kingdom if they would annex it for him. The former vizier had guaranteed that Babette's country could be taken without bloodshed, since Vladimirror had already won it with trickery.

Babette's mother recovered slowly, a bit day by day, but she wasn't up to ruling, and by the time Babette's father and brother were able to speak again, Babette had lowered the taxes, made sure the excess harvest was stored for the winter, distributed some of the land to the peasants who worked it, promoted Madeline to Lady-in-Waiting, seen to it that the dung-wagon driver was reimbursed for his lost cargo, and had generally promoted peace and prosperity throughout her land with all possible dispatch. Occasionally she would turn to Burl for advice or to ask a question, but most of the time he was out training with the palace guard, just in case.

Upon hearing that her father and brother were awake, Babette hurried to their bedsides; they were both in her parents' chamber, which had become a Royal Sickroom.

She had hoped her father would be glad to see her. She hoped he would approve of what she had done, preventing a war and the loss of the kingdom and all, and she told him all about it.

Her mother spoke up first. "Yes, and I thought I heard that you had been lost and starving in the woods for weeks and that you have been working day and night since you returned. But you're not a bit thinner!"

"*Mother*," Babette said in something of her childhood tone, "I *told* you I'm under a curse and I had to come home before I could effect the horrible cure proposed by that wizard who tried to take over our kingdom."

"Well, if you only had a bit of self-discipline I'm sure you could have..." her mother continued, but her voice trailed off as the King sat up.

"I suppose now you're here and have had a taste of ruling, you with your own sorceress and that hulking bodyguard of yours, you'll be wanting me to abdicate and name you as heir instead of your brother?"

"Hardly," she said, sighing. "I'm exhausted. I was just trying to keep the kingdom together for you until you get well, Daddy. You and Mother and Larry, who is welcome to the crown for all I'm concerned. I don't know what I'll do, but I'm not about to hang around here waiting for suitors. Maybe I'll go tend lepers or something instead. I rather liked being needed when I thought Fifi was blind."

But just then Burl rushed in and fell to one knee before her. "Barbara—I mean, Your Highness, Princess Babette, I know…" confused, he turned to the King and Queen and said earnestly, "I know I ran away before even attempting to take your tests. I was so ashamed I didn't go home, but got lost in the woods and took up woodcutting and adopted Fifi for my mother. But I love Barbara…I love you, Barbara."

"I love you too, Burl," she said. "But we were sort of in the middle of a family discussion."

"That's just it," he said. "I want to be your family; I want you to be *my* family."

"You can't be proposing to her!" the Queen exclaimed. "Her wedding day will be a disaster. We'll never find enough silk in the world to make her a gown."

Fifi appeared. "That's no problem for a girl with a fairy godmother." Fifi tapped her foot. "*Which*, I might add, she can certainly use when her own mother has her priorities so out of order."

"Barbara," Burl continued, "a messenger just came to tell me I've inherited my father's throne."

"You're a younger son, Burlingame," the King said. "I distinctly remember that. It's why you were placed at the end of the list of suitors to be tested."

"Well, my elder brother finally decided to run away with another prince he met while he was waiting to test for your daughter's hand, Sire," Burl replied. "And I am next in line for succession. So I have to leave. But I want you to come with me, Barbara."

Babette began to cry, with both weariness and happiness.

"Oh, Burl, I love you with all my heart, and being with you is the happiest place I can think of. Ever so much better than nursing lepers, though if you have any lepers in your kingdom, of course I'd be happy to run a charity on their behalf. Is Fifi coming too? And Madeline?"

"Anyone you want," he replied. "But we must be wed in a hurry."

"You must be mad!" the Queen scoffed. "Surely you want to wait until she's done her cure and had her curse removed!"

"Madame, my Barbara is a princess fit for any king," Burl—King Burl actually, said formally.

"And in case you hadn't noticed," Fifi said, "the curse has ended."

"Nonsense," said Prince Larry. "Look at Babette! She's still round as a butterball." He couldn't hurt Babette's feelings now, though, and she peeked out from under Burl's armpit and winked at her brother.

"But…by my sword, Mother, Father, look at her! The curse is lifted! She is beautiful!"

Her parents both looked at her and her mother gasped. "But how can that be?"

Fifi shrugged. "It's the same principle as the frog thing. A little genuine affection does a great deal to improve anyone, and true love works miracles. So, Your Majesty, have you got a list?"

As it turned out, the wedding was somewhat delayed while King Burl and Princess Babette, chaperoned by Fifi La Fey and Madeline and their retainers, returned to Burl's kingdom for his father's funeral.

Meanwhile, throughout Babette's kingdom, the ladies of fashion who had watched their princess and her fiancé ride away said to each other, "Really, tell me honestly? I'm looking far too thin and pale, aren't I? Did you see Her Highness? Did you see how he looked at her? She was radiant! Such dimples! Such ample curves. Please pass the chocolates. I've ordered a dress to be made in the style of hers and I simply *must* fill it out in time for the wedding."

Ralph Gamelli says that he doesn't really remember how this story came about or evolved to its main point of class struggle. "I was working as an appliance delivery man," he writes, "and must have been venting. Three-hundred-pound refrigerators going up to the third floor frequently led to that."

A Hero, Plain and Simple
by Ralph Gamelli

"We close in twenty minutes, Mr. Kembley." Balancing his round tray, the bartender retrieved the empty glass from the table and replaced it with a full one.

Kembley had been the only patron in the observation lounge for more than half an hour. He checked his wristwatch, noted that it was 1:40, and looked up at the man in black vest and matching bow tie frowning down at him. "Right, twenty minutes," he nodded, wrapping his fingers around this latest glass, his fourth. "Just enough time to toast my good friend Captain Palmer there." He raised his scotch and soda in the direction of the bronze life-sized statue residing in one corner of the dimly lit room. "Without whose help, I might be off somewhere covering a real story."

The bartender started back to the bar, shaking his head wearily as he threaded his way through the scattering of empty tables.

With a weary motion of his own, Kembley turned slightly in his chair and stared out one of the lounge's several viewports at the growing blue marble that, an hour earlier, had been only one of a thousand bright pinheads punctuating the night.

Following their return to port just after ten A.M., a ceremony commemorating the twentieth anniversary of Captain Palmer's rescue effort would begin—the type of lightweight event a cub reporter should have been covering. Yet it was Kembley, after eight years at the *Observer*, who had been assigned this interminable round trip to Mars, conducting necessarily simplistic interviews with Captain Nicholls and other members of the *Starbright's* crew, slapping together—once again—the kind of fluff human-interest piece he considered the lowest rung of the journalistic ladder.

He drew his glass up to his mouth and found himself staring into the eyes of a janitor who was moving a push-broom across the floor a few yards away.

The green-uniformed man nodded at him. He was middle-aged with thinning hair, a weak jaw, and about fifty extraneous pounds of flesh that tested the stitching of his bulging work shirt. He had such a solemn look about him that Kembley suspected it might be due to something more than the fact that he was pushing a broom across a floor at close to two in the morning.

Kembley returned his nod, and upon completing this gesture watched the large man lean his broom against a nearby table, pull back the chair across from him and, without waiting for an invitation or even asking for one, sit down.

"You're that reporter, aren't you? Kembley? The one covering the anniversary of the rescue?"

"The news event of the century," Kembley said, and took a generous mouthful of scotch.

"I've seen you around the ship the past couple of days, talking to the crew. I thought maybe you could interview me, too."

"Sorry, friend, but I left my recorder back in my cabin."

"Even so, I think you might find what I have to say interesting."

"No doubt. But like I said, I'm not ready for any interview; don't even have a pencil on me. Maybe if I'd noticed you around earlier…"

"You didn't, though."

Kembley shrugged lightly. "Sorry."

"Not many people do. I'm not exactly the type that attracts attention."

He didn't know how right he was. Kembley hadn't even known the man was in the room until their eyes chanced to meet.

The janitor tilted his head toward the corner of the lounge where the statue dwelled. "Now, Captain Palmer over there—he was a man worth noticing. A hero, plain and simple."

Kembley followed the man's gaze.

In the corner, Captain Palmer stood proudly, majestically, in the classic pose of a true hero: feet spread wide, hands firm on hips, square jaw jutting prominently into the air. An elegant plaque was mounted in the wall beside his likeness, and even at this distance it was easy to read the bold, dignified letters engraved in it:

> IN PROUD MEMORY OF CAPTAIN ANDREW S. PALMER,
> WHO, UPON 8 OCTOBER 2093,
> ABOARD THIS VESSEL STARBRIGHT,
> GAVE HIS LIFE IN RESCUING FOUR PASSENGERS
> AND ONE CREWMAN FROM IMMINENT DEATH.

Kembley had, in some way, been blaming the deceased captain for his assignment to this "story", for lack of a better word. In reality, he admitted to himself now, he had just not proven himself worthy of handling a major story yet, and he regretted his sarcastic toast to the statue bearing Palmer's likeness. "Yes, a hero," he said. "The kind of man who someday, I hope, I'll be writing about an hour after his death, not twenty years."

"The kind of man who gets credit for another's actions," the janitor added.

Kembley looked across the table at him for a long moment. "What are you trying to say, Mr…?"

"Morris. Joe Morris. What I'm trying to say, Mr. Kembley, is that you can't believe everything you read on plaques."

Kembley grinned thinly and swallowed some scotch. "You were right, Mr. Morris. You do have some interesting things to say. But interesting and truthful aren't always one and the same."

"Oh, it's the truth. I promise you that."

"Mr. Morris, I've interviewed over a dozen members of this crew, and none of them suggested anything even remotely like what you..."

"Doesn't make it any less true," Morris cut in. "None of them were here twenty years ago. None of them were aboard ship when the hull breach happened. All they know is the same story that everyone was told. Only a handful of people know who did the *actual* rescuing."

"*Actual* rescuing." Kembley shook his head, looked into the corner of the lounge once more, then back at the solemn-faced Morris. "All right, I'll bite. Who, if not Palmer, did the actual rescuing, then?"

"A janitor."

Kembley glanced down at his drink, didn't say anything.

"You don't believe a janitor could do such a thing?"

"I didn't say that."

"You also didn't say I'm crazy, but with a look like that on your face, you don't need to."

"I don't think you're crazy. Just someone who's not all that satisfied with his lot in life, maybe."

"I'm not ashamed of my job, if that's what you're implying."

"Look, even if I was totally off the mark with that last comment, I can't just accept your word for it that the Palmer story is a fake. You said only a handful of people know about the real rescuer. If you could get me in contact with one of them, assuming you know who they are and how to reach them..."

"You're in contact with one of them right now."

"You? You've been aboard ship for twenty years?"

Morris nodded. "And you have no idea how maddening it is to have to see that statue every day, to watch passengers drink in the lie along with their gin-and-tonics."

Kembley was still uncertain if he was only dealing with someone venting frustration at his station in life—something he himself had just been guilty of—but he put on a serious expression and folded his hands on the tablecloth. "All right, Mr. Morris, if you witnessed something here twenty years ago, tell me about it."

When he realized he was getting a chance to talk, Morris' hard features seemed to relax for a moment. "Are you familiar at all with the story?"

"Research isn't one of my strong points," Kembley admitted, and had to admit inwardly that that was likely a contributing factor in his lack of progress at the *Observer*. "But yes, I thought I was."

"Then you know the *Starbright* was one of the first ships to start taking people over to the Mars colony. We mainly carry tourists now, but back then, with the colony being brand new, we carried over settlers. The ship was less the cruise ship it is today than a basic transport, but there were still three of us aboard serving as custodians. Anyway, with a new pioneering era beginning and there being a sudden rush to get ships into space, the *Starbright* was put together a little too hastily. On the seventh flight over to the colony, there was a catastrophe, right here in this room, which was just an observation area in those days. No meteors were involved, no exploding engines, just simple poor construction. A girder collapsed, a seam buckled, and the air began to hiss away. There weren't as many luxuries back then, so we were able to carry a larger number of passengers, and a lot of them were in this room when it happened."

"And just what *did* happen?" Kembley asked. "In addition to the breach, that is."

"There was a panic, of course. People tried to clear out in one big wave. Screaming, shouting, and bowling over anyone who didn't move fast enough. After the smoke cleared and most everyone had made it over to a safe area of the ship, there were more than a dozen people lying hurt on the floor—some trampled, some knocked out by the falling girder, all of them slowly suffocating."

"That's when Palmer came into the picture," Kembley said. "He carried some of the injured to safety, then found himself trapped on the wrong side of an automated airlock."

"According to what you may have read, yes. But in reality he carried out only one person—the crewman mentioned in that plaque. To get to that man, he had to ignore a dozen passengers. And when he'd seen that crewman to safety, he went back for another of his men. Went back for men trained for just such disasters, but not the passengers who weren't. He never made it back out, though."

"So it was this janitor you mentioned who actually saved the other four people, is that what you're telling me?"

"I am."

"And you saw him rescue those people with your own eyes?"

Morris nodded. "He came on the scene a little before Palmer. He dragged four passengers out, then wound up with Palmer and the rest of the injured on the wrong side of the emergency doors." He peered with undisguised contempt at the shadowed form of Captain Andrew S. Palmer, and Kembley again could not help but reflect on the dichotomy of the stately space captain and the lumpish custodian. "They spent plenty to repair the ship and plenty to put up that statue, but I think more money was spent on hushing up witnesses. Because it wouldn't do to have a mop jockey standing there next to that plaque, would it? Wouldn't exactly inspire confidence in passengers to know that in case of an accident in flight their lives may depend on one of us."

Kembley drank slowly from his glass. "I don't know what to say, Mr. Morris. Everything you said may be true, but without proof…"

"Without proof, that statue will continue to stand in the corner, and someday you'll be covering the *thirtieth* anniversary of Palmer's rescue."

"Hopefully, I'll have moved on to bigger things by then," Kembley said. He felt an abrupt urge to drain the remainder of his scotch in one gulp, and obeyed it. "Hopefully," he said again, although this time it was more a self-addressed mutter.

"There's one way I can think of for you to move on."

Kembley grinned mirthlessly. "I've seen my editor's daughter. It wouldn't be worth it."

Morris's face remained solemn. "You said you'd need to contact some of the people who were there, so you wouldn't be just taking my word for it. You could track down a copy of the *Starbright's* early passenger logs, then try to locate anyone on that flight who may have been a witness. Maybe they'll speak now. Speak the truth this time. That way you'd be able to corroborate my story and we could all move on."

"Do you know how many people are on that colony?" Kembley asked incredulously.

"I didn't say it would be easy. And there are no guarantees, either. No guarantee you'll get a printable story, just like there was no guarantee that that janitor was going to make it back to a safe zone. But that doesn't mean you don't make the effort, does it?"

Kembley studied his drink. Effort. Had he ever, truly, made one, he wondered? Had he ever really given himself an honest chance to advance?

"Does it?" Morris persisted.

"I'll give it some thought," Kembley said, playing uncomfortably with his empty glass.

Morris gazed at him sullenly. "I wish I could believe that."

Meeting his eyes, Kembley suddenly grew defensive. "You haven't even told me his name—assuming, of course, that he ever actually existed." He didn't know if he raised that doubt as a counter against Morris' insinuation of laziness or if he was trying to rationalize his instinct to ignore the man's story.

Morris nodded slowly, the gesture of a man long resigned to disappointment. "You'll learn it, if you really want to." His gaze flicked toward his antithesis in the corner one last time before he hauled his ample frame out of his chair and retrieved the broom.

Kembley shook his head and gave him a half-mocking good-bye wave, then turned and signaled for another round from the bartender, who was busily smothering a shot glass with a towel. When he turned back around, he was glad to find that Morris had already left the room.

"We'll be closing in a few minutes, Mr. Kembley. This will have to be your last round."

Kembley grinned up at the frowning bartender and accepted his drink. "How well do you know the janitor who was just in here? He told me a story you wouldn't believe even if you were finishing your fourth scotch."

The bartender's frown deepened. "We've been using robots at that position as long as I've worked aboard the *Starbright*, Mr. Kembley."

"Robots?" Kembley said weakly.

"Captain Nicholls prefers them."

Kembley nodded dully. "Yes…yes, of course he does." For the second time that evening he raised his glass into the air. "I'll do my best, Mr. Morris," he said to the vacant chair across from him, to the ceiling, to the empty room in general. "I'll do my best to see that we *both* move on to better things."

The bartender only frowned.

The Year 2000 marks Cynthia McQuillin's 30th as a singer, 25th as a songwriter, 20th of recording and publishing her music, 15th of running her own publishing, recording and jewelry-making business, and 10th as a science fiction writer. In honor of the synchronicity of such numbers, she is officially retiring to spend her time writing fiction, puttering with music, hanging out at conventions just to see her friends, and spending time with her partner in life, music and laughter, Dr. Jane Robinson, and their beloved cats.

Cynthia frequently features large, successful characters in her stories, of which her (currently unsold) first novel *Singer In The Shadows* is a prime example. Another is the beautiful piece that follows, which she tells us was written after she was mesmerized watching four juvenile walruses in a Marine World habitat. Ungainly and comical on land, they seemed blissfully unselfconscious about it. "What moved me most profoundly," she continues, "was watching their seemingly endless swoops and dives, the way they moved with power and grace through the water, totally at one with their environment." Cynthia further reports that, unlike her usual writing method, she reached for her laptop and wrote this one all at once and only once.

Seliki
by Cynthia McQuillin

Gunnar Apperson closed the door quietly behind him as he entered the sheltered alcove of the massive bathing area he had constructed on the seaward side of his estate. Carved into the cliff itself, the chamber housed a pool as large as a pond. Seawater ebbed and flowed with the tide through a series of underground conduits, entering the pool through a heavy iron gate.

At the sound of a loud splash, he stepped forward to gaze in fascination at the woman who propelled herself effortlessly through the water with impossibly sensuous undulations of her enormous body. Powerful muscles rippled beneath her flawless skin as she turned to dive, resurfacing, then diving again and again. The dark mass of her hair flowed behind her like a shadow, cloaking her ample curves one moment, then revealing them the next.

It was wrong to keep such a creature imprisoned, even in so comfortable a cage. But from the moment he had watched her haul herself clumsily out of the sea and wriggle free of the cumbersome walrus skin that enveloped her, Gunnar had been as much her prisoner as she was now his. He despised himself for his obsession, but he could not let her go.

The mingled wonder and longing that had filled him that first day as he watched her sprawl, spent and flaccid, across the sun-warmed rocks of the desolate strand, woke within him again each time he saw her. Recalling the stories his grandmother told of selkies—magical beings who swam the sea clad in seal skins or, discarding them, walked as men and women upon the land—he had stolen quickly down to the shore and snatched up the discarded walrus skin.

Since then, she had been his, though never as he truly wished her to be. She understood his words well enough and was able to converse with him when she chose, but if she had a name, she refused to tell him what it was. So he called her Seliki, after his grandmother's selkies.

A joyful cry followed by another loud splash recalled his attention to the pool, and he crept to the grotto's entrance, the better to watch her frolicsome sport. Repetitive and limited as her activities were, he never tired of watching her, longing to swim happily through the swells with her as a selkie lover might. But he didn't dare. She was too strong and he couldn't trust her, for all his grandmother's stories had promised that selkie-maids were loving and submissive wives as long as their seal skins remained hidden from them.

Without warning, Seliki hauled her sleek, massive body up onto the strand beside the pool. Startled by the suddenness of her movements, Gunnar stepped back a few paces, pressing himself to the side of the sheltering wall of the grotto. It seemed, for just a moment, that the enormity of her weight might overwhelm her as she rose to balance precariously on small, perfectly-formed feet, then tottered forward. No matter how often she came ashore, she never seemed quite at ease; her movements were less powerful and certain, sometimes even graceless. But Gunnar found whatever clumsiness she displayed to be charming, almost puppy-like.

Her ample flesh rippled gently as she settled onto the smooth stone couch Gunnar had had placed to one side of the grotto that enclosed the pool. Seeing this, he stepped from the shadows to get a better view of the charms she so carelessly displayed. He smiled appreciatively as she arched her back to scratch one shoulder against the edge of her rocky perch.

"Let me go, Gunnar Apperson," she softly said, turning liquid eyes filled with reproach upon him as he came nearer still. Her voice was as deep and vast as the sea.

"You may leave anytime you wish," he airily replied, watching her with a wary eye. Docile as she now appeared, she was capable of moving quickly indeed when her anger was roused, and massive enough to crush him with any sudden movement, unthinking or deliberate. "The door is never locked, as you know, and I couldn't bar your way if I tried."

"What need have you of locks when you hold my very soul?" she countered, heaving herself up to face him. "I have kept my bargain. One year I have given you. Now give me back what you have stolen."

"I cannot," he whispered, his tone one of mingled shame and hopelessness. "I love you too much to let you go."

"Well," Seliki said, her expression as cold and bitter as a winter storm, "I do not love you. How can I, when you have taken my freedom and torment me daily with your petty wanting and needing?"

"I have never 'imposed' my wants or needs on you," he countered with equal bitterness, stung deeply by her words, "and I have seen to your every want or need without complaint and at great expense and inconvenience." It was amazing how much fresh seafood she could consume in a day, let alone a year.

"I want and need nothing but my freedom," she replied in a distant, weary voice, all the anger and indignation suddenly draining from her tone and posture. "Since you continue to deny me that, I shall accept nothing else you offer me from this moment on."

"What?" he demanded, dismayed by this sudden change. "What are you saying?"

"Simply this, Gunnar Apperson. Though I pity you for your plight, I cannot live as you would have me live. So from this moment on I will neither eat nor drink."

"But you'll die!" Horrified, he stumbled to her side, the thought of her wasting slowly away driving all caution from his mind.

"Then I will die," she said, sinking into a pose of utter dejection.

"Seliki, please," he whispered, kneeling to lay his head against her massive thigh. "I cannot bear it if you die."

"Then let me go," she said, laying a hand gently upon his head. "Love is not selfish, Gunnar Apperson. Love cares for the loved one even before the self."

"But the selkie legends…" he whispered, eyes glistening with childlike stubbornness and hurt.

"…are pretty stories based on bits and pieces of half-forgotten truth." She met his disappointed gaze with a sad but defiant look. "No matter what you say or do, I will never belong to you. You may bind my body to the land, but you cannot force me to love you."

"In time you will learn…"

"In time I will die." The sadness in her strange dark eyes deepened to despair. "It is only the hope that I might someday return to my home that has kept me so long from sloughing off the burden of this awkward human flesh that once I took some joy in wearing. With the breaking of your vow, that hope is gone."

"No! Please," Gunnar sobbed, fear and sorrow piercing his heart like a shard of ice. "How can I live if you are not in the world?" Tears streamed unchecked down his face and he clung to her.

"Then return my walrus skin and let me go. It is the only way."

"Alright! Alright," he murmured at last. "I will do as you say." But I must have something…something I can keep when you are gone."

With a soft, joyful cry she turned, engulfing him in the gentlest of embraces. Her breath was the ceaseless sighing of the sea caressing the shore, and the heaving of her massive breasts was like the swell of the waves as she drew him down. Drowning deliriously in the saltwater sweetness of her kiss, he was once again overcome by the childlike sense of wonder he had experienced the day he had found her.

The sun was almost down by the time Gunnar became once again aware of his surroundings. He lay spent and content across the broad, firm plain of her belly, knowing with a wistful certainty that, come morning, he would keep his promise and release her. But he also knew that, though Seliki had spoken the truth when she said she would never be his, as long as he lived she would always be with him.

According to Marian Crane, the story that follows "began eleven years ago, with a dream-image of dryads in the desert." An early version won an amateur short story contest at the 1991 World Fantasy Convention, but never saw publication. This is Marian's first "pro" sale.

The Blood Orange Tree
by Marian Crane

Who runs out of gasoline three days in a row in the same place in the Arizona desert?

The first morning I thought 'poor kid', drove on, and felt guilty the rest of the day. The second morning, I imagined a murderer's unmarked van, its interior bloodstained and littered with duct tape and makeshift gags, lurking behind the mesquite groves just off the highway. The third morning, seeing the same weary figure trudging past the same milepost, I stopped.

"Where you headed?"

"Just into the city."

"You okay? Car break down?"

"My bike's a few miles back." He shrugged a shoulder back toward the northwest, where the highway dropped from a maze of red sandstone mountains. "Thanks, lady. My own fault. I thought my gasoline would last all the way down from Nevada."

When mall kids his age said 'lady', it meant 'forty-something fat bitch'. His 'lady' was different enough that I said, "Join me and Gray Mare then."

He bent down to look through the open side window. "You have a horse?"

"The Saab." I patted the cracked dashboard. "From a Tolkien short story. It featured an old gray mare of uncommon good sense and loyalty."

"Ah," he said, nodding. "Sympathetic magic."

"Better than naming it 'Chrysophylax,' after the dragon. That was going to be my sportscar, after I made my fortune from painting."

"A dragon's name."

"I was nineteen in 1974. Go figure."

I had to remind him about the seatbelt, and he fumbled with the catch. He jumped at the Mare's stuttering engine. I smiled; he turned away to look out the window, a study of young nonchalance. Jackrabbits and mourning doves burst from cover as we passed. A hawk soared high enough over the desert, to be gilt by dawnlight. The boy frowned at the hawk.

When the road let me, I watched him. Sixteen, I thought, maybe seventeen. Thin, tall, knobby at the joints like a colt. Bronze hair curled against high, olive-toned cheekbones. A face I'd paint into a Florentine-style fresco. If I could paint well, or if a kindly muse stopped by to coach me. No artistically-ripped mall-rat clothes, either: jeans dark and crisp, a clean gray T-shirt, a storm-blue jacket with the rough sheen of raw silk. He didn't smell of three days in the desert, or even an hour. I didn't think the jacket hid a gun.

On the floor, the gas can rocked. Red-orange dust stained the boy's jeans. I saw the side of the can that he'd hidden from me. The metal was a pitted lacework of rust, a desert relic dry of gasoline for years.

The Mare jittered over the center line.

He looked at me, then at the can. "I'm sorry. I needed a lure, to make somebody stop. I don't mean to hurt you, lady."

"What do you want?" My knuckles whitened on the steering wheel, but I kept my voice light.

"You have to promise to help me. Before sunrise."

My luck. A juvenile detention center, heralded by Do Not Stop For Hitchhikers signs, lay not too many miles eastward. Gently I asked, "What happens at sunrise?"

"Nothing, to you." More hawks wheeled over a salt flat ahead, bright bronze shapes against garnet hills. "Can you get me into the city? I have an urgent business appointment at nine."

With his parole officer? I glanced east, saw the first sliver of sunlight pierce a gap in the mountains. Road mirages stole the gleam, sent it rippling down the asphalt a quarter-mile ahead.

On the straight road, I had time to watch my passenger watch the bar of sunlight blaze across the road. "Please?" he whispered, his fingers clenching the seatbelt.

"All right." Why not? "Into the city."

Peach-golden light spilled across the desert and into my car. The boy cast a watery shadow against torn upholstery. He forced one hand against his lips. A large russet hawk dipped by my side window, pacing the car, its wingtip almost brushing the glass. A dark eye blinked white, twice, then the hawk lifted away. I heard it scream over the Mare's laboring engine, the cry Doppler-shifted into distance as we left it behind. Then the light was only sunlight. The hawk was gone, over the hills or high up in newborn morning thermals. The boy's shadow was as solid as mine. His smile was unsteady, his gray eyes bright.

"Thank you," he said.

"For helping a kid from Nevada find his fortune in Phoenix? You're welcome. Just send some luck my way."

"On my honor, I will."

Such words. He must have gone to a Catholic school. I had a sudden vision of a young European prince, ten years later, buying my paintings. "You're really a billionaire's son. Your motorcycle really did run out of gas, three mornings in a row."

"And somebody stole my real gas can, about ten miles back past that town…"

"The town is Wickenburg. Better make it twenty miles. I live ten miles past it."

"Twenty then. I'm just down here to see the city. Run a few errands."

"Gems? Precious metals? Stocks?"

"Oranges."

"Oranges?"

"My father owns an experimental nursery—hybridizing plants to adapt to arid regions and grafting delicate strains to strong stock. He sent me down to look at an odd old variety he's interested in, at a private ranch. If it's what we want, I'll try to buy some cuttings. Our orchards are dying out. This hybrid seems like it might be the only type really adaptable to our area."

The mile markers surged by. I began to wonder about our game. "I've heard all sorts of legends attached to oranges."

He humored me. "Really?"

"The golden apples of the Hesperides. One of Hercules' tasks, I think. A 17th Century Dutchman said they were oranges. Maybe the Hebrew's Tree of Knowledge was an orange tree. Or was it apricot? And I read a fantasy book once, long ago, that said every thirteenth fruit of the orange tree held a wish. They were only folktales, but beautiful."

His voice was suddenly sharp. "You're a scholar?"

"Hardly. My family lived in a good part of the city. I was young when we left, but I remember all the houses seemed to come with their own transplanted English gardens. Whoever designed ours was a citrus addict. He'd left his books in the attic."

"Do you still have them?"

"No. My mother sold them in an estate sale years ago. To help me pay for art school. For all the good it did us, we should have kept the books and the house. I don't live downtown now. It's too depressing."

"I thought the city was magical, when I saw it at night from the mountains," the boy said. "A lake of light. What is it in the daytime? Steel and glass towers above, a deep green oasis below? I smelled orchards blooming, before dawn..."

"Most of the orchards are pastel subdivisions by now. It's only February; you smell the old orange trees in yards and along the freeways. Wait until summer. Did you know that hot pavement in central Arizona smells like dead animals? By August, anyone who hasn't run away from the heat goes insane. The steel and greenery don't even belong here. Phoenix is as much a mirage as Vegas."

"Vegas?"

"Never mind." I wondered where he really lived.

"I wish you could see it through my eyes, lady."

"I can't see around the past."

"What past?" His hand flattened on my forehead.

"Oh," I said.

The Arizona Tourism Board must marshal legions of photographers on mornings like this, I thought. Fifteen miles away, skyscrapers rose like Waterford-crystal blocks. Surreal mountains ringed the city, speared up through it in seven-hundred-foot-high scarps of russet and amber sandstone. Golf courses and swimming pools were beryls and sapphires bejeweling a golden valley. The abomination was beautiful because it had no right to exist, an ephemeral kingdom made as much of illusion as water and steel.

"Treasure it. It can't last," he whispered. His fingertips left my skin, but some of the sudden glamor stayed. "I know deserts. This one waits below the surface to take back its lands. People lived here once before. Who were they, and where did they go?"

"Hohokam," I dredged up high-school memories. "Native Americans. Canal-builders. Some of the new canals follow the old channels. They're gone. Maybe some of the nearby tribes are descendants. I don't know."

The boy nodded. "Whoever rebuilt those canals made the same bargain as before, maybe without knowing it. The desert's magic in exchange for desolation later. Whatever lives and grows here has the power to defy time and entropy, at least for a while."

"This is just Phoenix."

"This is *Phoenix*, lady. A city twice-risen from sand, called after the Benu, the Firebird? There is great power in names. Anything can happen here, while the city stands and water flows through it."

"You're nuts."

"You're blind."

"Perhaps, but I'm the driver."

"Then watch where you're going."

So I did, and saw the surviving citrus orchards yield to pink-walled, fake-adobe subdivisions and seedy strip malls. The painterly part of my brain stopped its habitual self-doubt long enough to piece together a sketch. Under a hot, white noon sky, three orange-tree dryads danced in a desert full of shattered glass and metal. Their bodies were lush, heavy as mine, relics of a beauty centuries out of style. I had never thought of myself as beautiful—but the dryads were. I tried to analyze the imagery. A manifesto railing against over-development? A 20th century take on Classicism? A size-wise fairy tale?

Stubbornly, the vision refused an explanation.

"Where are we going?" asked my passenger, pulling me out of the reverie in time to realize I'd been pacing traffic at an effortless seventy miles per hour instead of my normal plodding fifty-five.

"I work downtown. Where do you need to be dropped off?"

"Are you a painter there?"

"I wish. I don't even know what art is anymore. Did you know there's a guy in London who makes art from dead cows in formaldehyde tanks?"

He made a disgusted noise. "We have people like that, too. Are they valued here?"

"Enough to be famous. Sorry about the rant. I tell myself my day-job is desk jockey for a construction company, and that I'm only waiting for the big break. Let's worry about your future first. The bus connections aren't the best—okay, they're almost medieval—but they'll get you close to your orange tree."

"Bus?" he asked.

I was late to work, helping him find the right bus and giving him cash to buy an all-day transit pass. It was the best workday I'd had in years. I got through ten hours of data entry by planning another painting during my breaks. A twilight scene of tropical fish, swimming between weathered-wood fences and cacti. In the background, I imagined city lights blooming down in a valley, like lost Atlantis in an undersea rift.

Like the dryads, it refused to be nailed to a cause. It merely wanted to exist.

I pushed my last sketch aside and concentrated on work. Downtown Phoenix intruded through the window. By late afternoon, an unfamiliar city built itself outside the office window. Dusty sunlight slanted down in ramps between the skyscrapers. Palm trees, reflected between the glass canyons, stretched into an infinite oasis. A Precisionist painting might capture it: all angles, color-washed planes, clean lines that echoed back to the 1920's ideal of glorified technology and a bright future.

So many ideas. Could I paint even one of them? Trying would cost me nothing but the old watercolor paints slowly drying in their tubes. Blank paper waited in my studio, a dozen white-shuttered windows that didn't need reasons or markets or clients to exist.

I walked outside to the Mare.

Go home right now, sang the sun and the wind in the green palm-fronds*, and you can paint whatever you want. Only go now, and don't stop.*

I saw the boy leaning against my car, his head bent over something in his hands. The lines of his body, outlined by red-orange sunlight, almost made me reach for the tiny sketchbook in my purse.

"Any luck?"

He looked up, face set in a scowl. "No. I need your help again."

The muse's moment began to ebb. I might still paint. If I got in the Mare without involving myself any further. A rent-a-cop lounged against a marble fountain seventy feet away if I needed more backbone. The orange-tree dryads, the desert seascape and the crystal towers begged me to call out, turn over the boy's problems to someone else.

"The owner wasn't cooperative. No grafts. Not even a single rotten orange," he snarled, taking my continued presence on faith. He tossed away the object in his hands. It was a dead brown twig from a citrus tree, garnished with a few desiccated leaves. "He wanted things I didn't have. Credit cards, check guarantee cards, my father's tax number. And he wouldn't take what I had for payment! All for a wretched, half-dead tree that no one will be able to save in a few years!"

"What did you try to give him? Not the damned gas can, I hope." My moment of perfect creativity had fled, along with the dryads and the shimmering fish. I might as well go paint green and pink coyotes on black velvet. Tourist junk like that, I could sell at almost any weekend swap-meet.

He upended a palm-sized bag. I winced at the noise, then forgot to breathe. Finger-long bars of gold, chased with wavy interlocking designs, clanged against the Mare's hood. Polished nuggets caught the sun in their hearts and flamed Gulf-stream blue, dark carmine, jungle-green. A water-clear stone big around as my thumb sprayed a perfect spectrum across the pitted paint.

The boy glared at the trove. "He said I was probably a thief. Then he threw me out. Threatened to call the police. So I found you again."

I leaned back against my car. "How..." Did I really want to know how he found me in all of central Phoenix? "What do you want now?"

"You helped me once." He scooped up a handful of sapphires and gold, let it sparkle. "You're poor. You'll know better than I how to turn this junk into real money. It's yours."

"If I can get you back to that ranch tonight."

"Yes."

I looked at my elderly car and remembered the fourth-floor office above me. Maybe it was time I tried being rich and talentless.

We spent the time until midnight in coffee shops, where the boy pretended he knew what coffee was until it burned his tongue. I wasted gasoline conducting him to parks and galleries and shopping malls as we followed a slowly closing spiral. We idled through historical districts, along quiet streets curtained in the deep greens made possible, in the desert, only by water and money and care.

I parked half a block from his objective. "We'll get caught."

"I'll get you out of it."

"I suppose you'll flash gold in front of the security guards?"

"Aren't any. Just wires and sizzling lights."

"Electronics, then. Oh, how very easy."

"I didn't come this far to let a fence stop me."

Black shapes loomed ten or fifteen feet from the floor of the night. I was accustomed to the airy native trees around my adobe studio. The orange orchard seemed a threatening, alien labyrinth inside its wrought-iron fence.

Peacocks launched into a distant racket.

The boy ghosted by a gate interwoven with quiescent wires. I expected him to have tools. Then again, remembering the golden bars, I wasn't startled when he simply raised a hand to the gate. Something crackled. I smelled acrid smoke. The gate swung open. All the nearby crickets stopped chirping.

"Come on," he whispered. "I'll need your help inside."

I followed him, my high heels catching on twigs but making little sound. Tree branches drooped around us, offering leafy boughs and thorns, sweet fruit and rancid windfalls, a wild scent shifting between early blossoms and winter decay.

Vague coppery light, a second-hand gift from the city's sodium-vapor streetlamps, reflected down from the clouds. It lit a clearing occupied by one weathered shed and a tree. The tree had been grafted to a stock—bitter orange, I thought, recalling the old citrus-grower's books and sketches. The root-stock's branches, carrying a few withered green-brown globes, angled upward around a smooth grayish trunk shrouded in waxy leaves.

The main tree, the scion, looked unreal. Yggdrasil masquerading as a Fabergé jade and zircon toy for a Tsarina? It should grow from a golden urn in a museum. In the morning it would be only nine or ten feet high, and look as sad as the shed and the dying root-stock.

"What now?" I asked, my voice just above a whisper. "Do we dig it up?"

"Start the count. You pick where."

I considered one heavy fruit among many. An orange. Unmysterious. I might go to an all-night supermarket and buy its cousin. But I remembered childhood and hand-colored books: the apple growing in Eden, Hellenic myths, Arabian Nights tales where the forbidden orchards hid fruit of diamonds or genie-inhabited pearl.

Another dour medieval legend surfaced. "I can't," I said. "Women supposedly blighted orange trees with a single touch."

"Are you a virgin then?"

"Watch your mouth! I went to college in the seventies."

"And you remember them?"

"That was the sixties, infant. The only people who want to re-enact the seventies never lived through them."

He shrugged and said, "We'll chance it. Have you gloves?"

I saw his grin, in the copper light. "Gloves, he wants," I told the tree. "We'll need a lawyer if we get caught."

"For an orange or two? From necromancers who put pickled animals on pedestals? What a world you live in. Choose, lady."

The half-hidden oranges seemed to float like moons in a space made of sleeping dark green leaves. The one I chose was no different than its fellows—merely the first orange my eyes found. "That one."

He followed from that one, whispering each number. Then—"Thirteen!" The last orange snapped off its twig with a tiny snick. He tucked the fruit into his jacket. Then he reached up and snagged my orange. "Here. They're blood oranges. You can't find them often in the markets you frequent, I'd guess. Your wage." The easy arrogance in his voice stung me, did not sting me at all. The strong, clean citrus smell was worth that much.

A lone cricket rasped, somewhere in the tree.

A tardy alarm shrilled perhaps a thousand feet from us, near the main house. We'd left the gate open. A sensor woke and realized it. Lights flicked on. The peacocks cackled. A dog yammered, and I heard a man's voice raised in a question.

We ran. Like Cinderella, I lost a shoe on the way. The boy darted through the gate. As I passed, it brushed my arm and bestowed a kissing shock. But the Mare waited, her ignition blessedly loyal for once. Probably before the lights even reached the blood orange tree, we rocketed away laughing like fools.

Later, I stopped near an all-night grocery. Untrimmed palm trees screened out the sky, their papery brown fronds creaking in the breeze. In the parking lot, low-riders whooped and made their cars buck to tinny music. I didn't hear any sirens.

The boy dug out a knife from his jacket and began to open his prize.

"What about your father?"

"He wanted the cuttings to renew our orchards; the ripe fruit, he said, was useless unless it had grown from our soil. I don't see why. One orange might spawn more trees from its seeds than one cutting."

"No," I said, remembering another fact from the citrus addict's books. "Cross-pollination. The tree bloomed in that orchard with other oranges. God knows what you'd get from the seeds. Only a cutting would grow true to the strain."

His knife trembled across the orange's pitted skin, stopped in mid-cut. He looked at me, then out across the city. He smiled.

"No." I made it final by turning off the Mare's engine. "We are not going back."

"I'm not, either. Going back, I mean. To my land."

"Your land."

My companion shrugged. "I thought I had failed. But if I stay here, I haven't. The cuttings were for my people. But this orange, this magic—this city!—is for me."

"All this for an orange?"

He gave me the knife, hilt-first in a courtly flourish. "For this orange, yes. Try yours."

I held mine untouched in my hand and watched him. He peeled thirteen sections away from the pith. Blood, garnet, ruby—our oranges already had a wine-flush on their skins, hinting at the bruised colors within. The boy bit into the first red wedge. "Not hungry?" he teased.

I felt like a drunk teenager on a dare. One wish. Love or talent? Or wealth, which might buy facsimiles of both? A better life, certainly. It wouldn't be wrong to eat this orange. Only wasteful. I might never paint again. But I'd never forget how I'd felt in that sunset moment when I could paint whatever I chose—and let lapse the gift to help a stranger.

"It's lovely enough to keep." I handed back the knife. "How is it?"

"Beautiful."

In the brief, silken silence I remembered the day's embryonic pictures: fish flickering between night-blooming cacti, jade-skinned dryads sheltering from the noon sun under their leaf-bound braids, a thousand more images too jumbled to recognize all at once. If I reached for them, tried to quantify them enough to sell, they'd vanish. Remembering them was a torment; forgetting them, unthinkable.

The boy tucked twelve orange segments into his jacket, then opened the car door.

"Where are you going?"

"To find real magic. The kind you have, lady. There's more power here than in any place I grew up, and I want it.

Thank you for showing it to me." He leaned over and kissed me. The scent of the orchard rose from his hair and skin.

"How will you get back to…to Nevada?" I asked, as the secondhand taste of the wishing-orange swam through my mouth.

"Who cares? I could be a hero there, if I returned. But I'd rather see this world first." He set the treasure bag carefully on the seat, my other wage. It chimed from the wealth inside. Then he leapt away from the Mare, darting euphorically into the lake of light, noise, misery and hidden beauty that was my city.

"Wait!"

Some of the low-riders looked over and laughed, not viciously—a plain, heavy, middle-aged woman calling after some jail-bait hustler, imagine! The boy didn't look back, and the palm-fronds closed behind him like a wall.

"You can't survive here…" I began. "Oh, hell." How would I even report him to the police? "Yes. A lost boy, who came from very far away to steal an orange. No, I don't know his name. Here—he left an old gasoline can, try it for fingerprints. Though if they come out looking like Norse runes or alchemical symbols, don't blame me!"

He'd vanished again—beyond my finding, I guessed, even if I quartered the neighborhood in the Mare.

Who'd believe me? I looked at the top half of my face in the rear-view mirror. A clerk. A non-entity who thought she was an artist. Whose paintings died stillborn between mind and canvas.

The scent of the orange was still strong in the car.

I had never wondered why my paintings died unfinished. All those grand ideas, needing only a little adapting to fit them to this contest or that market. But I was always last, even when I completed something. My visions came too late to serve the cause, the creed, the trend.

Who started trends, I wondered, warming the orange in my hands. The wise, the powerful, the unconventional, the fearless, and the frightening. Maybe I should be grateful for being last, compared to a dead cow.

But I'd seen something different today. Dryads dancing between ruined skyscrapers. Fish swimming in desert air. A palm forest a thousand miles wide, the trunks like the gilt hall-columns of Xanadu. Dreams that deserved to be painted, whether I sold them or not.

"I can try," I said to the orange.

A low-rider Cadillac backfired in tempo with a loud Latino version of Duran Duran's "Rio". I jumped, then laughed, and wiped a few decades of useless tears from my eyes. When I looked up again, I saw a rich, sensual composition of neon signs, glossy automobiles, and jeans-clad flamenco dancers. Women laughing. Men making love to women in a roundabout way, their cars hopping like courting birds. I saw joy—and I saw how to paint it.

I felt the muse's moment stretch into a minute, and then eternity.

I truly don't know if I have the thirteenth orange. If the boy cheated himself with a delusion of discovery, while the real magic sleeps above my worktable.

I work—if doing what one loves can be called work—in the same adobe studio, under a grove of feathery mesquite trees at the top of a low red hill. I kept my Gray Mare but gave her a new engine and ignition.

I stuck cloves into the orange, dusted it with orris root to counter what little damp could harm it, and knotted it into a tether of ribbons.

The scent was, and will be for years, strong enough to flavor the entire studio with lush night and wheeling stars. It astonishes the people who commission artwork from me.

When I paint, one window looks south over the desert, to the mountains and mirages of Phoenix. The other gives me pure north light and a view down a winding dirt road toward the highway to Nevada.

Jon Hansen credits a Terry Bisson story, "The Toxic Donut", and the season of the year in which he read it as inspiring the story that follows. It was, he said, at the end of a Christmas trip. "Such holidays are a time when adults visit their parents' homes and end up feeling like kids again."

Eater
by Jon Hansen

Hank Orlean stood in front of the door to his mother's house, hesitating. The cab had long since gone, but it wasn't too late to change his mind. Just turn and start walking. Walking and walking. "Oh hell," he said to the empty yard, "let's get this over with."

He wiped his brow, slick with sweat despite the chill autumn air and wondered for the thousandth time how his family would react when they saw him. Hank had always been heavy, but now he pushed three hundred, easy. His brother had worked for Greenpeace in college, done some cleanup work; he knew what it meant to be an Eater, what was involved. But his mother....Hank shivered.

Lehman, his team leader back in Seattle, had just stared at Hank when he said he was going to his mother's in Chicago for Thanksgiving. Lehman was an cynical man, a former Eater himself, veteran of a hundred cleanup jobs. He knew the other pressures of the work.

"Your mother's house, Hank," Lehman said. One pale blond eyebrow arched, ever so slightly. "Isn't this the same woman who, right after your first tanker spill, said that at least the hospital would be able to limit your meals?" Hank's heart pounded louder at the memory.

Finally he took a deep breath and opened the door. His younger brother Jesse looked up from the evening news and roared with delight. "Hank, you came!" he shouted as he stood up, arms stretched wide. They hugged, good and hard. Jesse felt like a child in his arms; he barely felt his brother pounding him on the back, as they had since they were kids. Finally they pulled free of each other, identical grins on their faces. Jesse jerked a thumb at the door. "You got any luggage out there?" he asked.

Hank shook his head and slapped the black canvas bag hanging off one shoulder. "Nothing but this, bro'," he replied. Hank had gotten pretty good traveling over the last three years, since he'd become an Eater. Three years, eighty pounds, and a lifetime.

From the other room ran Jesse's girls, Lisa and Jamie, eight year old twin streaks of lightning. They each latched onto a leg, hugging and giggling like mad. Hank roared like a movie monster, waving the girls from his legs as they shrieked in delight.

Their mother, Angela, emerged from the kitchen, apron tied round her trim waist, smiling in welcome. "Hey, Angela. Good to see you," he said, and kissed her on her cheek. He thought he could see the surprise in her bright blue eyes, surprise at seeing *him*.

"Hello, Hank. I should have known it was you from all the noise." Hank turned. In the doorway from the hall stood his mother, silent and gray, watching him. Hank didn't meet her eyes at first. He waited as Angela pried the kids off his legs. Then, finally, he turned to his mother.

"Hi, Mom. How are you?" He wondered if he sounded as calm as he hoped he did.

"Fine, Hank. Are you hungry? We just finished dinner." The words were toneless, but Hank felt himself reacting. How quickly they fell into old stances, ready to take up arms again. Not this time.

Hank shook his head. "I'm fine, Mom," he said. On the way from the airport he'd sent the cab through a drive-thru and picked up several cheeseburgers. Then he'd eaten them all before he arrived. Just like when he was a kid again, hiding the evidence before someone found out.

His mother sniffed. "Let me show you where you'll be sleeping." Hank started down the hall, heading for his old room, but she shook her head and led him downstairs to the rec room. *Déjà vu* swept him as he went down the steps.

When his dad was still alive, this room had been his space, his little chunk of paradise away from the fire station. His dad had been a loud and hearty bear of a man. Deer heads and rifles had covered the walls, overlooking a pool table. The animal heads with their staring eyes creeped him out, but Hank loved the table. Every time his father went to fight a fire, he would spend hours rolling the balls back and forth across the glowing green felt, until his dad came back home.

Now it was all gone, sold at a tag sale or given to Goodwill or just carried out with the trash. Boxes filled the room, miniature buildings crowding over brown carpet roads. Along the wall a spot had been cleared, and an old sleeping bag laid out with a single pillow on top.

His mother said something, and Hank looked at her. "We put Lisa and Jamie in your old room," she was saying. "We weren't sure if you were coming and besides, the girls are getting older. They need their own space." She gave a tense little smile. "They're getting so much bigger, you know." She leaned closer and put her hand on his arm. "You don't mind, do you?"

"No," he answered. "It's fine. I've been sleeping in less comfortable places recently." He dropped his bag on the sleeping bag and headed back upstairs.

It was one of the stranger evenings Hank remembered in his mother's house. Certainly the quietest. Usually his mother took these opportunities to pick and chip away at him, acid comments on his choices. Clothes, friends, work, and always how his weight affected those things, always for the worse. The good things, which he denied himself through his gluttonous ways.

Not this time. His mother sat on the far end of the sofa, heavy ashtray beside her, silently smoking and watching as he and Jesse and Angela talked and the girls watched television. Three years of little details to catch up on: Jesse's job in the programming field, how Lisa and Jamie had grown, changes in the friends and places Hank had left behind long ago. All the while she sat and smoked.

Then Angela asked The Question: "So how's the job, Hank? How do you like being an Eater?"

As the words left Angela's mouth Jesse started shaking his head, a quick *no no no*, trying to stop them too late. The words slipped out and hung curling in the air with the cigarette smoke.

His mother's eyes widened slightly and her lips mashed together, forming a cold slash in her wrinkled face. With one movement she ground her cigarette out. Hank cringed and prepared for the torrent.

That never came. Instead she stood and marched from the room, leaving behind the smell of smoke hanging over the lipstick-stained cigarette butts in the ashtray.

Jesse sighed and Angela looked apologetic. "I'm sorry, Hank, I didn't…"

Hank waved his hand. "Don't apologize," he said. "Truth is, I appreciate it."

"You want her upset?" asked Jesse, his face in his old expression of dismay. Jesse, ever the peacemaker, seeing both sides and taking none, supporting whoever wasn't there to make the explanations that would never come.

"No, but it wouldn't make any difference. This is my life, and she doesn't like it. I'm tired of apologizing for it." They all sat silent for a moment, the only sound coming from the television, an argument set to a laugh track. Then Hank smiled at Angela. "I like my job very much, thanks."

Then he talked about living in Seattle, keeping it light and interesting: the way Mount Rainier floats in the sky on foggy mornings like a majestic god; the morning, deep in the heart of winter, he awoke early to find the city encased in gleaming ice, silent and still, waiting for the sun to free it.

As for his job, they both knew a fair amount about Eating, or thought they did.

Hank told them about the *Heir Of Perseus* tanker wreck last year off the coast of northern California. Some celebrities had shown up to help with cleanup and shape their images as environmentally correct. Hank had gotten some autographs. Angela's eyes widened when he told her who he met. He left out a lot, particularly the two weeks he spent in intensive care recuperating from the Eating.

"What about Mt. St. Helens?" asked Jesse. "Some scientist on CNN thinks it's getting ready to act up again. If it erupts, is that something you would be handling?"

Hank shook his head. "In the first place, that's a natural disaster. Eaters handle man-made problems, mostly waste spills, that nature can't clean up. Besides, we can't eat hurricanes or earthquakes."

"But the ash…"

"For all the mess it makes, the ash isn't really pollution. It's actually good for the soil, once it settles." Jesse frowned, not agreeing but not arguing. Hank shook his head, and made a strategic yawn. "Sorry, guys. It was a long trip. See you in the morning." The girls lay asleep in front of the TV, gently-snoring bundles that barely twitched when Hank bent down and kissed them. He waved goodnight and headed downstairs.

As he got ready for bed, he found a cold cheeseburger at the bottom of his bag. He took it out; the congealed cheese felt like plastic under his fingers. He sighed. "Sometimes I hate this job," he said as he choked it down.

Turkey, both white and dark meat, honey-glazed ham, mashed potatoes *and* stuffing, steamed carrots, green bean casserole, cranberry sauce, and three buttered rolls. Every time Hank put something else on his plate, he sensed his mother's eyes narrowing, her lips thinning, an objection starting to form on her lips. She never spoke, however. And with everyone dressed up and looking nice, things might have been all right, if it hadn't been for the call. Hank took it in the kitchen. It didn't last long, but long enough.

"You've got to work?" asked Jesse.

"But it's a holiday! They can't drag you away from your family like that!" The anger in Angela's voice comforted Hank a little. He shook his head and smiled.

"That's the way it goes, guys. Besides, this is local. You should be grateful." He waggled a finger. "They're sending a car. I've got about twenty minutes, so I'd better hurry." With that, he sat down and began to eat, choking down the food as quickly as possible.

"What are you *doing*?" He looked up, his mother's horrified face glaring at him. "You're still going to eat?"

Jesse raised up a hand, trying to pull her back to her seat. "Mom…"

She pulled her arm away and glared at Jesse. "They're coming to take him away *now*, to do this dirty, filthy job, on Thanksgiving of all days!" She wheeled back to Hank. "You're throwing your life away like your father, and all you can think to do is eat? My God!"

Hank made himself keep eating. "Mom, I've tried to tell you before; this is how it works. This is my job, and in order to do it right, I have to do this. Now please stop yelling. I'm trying to eat."

She straightened, looking down her nose at him. "Fine," she said in a cold voice. With that, she stormed out, leaving frost in her wake. After a minute, a distant slam came from down the hall. Jesse blew out a deep breath. "Hank, you could've handled that better."

"Jesse, gimme a break, willya?"

"You know she's got trouble with what you do. Can't you just be a little more patient with her?"

"I've tried to talk to her about this a hundred times before, but all she does is start nagging me about my weight, which, frankly, I don't need to hear. I know I'm heavy.

That's the whole point here. I have to be, remember?" He risked a quick glance around the table; Jamie and Lisa looked like they were about to burst into tears. He forced his voice a little softer. "Now, I'll be happy to try to explain it to her again if you like, but *not now*." They all sat in silence then, quietly eating. Lisa started to whisper something but Angela shushed her. Finally, mercifully, Hank finished. He pushed back his chair and dropped the napkin on the table. "I've got to go change."

Downstairs he opened his bag and pulled out his clothes. His Eater suit, he called it: comfortable shoes and a black sweat suit. He'd packed them on reflex, not even thinking about it. Now he was glad he had. After getting his jacket from the hall closet, he simply sat in the front room and concentrated on his breathing. In the dining room he could hear Angela and Jesse still at the table, trying to pretend everything was fine for the girls. Five minutes later came the knock at the door. Hank didn't bother saying goodbye.

The state patrolman was a young, blank-faced guy with a marine haircut. He didn't make conversation, just drove fast, his siren wailing like a banshee on speed. Hank closed his eyes and felt his dinner shift each time they rounded a curve.

Near the interstate, traffic stood still, rows of red taillights staring at them like little eyes. The cop slowed only a little as he crossed into the emergency lane and kept going. The stopped cars seemed to go on forever. Finally, up in the distance, the flicker of emergency lights appeared. The cars ended at a roadblock of sawhorses and tense state patrolmen. Beyond them a cluster of emergency vehicles sat. The patrol car crawled to a stop beside them, and Hank sighed in relief.

A tall man in a dark green trench coat strode up as Hank climbed out of the car. "Good to meet you, Mr. Orlean. I'm Fullerton, with State Disaster Management." He stuck out his hand, and Hank shook it. He had a cool, firm grip.

They started walking through the emergency vehicles: fire trucks, police cars, ambulances. Hank squinted against the glare of the lights; Fullerton didn't seem to notice. "Sorry to take you away from your family on the holiday, but we really needed someone of your abilities. The spill is damned close to the reservoir—too close. It provides the water for three counties." Fullerton glanced at Hank. "The local agencies are all unavailable, so we called your department for help. Mr. Lehman said you were in the area and might be available."

"Lehman, huh?" Hank chuckled. "I'll have to remember to thank him later."

They passed through the emergency vehicles, all gathered around one point on the highway, where the ground fell away. Hank walked to the edge and looked down.

The train tracks ran parallel to the highway at that point, and it was there the train had derailed. The last three cars lay on their sides, but only one of them mattered, a tanker car, ripped open, sides slick and wet. Past the wreck Hank could see the sun hanging low, bleeding red reflected in the reservoir. A whipping noise came from overhead. A news helicopter, he knew. He didn't look up.

Hank pointed at the tanker car. "What was in it?" he said. He recognized it already by the stench, but he wanted to hear Fullerton say it out loud.

"Fuel oil, several thousand gallons worth."

Hank nodded. "Most of my work has been with tanker spills, crude oil, but I can handle this." His heartbeat started picking up, excited at the prospect of action. "Where are the paramedics?" Fullerton waved them over.

They were a study in contrast, a tiny black woman in late middle age with a guarded expression, and a handsome young man who looked like a *GQ* model. "Either of you treated an Eater before?" Hank queried as he took off his jacket.

The woman nodded. "Three years ago, at a chlorine spill near Gary," she said in a clear voice. "Three of 'em came and cleaned it up."

"Good, then you know the drill. Wait *until* I finish. When I'm done, give me plenty of oxygen and keep your eyes open." Hank handed his jacket to Fullerton, who folded it over his arm.

The woman nodded, but the male paramedic looked puzzled. "What's he gonna do?" he stage-whispered, but Hank had already started down the side toward the spill.

It was steeper than he thought. Near the bottom his feet slipped. He fell, landing on one knee with a wet gooshing sound. He cursed. The fuel oil had begun seeping into the earth. He'd have to hurry.

Hank circled until he found a dry spot, the edge of the spill. He closed his eyes and pictured the signs in his head. They hung before his mind's eye, clear and gleaming, showing him what to do and how to do it. The tension began to build along his shoulders and back, muscles tightening like twisted rope. "Now," he snapped, activating the change.

He took three breaths, each deeper than the last. On the final breath he *swelled*, his neck thickening like a tree trunk, his jaws stretching wide like a python swallowing a pig. A great emptiness filled him, crying out to be filled. Then he bent down and began to Eat.

He began shoveling dirt into his mouth, the dark earth filled with stones and bugs and dead grass, and all of it stinking, reeking with the smell of oil, the stench of it filling his nose and his mouth. His eyes streamed tears, but he kept shoveling. The oil turned the dirt to mud, black dripping muck that marked his skin. He kept shoveling it in.

Finally, when he could hold no more he climbed out of the shallow pit he had dug. His insides twisted in protest and he closed his eyes from the pain. He suffered it as long as possible, long past the point any one could have.

Then his stomach clenched and he voided up the earth and stones from within him, now clean and pure again, like some ancient god of creation bringing forth the land from within him. When he finally finished, his belly empty, he staggered back into the pit and began shoveling more earth into himself.

For an eternity he ate and voided dark earth, time melting away in an endless cycle. Finally he finished, and climbed from the pit he had gouged. The smell of the fuel oil no longer itched his nose. Not bothering to turn away he bent and emptied his belly of the last of the cleaned earth. Inside he could feel the fuel oil burning within him, its fiery warmth itching from the edge of his skin all the way to the inside of his bones. Now, like a factory, his transformed body worked, feverishly breaking down the oil boiling within him. Here his mass worked in his favor, diluting the poison within him, giving him a chance to finish purifying it before it killed him.

Hank staggered away from the torn earth. Suddenly weak, he felt himself start to sway.

He didn't remember falling, but a hazy moment later he could feel hands touching him, rolling him over, and a mask being slipped over his face. Sweet oxygen filled his lungs, and his stomach spasmed again. He pushed the mask away and coughed hard, blowing out dirt and stones. He heard the male paramedic curse.

Hank grinned. "Told you to watch out," he breathed before he slipped away into the black.

He awoke surrounded by starched white linen and green tile walls. Every inch of him ached, and a vile taste lurked in the back of his throat. At a coughing sound he turned his head, slowly.

Lehman sat there, shaking his head. "Honestly, Hank, I told you going home would be a disaster. Didn't I? You should take a page from me. I haven't been home for Thanksgiving in eighteen years." The corner of his mouth tugged up. "Of course, that might be because my parents moved and didn't send me their new address."

Hank's chuckle started a coughing fit, which lasted until Lehman offered him some water. The water felt like a melted glacier sliding down his throat, wiping the taste away. "Thanks," he managed to croak.

"No problem," said Lehman. "Now that you're awake, let me give you the good news. Working on a holiday gets you a nice bonus, this time paid by the ever-so-grateful Mr. Fullerton's budget. Lucky dog. Now you can get that Perry Como box set I know you've been eyeing. However," he paused as he stood. "Remember those family members you left when you hustled out the door? They're outside, waiting to see you." Lehman smiled and left.

Hank closed his eyes for a minute, expecting to see Jesse and Angela there when he opened them. Instead it was his mother, looking pale and somehow *smaller* than before. Hank blinked, startled. "Mom?"

She leaned down and hugged him tight, her familiar smell of cigarettes filling his nose. "I'm glad you're all right," she said. "I'm so sorry, I just think about what happened to your father…" She broke off as the tears started.

"It's all right, Mom. Honest." He closed his eyes. Later they would end up yelling at each other, but for now this was enough.

Being a serious student of Middle Eastern dance has given Teresa Noelle Roberts "an added appreciation of the power and beauty of the female body in all shapes and sizes." Her dance experience, quite understandably, colors the story that follows. She credits Dayle Dermatis for helping her get the story back on track when it wandered off into the wrong subplot.

Demon Bone
by Teresa Noelle Roberts

Masyra's bruises made her wince slightly as she sauntered into the inn's dining room. Each step created a series of small earthquakes on her plump body and set the many strands of semi-precious stones on her hip belt and on the ends of her eleven long brown braids dancing. Her entrance caused several of the diners to look up and nod politely to her—a tall, fat woman dressed in a long green coat and baggy trousers striped in green and brown.

In the flickering candlelight, the bright mosaics on the walls and floors appeared abstract at first, but as Masyra looked more closely, she made out that they depicted scenes out of legend or history: famous banquets, she noted, not famous battles. The few patrons dining at this early hour were as striking as the artwork, the men in long fur-trimmed robes, the collars and cuffs of the shirts underneath marked with geometric embroidery, the women in heavily-embroidered, utterly useless silk aprons over tightly-laced, full-skirted dresses in deep jewel tones.

Even more impressive were the smells that filled the air.

Baradic, the air-mage attached to the Ebanni's court, had literally bounced Masyra out of bed with the urgency of the dream summoning her to Illach. But, she thought as she made her way to a table, she was willing to forgive him the bruises for his booking her a room at this inn.

She was less willing to forgive the vagueness of the information he'd given her. As an earth-mage, she could not be expected to read all the nuances of the airy medium of dream messages. The note that caught up with her half-way to Illach hadn't been much clearer. "I have a problem with a demon," it had read. "Its manifestation is much too physical for my magic." Then he had given her directions to this inn. She had sent a messenger to him on her arrival, but as yet there was no response.

Impatient as she was for more information, she was just as glad to wait until after dining. Air-mages drew so much of their energy from meditative breathing that they tended to forget earth-mages like Masyra had to eat. An earth-mage needed a solid, abundant body that echoed that of the earth herself, and after many days of eating catch-as-catch-can on the road, Masyra was feeling a little frail.

As she enjoyed an excellent dinner of spicy carrot soup, roast lamb, and rice studded with nuts and dried fruit, she observed her fellow diners, who were arriving in greater numbers now. By their dress, all were as prosperous as she would expect in such an elegant hostelry, notably prosperous even for Illach, where she'd yet to see anyone who looked truly poor. Yet all the women were somewhere between slender and emaciated, and none of them were actually eating. One pushed some cooked greens half-heartedly around her plate. The others weren't even making a charade of dining.

Finally, when she had finished the last of her cream-drenched berry cobbler and the innkeeper came over to her table to see if everything had been satisfactory, Masyra couldn't resist asking. "I'm newly arrived in Illach. I notice that I am the only woman here who was actually eating this wonderful food. Did I violate local custom by dining in public?"

The innkeeper laughed ruefully. "No, it's fashion that obliges women to starve themselves so they look like survivors of a siege."

"It's embarrassing sometimes, how foolish some people can be."

"It's obscene, if you ask me! There's no real hunger here anymore; the Ebanni and Ebanna see to it that food is distributed to even the very poor. And now people are starving themselves deliberately!"

"Have they gone mad?"

"That's the ridiculous thing," the innkeeper sighed. "The Ebannina Casilla was a healthy young woman until about six months ago. A fine-looking one, too, from what I hear them say." He gestured broadly, encompassing his wealthy patrons. "Then she started losing weight. It might be that she thought she had a touch of baby fat. She's only fourteen, and girls are silly that way sometimes. My own daughters are forever finding some fault with their looks that I can't see for the life of me. But she eats so little now they say she's practically a walking skeleton. Yet because she is the Ebannina, and because she's known for her beauty—or at least she was when she was eating properly—the fashionable ladies are imitating her. It's terrible for my business! The difference is, sooner or later they break down and eat, but the Ebannina won't or can't."

Masyra shook her head and said, "How peculiar!" Inside, though, she was excited. This might be her demon! A natural illness might cause similar symptoms, but the court physicians should be able to recognize illness even if they could not cure it. And if a demon possessed the heir-presumptive to the Kannish Confederacy, the possible ramifications were ugly. The peace and prosperity of the whole Confederacy could be at stake, threatening the land itself.

Baradic was an air-mage of the Brotherhood of the Owl, a specialist in prophecies and visions. A demon invading the earthly realm was not really in his line, especially when it was causing bodily distress. Such a problem needed the grounding and healing qualities of the earth-gift, and the earth-gift was rare among the people of the Kannish Confederacy, who tended to be fine-boned and of medium height. No wonder the court mage had sent as far as Ballyria for her.

Despite the gravity of the situation, she grinned. Air-mages liked to cultivate an air of mystery. It would be a pleasure to meet with Baradic and tell him what the problem was rather than wait for his explanation.

Baradic had confirmed her suspicions and told her more about the situation when they finally met, but no words could have prepared Masyra for seeing the Ebannina. Lost inside a sea-green brocade gown and pale rose embroidered apron that had once been tightly fitted, Casilla was a skeleton over which ghost-pale skin was stretched. She was pacing up and down the mosaic floor with more vigor than her frailty would suggest, and her eyes, blue-gray and several sizes too large for her skull-like face, glittered with energy. Some of the energy was unhealthy, demon-fed, but some of it was a fierce, fiery curiosity that lit up as soon as she saw Masyra's foreign clothes and appearance. Once she had been a remarkably beautiful girl. Soon she would be a dead one.

"Greetings, Ebannina," Masyra said with a neat bow. "I am Masyra of Ballyria."

"Greetings, Masyra. If you are here to trick me into eating more, you might as well leave." Her voice was sexless and ageless and icy, the voice of bone, as if the demon that possessed her made use of her lips and vocal cords without touching her emotions. "Actually, I would be glad to have you stay," she continued. "You have a wise face, Masyra. Perhaps I can make you understand what no one else seems to, so you can relieve my parents' minds."

With a gesture surprisingly graceful for a creature of bone and demon-will, she motioned the sorceress to sit down. She herself did not sit, but continued to pace as she talked. "You have traveled far from your homeland. In your travels, you must have seen much suffering." Her voice had changed subtly. No demon could counterfeit the tone of a idealist young enough that her ideals were not yet tempered by grim reality.

"And much joy as well, Ebannina." She smiled. Casilla's expression softened no more than a skull's would. "But why should we speak of such things? Here in Illach, there is little enough suffering. Why, the very beggar in the market square is rosy-cheeked and healthy."

"Indeed," and Casilla smiled, though only the beauty of her haunted eyes made it a smile and not a ghost's mad grimace, "if a man is a beggar in Illach, it is by choice. Finding employment is easy, for there is more work to be done than there are folk to do it. If someone cannot work and has no family, the temple of Garra will care for them." She added proudly, "My grandfather and grandmother saw to that."

"Your family," Masyra said, choosing her words with care, "has done the work of twenty in helping to wipe out misery in Illach."

"But we haven't wiped it out! We haven't conquered illness or grief or crime. And outside the walls of Illach, nothing has changed." She clenched her fists with frustration as she sought the words. "Think what the world would be like if no one went hungry, or got ill-treated, or suffered from a curable disease, and if no country ever waged war on another."

"It would be wonderful," Masyra agreed. "Unfortunately, the world's problems can't be solved completely, even by great and wise rulers. It would take magic far greater than mine to make even one city anything like your vision."

"I know! That's why I need to learn magic. How else can I do what I must?" She seized Masyra's strong, sunbrowned hand with her bony ones. "My parents are so worried about me. They think I'm ill and that I don't eat enough. I'm just trying to discipline myself as Baradic does. Perhaps you can help my parents understand that."

"That makes perfect sense," Masyra lied. "But I know it would allay your parents' fears if I can say we ate together. Would you share my luncheon? It's almost noon, a most suitable time for a bite of something tasty."

Masyra opened her basket, unfolded the linen napkin within it, and lifted out a small covered dish. With a flourish, she removed the lid and displayed a perfect baked apple. It was glazed with caramelized sugar, fragrant with spice, almost irresistible, but not so rich that it would hurt Casilla's weakened body. Casilla stared at the dessert with the fond gaze of a lover.

There was a small silver spoon in the dish. She reached for it, practically drooling. Just as she touched the dish, though, a grimace of pain twisted her face. Casilla managed to swallow two small bites of the baked apple, then pushed the dish away with such force Masyra had to catch it to prevent it from landing in her lap.

"It's delicious," Casilla said, "but I'm not very hungry." Her voice was sincere, but every sinew of her fragile body proclaimed the lie she no longer knew she was telling.

Masyra sat back and waited. As she expected, it didn't take long for the drug with which the apple was laced to affect the demon. Unfortunately, quieting the creature temporarily was the best she could do with drugs. Anything powerful enough to cast it out was also powerful enough to kill someone stronger than Casilla. Masyra could actually see the demon-energy dimming, leaving the girl weaker but more relaxed.

Her eyes filling with tears, Casilla reached for the dish with convulsive, jerky movements, as if some force was still holding her back. "I'm lying," she whispered. "I *am* hungry. I'm terribly hungry. It was self-discipline at first, but now I can't make myself eat. Something seems to stop me!"

Masyra pushed the baked apple toward her. Casilla's hands shook as she picked up the spoon and raised it, laden, to her lips. She managed one spoonful, though she was trembling. As she tried to take a second bite, she began to shake so violently that the spoon flew from her hand. "I can't!" she cried, and the demon-grimace flickered again over her face. She threw the bowl onto the floor and collapsed sobbing, her head buried in her matchstick arms.

Masyra wasn't sure of courtly etiquette, but she was sure how to treat a crying girl. She put her arm around the Ebannina's shoulders. "Talk to me," she said. "Together we can reach the root of this mystery."

Casilla sat up and wiped her eyes with her sleeve. "I suppose it all started when I became interested in learning magic. Baradic tells me I carry the seeds of magic, but he refuses to teach me. I think it's because I'm a girl; they don't take women in his order. I asked him to speak to my parents about finding someone who would teach me, but I think he forgot."

Masyra shook her head. Typical of an air-mage not to explain himself. They spent so much time in silent contemplation that they sometimes forgot how to communicate. Typical, too, for one to be so focused on his visions and dreamlore that he forgot something as important as a magic-talented royal child in need of training. "You could never be in the Brotherhood, it's true, but he could give you basic teaching if you had an air affinity. His path is not the right one for you, though." She considered the girl's restless energy, her intensity. "I would guess yours is the path of fire." As she spoke, Masyra put her hands on Casilla's head, closed her eyes and opened herself, feeling for the seeds of magic.

Casilla's skull, to a normal touch, was solid. Masyra was feeling for something beyond the physical. Her hands sensed heavings and writhings, as if the girl's head was the belly of a woman about to give birth. The demon, Masyra thought. Then she realized there were two presences there, one alien and demonic, the other sprung from Casilla. An ember to the full-fledged fire of a trained fire-mage, it was magic nonetheless. Flavoring that magic was a trace of earth, which confused Masyra until she recalled long-ago lessons she never thought to encounter in her own life. All true-born rulers were touched by earth because of their bond to their land, and a magic-gifted ruler, no matter what their dominant path, would always have a minor affinity for earth-magic. "Did Baradic teach you anything at all?" Masyra asked.

"Very little, but he let me spend some time in his company, and I saw the disciplines his order uses: fasting and silence and meditation upon the breath. I have been practicing them on my own, so I would be ready when a teacher was found."

Masyra, her hands still on Casilla's head, winced. Not only had she learned just enough to jar her magic awkwardly awake, what little she had picked up was suited to a path diametrically opposed to her own. Fire talents thrived on trance-dances around bonfires, drums and bells, passions both intellectual and physical. And they needed plenty of food to replace the energy they blazed through in their very active magic. Casilla's earth talent, minor as it was, needed outdoor activity, communion with nature—and again, a well-fed body. Even without a demon, the young woman would be suffering. But it didn't explain how she had become possessed.

Figuring that out would help determine how to rid her of the demon. But to get an answer to that question, Masyra would first have to get more information. "What you have been doing is dangerous, Ebannina," she said. "You have magic in you, and you have awakened it with your efforts, but you are going about it the wrong way for one with your particular gifts. It's hurting you. What earthly good can you expect to do when you're dead of starvation?"

"It was working at first!" she argued. "I was fasting for a day or two at a time, like the Brotherhood does, and I could influence things."

Because she was burning up her own flesh for energy, Masyra thought, *but I won't explain that to her just yet.*

"It was minor, I suppose, but I could do small magics, like making lamp oil last longer than it should have, and causing lost objects to turn up in my lap, and seeing solutions when people came to my father with a dispute that had no clear answer. I was in control, then, but now…I want to eat so badly, but I can't. It's been like this ever since I found those manuscripts in the library…" She cut herself off abruptly.

Masyra raised her eyebrows. "Manuscripts? What kind of manuscripts?"

"Books of spells."

"You didn't actually try any of those spells, did you?"

She shook her head. "I knew I didn't know enough yet, so I just read them over and over and meditated on them, so I would remember them."

Don't you know that's almost as good as casting them? Masyra didn't actually say it; obviously Casilla didn't know. "Were any of them spells for calling demons?"

"Let me think." She got up and began to pace the room again—typical of a fire-mage trying to concentrate. "No. Oh dear, yes! One was called *To Summon Demon Bone*, but I thought it was a metaphor. It was a way to cause a famine. Horrid thing, but I couldn't help reading it and thinking about it. I thought... I thought it might be important to see how such evil magic worked in case someone tried to use it against the Confederacy. It really worried me. I kept going back to it, trying to figure out how to guard against such magic. It scared me so much that I vowed I would give my life gladly if it would protect my people…" She stopped and looked at Masyra, her face heartbreakingly young. "Was that wrong?"

"It was very foolish, Ebannina, but you did it for the best of reasons." *She will make a good ruler, if I can bring her through this alive. And she will make a good mage as well.* "Fire-mages are very attractive to creatures of darkness, because you are so bright and full of energy. Your bond to the land made you even more appealing. Your study caught the attention of the one called Demon Bone and, I fear, called it here. I'm sure it thought you would be easy prey, untrained as you are, and an easy gateway to this world. But fire is a defensive magic, a magic of guarding and warding, and it made your vow to protect your people at all costs into an all-too-effective one. The demon can't get out unless we banish it with magic or it kills you, which it's trying to do. Fortunately, I think I know how to banish it."

Two days later, Masyra dressed in a calf-length coat of deep green silk, ornamented with realistic autumn leaves embroidered on the hem and up over her knees. The trousers underneath it were a woven brocade, also in a leaf pattern. On a chain around her neck hung a vial of her native earth mixed with the ashes of her long-dead teacher, and under her arm she carried a small wooden drum. She also had a covered basket full of food.

She had arranged to meet the Ebannina in the least-groomed part of the palace garden, a grove of oak trees, deep red with autumn, and underplanted with evergreen laurel. She knew the Ebanni and Ebanna and any number of guards must be lurking just out of sight, but the grove still felt wild enough for her purposes.

When she actually saw the girl, she was shocked. Casilla looked worse than ever, slumped in a chair and so thin she almost seemed transparent.

Masyra murmured reassurances as she opened the vial and touched the contents to the girl's forehead, lips, the palms of her hands, the place that should have been the valley between her breasts. Without her needing to ask, Casilla slipped off her little velvet shoes and lifted her feet, first right and then left, so Masyra could mark their soles. "With earth and ash I mark you," the earth-mage said, so softly that only Casilla, the demon, and the gods could hear. "Earth for life, and blessed ash for death, and earth for life again. Earth for the body, and ash for the soul, and earth for the spirit in all creation. Earth for instinct, and ash for human knowledge, and earth again for the ancient wisdom it teaches us. Have the strength of mountains and the aspiration of flame and soul, Casilla. It is time for you to cast away all that oppresses you!"

Casilla suddenly convulsed, and Masyra barely caught her before she fell off her chair. The girl seemed to be choking on demonic laughter, but in her fit, Casilla had managed to cover her ash-touched lips with her ash-touched hands. The demon could not use her mouth.

Casilla was shaking from the effort of moving at all, but her eyes were bright with healthy determination. Smiling, Masyra picked up her drum and said, "Dance with me, Casilla." She began to beat out a rhythm, moving her rounded hips and belly in that most ancient of dances, both sensual and sacred.

"I can't. I don't know how."

"You know how; every woman does. You just don't know you know. Listen to the drum and let yourself move." Even as she said it, she hoped her instincts were correct. Casilla was frail, dizzy from lack of food, and it seemed against all sense to make her dance. Yet for a fire-talent, dancing and drumming were sources of power. Masyra had drummed for fire-mages before, for the music of Ballyria was rhythmic and entrancing, well-suited to such use. She only hoped she was a good enough drummer to reach the fire in a half-dead girl.

Casilla moved stiffly, but Masyra drummed with controlled abandon, like the heart of someone making love. "Feel your blood flow," Masyra urged. "Feel the fire in your heart." As she drummed, she pulled power from the autumn earth, the strong oaks, the still-green shrubs, and directed it toward the girl in waves. Some she directed toward healing the physical effects of starvation and bolstering up Casilla's weakness, some toward augmenting the energy the dance raised. Gradually, the girl's movements eased into grace. Her cheeks flushed with exertion, and she smiled as her hips rolled and snapped in time to the drum. Instinctively, she moved toward the fire and danced around it, its energy adding to her own.

Finally Masyra sensed the time was right. "Now, Casilla! Cast the demon out!"

"Can I really do that?" she panted. She sounded slightly dubious, yet excited by the prospect.

"You can. You have great strength—strength of love, strength of honor, strength of a young mind and heart and soul." She pitched her voice even lower. "Strength of magic. Tell it, child. Tell it you are no demon's toy."

"Leave me, demon!" the girl said. Though barely louder than a whisper, her voice was firm. "Leave me in peace!" An unnatural wind picked up, buffeting at her, but Casilla was unfazed. "Go back to the darkness from which you came, for I am not going to be your amusement any longer, and I shall not tolerate you tormenting any of my people!"

The demon-wind continued to punish her. She gripped Masyra to remain standing before its onslaught, but the dance, while it must have taken a toll on her body, had sent magical energy coursing through her, reinforcing her own strong will. "I claim my body and my mind as my own! I am a free-born woman and no one, neither demon nor human, man nor woman, enemy nor lover nor prankish spawn of the spirit world has a right to use me against my will! Begone, Demon Bone!"

There was a great clap of thunder, and the howl of a demented wolf burst forth from the vicinity of Casilla's rib cage. Something shot out, disembodied yet visible. Masyra put her drum down and stepped in front of the demon. "You don't want me," she said calmly. "I am stronger than you are, as life is stronger than death." She reached out her hands, grabbed where the neck would be if the faintly humanoid shape was corporeal enough to have a neck, and hoped for the best.

There was a moment of intense physical activity as something with no body tried to wrestle a magic-charged mountain of a woman into submission. Briefly, Masyra thought it might succeed. Then she wrestled it down, pushing it against the good clean earth. "You have no place here, Demon Bone. I send you back to the darkness." She pulled a strand of power from the earth, envisioning it as a green, translucent, glowing rope against the demon's black, translucent form. She wrapped it around the prone demon as if she were wrapping meat in a butcher shop. "Door, open!" she cried. When the spirit door opened a crack, she tossed the demon in and quickly ordered the door to close. It did, first closing like a normal door, then closing in on itself until there was nothing left.

She checked the area for any signs of demonic residue and found none. She let down the defenses she'd put up and ran to Casilla, who was sitting in the leaves.

Casilla was still dangerously thin, and her frailty made the life-force flowing in her almost visible through her pale skin. "That was wonderful!" Casilla exalted. "The door…and wrestling the demon as you did…and the way the dancing felt. Thank you!"

"I couldn't have done it alone," Masyra said, and it was true. "It took my powers to build the gate and push the demon through, but only you could force it to leave you. How are you feeling?"

"Much better, but I'm soooo hungreee..." She let her words trail off into a comic wail.

Masyra took the girl's hands between her own. "Did you say you were hungry?"

"I could eat the world!" she cried.

The Ebanni and Ebanna ran across the clearing toward them and embraced their daughter. "Bring forth a feast!" the Ebanni ordered. "The best of everything! Our daughter is cured!"

"And while it's being prepared, let's have a snack," Masyra said, opening the picnic basket. Casilla pulled out a cheese sandwich and began to munch.

Martha A. Compton credits "a lifetime of co-habitating with felines," an explanation she once heard for one facet of common cat behavior, and her regret at having to bypass Glastonbury and the Tor on a recent trip to England, for the story that follows. This is her first professional fiction sale.

The Fat Cats' Tale
by Martha A. Compton

At the center of time and space dwells the collective cat. This truth was made known to me one fine, soft summer morning by a trio of felines.

The human mind is a funny thing; there are times when it forgets that it is incapable of certain things. This may be due to stress, fatigue, various dream states, lack of sleep or any number of other causes. In this particular case, I believe it may have been due to jet lag.

Using most of my savings and all the grant money I could scrape together, and with an enormous assist from some of my Dad's about-to-expire frequent flyer miles, I had been abroad for about ten weeks doing research for my doctoral thesis. The preparations for the trip had taken months, with permissions to obtain and appointments to be set and both accomplished with a fair amount of begging. But it was worth it. I'd had damn-near religious experiences while actually being allowed access to certain private libraries and special collections in various parts of the world.

I was in my hotel room, time-zoned out and happily exhausted from the long hours of study. I was about to use my laptop to update my faculty advisor on some things when I discovered an e-mail. It was from an old friend, kindly offering her home in Somerset for a little R&R for a few days before I flew back home to Texas. Knowing that I was near the end of my schedule, I checked my itinerary and was instantly preoccupied by just one thought; in nine days' time I could be peacefully sleeping late in the quiet English countryside. I accepted with a resounding "YES. PLEASE!"

So it was that I arrived in Glastonbury, got my bearings, and proceeded to walk down the high street, my wheeled luggage in tow, to a local bookstore. The owner, my ever-smiling friend, greeted me with a warm hug. Hilary was a tall, fair-skinned, copper-haired Rubenesque beauty, who looked as if, in another age, she would be the revered wife of a clan chieftain. Few would have doubted that she would have been more than worth the enormous brideprice paid to her powerful family.

We were both happy and excited to see one another and, soon after, spent hours catching up over a fine meal and a pint (or two) at a local inn. Afterward, we drove out of town, down a country lane, to the front door of a two-story Victorian-era cottage.

I was asleep as soon as my head hit the pillow in the airy, chintz-festooned guestroom.

The house was quiet, Hilary having left for work hours before, when I awoke to a persistent sunbeam warming my face. I padded downstairs in my long white cotton nightgown, found the fridge, and was able to locate a can of my favorite soft drink as an eye opener. Breakfast with a pot of tea could wait; I prefer my first-thing-in-the-morning caffeine fix to be a cold one.

With a certain amount of difficulty, I navigated through the house and out the open French-style doors to the brick terrace. There I found a waiting wicker lounge chair to settle into and tried to wake up while finishing my soft drink. As I sat there in the calm, verdant and utterly charming traditional English back garden, I heard something that I shall never forget.

"What's with him?"

I looked around to see only my own shadow and two of Hil's three cats.

"Him? He's all done in. It were his to do this morning."

"Must have been a right big one."

"Aye, and he's the only Tabby 'round here could have done it."

A fresh easterly breeze caused a drape of red roses to nod as if in agreement. A cloud shadow fell over the terrace as I considered the thought that I was, at the moment, asleep in some badly-decorated, two-star Venetian hotel.

"Mind you now," the voice continued, "his size is not the only thing what done it. Those hind legs of his were just the ticket. Oooooh, would you look at the power in that one and the passion, he has it!"

After taking another long draw out of the cold can, I saw that an enormous orange-yellow tabby was sleeping on the cool bricks under the bough of a potted fern. Nearby the other two cats were busy bathing and grooming one another beside a bed of flowers in full bloom. The male tabby was a fat cat, large and massive-looking. The other two, both females, were somewhat smaller—probably due to their gender—but healthy and ample in form and robust in appearance.

"Sure, I remember the time you and I had, a-setting it to rights last winter's eve. I thought between us it were a corker!"

By this time I was either going to question my sanity or just revel in the hallucination. I chose to do the latter, as it was obviously the path of least resistance.

"Pardon me," I asked, "what are you two talking about?"

My inquiry was greeted with mild indifference and just a tad of annoyance. Having been owned by a cat or four in my lifetime, this came as no surprise. But the answer I received did.

"Oh, so you can hear us now, can you? Well, no matter. It will soon pass," purred The Tortoise-Shell without looking up. "Big Thom there was called upon to reset the balance of the universe this fine morning."

"Sure…uh huh….OK." I obviously was not convinced, dementia not withstanding.

"Human, if you doubt us, why do you ask?" The Gray asked in a tone of exasperation and near-tolerance. "Have you ever seen a cat running pell mell to and fro for the length of your house? Upstairs, down and back again? Did you never wonder why?"

"Well, sure. I just thought that it was a cat thing." (Hey, *you* try and defend yourself to a cat first thing in the morning!)

"A cat thing, indeed!" spat back The Gray while her green eyes flashed at me. "Cats have collectively kept the universe and this world in time with what is. We have a grave responsibility and have never questioned our duty."

"Don't be getting your fur in a fuzz, Dearie. Your tail is looking like a bottle brush," The Tortoise-Shell soothed. "This may be beyond her ken—she is a human after all. But if she can hear us, she may be one of the enlightened ones." She looked up at me for the first time as she added, "We will just have to explain it in terms that she can understand."

The Tortoise-Shell then walked over to my chair and nonchalantly hopped into my ample and appropriately-queen-sized lap. She settled in comfortably and began to explain as if telling a fairy tale to a child.

"So long ago that no living cat knows when or why, we were given our task of stewardship. Cats are all over this Earth we all share; we live in every climate and culture. We are the big cats living in the wild and the smaller ones on prowl in both the most humble and most regal of homes. We live on land and on ships at sea. We were once worshipped by the Egyptians."

"A superior race of humans, to my way of thinking," added The Gray as she determinedly walked away from us, off the bricks and into the yard while holding her tail straight up. (Attitude is everything, you know.)

"Individual cats, but sometimes in pairs, are called on to move about in a certain way at a precise time and place," continued The Tortoise-Shell. "In this way we use our energy to alter, fine tune, repair, speed up, slow down or wind the clockwork that is time and space. We, the cat collective, keep the universe in its proper motion."

"Is that why cats sleep so much, to conserve energy for when you are called on?" I asked, not wanting to be left out of participation in my own delusion.

"Aren't you the clever girl!"

In appreciation, I reached over and scratched her behind the ear. This mid-summer madness wasn't so bad.

The Tortoise-Shell turned as I continued to pet her and beamed down at The Gray, who was now sitting in the sunshine with her back to us. "There now, I told you she was one of the better ones."

"Oh, very well. Do get on with it," replied The Gray with a switch of her tail. "I will want to sharpen my claws soon."

Looking back up at me, The Tortoise-Shell continued, "Oh, give her no mind. She's always such a sour puss in the mornings." I glanced at The Gray and saw her ears go back, nearly flat on her head, at that last remark.

"Oh there; that's it!" The Tortoise-Shell's golden eyes closed as she raised and turned her head. "Now just a little to the left. Oh, thank you." (Feline ear manipulation is a specialty of mine.)

"Now let's see, where was I? Oh, yes. All that exists has many of what you might would call 'navels'—areas that conduct the ebb and flow of energy. Cats concentrate in numbers around these places, where we are most needed and our task best accomplished. See that whale-shaped rise over there? The hill, the one you humans call the Tor. That is one of the navels of this world."

I looked up and over the back fence at the top third of the seemingly-stepped Tor, awash in the full sunshine. I could see clearly, on the small plateau at its summit, the ruins of the tower of the Chapel to St. Michael the Archangel. So, I thought, the Tor is a navel. Wow! It's an "out-ee"!

Zing! Whoa! With that last thought my brain skidded to a full stop. I stared until I was called back to the surreal reality I'd been experiencing by The Gray's soothing low tones, purring admiration spoken to the now-awake Tabby.

"Did you have a nice lie-down, now? A busy morn you've had this day. We are proud of you, to be sure." She slinked over to him and began to bathe him in true cat fashion. He stood and stretched to cast out the last of his nap from his powerful mass, and said something that I didn't catch. I knew there were words being formed and that I should be able to understand him, but…

"I'm sorry, what did he say?"

"Oh, so you didn't understand him? It must be that you are having trouble with the accent. He's Welsh, you know. He came here—oh—it must be five springs ago now. We knew he was a-coming long before our human did. He arrived here in a motor-car with her littermate."

Huh? Hilary's littermate? Must be cat-speak for sibling, I told myself. I knew she didn't have any sisters, and I've known her only brother for years.

For my benefit, The Tortoise-Shell translated for The Tabby. "He said that we woke him, but as long as he was up, he could do with a nice tin of meat and a bit of cream. Would you?" she asked. "Come on, be a love and set our Thom a well-deserved meal."

I nodded but was slow to move, vaguely aware that the forgotten cola was now becoming tepid.

"Shake a leg there, human!" wailed The Gray. "I'll show you where she stows the goods. Sprightly now, our Thom is waiting!"

Up I went into the house, with all three cats leading me into the kitchen. At The Gray's directions, I found and opened a can of cat food and poured out a saucer of cream before the assembled troops. The two females watched as The Tabby ate and drank the hero's portion. Then, only when he was sated, did they begin to finish off the rest of the requested meal.

By this time I was seated cross-legged on the kitchen floor. The Tabby, now full, ambled over to me and gave me a head butt. The action needed no translation, as the meaning "PET ME NOW!" was very clear. As I stoked his soft fur, I could not only hear but also feel his purring. I looked over at the two female cats cleaning up the last of the food from the dishes and saw The Tortoise-Shell pause to lick some cream off of her whiskers.

She saw me looking at her and said, "Was a fine thing you did, feeding our Thom. He don't take to just anyone, you know. Thank you very much indeed."

The Tabby spoke to me, but again I was at a loss. (This Texas ear of mine just doesn't do cat Welsh.) I kept on petting The Tabby as The Tortoise-Shell came to my rescue. "He said, 'You mustn't dwell too much on what you have learned this day, as it will only muddle your thinking.' I must say, I agree with him. Few humans come to understand our ways. You have come far in this world."

The Gray lapped the last of the cream from the saucer, strolled over to me, and rubbed up against me, starting with her cheek and then along the full length of her body. I was now a marked woman.

"You may be of some value after all. You did a fine turn with that tin opener." (The Gray obviously knew that too much praise can ruin a human.)

I stood as the trio left for familiar places in the house to sun themselves, bathe, sleep or—I began to suppose—just await the next assignment. I prepared myself a breakfast. Doing something considered normal, and consuming some proteins and carbohydrates, would be a good start toward regaining my sanity. Or so I thought at the time.

I finished breakfast and went upstairs to take a shower. Hot soothing water, a good shampoo and some down-time would do me wonders, I knew. I couldn't help but go over what I thought I'd heard that morning and, remembering, I laughed out loud. I must get more fresh air, I told myself. All that time spent poring over old, dusty and probably micro-fungus-laden tomes and manuscripts has taken its toll. I remembered reading about a small village in France, sometime late in the nineteenth century, where a mold that developed in the local bakery had everyone who'd eaten the bread baked there doing swan dives off the roofs of their houses. Who knows what I may have come in contact with! Imagine, talking cats explaining their metaphysical mission statement to me, indeed!

I dried my hair, dressed and returned downstairs. One of the cats was sunning herself in a bay window, the other two were asleep on top of a massive bookcase. But no one was speaking to me, or near me, either. I stopped still to listen. No voices of any kind. No talking teapots or bedtime stories as told by the flower bowl.

I spent the day in glorious sloth, the morning's lesson forgotten or filed away with a nap. I was just awake good when Hilary opened the front door and, on three different vectors, the cats appeared at high speed. The meowing and rubbing up against her legs commenced as if on schedule. All three of them were visibly happy to see her.

"Goodness, I must feed these cats or I shall never be able to sit down. I take it you have met my small pride?"

"Oh yes," I replied, "we're old friends. They're a real fixture around here, aren't they?" We walked into the kitchen together accompanied by the furry fury.

"The two females were here when I bought the house. They seemed to own it and allowed me to move in with them." Hilary explained as she fed the cats. "The big tom was a surprise gift from my twin brother; he brought him here from Wales about five years ago."

She began to laugh as she continued, "I wonder that he didn't wake you this morning. Just as I was dressing, he was madly dashing about as if the devil himself was after him. It was a jolly sight, his tail up and flying like a battle flag. I have no idea what he was on about. There he was, using all his strength, running fiercely about the house and back garden like he was on a mission for Queen and Country."

I went into the sitting room and sat down slowly. "Hil, you never told me that you and Will are twins."

"Haven't I? Is it important?" she asked, joining me on the couch.

I was slow to answer. "No…you just never said so."

She eyed me quizzically for a moment, until we started chatting about the day. Then the subject turned to plans for the evening, and Hilary went upstairs to change clothes.

I stood and looked out the window at three cats in the golden, rose-tinged light of the quickly fading afternoon. All three of them were sitting on the back fence, their backs to me. Just sitting there attentively, as if on watch.

I looked at the cats. I looked at the Tor. Then I yelled up the stairwell.

"Hil? You got any tequila?"

Catherine Lundoff says this story began with the desire to write a "different kind of heroic character", one *not* in the "babe in the battle nightie" mold. The result was "someone a little like me and many of my friends: an aging woman of substance coming to terms with who she is and what makes her special."

Vadija
by Catherine Lundoff

I have heard it said that even Vadija the Merry could not lift the sorrows from Laith. In all the tales, the sadness swam sluggishly through the streets of the city like the giant carp in the slow moving River Omphere or the mist clouds from the Kaleva Mountains. Each inhabitant carried the misery balanced precariously on their packs or on their bare shoulders as they walked the gray avenues, one foot dragging up to collapse down in front of the other.

So it was said. Said with a kind of pride, at that. But I didn't believe it. I knew the city wasn't a happy place, mind you. And I knew that Vadija had a merry and glorious laugh, a laugh that changed things. It was like a clarion call to arms if you were a soldier and liked being one. Or the wind whipping through the Forest of Anma Bekash if you were a hunter. Once Puar the Moneylender even said to me, "Ah, Sira, her laugh is like a rain of gold coins poured down a chimney and ringing on the stones below." From her, this was the highest of praise.

I thought I heard Vadija laugh once myself. The sound rode down on the wind and sang around the chimney of my farm, making the little bells on the door ring and the dogs howl with the shock of it. Swirling and roaring, it swept around me until I came near to howling myself. I didn't know what it was then, but I left that day. There was nothing to hold me once I heard it. Her laugh is like that.

But even she couldn't change Laith of the Sorrows, or so they told me as I followed the news of her laughter from my distant valley and days of unending work. Always she went a little before me and I had to make my own way. But I kept walking, for I had no laugh of my own in those days. I thought she might tell me how she found hers.

In the beginning, I washed and cleaned at the inns and little farms to keep bread in my pack and a roof over my head. I told tales to the children, for they were the only ones who heard them. When I could, I sat and listened to the rare talespinner who would venture so far from the cities of the coast, letting the words wash over me and wondering always where they had found such things.

It was then I first heard Vadija's name and learned that it was her laughter which drew me from my home. But though I listened until I could repeat the tales, I had no thought to become a talespinner myself, not at first. Certainly I knew I could not be one because everyone said that I was not the way a talespinner should be. After all, talespinners are long and lean where I am soft and round, dark where I am golden, mysterious where I am open and speak what I mean. So it was said. But sometimes I remembered Vadija's laugh. Then all things seemed possible.

As I followed her, I began to see words growing in the hedges and drifting on the breeze. It terrified me then, for I knew no one else who could see them. At first, I tried to ignore them, turning away from the small whispers of sound and the touch of dreams. Soon I could see them even while I slept. They followed through the dreamlands and my waking days until I could stand it no more and I reached out to one. Then another. I called one to me and it came. I was no longer afraid.

With the words I began to weave the webs that drew in those who listened. One night, a circle at the fire followed me up Princess Miaqi's rainbow stairs. I made the steps glisten with color and shine with the firelight's glow in the eyes of those who heard until I could see them myself. The next night, another circle swam behind me with Gregoth of the Sea, gasping at the vengeance that he wrought on those who slew his people and at the sudden tang of salt in the air.

After that, I began to tell stories at the inns and wayside traveler's rests. These were tales about strange lands and mighty warriors, like those I told my little ones before the wasting fever carried them off. Lord Death took them, just as he had taken their father before them, and I could do nothing but watch. Until I heard Vadija, I wished that he had taken me, too.

I found these tales hard to tell at first, but the words flowed around me and I went with them until I could no more stop telling stories than I could stop following Vadija. I went on telling the tales I had heard and, after a time, I even made up new ones. Kingdoms fell, lovers were reunited, evil was conquered; such were the stuff of the tales that I told. I began to feel joy in the telling of what could be and what should not, and soon I could laugh a little.

But my tales about Vadija were best of all, at least to me, and they came to me often when I walked or when I washed and tended. I told them only to the women and children and those who were worn from their day's work. In those stories, she laughed and armies crumbled. Tyrants flew away on the wind. Always her laugh changed things for the better. So I said and so I believed, though I had done nothing but follow her trail, never once laying eyes on her.

Still, I talked to many on the road who had heard her laugh. Some of them even claimed to have seen her. She was young or old, lean or fat, beautiful beyond a winter's frost on lacy tree branches, or ugly and grim like the burning lava in the mountains on the southern edge of the world, depending on who told me the story.

I had my own idea, held close within me with the tales that I told no one else. I knew that she must be a big, queenly woman with strong arms and a great soft belly, bigger even than my own. For how else could she have the power to laugh such a laugh that changed those who heard it? But I didn't know, so I followed her to see for myself. Before I heard her, I never could have wanted such a thing.

After a time, people began to know my name, and my tales kept my belly round as I walked leagues each day, following the trail she left behind her. Finally, she turned toward Laith of the Sorrows, a city out of legend, and there I went also. It was midday when I arrived and stood before the walls. I paused and trembled outside the gates long before I was willing to follow her inside.

There were many tales of how Laith gained its sorrows. In some, they sacrificed their children to one of the Old Gods to save themselves from siege. In others, they betrayed their king and brought his curse down upon the city. At the end of each, they were left gray and solemn, bereft of joy and music from seasonturn to seasonturn from my grandmere's time onward. I remembered each story as I paused between the cold metal gates before stepping forward. They closed with a bang to swallow me as I set foot on the flagstones of Laith.

Once inside, I could see no more of the lands outside, for Laith's sorrows are sealed in by the high walls. There were no inns and no other places where people could gather to hear my tales, so I instead walked through the city looking for Vadija. As I searched, the gray walls to each side and the gray paving stones beneath my feet sent icy fingers through me and I shivered, warm though my cloak was. The sun's dim light barely lit my way as those who lived there shouldered past me unseeing, and my heart grew colder and colder.

When I had wandered some time down the long avenues where not a single flower bloomed, I could feel the wings of the city's sorrows settling around my shoulders. "Why, why had she come here?" I wailed in a whisper, fearing to speak aloud and draw the misery closer. I could see no one who could be her in the dismal faces that passed me, but I knew she must have come here. There was nowhere else for her to go unless she flew over the mountains that circled the city on three sides. *Besides*, a voice whispered inside me, *how could she deny such pain*? *Or such a challenge?* How I longed then to have her power!

I tried to ignore my thoughts and listened hard for her laugh, but there was nothing. No chime of bells or laughter or dogs barking. I could hear only the creak of passing wagons the color of twilight and the soft, whispered exchanges between the few merchants and those who bought from them. The words were so soft that none fell to the cold hard ground, so light that no tales could grow from them.

The weight of despair settled heavier and heavier upon my shoulders until I must sit or fall to my knees. I sank onto a cold step, cursing Vadija for coming here and myself for following her. My tales begin to fade when I did this, gliding away like water with no basin left to hold it. How long I sat like this I do not know, for the hours pass strangely in Laith of the Sorrows. Soon there was no joy left in me, and I began to forget Vadija's laugh and the world beyond the city walls.

Still I sat and drifted into the sorrows until I gazed at nothing but the gray stones beneath my feet. After a great while, I knew that someone stood before me, but by then I had not even the strength to look up. "Outlander, you must leave here," the voice whispered down at me like a breeze. I knew that what it said was right, but I could not lift my head to go. A gnarled hand clasped my shoulder hard, but it was nothing compared to the despair that held me and I scarcely felt it.

The hand reached down for my own hand and tugged upward, until I was dragged unwillingly to my feet. The bony fingers reached under my chin and forced my eyes up to meet those of an old, old woman, her face gray and drained like the others I had seen. But her eyes were something else. In their black depths, I could see a tale growing, a story of gray and cold, but a story nonetheless.

"Tell me what you seek, Outlander," the voice licked at my hearing like a small wind, like a sigh.

I tried to remember, and all that came to me was my dream of Vadija. I saw her as I imagined that she must be. She did not laugh, not here in this twilight place, and she shrank in size with the loss. I shrank with her, folding in around the vision, bright garments dimming. She was little more than I had been before I left the farm, and the sight pained me. "I was looking for Vadija," I whispered back to the woman, tears rolling down my cheeks.

"I thought you might be." The dark eyes twinkled slightly, and I found that I could lift my head on my own, without the support of her hand. I still had no words, no tales to tell, until she spoke again. "Tell me about her, talespinner."

I wondered how she could see the words to know me for what I was, until I looked and saw those that had fallen to the gray stones around me. Many were fading away, but a small few still glowed brightly against the dim light and the cold. "Vadija..." I stumbled over her name but I whispered on, coaxing the few remaining words back to me, remembering a tale that I had told no one else. "Vadija came once to a valley far from here. There I heard her laugh for the first and only time." The woman's sparkling eyes were closed for a moment.

"What did the valley look like, talespinner?"

I told her what I could still remember of my home and my family. Sometimes the words came to me and sometimes I made new ones as I told her the tale of how I had come to seek Vadija. With each turning of the tale's web, I could feel the city's sorrow loosen its grip upon us both. She wore the ghost of a smile and I stood on my own, my voice more than a whisper, growing in strength. There was a wind now that night had fallen and, though it was a cold one, I welcomed it and the words that it brought.

She asked me many questions as we stood shivering in that wind. Twice the merchant on whose steps we sat came forth to drive us away but, terrified by the strangeness of that which she did not know, retreated inside. With each answer and each word, I grew warmer until I slipped my cloak from my shoulders. It was then that I saw the little blossom growing in a crack between the gray stones, drawing itself up from where my tears had fallen. It was but one against all that gray expanse, but it was enough.

I pointed to it and laughed. It was just a little laugh, but I saw her eyes grow wide at hearing it and she smiled a little. I laughed again for the little joys of seeing her smile and the small flower struggling against the sad city. The wind caught the sound this time and sent it upward to dash against the gray stone walls and the closed windows of Laith. The stone sent my laugh back, flinging it between the wind and the stone until I saw the chink of windows and doors opening as those who lived in the city looked out to see what was wrong.

The bits and pieces of my laugh danced around them on the wind and they drew back, many of them, retreating into the gray insides of their chilled homes. Only one, a young man with dead eyes, came out to stand beside the woman. His glance fell upon the flower and upon the words that lay on the stone and he blinked slowly, carefully, as though trying to understand what they meant. I wondered that one with eyes so dead could see the words, but perhaps he did not.

He reached out to the flower at my feet and pulled it up. Its delicate beauty vanished in a moment and he held a gray blossom in his palm. His face opened somewhat in astonishment, then closed as he laid the flower back at my feet. Without a word, he turned and walked back into his house, and his door and all the others that remained open shut against the small remains of my laugh and the tiny petals of the gray flower.

I met the eyes of the old woman and found their gentle spark fading. "He does not need your gift yet," she whispered softly, but I did not understand. I tried to force a laugh, but it would not come. The cold crept up my limbs, tendrils reaching once again from the stones beneath my feet to root me to the spot. My spirit cried out for Vadija, but still I heard nothing until, at last, I grew angry with cold and loss.

I threw my head back and I howled her name out upon the wind that carried no more words. Once more, it dashed my voice upon the walls and flung it at the city gates at the far end of the street. They swung open, but I could see no one standing outside waiting to be swallowed by the city.

Quickly I grabbed the old woman's hands and marched down the street, pulling her unresisting behind me. If Vadija would not come to me, then I would wait for her at the city gates until she emerged. So said the voice of my anger as it buzzed and crackled around my ears. How dare she do this to me, dragging me from hearth and home to this place? The despair I had left with the telling of my tale began to return, but I fought it until we reached the gates.

The woman stopped and would go no further. "I can't leave."

The whisper made me pause in my headlong rush to leave the city behind me. "Why not?" I demanded, bathing my eyes in the lands beyond the city gate.

"Because I built this place, I and all the others. It is part of us and we of it. I must stay and help those who want to leave weave tales of their own. There is nothing for me there," she gestured at the lands outside. In my anger and my astonishment, I threw back my head and I laughed, a harsh noise in that quiet place.

She flinched away from the brittle hardness of the sound, which dashed like ice on the wind, tinkling against the stone walls and shattering. For a moment, I was tall and lean and mysterious, as it was said a talespinner should be. My laugh rose until bitter tears flowed down my cheeks and I sought outside for the words that would break the stone wall. I wanted to succeed in my anger where Vadija had not in her merriment.

"Please don't." I barely heard her speak, but it was enough. I stopped laughing and looked at her. Again I was short and round, though not as merry and frank as I had been since I began to follow Vadija. The old woman stood before me, thin shoulders bowed with the weight of the city's grief, but still with a little light in her eyes for those who could see it. Now I began to understand. I knew where Vadija came from. With a small shove, the woman pushed me outside the city gates and backed away from them as they began to close once more, sealing her in.

The lands beyond called me, their words caressing my face and pulling me back to them, but I stood for a time looking upon the walls of Laith of the Sorrows. As I stood, my laugh grew strong within me, filling me with tales, and I could feel myself grow with them until I was rounder and taller than I had been before I came to this place. I thought about my children and my husband and the man with the dead eyes and I wept, the tears pouring down my cheeks in a steady stream until a small creek flowed away from my feet. Tiny flowers sprang up against the walls of the city and I laughed, even in my sorrow, and I grew no smaller.

Long I sat and thought about what had been and what could be, until I looked to the lands beyond the city. I thought of a funny story that Puar the Moneylender had told me, a simple tale unworthy of a talespinner but with a light of its own. I thought, too, of the old woman with her listening eyes and of what she had asked. After a while, I knew that I didn't need to see Vadija anymore. I went away without loosing my merriment against the grim walls.

My laugh went on before me on the wind, whipping away to ring around the chimneys of small farms and knocking on the doors of tyrants. But always it went ahead, never behind to the city that I left. For it was said that even Vadija the Merry could not lift the sorrows from Laith.

So it was said and so it would be.

Of the following story, Lisa Deason says, "This was written in basically one long, exhaustive session over three days. I emerged feeling rather dazed, but elated as well. I've always wanted to tell a fun adventure with a Big Beautiful Main Character, and I'm glad to have finally had the chance."

Lady Emerdirael's Rescue
by Lisa Deason

"I feel ridiculous," I muttered, tugging at my sleeveless, silver-studded black vest. My matching thigh-length skirt seemed in perpetual danger of flipping up over my sizeable rump.

I'm a warrior, darn it, I thought. *This is undignified!*

"You look fantastic, Darian," said my mercenary partner Rishauna a'Liuh. "Trust me."

I narrowed my green eyes and shot her a fairly murderous glance. "After this outfit, I don't think I'll ever trust you again, Ree."

She smiled, unconcerned, and adjusted the elaborate silver headdress crowning my upswept blonde hair. "There. You look like an Amazon Queen."

"Like something an Amazon Queen scraped off her boot, maybe," I retorted. "I'm going to stick out like a tank in a tea cup parade."

"Darian, at seven feet and three-hundred-some pounds, you don't blend in. But you should celebrate yourself, not try to hide."

Rishauna, who was one of the few women taller than me, knew what she was talking about. But, though we were of equal mass, she wore it exotically, with her smooth dark skin and bright blue eyes. She was the ideal Amazon Queen, except for the unwieldy plasticast encasing her left ankle.

"You could still go as Giganta, the Limping Barbarian," I suggested.

"I don't think so."

"Can't I at least wear my blaster?"

"An Amazon Queen uses a dagger," Rishauna said firmly. Then she patted the large holster hanging on her gunbelt behind her own. "Don't worry. Mr. Sparky will be safe with me."

A small droid rolled up. "It's your turn, Ms. Fairchild."

"You'll do great," Rishauna said. "Our so-called Sultan of the Unique will be knocked out of his chair."

"With laughter, probably," I mumbled darkly, but put on a big fake smile, strode down the narrow corridor, then pushed through the curtain.

Pulsating music blared to life as I walked the short runway. The blinding lights prevented me from seeing any faces.

Good. I really don't want to know what they're thinking.

But I figured it out a moment later when some sort of red squishy fruit came sailing out of the light and splattered my black boots.

My phony smile turned to a very real scowl. Another fruit soared in with much better aim. I drew the dagger I was wearing in Mr. Sparky's place and slashed out, cutting it in half before it brained me.

Surprisingly, that earned applause. Unfortunately, it also filled the air with fruit-missiles.

I spent the next few minutes trying to deflect the worst of it. When the music ended, I bowed grandly, like I had planned things that way, then made my escape.

Behind the curtain, a bevy of lovely women in glittering outfits gaped at me. Doubtlessly, they were shocked at my be-fruited state, or at all the plump, pale flesh revealed by my black leather. Probably both.

"It's a scary universe out there," I said.

This day just isn't starting off well.

My journey into sordid self-exploitation began with a kidnapping. Not my own, but that of one Lady Emerdirael of

Yatte. She had been snatched on her way to her new home of Chreah, where her presence would cement the fragile peace the two long-warring worlds had just achieved.

Or something like that. Rishauna and I had dealt with a Yattian envoy who gave his rank as Second-Nemian and whose Standard was atrocious, so the details were rather foggy. But all we really needed to know was who the kidnapper was, and the Second-Nemian had been clear on that.

The Sultan of the Unique. An enigmatic figure of vast wealth who traveled the known universe holding "beauty searches". Females of every species dreamed of winning one and getting to live in his "flying palace". Every female but Lady Emerdirael of Yatte, it seemed. When the Sultan personally contacted her, she declined his offer.

She had vanished shortly after that.

Yatte had hired the Chrythia Mercenary Company, and indirectly Rishauna and myself, to find the Lady and get her to Chreah by the appointed time. If she didn't show, the war could very well erupt once more.

Rishauna and I decided against a frontal assault, opting to sneak in the back door.

The Sultan never attended his beauty searches in person, but rather monitored the proceedings with an avatar droid. By using a modified signal scrambler, I would have switched Rishauna's identity for that of the Sultan's real choice, which would have gotten her to the ship. Remaining there long enough to liberate Lady Emerdirael would have been another thing, of course. But the mercenary business was all about improvisation.

We were reminded of that the hard way when Rishauna sprained her ankle earlier this morning. We were forced to swap places and run my ID through the scrambler instead.

They wouldn't have thrown fruit at Rishauna, I was sure of it. But as long as the scrambler did its job, it really didn't matter.

Much.

Backstage in a small dressing area, I crawled thankfully out of my "Amazon Queen" gear and soni-blasted the sticky mess out of my hair and off my skin. Then I pulled on normal clothes and was thrusting my chunky black hair pin through the casual roll of my hair when I received a visitor.

It was the faceless, humanoid-shaped avatar. "Darian Fairchild?" it asked in a bland voice. "The Sultan of the Unique requests your presence aboard his ship."

I picked up my packed bag. "I was hoping you'd say that."

"Only invited persons are allowed," the avatar said outside, blocking the shuttle's entrance.

That had been anticipated, of course.

"You're *so* lucky," Rishauna said, patting my shoulder as she hugged me. "I'm going to miss you. Bye!"

By the time we lifted off, I had no doubt that Ree was back at our ship, powering up to follow the long-range, low-power tracking agent she had just tagged me with.

When I caught my first glimpse of the Sultan's fabled ship, quite frankly, I was disappointed. It looked like a regular, if large, starcruiser. But when I left the shuttle bay, I also left behind my disappointment.

With one step, I went from a sterile environment into a lush garden teeming with an amazing array of plant life. In the distance, I could even hear a waterfall.

Holograms and sound recordings, I thought, but couldn't explain the cool mist on my skin or the heady fragrance of exotic flowers swirling on the breeze.

"It's no illusion," a deep male voice said. "It's all quite authentic. Controlled and pest-free, but real nonetheless."

I turned, but no one was there. The avatar had already disappeared with my bag.

"We'll meet soon enough, Ms. Fairchild," the voice said, floating no doubt from a speaker hidden somewhere in the glistening greenery. "For now, make yourself comfortable.

You may travel anywhere and avail yourself of anything you find, within the bounds of common courtesy, of course."

"Of course," I echoed.

"Would you like to meet some of the others now? They're down at the pool. Or would you rather retire to your rooms?"

There was an awful lot of decadence implied in that plural word. *Remember why you're here. This is not an episode of "Your Dream Vacation"!*

"The pool sounds great," I said.

"Then take the path to your right."

I nodded, starting that way.

"Oh, Ms. Fairchild?" the voice said.

I paused, looking back. "Yes?"

"Welcome home."

The words left a funny feeling in my stomach as I continued down the path. I realized why a moment later. The Sultan should have been asking where his real "beauty" was by now, and I should have been firmly into my best song-and-dance. So, why hadn't he, and why wasn't I?

Surely…

Surely, I hadn't won the beauty search for real?

Hey! I barked to myself. *Priorities, please.*

The fluttery feeling in my stomach faded as I focused on my task. But, I have to admit, my step was lighter than it should have been as I headed to find my target.

When I stepped out into the clearing, my first startled thought was *It's the Valley Of The Perfect People!*

The glorious waterfall cascaded down over shimmering white rocks into a tremendous, crystal-clear pool. But the magnificence of the setting was nearly overshadowed by the half-dozen females either swimming or lounging on the pale, sandy shore.

The Second-Nemian hadn't provided us with a holo-image of Lady Emerdirael, only with a rather sparse verbal description.

"Dark eyes, like deep space. Hair like gold."

I scanned the crowd of amazing, stunning beauties, but nowhere among the many colorful humanoids did I find the one I was looking for. I backed away before I was spotted, deciding on my course of action. I could go make friendly with the natives, but I didn't want to reveal my interest in Lady Emerdirael before I had to.

So, since the Sultan said I was welcome to explore…

An hour later, I had seen more stunning landscapes than I had ever imagined, much less imagined existing inside a ship. I finally found a series of lavish suites. In the fifth I came to, a short-haired cat was curled up in the middle of a large, rose-colored bed. The animal raised its head as I entered, blinking at me with glittering sable eyes.

"Hi, kitty," I said. "Who do you belong to, hmm?"

The feline stretched languidly, then bounded off the bed with boneless grace and wrapped around my feet. I held a hand down, carefully, and the cat purred as I stroked its tawny fur. "Good kitty," I said. "Nice to meet you."

When I left the suite, the cat trailed along after me, padding on the thick bronze and black carpeting in the corridor. After finding several other empty suites, I finally hit an occupied one. I crept across the expensive Mahsian rug to view the figure asleep on the bed.

She had hair so blonde it made my own look dull and dirty. She stirred, then opened her brown eyes.

I don't know if they're dark "like deep space", but they're close enough for me. "Lady Emerdirael?" I said. "I'm here to take you home."

She looked puzzled, but didn't say anything. The cat twined around my feet again. I scooped it up and absently stroked its silky fur. The Lady still didn't speak.

Is she drugged? Confused? A few cranks short of getting her engine started? Or maybe she just doesn't speak Standard.

The cat meowed and I glanced behind me, finding an avatar droid standing in the doorway. "Why, hi there," I said, trying to brazen it through. "I was just making a few new friends."

"Glad to hear it," the avatar said in the Sultan's voice. "Dinner will be in half an hour. Will you wish to dress?"

I was wearing dark brown stretchy-pants and a plain, tan shirt, which was about as dressed up as I ever got for a meal. "Naturally. Where's my room?"

"This way."

"Well, good talking to you," I told the confused-looking woman, then followed the avatar out. It guided me to a sumptuous suite, then retreated.

"Here you go, kitty," I said, placing the cat on the luxurious lavender bed. My bag sat on the floor, apparently undisturbed, though doubtlessly it had been thoroughly scanned. It didn't matter; there was nothing suspicious in it. I had only one concealed device with me and it was hidden in plain sight.

The clothes I brought were disposable, so that I could leave them behind and not lose anything of value. Unfortunately, they all reflected that. "It seems I'm going to have to go casual, kitty," I said aloud. Then, on a whim, I checked the huge closet and found it bursting with clothing, all tailored to my not-exactly-easy-to-fit size. Somebody's computer clothier unit had been hard at work. It gave me that peculiar feeling again, that I had been expected.

I reached in and pulled out a dress at random, then stripped out of my clothes and stepped into an incredible confection of red silk. It floated on me, draping in dramatic, flowing waves down almost to the matching soft-soled shoes. Without a doubt, it was the most delightful, feminine thing I had ever put on in my life.

I twisted up my hair, securing it with my thick black pin. There was a jewelry box on the dresser, no doubt containing a king's ransom of treasures, but I didn't even open it. I hoped that going without extra adornments would help me remember I was a mercenary on a job, not Cinderella going to the Ball.

"See you around, kitty," I said as I headed out the door. The cat seemed more than happy to stay where it was, holding down the plush bed that I would never—sigh—sleep in myself.

As I stepped into the corridor, I was met by an avatar. "May I escort you, miss?" it asked and led me on a long trip that ended at a set of ornate double doors. They swung open and we entered.

The room was quite large, but the massive table dominating it made it seem smaller. The avatar held out the chair at the right-hand side of the head of the table.

I made myself walk lightly. While I was dressed like a princess, I wanted to act like one as well.

After I was seated, the avatar offered me a wine selection. As this wasn't the time to dull my thinking, I asked for water. The avatar glided away, then reappeared in a few moments with a crystal goblet on a silver tray. It had just set that before me when a veritable parade of avatars came through a door at the back, all bearing silver trays brimming with delicacies.

"The Sultan has made selections for you," an avatar said, "but you may change them if you wish." Not being the gourmet type, I doubted I could name any of the dishes, much less choose among them. "No, that will be fine."

The etched, white plate before me looked rare and expensive, the sort of thing you would expect to find in a collection, not on a table to be eaten off of. But in seconds its exquisite design was buried in food. The avatars left and the room became very silent.

"So?" I finally said. "Am I supposed to eat alone?"

As if that were a cue, the room lights dimmed and the massive chandelier over the table flickered to life. Then a figure appeared at the head of the table, a privacy shield blurring his image. "Try the *vohca*," the Sultan suggested as avatars arrived to serve him as well. "I think you'll like it."

When he indicated the dark purple meat on my plate, I speared a piece with my heavy silver fork, then tried it. "It tastes like chicken," I exclaimed a moment later.

The Sultan laughed good-naturedly. I couldn't help but do the same.

The meal was a surprisingly pleasant affair, all considering. It would have been a spectacular first date if I could have seen his face. And, of course, if he hadn't been a kidnapper and if I hadn't been there under false pretenses.

"Well," the Sultan said. "I've had a lovely time, Ms. Fairchild. I certainly hope you'll choose to stay."

The conversation so far had been nothing more than dressed-up small talk, revealing nothing of import. But now he gave me the chance to probe into something more substantial than the various weather conditions on his ship. "If I choose to stay?" I asked. "I can leave?"

"Why, of course," he said, sounding surprised. "All of my guests are free to leave at any time."

I bit my tongue, literally, to keep from throwing the case of Lady Emerdirael in his privacy-shielded face. Obviously, he had exceptions to his own rules.

"That's good to know," I said, pushing back my chair. As I stood, so did his hazy image. He appeared to be half a head taller than me, though it was probably a trick of the privacy shield. "Thank you for the meal," I said, politely. "It was wonderful."

"Your company made it so," he returned.

Deliberately, I held out a hand to shake his. The privacy shield popped like a bubble when my fingertips came in contact with it, leaving behind an empty chair.

I returned to my suite and, a bit reluctantly, changed into my own clothes and hung up the beautiful red dress. The cat wasn't there when I arrived but when I went to Lady Emerdirael's room, I found it draped across her lap.

"My lady," I said. "It's time to go."

She didn't respond. I strode across the room and, gently but resolutely, got her by the arm and pulled her to her feet. The cat yowled at being abruptly dumped to the floor. Lady Emerdirael looked like she was about to do the same.

"It's all right," I said soothingly. "Here we go..." I got her to take three steps toward the door before she dug in her heels. "My lady," I said, trying not to sound annoyed. "We've got to *go*."

She attempted to yank her arm out of my grip and, when that failed, she decided it was time to use her voice at last. She screamed bloody murder.

My initial impulse was to lay her out flat with a punch. Of course I didn't; I was there to rescue her, not assault her. So I clamped a hand over her mouth instead. "Would you stop that?!" I hissed. "I'm with the good guys!"

The door flew open and an avatar came in. "That is unacceptable behavior," it said as sternly as it could with that bland voice. "Cease immediately."

"She...ah...stubbed her toe," I said, letting go of Lady Emerdirael and sliding the pin from my hair. As the avatar approached, I pulled the pin out straight, aimed with the rounded end, and squeezed. The avatar broke into a frenzied dance, then tipped over backwards. "Ah, the camouflaged electrical pulse gun: never go into hostile territory without it," I muttered.

Lady Emerdirael, still hollering like a banshee, fled into the next room. *This was* not *the plan*, I thought grimly, giving chase.

She may have been thin, but I was determined. I caught up with her, then slung her unceremoniously over my shoulder. She pounded my back with her tiny fists and kicked her dainty legs. "Knock it off or I'll drop you on your head!" I bellowed. She stopped struggling. Obviously an angry, desperate mercenary sounded the same in any language.

I ran, following the route mapped out in my head. Two droids rolled out of an adjoining corridor. I fired, leaving them spinning in circles. Lady Emerdirael started shrieking again, but I didn't have enough breath left to threaten her. Several other avatars and droids tried to block my way. I disabled them with the pin gun, beginning to worry how many more shots it had left in its limited power pack.

What I wouldn't give to have Mr. Sparky at my side right now! We'd clear the deck, that's for sure!

The shuttle bay doors loomed ahead of me and I slowed, certain they would be locked. They weren't. I hurried in…and skidded to a halt.

There wasn't an army of avatars between me and the shuttle. There was only a hazy figure whose image was distorted by a privacy shield. "Is this some sort of calisthenic workout?" the Sultan asked, his deep voice sounding unperturbed.

My mind went blank. Standing there with the struggling Lady over one shoulder and my pin gun in hand, I knew I looked utterly nuts.

Might as well go with that, then. I pointed the pin at him.

"I'm not a droid," he reminded me mildly.

"No," I agreed, "but I can turn off that privacy shield you're so fond of."

He paused. "You're trying to hold my *privacy shield* hostage?" he finally asked.

It was ridiculous, but it had been that kind of day. "Yes, I am," I said. "So back off."

He held up his blurry hands and took several exaggerated steps backwards. "A question, if I may, Ms. Fairchild?"

I nodded, keeping the pin trained on him.

"Why are you trying to kidnap that woman?"

I snorted. "Why did you kidnap her in the first place?"

He snorted in return. "Who told you I kidnapped her?"

"Believe it or not, everybody noticed when Lady Emerdirael disappeared right after she turned down your offer to join your little flying circus here."

"That's how you think she got here?" he said, incredulously.

"Are you denying it? I have proof right here!"

"I'm afraid you don't. That's not Lady Emerdirael."

Now *I* looked incredulous.

"Here, I'll prove it," he said, then called, *"Venga, timo sem Emerdirael?"*

The blonde woman dangling over my shoulder answered in the same language. *"Emerdirael? Nes! Ceves da Mericia!"*

"Her name is Mericia," he translated helpfully.

I carefully lowered her to the ground. "Lady Emerdirael?" I asked with waning hope.

"Mericia," she repeated firmly, poking me in the arm with a slender finger. She tossed up her hands and said something else to the Sultan. Then, giving me a final glare, she left the shuttle bay.

"I'm afraid to ask what she just said," I mumbled.

"She's rather annoyed, I'm afraid. She had pledged a week of silence and it wasn't up until tomorrow. Now she has to start all over again."

I flushed, hideously embarrassed.

"If you promise not to keep shooting my avatars," the Sultan went on, "I'll have one of them bring you the real Lady Emerdirael."

I was still covering him with the pin gun. After a moment of deliberation, I snapped it back into its camouflaged shape and returned it to my hair. "Sure," I said. The Sultan murmured into a small communications device and, in a few moments, an avatar came in.

Carrying the cat.

"Oh, you've got to be kidding," I muttered, but it made a gruesome sort of sense. *Golden hair? Tawny fur. Eyes like deep space? Sable black eyes.*

"I didn't kidnap her," the Sultan said, and the cat disappeared behind the privacy shield as the avatar handed her to him. "She was a gift, an exceptionally rare breed and very valuable. I was warned that a thief would try to steal her. In fact, I was told to use my 'considerable power' to defend myself."

"Let me guess," I said. "She was a gift from a Second-Nemian from Yatte?"

"And why do I get the feeling you were sent by a Second-Nemian from Yatte, who seems to have been busy defaming my character in the process?"

And why do I get the feeling that some Yattians don't want peace between them and Chreah?

"I'm not a thief," I said.

"I know that. You're with the Chrythia Mercenary Company." He chuckled at my reaction. "I know more about you than you realize. Your partner—Rishauna a'Liuh, correct?—tried to sabotage my beauty search avatar."

So, he knew all along. An unbecoming wash of disappointment flooded through me. Deep down, I'd hoped it had been real. "You let us think it worked, then," I said.

"I didn't have to *let* you. You were my choice."

"Why?" I asked, fighting an even more unbecoming wave of delight at the thought. "There were some gorgeous women there."

"I look for those who are unique as well as beautiful. I liked how you handled yourself when that idiot started throwing fruit. I was impressed, not just with your appearance, but with your style."

I flushed again, but for a different reason. "I, uh, am still going to need to take Lady Emerdirael back with me," I said, changing the subject.

"Of course. Shall I signal your partner to pick you up? She's out there following that tracking agent in your bloodstream, I presume. Or you could use my shuttle and come back…to stay."

All the little temptations I'd felt so far were eclipsed by what I felt now. *Sleeping in that fluffy bed. All those locales to explore, right at my fingertips. The incredible food. That red dress. I could be a princess every day.*

But…

Never going on another mission with Ree. No more real

adventures. Doing nothing of importance. Never carrying Mr. Sparky at my hip again.

"And if you can't stay for good," the Sultan went on, at the exact moment when I made my decision, "then perhaps you could at least visit?"

"I'd like that," I said.

He spoke into his communications device again. "Ms. a'Liuh will be here momentarily."

"So how did you know we were mercenaries?" I asked. "That kind of information is encryption-protected."

"Why don't I save that for next time?" he said.

Lady Emerdirael suddenly appeared out of the privacy shield as the Sultan held her out to me. She meowed, startled.

I stepped forward to accept her. Even at that close range, I still couldn't see through the privacy shield. "Do you want me to turn it off?" he asked softly.

I thought it over, then shook my head. "Next time," I said, preferring to keep the mystery for now.

"As you wish, Ms. Fairchild."

I smiled. "And maybe next time you can call me Darian and I can call you…?"

But he only chuckled.

"I should have gone with the Giganta, the Limping Barbarian thing," Rishauna said with a mournful sigh as we sat in the cockpit of our ship. "Then I could have been running around a magnificent flying palace, frying avatars and flirting with mysterious men while hauling around irate alien women."

"I *do* have all the luck, hmm?" I teased. My gunbelt was once more strapped on and I patted Mr. Sparky's comforting weight.

Lady Emerdirael suddenly leaped into Rishauna's lap, and purred loudly as my partner rubbed her ears. "So," Ree said, "shall we take the Lady to Yatte and expose the whole sordid tale?"

"And be responsible for starting up a war again ourselves? No, I think we should take her to Chreah, just like we were supposed to."

"And let that Second-Nemian get away with everything?"

"Well, I figure we should say hello to the First-Nemian while we're there, don't you?"

Rishauna grinned. "That's only polite."

I grinned in return, then got up and went back to my tiny room where my pack was sitting atop my cot. I opened it, intending to put away the contents.

Red silk spilled out over my hands like liquid fire, and a slip of paper fluttered to the floor. Three words were written on it in a bold, masculine script:

For next time.

"Next time," I murmured thoughtfully, then smiled.

It hadn't turned out to be such a bad day, after all.

I've been a fan of Laura Underwood's "Anwyn" stories since my first encounter with the reluctant-mage-turned-minstrel. I'm particularly fond of the harp Glynnanis and was delighted to learn that Ms. Underwood owns the original. This story, she says, was inspired in part by old Scottish folklore "and by Amy Huber whose abundance of friendship most certainly exceeds her abundance of presence."

The Wife Of Ben-Y-Ghloe
by Laura J. Underwood

Though it was a bright, clear afternoon, the thick trees and high mountains cloaked in mist made the path Anwyn Baldomyre traveled seem as dark and gloomy as twilight. He found himself wont to move cautiously along the rambling trail that wound its way between the great peaks. Mage eyes of silver perceived that the shadows before him held some strange mystery in the shapes of stones and shrubs.

"Perhaps I should have listened to the villagers," the young harper whispered aloud. His mind wandered back to the warnings they shared. "*Go not through the Mountains of Mist if you value your life*," they had said. But the alternate route was many more leagues than Anwyn cared to walk in the Lamborian realms where he wandered. "This place doesn't feel right, Glynnanis," he said.

"*About time you realized that*," the harp replied with a toss of its unicorn-shaped head. "*There's death in these woods. I can smell it.*"

"Since when does living wood possess a sense of smell," Anwyn half-heartedly teased.

The harp rang a note of retort in Anwyn's head that made him grimace.

The trail wound past a large grey boulder that was a little less than the height of a man. Ragged bits of moss fluttered in a barely perceptible breeze. Anwyn gave it but a glance as he passed, noting to himself that it almost possessed a shape…

And then it moved, unfolding from a crouch to reveal a hag's cadaverous face with a large nose and sharp teeth.

"Lords and Ladies!" he shouted and ducked the claw that lashed out to snatch at him.

"*Get out of here*!" Glynnanis cried. "*Use the Gate Song! Take us back!*"

But the Songs of Power Anwyn had learned from Rhystar of Far Reach required a certain amount of concentration. Not easily obtained when one was trying to dodge raking talons of death on an uneven trail. Anwyn misstepped and tumbled back. He twisted to keep from crushing the harp in the cerecloth sack on his back, and the motion proved to be disadvantageous. His head found the trunk of a rather stout tree. Pain flashed, and with it came the moment of panic in knowing he was likely to die here with no one to sing his dirge…

"Sweet blood of youth with magic blessed," the hag thing said in a croaking voice. Fetid breath assailed him as talons seized his tunic and pulled him closer to the wretched grey face. "I shall feast well this…Arghh!"

Anwyn heard a thump and smelled the sizzle of burning flesh.

"Not this day, foul hag," a woman said. Her words fell on Anwyn's ear with such strength, he felt certain, as he was tossed aside, he would find himself in the company of a great warrior. He fought to roll over and rise, to meet this benefactress who sent the hag scurrying with fright, but his legs and head refused to cooperate. The warm trickle that washed across his face and stained his clothes turned out to be his own blood.

Still, he got a glimpse of her as his vision swam. She was a mountain of a woman, decked out in the greens and browns of a forester. Her girth would have made four of him as she stood on the path, brandishing a rowan staff with practiced ease. Her long braid of fiery hair was pulled back from a beautiful face, set with hemlock eyes, that topped the great mass of her. She glowered beyond him, and he was faintly aware of the crash of someone fleeing into the lower depths of this shadowy land.

"My lady, I am grateful for your assistance," he said and tried to stand.

His head wound must have been more serious than he first imagined. No sooner did he gain his feet than he swooned, tumbling forward into the abundance of her. She, without a fuss, merely hefted Anwyn into her arms like a babe and started into the height of the mountains. Blackness took his senses from him for a time…

"*Anwyn?*"

The harp's gentle voice filtered through a darkness of dull pain, and brought Anwyn back to awareness. His eyes fought against opening, but he was determined to have his sight. So open, they did, on a room washed with warm amber light. Walls of stone, and a ceiling of thatch and logs greeted him. He was on his back, wrapped in the warmth of bear skins—and nothing more, he swiftly realized. He looked about in panic, struggling to rise to his elbows in search of his possessions. His clothes had been washed of their crimson stains and now hung by the fire to dry. Glynnanis had been propped at the base of the pallet, gem eyes glittering with mischief.

"*Welcome back,*" the harp sang.

Anwyn sighed and looked about once more. The large chamber was furnished, but otherwise empty.

"*She's gone for water,*" the harp said. "*She told me to keep trying to wake you. Said it was bad to sleep so soundly with a head wound.*"

"She can hear your voice?" Anwyn puzzled and reached up to touch his own forehead. Swathed in a bandage of linen, a great gash just under the line of his hair greeted his fingers.

His own probing caused the inflamed flesh to sing a hearty protest that made him wince.

"*Oh, yes,*" Glynnanis said.

"But her eyes are green. She's not a mage…"

"*No, but she's not mortal, either.*"

Before Anwyn could ask what the harp meant by that, the door fell open and the woman strolled gracefully into the chamber, carrying two large pails. She offered a faint smile as she set the pails by the door and closed it in her wake.

"Back among the living, I see, Master Anwyn," she said.

"So it would seem," he said, sitting up and clutching the pelt. A dizzy spell made him pause. "You have me at a disadvantage, my lady, so if you'll just hand me my clothes, I'll dress and…"

"Oh, you're not ready to go anywhere, my lad," she said. Drawing a stout stool over beside the pallet, she seated herself there. "You've lost blood, and you're weak as a child." To prove her point, she pushed a finger into his shoulder and sprawled him. The motion sent waves of nausea through him so that he groaned. "And besides," she continued. "I have not wasted time saving you once just to lose you to the Grey Hag."

"The Grey Hag?" he said, and frowned at the grim reminder of that hideous creature. "What is she?"

"A troll fiend," his benefactress said. "A creature from the shadow realms who sits by the gloomy path and feeds on the blood of those who come her way. It's dark out now, and she'd be on you the moment you stepped outside my protections."

"And just who are you?"

"I am the wife of Ben-y-ghloe, though you may call me Donella."

World mighty, Anwyn thought. A name worthy of her. "And where is your husband?"

Her smile was both secretive and sad. "Out and about, as he is always wont to be. Now, tell me, Master Anwyn.

What brings an untried mage like yourself and a magic harp with a saucy tongue to these parts of the world so far from his home in Nymbaria?"

"I'm merely a harper, my lady, seeking adventure and songs."

"Really," she said with a dubious look that made him flush. "Then welcome to my house, *harper.* You may rest here until you heal."

"I don't think that will be very long," he said.

"And why not?"

Should I show her? Anwyn thought.

"*She already knows what you refuse to admit you are,*" Glynnanis said. "*Your gifts will not be shunned here.*"

Anwyn cast the harp a surly glance. "Because I can heal myself," he said, and softly began to hum the notes of the Song of Healing.

Warmth flooded through him, dancing rainbows of color across his skin that grew more brilliant around his wound. Donella watched him, calm as stone.

The Song faded from his lips, leaving its magical tingle on his skin. Cautiously, Anwyn touched the spot on his forehead and found nothing, not even a hint of a scar, under his fingertips as he pulled the bandage away.

"Impressive," Donella said. "Perhaps you are the one."

"To do what?" Anwyn asked, eyeing his clean clothes longingly as he sat up and pulled the fur about him for modesty as much as warmth.

"To help me put the Grey Hag back where she belongs," she said, reaching over to touch his breeches. "I think these are dry now. You may put them on and I'll tell you what I know."

He nodded, grateful when she rose from the stool to pull his clothes from the drying rack and toss them at him one piece at a time. She gave him privacy as well, turning her great back to him as she spoke. He quickly shucked into his trews and shirt, lacing them.

"I came here when I was but a girl," she began. "I had no kin, having lost my family to bandits, and with no place to go, these mountains became my sanctuary. I was sleeping in a cave one night when he came to me, my husband. He made love to me, and in my dreams, he whispered that if I would consent to remain here as his wife, he would share his great wisdom and strength and immortality with me. He instructed me in the ancient ways of the world, and from time to time, men seek me out to learn these arts to improve their lives. Or did until she came."

"The Grey Hag?" he said.

Donella nodded, turning back and claiming her stool once more as Anwyn sat pulling on his boots.

"It's my own fault, of course. My husband warned me it was best I not go to the Valley of Shadows where he, long ago, had sealed the creature and her wretched kin. But it was late summer, and the blackberries were in season on the mountain across the other side of the Valley of Shadows. Being immortal does not stop me from craving their sweetness from time to time."

Anwyn smiled. Blackberries in season were hard to resist.

"I crossed the Valley of Shadows during the day when the sun was high and went on to the other side to collect my sweet fare. But it was getting late by the time I returned. Though the Valley of Shadows lives up to its name in the late afternoon, I was tired from the long journey and did not think there would be any harm in resting there for a while.

"Alas, I chose what looked like a well covered with a capstone upon which to rest my large bones. And forgetting that sometimes nature is a delicate balance, I suddenly found my comfortable seat tipping away beneath me. Naturally, I grabbed the stone to keep it from falling into the well, but what I did not know was that very well was the mouth of a dreadful prison. The Grey Hag suddenly sprang from those depths and raced for the dark wood, since the light of day will turn her and her kin into stone. I heard such a scrabbling in the well, and realized that I was about to free her kin, so I righted the capstone, sealing it back in place with more stones. But all around me, I could feel my husband's dismay.

"'You have undone the world, my woman,' he said, 'for long ago, I helped a good mage to seal the Grey Hag and her kin in that well to keep them from feeding on the blood of travelers and ravaging the villages below the mountains at night. Now that she is free, if she takes enough blood, the Grey Hag will have the strength to lift the capstone and set her kin loose to ravage man once more.'"

She paused, green eyes moist, and Anwyn felt his own throat thicken in sympathy. *Is that why her husband isn't here?* he wondered. *To punish her for a mistake?* "Since that day over a year ago," Donella went on, "the Grey Hag has plagued these mountains. No longer can I share the wisdom of Ben-y-ghloe with mortal men. I spend much of my time roaming these mountains, hoping to catch her, but she's an elusive creature, capable of disguise and deception, as you saw. She'll not come against me, for she knows I wield the power to trap her. The only thing that attracts her is the blood of men."

"How can I help?" Anwyn asked.

Donella sighed. "I would not ask any to risk life for my mistake," she said. "But, if you're truly willing…you could assist me by luring her to a place I have prepared. I've dug a well in the mountain in which to trap her, but I'll need the bait of your youth and blood to lure her there."

Anwyn glanced at Glynnanis. Visions of the cadaverous creature whose smile was full of long tiny sabers made him shudder. Still, how could he refuse when this woman had saved his life?

"When must it be done?" he asked.

"Tomorrow night, the moon will be nearly full and her craving will be sharp. We'll do it then. For now, I would suggest a good meal and a warm bed."

Anwyn smiled and nodded. "I could use a bit of food," he agreed.

"Blackberry tarts?" she ventured.

"How can I refuse?"

She served him the tarts along with a hearty bowl of stew made of rabbit and roots and seasoned quite nicely. The meal left him content and sleepy so that he had hardly pulled a few melodies from Glynnanis' golden strings before he found himself nodding into his chest. She encouraged him to lie down, and he did, vaguely aware of the gesture when she touched his hair as a mother would caress her own child's head.

Come morning, Anwyn awoke to find Donella by the fire, tending her griddle and humming an old ballad he vaguely recognized. Did she sit there all night keeping watch? he wondered, but did not ask.

She gave him warm oatcakes dipped in honey, and white cheese as creamy as fresh milk. Afterwards, when the sun rose, she led him from the cottage to the heights above the line of trees. He marveled that she moved along with such delicate ease and showed no sign of being winded by the ordeal, while he felt his own lungs strain in the thinner air of such lofty heights.

"*I once heard from an old storyteller who visited Far Reaches before I became a harp*," Glynnanis remarked, "*that the mountains of the world were once giants who laid down and fell asleep when the world was new*."

"Not all of them," Donella softly whispered.

She had stopped, and Anwyn was grateful for the pause. He sank to his knees on the ground to rest as Donella gestured to the area surrounding them. A wide plain of rock greeted Anwyn's gaze, and around its edge curled the ever-present mist. Above them, he could see a formation of stone vaguely resembling a man lying on his back. Perhaps the story of sleeping giants is true, he mused.

Donella turned away from the formation, stretching a finger towards the lower edge. "There," she said. "That is where it shall be done."

She started down the slope, and Anwyn was forced to rise and follow. He reminded himself that this direction would certainly be easier. Donella led him to a space where he spied a deep hole dug into the very rock of the mountain. How? he thought.

To one side lay a large stone that would more than cover the hole. Donella lowered herself majestically to sit on it, and bracing the end of her staff on the ground, she leaned against the swirling wood and cocked her head.

"Think you can run from the forest edge to this place without the Grey Hag catching you?" Donella asked.

Anwyn's brows rose. It was not so steep, but he had his doubts. "I think the more likely question is, can I lead her so far up the mountain?" he said grimly. "In which case, I fear I must admit that I doubt I have the strength to go so far so fast."

Donella grinned. "That won't be necessary," she said. "The Grey Hag will be lurking about in the valley below where the sun cannot reach her, but come nightfall, she'll catch a whiff of your sweet mage blood on the wind and be up here quicker than a hare on the run."

"All right," Anwyn said. "But where will you be?"

"Up in the rocks where she can't see me."

Anwyn glanced at the distance, feeling a bit of dismay. So far, he thought miserably.

"Have no fear," Donella insisted. "You lead her up here, and I'll manage the rest. Now, play for me, harper. Let me hear your pretty songs. We've hours yet to pass us by before the sun leaves this place."

Anwyn seated himself on the stone beside her, drawing Glynnanis from the cerecloth sack. The golden strings quickly warmed under his zealous touch. He raced from "Kid on the Mountain" to "The Black Bear's Amble" with ease while Donella clapped her hands in delight. At one point, she drew forth a small feast from the satchel she had brought, giving him a share. She coaxed him into telling tales of his youth and his adventures. In turn, she told him of her own happy days before the bandits stole what she had loved most. Yet the moment he asked where he husband was, she fell once more into that sad, secretive manner.

"Out and about," was all she would say, looking across the rocky expanse with a hint of longing. Anwyn wanted to take her hand and tell her it was all right to grieve, as his father had always told him, but the young harper feared Donella would take his comfort in the wrong light, for she did not seem to want pity. So he wooed her smile back with a humorous song of a stalwart maid who could not be convinced that the bold knight's attentions were as honorable as he declared.

"Will you write a ballad about this night?" she asked Anwyn with a waggle of her brows.

"If I should live to tell the tale, perhaps," he said.

She laughed, a hearty sound that ranged through mist and stone and forest, and the infectious boom brought him nearly to tears of mirth. Part of him thought, I could be content to stay in such a place and share her generous company…

"*Away from Rhystar*?" Glynnanis teased softly, and Anwyn felt his face grow warm.

Donella did not seem to notice, however, for her smile faded as she gazed out across the woods below. "I fear the time is drawing near," she said.

Anwyn looked as well. He had not noticed how dark the mist had grown. Time had flown like a hawk on wing, and the sun's rays were now splayed into streaks by the shapes of the mountain peaks. The valley and trees below were a blanket of verdant shadows, and he felt a crackle in the air that chilled him to the bone.

"Go just to the edge of the sun and wait," Donella said. "Sit yourself there and play your songs as though naught were wrong. As the shadows stretch, retreat from them slowly, as though you are in no hurry. But should you see her in the gloaming, run for the well as though your life depended on it."

Anwyn took an uneasy breath. "It shall," he said softly.

"Have courage," she said, patting his shoulder in a fond manner. "You have power, remember?"

And what good are songs against talons, he wondered. Even Songs of Power such as he possessed.

Donella rose from the capstone. "Lead her to the well," she said. "I'll do the rest."

Anwyn glanced at the far edge of sunlight and forest, which looked so much more distant to him now. He turned to speak to Donella, but she was no longer in sight. Indeed, as he rose and glanced around, he saw no sign of her among the drifts of mist and dark stone. How could she have moved so far so fast?

"*I told you, she's not mortal, not anymore*," Glynnanis said.

Anwyn shivered and gathering the harp, he made his way down to the edge of the light and the forest. Seating himself there, he played a simple tune.

After a time, he heard a faint rustle down in the dark. His eyes flitted warily towards the trees. Nothing seemed amiss, but then his previous encounter with the Grey Hag had taught him the creature was not to be trusted. Suddenly, every stump and stone became suspect in his mind.

"*Let's move up a bit*," Glynnanis suggested.

Anwyn was quick to agree. He rose, the harp before him, ready to dash towards the well.

"*Easy*," Glynnanis said, "*or the troll will know it's a trap*."

He shivered and pretended to do no more than stretch, then sauntered a few paces, keeping in the fading glory of the sun.

Yet now the light seemed to disappear more rapidly than he liked. The wind became cold and teased him with its icy tug. His heart quickened, and so did his pace, for now, it was as though the light fled his company. The last shards of it blazed in his eyes from behind the peaks, then slid away, leaving twilight to stretch a blanket of gloom across the land.

The snap of a twig in the forest to his back was all it took to make Anwyn's heart leap into his throat with fright. He turned a fleeting glance towards the mist and shadows, and saw movement. The grey shape almost blended with the drifting fog that now reached higher than before.

Lords and Ladies! His legs tried to become lead as he bolted for the rise, only to realize the dense mist and evening sky were obscuring the path. He could not say which direction led to the well of stone.

By the Four, how was he to find his way? He had no choice but to run. The creature's hot breath scoured the air to his back, and the swish of those talons sounded too close for comfort. The Grey Hag cackled as she dove at him. Only what little logic his fear-tattered wits allowed to remain kept him moving up the hill.

Straight, however, was impossible. Rock did not form a flat surface with wind and rain to erode its lofty face. He wove an erratic path, stumbling and tottering like a drunk over the irregular surface, the harp clutched feverishly to his chest. Glynnanis peered back over his shoulder crying, "*Hurry, Anwyn! Please hurry*!"

Which way? Anwyn wanted to shout, for even the ground was being obscured as the mist of the mountain folded itself around him. The only consolation he had was knowing it obscured the Grey Hag's path as well. But it did not stop her from scenting his sweet mage blood, while her cackling laughter echoed all around him until he was no longer certain where she might be.

In his distracted state of terror, he stumbled and went to his knees. Scrambling to rise, he only managed to overbalance himself. He fell, putting forth an arm to catch himself, and rolled sideways to avoid crushing the harp.

The Grey Hag loomed out of the mist like a phantom from one of the old stories Anwyn's father once told him.

Childhood terrors could not match the grim reality that smiled razors as the Grey Hag howled her triumph and dove. Anwyn balled himself up small, waiting for the terrible death she would bring.

Her sudden shriek of pain brought his attention back. He heard the thwack of wood striking and flesh popping. An ichor sprayed hot across him as the Grey Hag screamed, and Anwyn unwound himself enough to see why.

Donella had emerged from the mist, fierce as any warrior, to strike a dreadful blow. She was rearing back for another when the Grey Hag lashed out with those claws, snagging the rowan staff even though it burned the creature like a firebrand. For moments, the two titans were locked in a battle of strength. Pain forced the Grey Hag to let go. Donella reared back for another strike when the Grey Hag dropped low and snagged the woman's cloak hem. With a fast tug, the creature sent Donella tumbling. Anwyn cried out, for the mist parted enough to reveal the mouth of the stone well was right behind her. Before the harper could do much more than gain his feet, the wife of Ben-y-ghloe disappeared into the cavernous maw.

With a snarl of triumph, the Grey Hag lifted a loose stone three times the size of her own head and prepared to throw its smashing weight into the depths of the well.

"No!" Anwyn cried, ready to rush at the creature's back.

"*Song of Light!*" Glynnanis sang. "*Sing the Song of Light!*"

The suggestion seemed absurd for a mere moment. Anwyn called the notes to mind and felt their brilliance sparkle in his own soul. He threw back his head and sang the magical Song with all his heart. As those notes were pitched into the foggy air, the luminance that exploded around the Grey Hag was brighter than the midday sun. She screamed in agony, dropping the stone. The scream froze in her throat, leaving its echo to chase across the mountains as she turned into a grotesque statue of stone.

Anwyn released his song and sank to his knees to stare at the hideous formation. Of course, he thought. She can't abide the light.

"*A true mage would have known that*," Glynnanis scolded.

"Be quiet," Anwyn said. He put the harp aside and made his way to the edge of the well to peer into its depths. At first, all he could see was darkness and mist, and he feared the fall had killed Donella. He called her name softly, an uneasy thickness rising in his throat to think she had given her life for his.

But a hand suddenly reached out of the dark, seizing the rim of stone. Anwyn gasped as, before his startled gaze, Donella's greatness arose from the hole. She agilely heaved herself over the rim to sit at his side and catch her breath.

"You're all right," he said, blinking tears.

"Takes more than that short fall to shatter someone like me," she assured him with her smile before she glanced darkly up at the statue that now disgraced the landscape. "This shall not do," she said, and clambered to her feet. "It would be a shame to force my husband to look at this when the mist clears."

With those words, as Anwyn crawled slowly upright, Donella heaved and tipped the stone figure of the Grey Hag over, toppling the monster into the well. Anwyn winced to hear the snap of stone shattering in the depths, and held his breath as Donella pulled the capstone into place and dusted her hands.

"She'll trouble these mountains no more," Donella said. "Now come, young harper. The mist is fading, and my husband will be waiting to give you his thanks."

"But…I thought your husband had left you," Anwyn said.

"Left me?" Donella said. "Not likely. Where would you get such an impression?"

"A man who does not come home to his wife at night…"

"This is his home, Anwyn," Donella replied, gesturing to the world at large. "Come."

She grasped his arm with a gentle strength he could never resist. The mist was parting higher up as she drew him along, leading him towards the reclining stones washed in moonlight. There, she released him, then stepped forward and raised the rowan staff, closing her eyes.

The ground beneath Anwyn's feet trembled, and the mountain heaved like an old man rising from his bed. Anwyn was driven to his knees in fright, and at first, he thought an avalanche of stone was about to descend on them both. Instead, the reclining figure of stone sat up, and a craggy face smiled. Gently, a hand reached forth to lift Donella into a fond embrace. Eyes of granite turned upon the harper.

"Thank you for helping my wife to put the Grey Hag down," a voice rumbled.

"The mountain is her husband," Anwyn whispered in awe.

"*Of course,*" Glynnanis said. "*If you had made your proper sacrifice, you would know that in the ancient tongue, Ben-y-ghloe means 'The Mountain of Mist'. Now play for them, Anwyn. Show them your gratitude.*"

Anwyn's hands trembled as he drew forth the harp and plucked notes from the golden strings. Donella smiled, and Ben-y-ghloe nodded in time with the music. And all the while, the harper continued to marvel at what he had seen, and wondered how Rhystar would react to hear to tale of the beautiful mountain of a woman who was wife to the Mountain of Mists.

When Carol Huber got hold of the anthology guidelines, she decided to play fast and loose with the one about "no magical weight loss" and used her preferred form, poetry. Mike Baker came on board to help write the following short story using Huber's poem as a base.

Chance Hospitality
by Carol Y. Huber & Mike C. Baker

I was on my way to the annual archery tournament at Handover Creek. For once, my life-partner Mick wasn't with me. There's a big purse to be had at the Menzownly Faire and not only do they not allow women to compete, they don't like women who do compete. Silly rule, that, but I didn't make it up.

We agreed to go our separate ways for a while so that I could enter elsewhere. I remember the last thing he said before we parted. "Lysera, *please* try to stay out of trouble this time." I wonder, sometimes, if he thinks I'm some sort of trouble magnet.

I was strolling along, taking the Miner's Mistake to Handover Creek Road and expecting to make a little town called Hangum by dusk, when the skies went greenish-black and proceeded to dump water by the bucket. Then it picked up the pace and started dumping it by the barrel.

I'm a big person and in great shape (I don't make money otherwise) but storms don't discriminate. They don't care who they piss on or otherwise inconvenience, so I started looking for shelter.

Lightning flashed, revealing a small cottage set back from the road. I headed toward it. I had plenty of money in my purse, just in case I needed to convince someone that they wanted to be hospitable, and figured there would be no problem. Isn't hindsight wonderful?

I knocked briskly, wiping my feet off on the doormat. Mama taught me right, even if I don't always follow her rules. As I plastered my best "I really am harmless and wouldn't you like to help me?" smile on my face, I noticed some very fussy letters on the mat; they spelled out "Chance". Sometimes it works, sometimes it doesn't. The smile, that is.

The temperature was falling along with the sky, and I was starting to shiver. Though my bow, quiver and sword have the best waterproof leathers that money can buy, they didn't need to be out in that kind of mess. Neither did I.

The door opened up quickly and this tiny woman looked out. She had all of her grayish-mouse-colored hair scraped back from her face into a bun that must have hurt. It was so tight, it pulled her face back into a caricature of a rodent. Actually, it wasn't that bad a color…but it would have looked better on a mouse.

She stared up at me as if I had just grown a beard or something. "You're wet," she said.

"Rain usually does that," I replied with as straight a face as I could manage.

"Well, I guess you may come in."

The next words out of her mouth weren't your typical guest-greeting, either. "It's a shame you're so fat. Why did you ever let yourself get that way?"

I counted to ten—twice. I'm a fairly easy-going sort of person, you know, even-tempered. I'm a professional archer; I can't afford to lose it because someone is rude or nasty. Besides, I hear it all the time. Same song, next verse.

"Thank you for granting me shelter. It's miserable out, and without your kind-hearted hospitality, I would probably have caught pneumonia," I answered. All right, so I was laying it on a bit thick, but sometimes being extra polite reminds others that they are being rude.

Inside, the place was spotless. Not clean—spotless. Even Mama didn't clean like that. And why bother? It would be dirty again tomorrow. I tried not to drip on too many things as she led me toward the fire.

She brewed some tea on the stone hearth while I stood as close to the fireplace as I could without actually getting in it. Mouse-face peered down her nose at me some more as I saw to my steel, wood, and cord babies. They were, indeed, still dry within those costly leathers, proof again that my investment had been worth its while.

"You obviously don't need any sweetener," she said, oh so primly, as she handed me a mug full of the tea.

Sometimes truisms aren't. This time, extra-polite hadn't worked. Once again, I just kept my mouth shut. I'd heard this one before, too. On the other hand, I decided that I would give her the smallest guesting-gift I could think of. (I never claimed to be perfect.)

I drank the tea down. It didn't taste very good and it really did need some honey or something. But it was hot and I was cold.

Next thing I knew, I woke up with my head pounding. I'd been dumped on a pallet in a little room at the back of the cottage. I guess she thought I would be grateful for the pallet. I guess Mouse-face thought I would be grateful for what else she'd done, too.

Wrong!

Forge irons pounding in my head, I tried to jump up as soon as I saw what she had done. It took a minute to get my balance, in more ways than one. Whether through that nasty tea, or while I was out, she'd worked some gods-awful magic. Her damned spell had *re-sized* me! Made me *thin*! She had removed all of my comfortable padding, and most of the muscle, too.

I've heard of people seeing red.

Guess what? It's true.

You can.

I did.

The mouse-faced old biddy came prissing into the room, alerted, no doubt, by my mutterings. She proudly proclaimed,

"I have fixed all of your problems. I removed all that unsightly fat. Instead of wandering through storms, you'll be able to find a good, respectable man and get married. You'll finally be able to settle down, have children, live in a nice little house…with a fence, I think. Yes, definitely a fence. I have re-formed you so that you can have all those wonderful things you couldn't have before due to your immense size."

Mick says that I still go red when I tell this part. I'm certain that what he sees now is only a pale reflection of my original fury. I know I was too angry to speak as she continued blathering.

"You can be fruitful and happy. You can sew for your family, and no doubt you'll take up knitting. And you'll be cooking and cleaning and all those wonderful things that are so proper and fitting for a woman. I have reduced you to a nice, even ninety-eight pounds…which is, of course, the proper weight for a bride."

I just stood there for a moment. Sure, I'm used to the "you're fat" garbage, but this was something brand new. I was stunned and speechless for a moment longer.

But only for a moment longer.

"Ninety-eight pounds!" I yelled at the top of my lungs, volume crippled by the unwanted changes. "Did it ever occur to you that I *might* look like I do for a reason? It's what works! If I can't carry my own weight, I can't compete. If I don't compete, I don't win. If I don't win, I don't make money. And if I don't make money, I don't eat. I like food. I also like all the other interesting things one can do with money."

I gasped in an extra breath, fighting to calm down while battling my unfamiliar—and undersized—diaphragm. "I won't be able to string my bow, much less draw it. I'm not sure I'll even be able to pick up my sword."

I went on. "I'm a competitive archer, working the tournament circuit. If I wanted the fence and the house and the sewing, I could have had them, you meddler. I *like* traveling. I *like* archery. And I already *have* a good man. He loves me passionately, and he respects and understands me. He cherishes ALL of me—fat, muscle, mind and spirit. The whole package, not some bloody image."

"As for knitting," I continued after gasping for another breath, "I already tend to my own. Where else in this gods-forsaken world do you think I would find socks? Growing on the trail?"

By then, my anger had turned cold and even more intense. I wasn't finished chewing her narrow ass, though. "Get this, Mou…*lady*: I Do Not Want Children! I know everyone thinks it's strange, but I don't want children! I like my life just fine the way it is. Or at least the way it was 'til you reduced me to *this*."

Mouse-face tried to break into my tirade, but I wasn't done yet. "Put me back! Put me back *exactly* the way I was. Put me back and I won't haul your scrawny ass before the Hangum sheriff for misuse of magic, reckless endangerment, and generally screwing up my life. I like the person who came here. I don't have time to work back up to *my* proper shape. So PUT ME BACK, NOW!"

She simply stared at me for a minute, nose in the air. Then the interfering old bat started sputtering about all her hard work. "I have rules. I have standards. You broke them all, just by existing. How *dare* you object to me helping you! Such ingratitude! What a horrible temper you have. It was for your own good, you wretched, sort-of-almost-woman! But I don't need to be listening to your ranting and raving, and I certainly don't like this abuse or your language."

Not to mention my threat of the Sheriff, I thought snidely.

She continued with her not-phrased-as-such surrender. "I'll return you to your prior, malformed and unsightly self if only to shut you up. It will take time to make the tea."

The old biddy went over to the fireplace and brewed up a new pot. Then she walked back over with a full mug and told me, "Drink it all down. If you hurry you can get back out on the road and reach the next town by sunset. But first, pay me. You owe me for all of my hard work."

That almost set me off again. Instead, I basically threw quite a bit of money at her. I didn't even try to bargain. Although that was out of character for me, sometimes you just pay the price and don't argue. I learned that rule early on.

I grabbed the mug and drank the new tea down as quickly as I could. It tasted like dog piss. Well, maybe...I don't really know what dog piss tastes like and don't want to find out. But it was bad.

Of course, she didn't add any sweetener this time either. Even then, she was still trying to bend me to her rules.

I woke up with another pounding headache. This one didn't stop me from checking myself out and...blessed be!...I was back to my familiar round self. All the parts looked like they should, and I no longer felt as though I would blow over in a light breeze. Solid and sturdy, that's me. And that's the way I like it.

I got the hell out of there. People think I like to take my time and, usually, I do. But there are exceptions. I moved and I moved fast. Just in case Mouse-face changed her supposed mind.

I met up with Mick a few days later, after we had each won our respective tournaments. I told him the whole story. And instead of being properly sympathetic, he nearly busted a gut laughing. MEN! But it was also his idea for me to write it all down and see if I (reminder to self: we!) could make some money off of it.

Hey, why not?

The guidelines were specific: no "fat gene" stories. Then I got a letter asking if I would consider a "Fat Gene" story and offering the one that follows. Gene Wolfe says this piece "originated in the image of a fat man—one who was not merely fat but huge, a species of giant—sitting solidly in a great chair big enough and strong enough to hold him," and "concealing something by his very presence and position. Such thoughts led to stage magic, which I love, and to the art of misdirection." The narrator, Sam Cooper, has appeared in three earlier stories, "The Nebraskan and the Nereid", "Lord of the Land", and "The Eleventh City."

The Fat Magician
by Gene Wolfe

May 3, 2000
Franklin A. Abraham, Ph.D., Chair
Comparative Religion and Folklore
U. of Nebraska Lincoln
Lincoln NE 68501
Amerika

Dear Frank,

I have quite a tale to tell. It is not exactly folklore. Not yet, but it is fast becoming folklore. It is a mystery story if you will, and centers about a man in league with the Devil, who was on the side of the angels. It is also a story of murder, though there is no mystery about the murder. Most signally, it is a horror story, by far the most horrible I have ever been made aware of.

And it is a ghost story, on top of everything else. You will have to accept my own testimony as regards the ghost; so let me say here that everything I am about to tell you is true to the best of my knowledge. I am going to stretch nothing, because there is nothing that requires stretching. I am not, however, going to tell you the *whole* truth. I cannot do that without betraying the pledge I gave this morning to a most attractive woman who has been exceedingly kind to me. I know, Frank, that is not a thing you would wish me to do.

As you will probably be able to tell from the postmark, I am not yet in Vienna. Trains do not break down—or so I have always thought. It turns out I was wrong. I am not sorry, but I am very glad that I allowed myself a few days in Vienna before the opening of the WFC.

In brief, I woke up this morning and found my train at a dead stop between two flower-spangled mountain meadows when it ought to have been in the Vienna station. I have my demotic, as you know, and fair command of Spanish. My German, I fear, is merely amusing. Amusing to me, I mean. Actual Germans and Austrians are inclined to burst into tears.

By jumping up and down and shouting, I was able to make the conductor ("Herr Schaffner") understand that I wished to know why we were not in Vienna. Herr Schaffner, by shouting back, stamping, spitting in my face and wiping his own with his handkerchief, was able to convey to me that *ein gross Herr Shaft* (I suppose the crankshaft) of our engine had broken. In all fairness, I must admit Herr Schaffner's English is better than my German. Say, about ten percent better.

Soon we were joined by a handsome young guy called Heinz, a grad student who speaks English a good deal better than I shall ever speak German. Heinz conferred with Herr Schaffner and explained to me that the Austrian State Railway would not be able to spare us a new engine for a day or so. We were welcome to stay on the train until the new engine arrived, eating such food as there was in the dining car. Or we could walk three kilometers down the tracks to R___, where there would be restaurants and so forth. When the new engine arrived, the train would pull into the station at R___ and stay there for an hour or more collecting its passengers.

Heinz and I conferred and decided to walk to the village and perhaps take rooms there, I promising to buy his breakfast if he would interpret for me. We fetched the overnight bags that were all we were permitted to have in our compartments and off we went, hurrying along before the rest of passengers (they were still yawning and dressing for the most part) came along to overwhelm the village facilities.

"I myself am living not so far from this place when I was a child in Freistadt," Heinz informed me. "This R___, it is where the famous and terrible Ernst S___ lived."

Naturally I wanted to know what made Herr S___ famous and terrible.

"He is a Hexenmeister." Heinz grinned and made magical gestures.

"A master of bad luck?"

Heinz laughed. "He will make you a dog or a toad, Herr Cooper. This is bad luck enough, ja? Only we do not worry now. He is dead. When I am little, the older *kinder* scare us with him, the big children."

After that, I wanted to know a great deal more, as you can imagine, but Heinz could only tell me that "Fat Ernst" (this was the name used to frighten children, apparently) had been a giant, that he had disappointingly boasted but a single head and, most surprisingly, that he had been a living, breathing man in Heinz's grandparents' time. Heinz's great uncle, a traveling salesman, had met him more than once. Heinz thought that he had died during World War II and that he had probably been killed by a bomb.

We got to the village and soon found a snug *das Cafe* where Heinz quizzed our waitress on my behalf. She called Fat Ernst "Ernst the Great" (which interested me), agreed that he had been a bad man, but seemed to feel a secret sympathy for him. An older man with a bristling mustache stopped at our table on his way out and snapped something in German that I could not understand, but at which our waitress colored. When she had gone, Heinz explained in a whisper that the other patron had called Fat Ernst a liar and a thief.

Our *Fruhstucks* came (bread, butter, pastries, cold cuts, three kinds of cheese, and the wonderful Austrian coffee), and, with all the other things, an old man who had been drinking his coffee at a table in the back, speaking a German so slow and simple that even I could understand most of what he said: Fat Ernst had been a friend of the Devil's. It was better not to talk, or even think, about such people.

Properly chastened, Heinz and I confined our conversation to the excellence of the food and the length of our delay for the remainder of the meal.

When I paid our bill, the owner of the cafe said in halting English, "Quick you will want das Mittgassen, ja? In R we have ein fine Gasthaus." He pointed. "Der Romantik Hotel S___. Sehr alt. Sehr in-ter-es-ting. Gutes Speiss."

Well, Frank, I have never claimed to be the sharpest knife in the drawer, but even I could not help noticing that he was—yes, earnestly—recommending a place other than his own, and that the name of the "Romantic Hotel" he recommended was also that of Fat Ernst.

In retrospect, we should have found a cab. As it was, we assumed that der Romantik Hotel S___ was in the village. We found out (by asking directions on a street in which all the houses seemed to have been modeled on cuckoo clocks) that it was not, that it was nearby. As, alas, it was not. Frank, the Chinese are right; uphill miles *are* longer. So are uphill kilometers. By the time we had gone wrong, and found the right road again, and stopped a couple of times to rest and hold lengthy conversations concerning job opportunities in American universities, and Austrian folklore and American folklore (poor Heinz thought that Pecos Bill and Paul Bunyan were legitimate, but had never heard of the Boss in the Wall), and German and Russian and Polish folklore, to say nothing of the opportunities awaiting an unmarried man in Vienna…Well, it was nearly lunch time when we got there. I honestly think I could have sat down, taken off my shoes, and eaten Heinz's lunch as well as my own.

Now I'm going to describe Gertrun's hotel. Pay attention, Frank. This stuff is important.

Although the setting is lovely, the building itself is not. What it is, is old. It was built (Gertrun says) in seventeen fifty-seven as a hunting lodge. Her family, the S___s, took it over in eighteen sixty and has operated it as a hotel ever since. It is of weathered gray stone, is as square as a bouillon cube, and has three stories, with one of those high, pointed roofs you see everywhere here and (I suppose) a good-sized attic underneath it. Parlor, dining room, kitchen, hotel office, et cetera, on the ground floor, with a wine cellar and other cellars underground. High ceilings in all the rooms. Go up the stairs and you find a square landing on which you might drill troops, with a massive carved railing. This landing gives access to the twelve rather old-fashioned bedrooms on the floor. The stair continues to the floor above where there are more rooms; I did not bother to count those, but Gertrun says those are smaller, so sixteen up there, possibly.

Gertrun owns and runs the place. Picture a substantial woman between thirty-five and forty, very blond, with a round, smiling face, a toddler's complexion, and truly beautiful clear blue eyes. She showed us into a dark paneled dining room ornamented with the antlers of deer that had died before any of us were born, assured us that lunch would be ready in a minute or two, and stayed to chat with us. At first I supposed, as I think anybody would, that she was an employee; I asked if there were any members of the owner's family about.

"I am here, Mein Herr. I am Gertrun S___."

I apologized, and we introduced ourselves and explained about the train.

When I mentioned Ernst S___, I unleashed a flood of information. He had been Gertrun's grandfather. A giant? Oh, ja! She rose on tiptoe and stretched a hand as high as she could reach to indicate his height and embraced an imaginary barrel to show his girth. Three hundred kilos—four hundred. She did not know, but he had been *sehr gross*, huge.

Heinz asked several questions I was too dense to understand; Gertrun replied in German, and I caught the word *Jude*. Heinz turned to me, smiling. "He hid people from the Nazis when they took power in our country, Herr Doktor. Jews…"

Gertrun interrupted in German.

"She says he had a Jew, a priest, and a man that wore dresses in his secret room at the same time once." Heinz roared with unfeigned delight. "What a rumpus that must have been!"

"They wished to send them to the camps," Gertrun explained. "Mein Grossvater did not like." She shook her head violently. "He was before on die stage, ein performer."

I said that I had thought the Nazi sent only Jews to their concentration camps, at which Gertrun became very somber. "It does not matter what they say, Herr Doktor Cooper. When such mans have authority, they send to their camps what they do not like. They send Jews, und the priest does not like that, und so they send the priest. A man which does Lippenstift…" Her finger signaled lipstick. "He…" (She groped for a word, one hand on her own soft stomach.) "They grow sick from seeing it. So him auch. Him also, mein Grossvater hides him like those other mans."

I asked whether the Nazis had found them.

"Nein! To Schweiz they go." Gertrun's eyes, which were very round already, became rounder still. "Again und again der Nazis come! All night almost for many, many… Mein vater ist a little boy, Herr Doktor. He hears them up und down die steps, in den cellars, everywhere. Into his room they come, und under his bed look. If him they frighten, mein Grossvater will show where ist das Geheimzimmer. This they think, but they make der mistake."

"The secret room," Heinz translated.

"Never! Never his secret room he shows! Kommen mit, I show you his chair."

She led us back into the parlor. It was an enormous chair, like a throne. The seat was as high as a table and four feet across, and the legs looked sturdy enough to support a small house. "'Search!' he tells them. 'I sit till you are done. You leave, you close mein door.' So they think the secret room it is he sits on. They make him get up. They move his chair." She showed us a nick in the sturdy oak back that the Nazis had supposedly made. "They take up der carpet. They drill through our floor, but ist der Weinkellar they searched every night. There they find ein klein Judsch Mutze," she touched the back of her head, "und mein Grossvater laughs."

Naturally Heinz and I wanted to know where the secret room was.

Gertrun's face went blank. "I do not know, Herr Doctor. Nobody knows but mein Grossvater. I see in die Kuche. You will be hungry, ja?" She hurried away.

"She knows," Heinz told me.

"Of course she does," I said. "What I'd like to know is why she doesn't want us to."

From that time until our lunches arrived, Heinz tapped panels and moved pictures and ran up the stairs to the floors on which the guest rooms were located, without finding anything. He went back to the train after lunch, but I decided to rent a room at the Romantik Hotel S___ , enjoy a good dinner (there is excellent food all over Austria, but our lunches had been superb) and a good breakfast today before I reboarded.

"In Juni will be full," Gertrun told me. "Ist when young people ist married. They come then to hike und climb. Now you have mein best."

It was indeed a large room, and beautifully furnished with antiques. I have seen more dramatic views than the one afforded by its four wide lace-curtained windows, but few, if any, that were lovelier.

"There und there ist dem doors for des rooms next door," Gertrun pointed out to me. "Sometimes two ist rented together. For this die Hotelrechnung for number two ist half. But you have die Bolzen. Chains mit locks die handles of them both holds, you see?" She demonstrated, shaking the handle of one of the bolts. "Here ist keys to der locks for dem chains. So you know nobody comes und bothers you. You must give back to me mit der key of das room when away you go. If you not, I must telfonieren der Schlosser from R___." She pantomimed cutting the shackle.

I promised that I would certainly return all her keys, and asked whether she had been in show business like her grandfather, praising her appearance and melodious voice.

She laughed. "Nein! Nein! But I have picture. You would like to see?"

I thought she meant a picture of herself, but she led me to her office, a small room off the parlor, and showed me a framed theatrical poster on which rabbits bounded, rings flew, and maidens floated about an imposing man in evening dress. A man already portly, although from what Gertrun told me he must have been quite a bit younger in those days than his waxed mustache and full beard made him appear. Behind him a shadowy, Mephistophelian figure, taller even than he, stooped as though to whisper some dreadful confidence. Fat Ernst had been a conjurer!

"Till his vater ist no more," Gertrun explained. "Then he comes home to take care of mein hotel."

"With the secret room in which he hid the Jew and those others."

"Ja, ja." Gertrun looked a trifle flustered. "Many more also, Herr Doktor."

"No doubt. The room that the Nazis were never able to find, even though they searched this building repeatedly and no doubt systematically, since Austrians are every bit as systematic as Germans."

"Ja. Never." She was at ease now and smiling. She has good teeth and is very attractive when she smiles.

"You said that they found a yarmelke in the wine cellar?"

Gertrun nodded. "In die attic, too, they find something once. I do not remember."

"A rosary or a crucifix, I'm sure. A breviary, perhaps. Something of that kind." I took her hand, "Frau S___, I don't know why you're so anxious to keep the location of your grandfather's secret room a secret, but I want you to know that whatever harm others may intend to you or your family, I intend none. I like you—more than I should, perhaps. And yet I can't help being curious. Would it trouble you if I had a look at your wine cellar? And the attic?"

"Nein!" She shook her head violently. "I take you myself, Herr Doktor."

I told her she need not bother and went up to my room, where I immersed myself in thought as well as hot water.

Fat Ernst's having been a conjurer had given me the clue. When I had dried myself and changed my underwear, shirt and socks, I unlocked the heavy wrought-iron bolt on one of the connecting doors and tried to move it. It traveled a sixteenth of an inch, perhaps, but no farther.

Let me interrupt myself here, Frank. On the first page of this letter, I promised you a mystery. It is the location of Fat Ernst's secret room. You have all the facts that I had now. Where was it?

Gertrun and I breakfasted together the next morning in her private apartment—a meal large enough to last me all day. Over coffee, I asked her whether her grandfather himself had ever spoken of a secret room. Had he said, for example, that there was one?

She shrugged. "Gone he was before I am here to hear him, Leibling."

"I doubt that he did, although he may well have said that no one would ever find it. In that he was quite correct. No one ever will, because it does not exist."

She stared without speaking.

"Allow me to tell you, so you'll know I'm not bluffing. Then I will give you my word that I will never reveal the name or location of this hotel, or the name of your family. Never. Not to anyone."

"Danke." I had taken her hand as I spoke, and she managed to smile. "Danke schön."

"There's only one kind of secret room that can't be found no matter how thorough the search, Gertrun. It's a secret room that does not exist. Your grandfather put the people he was hiding into the ordinary rooms of his hotel. Many hotels have connecting doors between rooms, as yours does. And all of those I have ever seen have sliding bolts on both sides of the doors; I cannot enter my neighbor's room unless his bolt is drawn back as well as my own, and he cannot enter mine. In this hotel, however, those bolts are connected by a slot through the door. I don't know the word in German, but an American conjurer would say they were gimmicked. Or gaffed. That's why you think it necessary to chain and padlock them."

I waited for her to speak, but she just stared; I saw her lower lip tremble.

"When the Nazis put their room key into the lock, the person hiding in that room had only to slip into the next and hold the bolt of the connecting door closed until he heard the searchers leave and he could return. When the Jew's room was being searched, he could slip into the priest's, and when the priest's was searched he could slip into the Jew's. Or both could slip into the room occupied by the transvestite. I would imagine that they were careful to sleep on the floor, and so on—not to leave any indication that the room had been occupied that could not be snatched up and carried away. As for the yarmelke in the wine cellar, and whatever may have been found in the attic, they were false clues planted by your very clever and very brave grandfather to throw the searchers off the track."

She nodded and gave me a shaky smile.

"How did he die? Was it an Allied bomb? That's what Heinz thought."

"Nein. These Nazis here take him."

That puzzled me. I said, "But they can have had no evidence if they never found…"

"For ein trial, Herr Doktor?" Gertrun's smile was bitter then. "Evidence they do not need. They take him, und he ist dead."

It required some time to digest. That immense body sprawled in a gas chamber. Half a dozen Storm Troopers to drag it out and get it on the truck. Then I said, "You keep his secret…"

"For nachst, Herr Doktor. For next time."

There you have it, Frank. But my train has not come yet, so let me tie up a few details. I promised you a mystery, and I think you will agree that I gave you one.

A murder, as well. Was not Fat Ernst murdered by his government? If not, how did he die?

That seems to me the greatest of all horror stories. When the millennium now ending began, government meant a king, and that king, whatever else he might be, was his nation's leader. He might wage war upon his neighbors, but he would have been thought mad if he had waged war upon his followers. Bandits and cutpurses abounded, and they constituted a very real and present danger to everyone except the strongest; the king was the sworn foe of all such criminals. In the century we are just now closing out, we ordinary men and woman have been in much greater danger from our own governments than from all the criminals in the world.

In Nazi Germany, and not long afterward here in beautiful, smiling Austria, the government declared that Jews must die. The priest objected, so the priest had to die, too. The man who cross-dressed disgusted the government's functionaries, and he was added to the list.

Which is more disgusting, a man in a dress or a government that murders the people who created it to protect them? Which is more horrible, Frank? Is it the werewolf of our folklore, or this soulless monster squatting over the corpse of its nation, its hands running with innocent blood?

Sincerely,
Sam Cooper

P.S. Still no train, although I spent nearly an hour sipping coffee in *das snug Cafe*. Thus I have time to tell you that, last night about one-thirty, I woke to the sound of footsteps, footsteps slow and so heavy that the timbers of the landing creaked and groaned. Very distinctly, I heard the door open and saw a vertical bar of very bright-seeming light from the stairwell. Somebody standing not more than a step from the bed in which I lay said softly but unmistakably, "Ist gut," and the door closed again. I got out of bed and turned on a light, but the only other person in the room was sleeping soundly. All three doors were securely fastened, as we had left them.

I intend to return here to R___ for a week or so after the conference, to investigate this and other matters.

Sam

What happens when a writer gets tired of reading about "pale, thin, languid twenty-something vampires?" In the case of Joette Rozanski, she starts asking questions: "What about creatures of the night who looked like the rest of us? What if they were considered 'second-class' by the more typical undead?" And the answers come in the form of the following story.

The Search For A Sipping House
by Joette M. Rozanski

Eleanor saw it coming and braced herself. The man's big sweaty hand swooped down and lifted her off of Edgar.

"Don't you wanna keep any of this stuff, George?" the man asked the landlord, who hovered in the shadows of the doorway. "Some looks pretty good."

"I don't want any of it," George snarled. His beady eyes glanced from side to side and he shivered. "He's gonna be in the big house a while. Just dump it at the curb where the scavengers can haul it away."

"Okay, George."

The world became a pendulum for Eleanor as the man carried her down the stairs and out into the hot summer sunshine. He swung her so enthusiastically that he tripped over her long black cord several times, nearly sending the both of them crashing down several flights. Eleanor became so distraught that she almost forgot to bite.

"Ouch!"

With a resounding clang, the man dropped her onto the curb. His co-worker stared.

"How'd that happen, Bill?"

"I dunno." Bill sucked at his hand. "Glad I got that tetanus shot last year."

Warm blood thrilled through Eleanor's substantial brass body as she watched the movers bring out the rest of the apartment's furniture, which included a beautifully sculpted piece of black marble, an elegant end table, and a rather homely rocking chair. These were, respectively, Yolanda, Edgar, and Martha—the vampire Brood.

"I still think we could take some of this," Bill said, wiping his brow. "The dealer had class."

Eleanor became anxious; she didn't want to be separated from the others.

"Nah," his companion said. "George wants us to go to his Woodlake apartments right away. Gotta beat—I mean evict—somebody."

"Okay." Bill shook his square head. "Shame, though. About the stuff, I mean."

Eleanor watched as the men's battered pick-up truck, followed by George's sedan, disappeared down the street. Then, one by cautious one, the Brood blurred into their human shapes.

"Is this wise?" Martha asked, her small hands clutching her wrinkled face. "Shouldn't we have waited until full dark? What if someone saw us?"

"Then they're that much closer to rehab," Eleanor said bitterly from her perch upon the soiled mattress. "I'm glad we're leaving this dump." She scowled at the dirty brown clapboard duplex that squatted before them on its weedy lawn.

"Yeah, but where do we go from here?" Yolanda shook her head and her tiny tight braids swished across the shoulders of her black satin dress. "Only three months this time. I'm gettin' real tired, Edgar. Why can't you get French to fix us up with something better?"

Edgar, slim and elegant in his linen suit, shrugged. "I can only do so much with French. We're not his highest priority. Perhaps if we were to live in a morgue…"

"What we really need," Martha said in her soft librarian's voice, "is a Sipping House."

"Maybe so," Yolanda said, gnawing at her lower lip, "but that isn't going to happen for a while, and for now we still need a place to stay. Edgar, go see French—and take Eleanor with you. He seems to like you two best."

As Eleanor and Edgar strolled down the street toward the town's near East Side, all eyes turned toward them. Edgar's dark gaze and thin aristocratic sneer still fascinated the living. And Eleanor, with her waist-length red hair and two-hundred pound frame, swept past them with a powerful, graceful stride, as irresistible as an ocean wave.

Eleanor dreamed as she walked. She dreamed of the tall vampire who had ushered her into the shadow world. He could transform into a great golden wolf that would roam the night and claim numerous victims. How brilliant his eyes as he loomed over her, his shadow bride.

Eleanor also remembered the disappointment in those eyes the first time she'd translated into a brass lamp, her favorite form. Out the window flew both her first and only lover, and the eternal romance he'd promised her. "I may bestow immortality upon you, but not creaturehood," he had said before making his exit. "Your character determines that. You are too staid and proper to be Animated, my dearest Eleanor. Furniture is *your* future."

And so Eleanor discovered that vampires came in two varieties: the Animates, who could transform into animals, and the Inanimates, who took on manufactured shapes, such as furniture. The two clans did not get along.

Abandoned, Eleanor wandered about until she found an Inanimate Brood, several hundred strong, that occupied a large country mansion, but soon wearied of her humble position in the pecking order. The eldest always got the best blood-lettings, even as the others grew faint with hunger. So when Yolanda offered her the chance to become an Elder in an infant Brood, Eleanor had gladly followed her.

However, there were few homes for new Broods. Large houses were best, since living victims tended to dismiss the regular flow of "accidents" to the occupying humans that occurred in such places. But the established Broods owned the majority of these homes and jealously guarded them from intruders. Smaller Broods had to content themselves with whatever French the Ghoul found for them.

"Wake up," Edgar said, nudging her. "We're here."

The evening's clean pink light had faded into a sticky purple glow that made French's Pawnshop seem almost jolly. A huge plate-glass window, filled with jumbled glittering goods, reflected the evening's first dim star. Eleanor's gaze ranged over radios and television sets, gold and silver, furs and velvets. "French believes in tempting fate, doesn't he?" she asked.

Edgar's lips twisted into a bitter smile. "Welcome to French's mousetrap. Doesn't the cheese look delicious?" He pushed open the door and they walked in.

Eleanor, who'd met French numerous times in cemeteries and outside dilapidated homes, had never visited his place of business before. The inside of the shop was quite small, but mounds of valuables were piled nearly to the ceiling. Bare bulbs provided ugly yellow light, which sparkled off many watches, rings, necklaces and bracelets. Here and there someone had scattered earth-stained clothes that smelled of embalming fluid; they reminded Eleanor of discarded candy wrappers.

"Aha!" a deep voice rumbled. "My two favorite Inanimates. Come over here and let French have a look at you."

They walked toward the back of the shop, where French sat behind a counter. He was huge, his skin as pale as tallow, his flesh straining against dirty black jeans and a black t-shirt that read "Reality bites and so do I." Tiny eyes twinkled behind fat lids; the sparse, greasy strands on his scalp were pulled back into a tight ponytail. His smile revealed gorilla teeth and a gray tongue that looked rough, like a cat's.

"I assume," he said, "that your presence here indicates domestic trouble." The Ghoul placed his hands on the counter. Each hand sported six well-formed fingers, their nails encrusted with dirt.

Edgar turned away in disgust, but Eleanor said, "Yes, French. We'll need your help again."

French closed his eyes and sighed, blowing foulness mixed with breath-mint sweetness into the dusty air. "Eleanor, Eleanor, built like a diva with a voice to match. What a Ghoul you would have made—we all have operatic-level lungs." His eyelids flew up. "But you're in luck! Phenomenal luck! Only for his dearest friends would French produce such a treasure."

"Really?" Edgar asked. "What now? A cardboard box?"

French shook his head and tut-tutted. "Friend Edgar, so beautiful and yet so bitter." With much creaking and groaning, the Ghoul stood up; he leaned across the counter and stared at them.

"What would you do," he whispered, "if I could guarantee you a Sipping House?"

A Sipping House! Eleanor had heard of such things, but only as legend. They were vampires who could masquerade as entire buildings, sheltering their Broods for centuries. Over the years, many became extremely powerful, and the very oldest in Europe had grown into castles. But Houses were so rare that only the largest Broods associated with them.

"How did *you* find such a prize?" Edgar asked suspiciously. "And why offer it to *us*? Any big-name Brood would kill for a House!"

"Hah!" French snorted. "I haven't met an In yet that could harm a fly, much less kill one." He leaned back. "Besides, not many Broods like me; we are not exactly on speaking terms. And I must warn you, this House is a loner who distrusts his fellow vampires. You know the story: sire saw what he was, abandoned him, and the fellow freaked out. All you Ins need therapy."

"Assuming that we might bite," Eleanor said, ignoring French's remark, "how much will this information cost us?"

French raised his hands, hairy palms up. "All I want is a favor. From you." He pointed at Edgar, who snarled and stepped back.

"No need for that," French said soothingly. "I need you in your professional capacity. You appraised jewelry and antiques in your previous life, dearest Edgar, and last night I scavenged up a new lot." He jerked a thumb in the direction of the shop's rear. "Interested?"

Edgar glanced at Eleanor. "Are we?"

Eleanor shrugged. "Why not?" She looked at French. "We're all yours."

"Excellent!" the Ghoul said, grinning and rubbing his hands together. "Come along, Edgar. You do your thing and I'll do mine. Satisfaction guaranteed."

The next evening, Number 42 bus rattled down a narrow street lined with huge old horse chestnut trees. Their branches nearly met overhead, casting dense shadows speckled with sunset light. Small wooden homes, most of them neatly maintained, sat upon patches of lawn burnt brown by the summer heat. It was a worn-at-the-edges kind of neighborhood, but nice.

The bus lurched to the left, shaking Eleanor so hard that she felt her teeth rattle. At this hour, the Brood were the only passengers, but no one wanted to talk; their situation was just too humiliating. While Animate vampires prowled on wing or paw, they had to use public transportation—and only if Eleanor collected enough spare change while posing as a sofa.

"The next stop," Edgar announced. "French said our House is just to the right of it." He pressed the yellow strip near the window's edge and the bus rumbled to the curb. The doors wheezed open and the Brood tumbled out, their eyes eagerly ranging over the nearby homes.

Eleanor immediately placed the Sipping House.

Despite a bowed roof and knee-high grass, the House was amazingly intact. Sparkling glass filled every window and the walls were painted an immaculate white. The House either repelled vandals or continually repaired itself.

Yolanda marched onto the front porch and inserted the key into the door. She pulled and twisted, but could not open it. "He won't let me in!" she shouted. She pounded on the door. "Come on! We've come to claim you, so talk to us right now!"

Abruptly she stopped, frowned, and pressed her face against the door's smooth wood. "He's saying something." She gestured to Martha to join her. "You can hear better than any of us. What's going on?"

Martha laid her soft cheek against the door and listened intently. At last, she said, "After all these years without feeding, the House is pretty much stuck in this present form. He needs blood—a good splash of it."

"We can get him blood," Edgar said. "French knows people at the blood bank…"

Martha shook her head. "No, he wants to be certain of our sincerity. He wants to feel that we really, really value him for who he is, not just because he's considered a prime Brood commodity. We have to bring him a victim and bleed him or her right there in the living room. Otherwise, we can forget about the House serving us."

"I think we've got a problem," Eleanor said.

They sat in the House's backyard and considered the necessity of violent deeds and vile plots; even the approaching night added to the sense of dark doings. Strange shadows stretched like crooked fingers from the base of the little plum tree in the far corner. Rats squealed in the high grass; unseen creatures passed through the alley at the yard's eastern side and blinked their red eyes at the Brood.

The Brood's stumbling block: no Inanimate had the heart to risk the life of a warm, breathing human being. Inanimates, even the greatest Houses, sipped their meals over long periods of time. Only enormous Animate greed could steal the required blood that this House demanded. And so each Brood member's plans for waylaying drunks or dopers or smug businessmen trailed into silence.

"At last!" a voice chirped from the wooden canopy above the back door. "Just the ones I wanted!"

A small black cat soared through the air and settled before them. In an instant, it became a black-clad young woman whose long dark hair swished against the ankles of her bare feet. She regarded them with brown, almond-shaped eyes.

The Brood drew back. All Inanimates distrusted their aggressive cousins. They remembered the adoration their makers showered upon them, only to be replaced by revulsion and abandonment.

"What do you want?" Yolanda snarled.

"French told me where you were," the Animate said. "My name is Kim. We can help one another."

"Ins help Ans?" Edgar snapped. "Won't happen."

Kim smiled sweetly at him. "Pretty brave talk from an armoire." She laughed—a low, seductive sound. "I've been listening to you. You need blood so you can wake that dump, but you're too squeamish to do anything constructive." She bared her small, perfect fangs. "I can provide a victim, but then you've got to do something for me."

"Why would you need the likes of us?" Eleanor wondered.

"I'm in love," Kim said, and sighed.

Edgar made a vile sucking noise with his tongue and front teeth. "So go to it."

Kim stomped her feet and growled. "I should have known frigid lumps like you can't understand the emotion, the *passion* involved in the courtship process. I want to *please* him—he's got to love me back." She smiled nastily. "But what do *you* know? *Your* kind can't make vampires."

"How true," Martha sighed from her place on the stoop. "So how can *we* help *you* in matters of the heart?"

Kim smiled at her. "My beloved is a brilliant associate professor of English literature at the University where I take classes. Despite his genius with words, his life's obsession involves the investigation of our shadow world. He wants a haunted house—a place where doors open and close on their own, where tables dance and dishes fly through the air. And he wants all this on film."

"So we do the special effects," Edgar sneered. "Then what? You take him and allow a little on the side for our House?"

"Never!" Kim exclaimed. "I shall take him in a far more intimate setting." She made a dismissive gesture with her right hand. "You may have his wretched little cameraman."

"But *how*?" Yolanda insisted. "We're not made like you. We can't…kill."

"That's not necessary, is it?" Kim asked. "Does your House need that much blood?"

They all looked at Martha.

"Oh, I think not," she said. "Perhaps a cup full."

"There you are!" Kim exclaimed triumphantly. "Someone becomes a chandelier, drops onto the cameraman's head, opens a nice scalp wound, and voila! Instant House!"

Yolanda pondered Kim's proposition, then sent Martha to ask the House its thoughts. Martha laid her head against the back door, listened closely, then turned to face the Brood. "He agrees to let us in if we provide the promised victim," she said in her high, quavering voice. "But if we dare cross him, he'll crush us all into jelly."

Later that night, the Brood entered the House and went about making it looked lived in. Edgar stocked the living room with battered furniture provided by French and worn curtains provided by curbside. The effect was ugly but plausible.

The next evening Eleanor, dressed in a drab housecoat and fuzzy pink slippers, took one last look around. A single floor lamp shed dim yellow light. Toward the back stood Edgar, who had assumed the bulky dimensions of a chest of drawers; Yolanda—a slim-legged coffee table—was several feet away from him. Overhead Martha, resplendent in silver and crystal, awaited her moment.

Someone knocked on the door and Eleanor, as official "woman of the house", opened it. French, wearing his customary black denim and too-small oval sunglasses, stood on the threshold and grinned at her.

"French?" she asked. "What are you doing here? The Brood is in the middle of something…"

The Ghoul squeezed himself inside. "I know that, dearest Eleanor. Since I've never actually seen a House in action, I've come to watch the proceedings. Don't mind Kim; I'm posing as her ex-boyfriend and she is not at all happy with me."

Kim, radiant in a yellow shift and sparkling white sandals, barreled past French; her left hand clutched the tweed sleeve of a tall, thin, dark-haired man. "Hello, Eleanor," she said, "I've brought James, the man who is going to exorcise your house."

"Oh, no exorcisms today," James demurred, his eager gaze taking in the living room. "Just basic fact-finding." His glance lingered on Eleanor and he smiled. She quite liked that smile .

A short, frog-faced man, dressed in dusty jeans and smelly black t-shirt and holding a camcorder in his hands, waddled in. *Walter*, Eleanor thought, feeling queasy. *Our victim.*

"Isn't he a delicious little tidbit?" French whispered.

"Shut up, French!" Kim hissed.

As James proceeded to ask Eleanor a series of questions, Kim looked at him in adoration. Walter merely yawned and picked at a pimple on his chin.

"Have you been under a lot of stress lately?" James asked. "Stress triggers poltergeist activity in the majority of published cases."

Eleanor nodded dutifully and noticed how kind James's eyes were—soft and dark, and surrounded by laugh lines. His entire demeanor suggested a gentle and mild-mannered personality.

This man has recliner written all over him, she thought

with sudden glee.

James continued his interrogation. "The house isn't built over an old cemetery, is it?"

"I don't think so," Eleanor replied. She shuffled over to Walter and tried to nudge him to a spot beneath Martha. "Why don't you stand there? Isn't the light perfect?"

"You tryin' to tell me my job, lady?" Walter snarled. He looked her over and leered. "Hey, you ain't bad for a fat broad."

"Have you ever seen blood on the walls?" James persisted. "Strange swarms of insects? Green ooze? Demonic voices telling you to get out?"

"No, no," Eleanor said, trying to block Walter's progress toward the sofa. "Just moving furniture. Like that!" She pointed dramatically at Yolanda, giving the coffee table her cue.

Yolanda slid toward them across the bare wooden floor.

"This is fantastic!" James gasped. He grabbed Kim by her shoulders. "Kim! We'll be famous!"

"Oh, James," she sighed.

"*Oh, James*," Walter mimicked as he prepared his camcorder. "Leave the broad alone and pay attention. I never seen anything that can move like that!"

Shoving his drawers in and out in manic syncopation, Edgar skittered toward them. Walter yelped and backed away. "Hey! That thing looks dangerous. I…"

Eleanor grabbed him by the soiled collar of his t-shirt, twisted it, and turned him toward Martha.

"Gently," French cooed. "You'll ruin that marvelous blanched skin."

"Lemme go!" Walter squealed.

Eleanor immediately twisted harder. "I thought you *liked* fat broads, you little creep."

Kim screamed, "NO!"

Stunned at Kim's sudden change of heart, Eleanor said, "Huh?" but then she saw that Walter's welfare was the farthest thing from the Animate's mind.

In a blur of cherrywood and brass, Edgar slammed into James, who, with arms windmilling wildly, stumbled toward French. The Ghoul, a bland smile stretched across his face, shoved him directly beneath Martha. The chandelier swayed to the left, then the right, and then, after circling indecisively, snapped free of the ceiling. She connected solidly with James's head and blood sprayed all over the floor. James dropped like a stone.

Everybody froze. Except for Walter, who gagged and gasped for air. Eleanor released him.

A sudden humming and pattering filled the air, sounding like millions of angry bees throwing themselves against a hundred panes of glass. The humming quickly descended into deep, thunderous rumbling which accompanied the suddenly vibrating walls.

Eleanor watched the room grow smaller. The walls were closing in! "Earthquake!" she yelled, pushing Walter toward the door. "Let's get out of here!"

Eleanor lifted James and settled him across her shoulders as if he weighed no more than a feather boa. The rest of the Brood transformed and followed her out of the House.

"Hey, who are all of those guys?" Walter asked as he watched Yolanda, Martha, and Edgar run down the porch stairs. He glanced at Eleanor and James. "Gee, lady, you're really strong!"

"Shut up, Walter," Kim snapped as she grabbed James from Eleanor and slung him into the back seat of his coupe. "Get in. We've got to drive James to the hospital." As Walter complied, Kim turned toward the Inanimates. Her face became suffused with feline anger and she hissed.

"I'll remember this! I'll never forget what you did to my beloved!" She snarled at the Ghoul. "And don't think I'm finished with you, you big tub of cremains!"

"And my little dog, too," French drawled. He waved as Kim hopped into the car and sped away.

Edgar snickered. "We'll see how long that beloved stuff lasts," he said. "I bet we'll be inviting old James into our Brood within the month."

"Look at the House!" Martha shrieked. Everybody turned around and looked.

All the used furniture and curtains that Edgar had collected for the twilight drama came shooting out the front door, down the porch steps and onto the lawn. Then, like some great gray gelatin, the House shimmied and shook. It groaned and moaned and complained in a giant's voice composed of snapping boards and cracking nails. Finally, it melted down, first into an ashy heap and then into the figure of a short, stocky, fiftyish man dressed in a gray suit. He sat in the middle of a patch of bare earth and dragged his left hand across his eyes.

"You care," he sobbed. "You really care. You gave me the nice man instead of that vile little toad." He sniffled a couple of times, stood up, and bowed to Yolanda. "My name is Stanley. Thanks for bringing me around."

Yolanda cocked her head. "So, you really do know who we are? What about the year? Do you have a lot of catchin' up to do?"

Stan grinned. "I may have been stuck in that form for a couple of decades, but I could hear the television. I know what's what." He stretched. "Hey, mind if I walk around for a while? I could use the exercise."

Edgar, Eleanor and French watched their new House chat with Yolanda and Martha. "Was it wise to antagonize Kim?" Eleanor asked Edgar. "Why did you go after James?"

Edgar shrugged. "If I were Stan, I wouldn't have touched Walter's blood, no matter how thirsty I felt."

"Picky, picky." French said, smiling benignly. "He'd have made a perfectly lovely casserole."

Exactly one month later, the doorbell of their new House rang. Eleanor, who was alone, rushed to answer it. *I hope that's someone answering our ad*, she thought. *Some rent would be nice, not to mention fresh blood.*

James stood shivering on the threshold; he barely managed a wan smile. "Kim doesn't want me," he said. "I…I didn't meet her expectations. She has something against recliners."

Eleanor drew him into her large, soft, loving embrace. "You're always welcome here," she whispered into his ear. "We are your home."

We're told that this one started with a fact (that only one in 40,000 women can look like a fashion model), a puzzlement (what about the other 39,999 of us?) and questions. Why is it we don't value our individuality? Should we declare ourselves worthless because we don't meet someone else's pre-specified criteria? K.D. Wentworth says she wanted a main character "who was already strong, but didn't yet realize her strengths, someone who had choices but hadn't learned to see them." She continues, "I have known many like 'Mari' over the years; they are a dime a dozen, it seems. But if I were in trouble, I would want a 'Lia' by my side."

A Taste of Song
by K. D. Wentworth

That summer, even halfway up the mountain, the mornings were always hot. The mingled scents of a thousand different spice plants hung low and heavy inside the compound's walls, and the sultry air hummed with the bees kept by the Order of Spices to pollinate its fabled gardens.

Other guard trainees, their faces flushed, complained about the heat, but in truth Lia preferred sparring out in the sweltering sun. She would plant her sturdy legs like trees and relish the solid feel of a quarterstaff in her callused palms, the breeze-borne scent of sage, vanilla and saffron in her nostrils. Each time she knocked an opponent into the dust, she felt important and useful, as she never did otherwise.

One torrid, sun-drenched afternoon, as the familiar crack of staff against staff filled the air, she was summoned from drill by a sloe-eyed handmaiden. Lia bowed to Master Locolo, who merely glared at the interruption.

"If you dawdle," the handmaiden said, "Mother Warden will be angry." The slender girl's skin was as ivory as rosemary blooms, her cheeks smooth. Lia had a knot in her throat; it hurt just to look at her.

Wiping the dust from her face with a sleeve, she followed the handmaiden through the vast gardens. Terraced beds and orchards covered the vast grounds, and it was said every spice known to man was cultivated within these stout stone walls. The girl did not look back as they walked. She was far too beautiful to acknowledge a great clumsy creature like Lia.

She tucked sweat-soaked hair behind her ear, acutely aware of how her wet cotton tunic clung to her big body. Her pulse was racing as it never did in combat. Had she unknowingly committed some error that would cause the Mother Warden to dismiss her from the only home she'd ever known?

The handmaiden led her into the Warden's fabled limestone tower, then up a spiral staircase and through a pair of oak doors carved to portray the Six Essential Magical Spices. Inside, the audience room was dim and cool as a cavern, as richly appointed as she'd always heard. The floor was made of rare imported woods and inlaid with onyx. The chairs were upholstered in sable. Shelves of gleaming jars stretched to the ceiling. The scent of nutmeg, ginger and vanilla filled the air, along with the bite of black pepper and the subtle menthol of clove. Lia also detected other, less familiar aromas that might herald the rare magical spices.

The Mother Warden looked up from a low mahogany table that reflected the light of a single lamp. The woman herself was diminutive, old and nearly toothless, her skin wrinkled and sallow as last year's apples. Clad in black linen, she waved a careless hand. "Sit, child, sit."

"Yes, Mother Warden." Lia settled awkwardly onto a stool far too short for her long, muscle-bound legs.

The woman's tiny eyes, black as a crow's, studied her. "Master Locolo names you the best of the current lot of guard trainees, a reliable girl who is not afraid to ask questions." She leaned over the highly polished wood. "Through unforgivable stupidity, a packet of rare spices intended for a far-off patron has been stolen. You will retrieve it for me."

"Of course, Mother Warden!" Lia dropped to one knee on the floor, fist over her heart. Was she to be allowed to serve the Order at long last? She had waited for such an opportunity her whole life. "I am yours to command!"

"Of course you are." The old woman waved imperiously. "Bought and paid for since the day of your birth like all the rest, but that alone is no guarantee of loyalty."

Lia blinked as though the warden had struck her. She knew a great, ugly girl like herself was fortunate to have a place here. Had she been raised in a village, no man would have taken her as wife. Those with charge over her had made it plain, from earliest memory, that she would never be clever enough to keep the Order's accounts, never comely enough to serve as a handmaiden, nor possess the wit of a courier or gardener. The strength of her body was all she had to offer. She lowered her head. "I live to serve."

"And serve you shall." The old woman's eyes flashed. She turned to the shadows. "Well?"

A hooded figure emerged. A lock of golden hair strayed across one cheek and caught the lamp light. "Surely you cannot mean to send her. She is an ox, sure to be clumsy, as well as lacking in wit. We would not get ten paces down the road before she babbled our mission to the first passerby."

The warden's laugh rang out in the spacious room. "She would betray us, Mari, as if you had not already?"

"There were ten of them!" The girl threw back her hood. Not more than two and twenty, she was perfectly proportioned and lovely, as were all those who represented the Order to the outside world. A livid bruise marred one otherwise flawless cheek, and her right eye was swollen nearly shut.

The warden snorted. "One, perhaps two, at the very most, and I suspect your foolishness invited all that happened." She shook her head. "Would that I had sent any other courier, rather than this vain, empty-headed wretch, but that bread has already been burnt. Now we must rectify matters."

"After they attacked me," Mari said, "the thieves fled into the thickest part of the forest. It's no use now. We'll never find them."

"There is one way, old and secret, to track them." The warden picked up a bit of bark from the table and rubbed it to powder between her fingers.

Mari paled and retreated a step. "That's songwort!"

A sharp scent filtered through the room. She gestured to Lia. "Come here, girl." Lia walked around the table to loom over the Warden. "Open your mouth." The old woman reached up to sprinkle the powder onto Lia's tongue. The taste was strange, hot as red pepper, sweet as honey, with an underlying tang like lemon.

"And now you, wretch." The warden motioned to Mari.

Mari backed farther away, her face stricken. "Surely one so afflicted will be enough."

"Don't be impertinent." The old woman gestured impatiently. "Two heads are always better than one. Come here at once!"

The girl whirled and ran toward the doors.

The warden turned to Lia. "Stop her!"

Lia caught up in two strides, then wrenched the girl's arm behind her back just enough to compel obedience without damaging bone or sinew. The warden nodded her approval. "I see Master Locolo did not exaggerate your skills." She picked up another fragment of bark. "Now, hold her!" Pinching Mari's nose, she administered the powder when the girl finally gasped for breath.

Mari shrieked and fell to her knees, tried to spit the powder out. "You…had no…no right!"

The warden's black eyes narrowed. "I had every right. You damaged the Order by your foolishness, so you must make restitution. If you knew your duty half so well as this one, you would understand that."

Mari wiped her mouth with the back of one trembling hand. "I'll go mad." She tossed her disheveled golden braid back out of her face. "They always do!"

Lia's mouth burned. She wondered uneasily what she had swallowed. Her throat seemed swollen now and her ears rang, as though every bell in the town outside the walls tolled at once.

"A few survive," the warden said, packing the remaining bits into a velvet-lined casket. "There is an antidote." She could have been remarking upon the weather. "If you recover the spices, the Order might authorize a dose for a deserving soul."

Mari pulled herself up, using the stool for support, then tottered toward the carved doors. The warden thrust a pack toward Lia. "Assist that wretch in recovering that which she so carelessly lost." She turned away. "Don't you dare return until you have the shipment in hand."

Lia retrieved her staff, shouldered the pack, and followed.

The spice gardens, along with the tower and accompanying outbuildings, lay just above the mountainside town of Norr. Mari stalked out through the orchards, then the wall, into the town proper, paying no attention to Lia as she trailed after.

The streets were dusty and crowded; it was market day. Mari wove through the bright stalls of cloth and vegetables without comment, but Lia could not have heard her if she had spoken. Everyone seemed to be shouting, and when they left the town behind, the voices grew oddly louder, though Lia saw nothing but scattered trees. Where were all these unbelievably noisy people?

"I hear voices," Lia said, when Mari glanced back over her shoulder, "but no one is there."

"Fool!" Mari stalked down the road. "No wonder your mother sold you off. You still have no idea what has been done to you!"

"What?" Lia called after her, but Mari would not answer.

A short time later, she tried again. "Who are these men we're following?" She had to shout to make herself heard above the voices which seemed to come from everywhere.

She rubbed an ear in irritation. What was wrong with all these people, skulking about just out of sight?

Mari turned off the road and stopped, head drooping. "This is where they robbed me." She ran a finger down a fresh bloodstain on the bark of a slender ash tree. "Now we'll have to ask which way they went."

"Who are you going to ask?" Lia craned her head, scanning the landscape. "These idiots who don't even have the courtesy to come out and introduce themselves?"

"The trees," Mari said, and Lia had to strain to catch her words. "And the underbrush and, if we're very desperate and not too particular, we'll even ask the sodding weeds!"

The clamor grew ever worse. Lia fought to make her voice carry. "What are you talking about?"

"The songwort," the girl replied. A bead of sweat trickled down her temple and she dabbed at it with the back of one hand. "Mother Warden is nothing if not efficient."

Lia covered her ears, trying to shut out the ever-present roar of voices. "I don't understand."

"Idiot!" Mari put her fists on her hips. "If she had to do this to me, why couldn't she at least send another courier, not an uneducated ox who doesn't know songwort from cumin?" She faced the ash tree. "All right, you witless, overgrown shrub, stop babbling and tell me which direction they went!"

The din grew louder, as though everyone in the whole world was trying to speak at once. Lia could not make out one word in twenty. She felt as though she was drowning, as though, if the relentless flow did not stop, she would lose her mind. "Silence!" she shouted at the top of her own voice. It did no good.

Mari's laugh had a bitter, hollow edge. "If it was that easy, don't you think everyone would take songwort and talk to plants?"

Plants? Lia blanched. Could plants really be making all this noise? And if they were, how would she ever find peace again? The world was full of plants. A terrible panic rose up in her throat. It wasn't fair! The Mother Warden should have warned her. Doing this to her with no preparation was worse than foolhardy; it was stupid and cruel.

"Only the ash!" Mari ordered. "The rest of you be silent!"

The clamor redoubled and the courier wilted to her knees, hands pressed to her ears. Lia reeled back against a monumental old oak. The noise was like a storm breaking over her head, like a wall of water drowning her, cutting off light and air.

She drew her knife and slashed the ash tree. Amber sap welled in the cut. "Make them stop or, so help me, by all that is holy, I will hack down every tree in this forsaken grove!"

A thin-edged wail rose above the rest. *Pain!* it cried. *Violation! Invitation to rot and disease!*

Despite her anger, Lia felt ashamed, even as she gripped the knife in a sweaty hand. "Tell us what we want to know!"

The two-leggeds took the direction of the breeze, trampling grasses, breaking limbs, heeding none who lay in their path.

Mari held up a finger. "Windward…west." She struggled back onto her feet, her face pinched.

Shaken, Lia sheathed her knife. The voices resurged, a thousand voices demanding to be heard. Mari wove through the trees, examining the ground for tracks, and Lia followed as best she could while avoiding flower and bush, grass and leaf, and taking great care not to break even a single twig. The ceaseless voices thrummed in her bones.

Mari trembled as though possessed by fever. Each time they lost the trail, they queried another tree, sometimes old giants whose roots fed from the heart of the world, sometimes callow young saplings. Those reluctant to answer, Lia threatened with her knife, going so far as to prick several, but never again wounding another in the grievous fashion of the first. That agonized cry would ring forever inside her head.

From time to time as they walked, it seemed as though she detected an underlying rhythm in the ceaseless voices, a pattern that almost made sense. She grasped at it even as it slipped away but never could quite make it come into focus.

By midafternoon, they came upon a marsh where the sunlight glimmered down on still green water. The sultry air smelled of sun-heated mud and decaying plants. Herons stalked through the shallows like self-important old men, and, over at one side, two figures lazed back on the grass, speaking in low voices Lia could not make out over the hiss of marsh grass and murmur of cattail.

She jerked her head at Mari. "Are they the ones?"

The courier nodded, her skin so pale, her lips seemed stained red in contrast.

"Well, come on then!" Lia skirted willow and deadfall to approach from their blind side.

Wait, said a clump of sedge. *These two-leggeds have swords. See how they gouged us, for no reason save sport!*

She touched the gash and shuddered.

Quiet, quiet, whispered the rushes. *They are waiting for you. They said the Order employs only women. They mean to use you for their pleasure, then spill your blood to feed the gnats.*

Lia drew her knife with one hand, held her staff ready with the other.

A muscle twitched beneath Mari's bruised eye. "Hurry up!" she hissed. "Cut their thieving hearts out and be done with it!"

The two men bolted up. "Well," said the first, who was short and squat as a boulder, "I thought the Order of Spices was known for its beauties." He scowled at Lia. "*You're* sure no treat for the eyes."

The entire forest clamored for her attention—giving advice, predicting ruin, shouting warnings. Lia threw her shoulders back, stood straight and tall so that she towered over the first man, and looked the other, who was also shorter, full in the eye. "Return what you stole and the Mother Warden will take no further action."

"No!" Mari lurched to her side. "Kill them!"

The first man snickered, said something Lia could not make out above the screech of the underbrush. She edged closer, concentrating, trying to think past the distracting noise and weighing the odds. There were only two of them and she was well trained, if only the plants would shut up and let her plan.

Mari snatched up a rock and darted past Lia. She was light on her feet, far faster than Lia would have credited her.

"No, wait!" Lia cried and ran after the foolish girl. A warrior would have known better than to expose herself so, but Mari had no such training. The girl heaved the rock, but it fell far short and rolled harmlessly in the grass.

Before Lia could catch up, the second man, lean and feral-eyed as a wolf at the end of winter, met Mari's charge. He seized a handful of golden hair and threw her to the ground where he planted a foot on her slender neck. Her arms jerked as Lia halted just out of reach.

"Little girls should not play at a man's game." He told Mari, then drew his sword and grinned crookedly up at Lia. "And you should stick to those womanly duties for which women were created. But then, with a body like yours, I suppose you'll never have a man." He leveled the blade at her chest. "She's yours, Beno," he said over his shoulder. He jerked Mari's braid, saying, "I'll take this one."

Run, run! shouted the cattails.

"Oh no, you don't!" The shorter one bristled. "Next you'll say all the songwort is yours, too!"

Songwort! The same spice that had flayed open her mind to the entire plant kingdom? That was what they had stolen?

Your companion is dying! cried the sedge grasses. *Help her!*

No, save yourself! the willow insisted mournfully. *These rootless creatures have no understanding of the evil they do.*

Lia spun her staff and caught the shorter thief full across the neck. He fell heavily. The forest shrilled its approval as she turned to the second man, circling in an attempt to draw him away from Mari. "Let her go!"

In answer, he only grinned and trod on the girl's neck so that Mari's eyes bulged and her arms flailed. "Come and get her, dogface!"

Sweat soaked Lia's back. The plants gibbered and shouted and screamed, inundating her in a veritable river of sound. Why had the warden done this to her? She could have taken out these two amateur thugs in a heartbeat, had she not been handicapped by having the whole of the marsh shouting inside her head.

Mari's hands scrabbled uselessly at the thief's boot. Her eyelids fluttered, then she went boneless. Time had run out. Lia had to find another way. "All right," she said suddenly, throwing both knife and staff aside and lowering her gaze as though intimidated. "All I ask is that you give me a taste of songwort before you go," she continued, gambling to divert his mind from mayhem to greed and self-interest.

The thief stooped to collect her weapons, never taking his eyes off her. "Waste a priceless spice on a pig like you?"

"Please!" The catch in her voice was real, though she was pleading for something far different than he realized. "I am big and ugly and stupid, but if I could have just a taste, Mother Warden said it makes a body smarter so you understand things beyond mortal ken. That way, perhaps I could find a husband someday." She ducked her head meekly and dropped to her knees.

"You don't deserve to be smarter!" He backhanded her to the grass, where she blinked up at the sun, tasting the salt of her own blood. She saw the boot coming, heard the plants cry out in warning, rolled—but too late. Blackness enveloped her, a cold biting presence that admitted neither sun nor air nor sound.

"Wake up!" A hand tugged at Lia's arm, jolting her head, which ached fearsomely. "Wake up, damn you!"

Lia groaned.

"It's all your fault!" A slap rocked her face. "You were supposed to stop them! What point is there in sending an ox like you if you just let them go?" Mari's voice shook. "Now we'll never get the antidote!"

Lia forced her eyes open. "I…did stop them. I think." She sat up, wincing at the throb in her right temple. Overhead, the willow crooned a sympathetic song as its fronds danced in the breeze. The other plants joined in, one voice weaving a descant through the others. She listened, surprised. It wasn't a painful cacophony anymore. It was almost…pleasant.

"Stopped them with your head, it looks like." Mari glared, her own face even more swollen, new bruises overlying the old.

Hours had passed, by the slant of the sun. The two thieves had gotten a long start. She heaved onto her feet with a sigh. "Come on," she said, though the marshy glade spun around her. "I don't think they will be far."

Mari sniffed. "Too busy laughing themselves sick, no doubt."

"I don't think they are laughing." Lia pulled herself along, tree by tree, fighting her dizziness by concentrating on the plant voices, listening instead of shutting them out. They all seemed to be singing now, or at least murmuring in harmony, cattail with marsh grass, pine with ash.

Mari trailed after her, complaining bitterly, but her words were lost in the swell of song. The thieves' trail was now easy to follow. They were obviously no longer concerned about being tracked. The few times she did lose the way, she queried the nearest oak, pine or ivy for help. Each answered at once.

Finally, Mari fell silent and put all her energy into keeping up. Forest faded into meadow, the land rising into low blue hills in the distance. Dark was near and Lia was so tired, it took all her strength to put one foot in front of the other. Then a bed of wild strawberries told her to look to the setting sun. In the shadows, she saw two forms huddled on a grassy stream bank, shivering as though in the grip of fever.

"It's them!" Mari seized a rock, but Lia caught her wrist.

"There's no need," she said, and the grasses hummed agreement. "Listen."

Mari cocked her head. Carried on the breeze was the unmistakable sound of weeping. "What's wrong with them?"

"It does not matter." Lia searched the surrounding ground for the precious packets of spice, marked with the Order's sigil, finally finding them safe beside the ashes of a small fire. Only one seal had been broken. The others were still intact.

"Find our pack," she told Mari, then closed her eyes, listening. The song of the meadow was different than that of the forest and marsh, more sweeping, lower-pitched. She hummed along, riding its currents, letting herself drift in its sweet melodies.

"Here it is!" Mari's voice jerked her back.

Over by the stream, the taller of the two thieves twisted around to look at her. "Make it stop!"

The steady beat of the moss growing along the stream bank kept time with the interwoven harmony of the grasses. Lia felt lighter just listening to it, as though she could let go of the ground and fly. "Don't fight it," she told the thieves before turning away.

Mari handed the pack to Lia. "Here, ox. Carry this."

Lia replaced each of the spice packets, taking special care with the breached one, then shouldered the pack. The music of the plants and trees flowed over, through, around her, as though she were made for this place, this time, this moment. As though she had come home. She felt as pliant as a new root, soft as the petals of a rose, crafty and strong as a vine wending its way inch by inch up the trunk of an ancient oak. "*Root, leaf and stem*," she sang under her breath in time with clover and thistle. "*Sun, rain and soil.*"

"What?" Mari demanded, but in answer Lia only shook

her head, then led the courier back through the forest until it was too dark to travel further.

They bedded down in a grassy hollow, where Mari tossed and turned the whole night, crying out in her sleep, begging the plants to be silent. Finally Lia took herself off far enough to be alone with the glorious symphony, then slept, bathed in song.

When they reached the Order's grounds late the next afternoon, Lia studied the surrounding spice gardens with a new appreciation. Before, they had been pleasant to look upon, enticing to smell, but symbolic mostly of profit. Now, she felt the life bursting within, the unending music. So much wonder was contained within these high stone walls, she did not know how the gardeners ever tore themselves away long enough to sleep.

She and Mari ascended the winding staircase of the main tower, the song of the gardens growing more faint with every step. At the top, Mari rushed through the carved doors to fling herself at the warden's feet, sobbing. She had not spoken a word for the last eight hours, save a frenzied, meaningless mumbling under her breath. Her slender body shook uncontrollably.

Dust motes danced in the shafts of fading sunlight. The warden stared down at the broken woman distastefully, then met Lia's gaze. "Did you recover the shipment?"

Lia swung the pack off her broad shoulders and placed it on the mahogany table before the old woman. "Yes."

The warden examined the contents and pulled out the breached packet. Her eyes flashed. "This one will have to be weighed and the value of the missing contents deducted from your pay."

It was still in the high-ceilinged room, with only the solitary voice of a poor potted vine to keep her company, a sad creature, hardly able to bear up in such dimness and isolation. Lia felt suddenly bereft.

Mari looked up from the floor, eyes crazed. She plucked at the warden's hem. "What about the antidote?"

"And the price of that as well!" the old woman snapped. She clapped her hands. "Bring the ivory casket from beneath my bed," she directed a handmaiden who appeared out of the shadows.

The girl bowed and hurried away, so beautiful to look upon, Lia felt wistful. Just a day ago, she would have given anything to possess that sleek dark hair, that elegance of form, but now, all she wanted was to return to the clean outside air and the elegant song being woven around unhearing humans every second of the day and night.

"As for you," the warden turned to Lia. "You could have been swifter, but you did well enough for a first assignment. I will instruct Master Locolo to assign you to my personal guard."

"I would rather have a different place now," Lia heard herself say, though only a day before, such an opportunity had been all she'd ever wanted.

"It doesn't matter what you want!" The warden leaned over the table, palms flat. "You belong to us. We'll place you as we wish! Perhaps scullery maid would be more to your liking?"

Lia searched for the right words. "I need...to be outside, to work among the plants."

"Don't be ridiculous. It takes years of training to tend the gardens, not to mention a certain innate talent."

Lia flushed. The look in the Mother Warden's eyes said it all. "And, great ham-fisted creature that I am, I would be too clumsy, too slow of mind?"

The handmaiden returned, bearing a small ivory casket. She bowed and left it on the table.

"Each of us serves according to her gifts and abilities," the warden said. She opened the casket and measured out a tiny spoonful of white powder, then mixed it in a cup of water.

Mari leaped to her feet, trembling hands outstretched, but the warden turned to Lia. "You first."

If she drank, the ongoing song would be silenced. She would lose the only beautiful thing she had ever possessed. Lia backed away. "No."

"You forget yourself, girl!" The warden was thin-lipped.

Mari plucked at her sleeve. "Mother Warden, please!"

"I have learned to hear," Lia said, "truly hear. I want to use this gift to serve the Order out in the gardens."

"You are confused," the warden said stiffly, "but once the antidote has a chance to work, you will think more clearly."

"I won't take it," Lia said.

Mari curled into a sobbing ball on the floor. "Make them stop!" she mumbled over and over. The warden handed the tumbler of antidote to her. She drank it down, then buried her face in her arms and wept with relief.

"There is," said the warden, "only a short time during which this compound is effective. More than three days after ingestion," she folded her hands, "will be too late."

Lia turned back to the doorway, straining to hear the gardens. It was so dreadfully quiet inside this stifling tower.

"Think." The warden gazed down at Mari's trembling form. "In the end, it will drive you beyond the bounds of sanity. If you refuse the antidote, you must tread this path all your life, never again to know the silence of your own mind."

Lia raised her chin. "Will you have me in the gardens then?"

The Mother Warden's dark eyes regarded her without warmth. "Our spices are priceless. Most of the magical varieties are no longer cultivated anywhere else. We cannot allow someone with impaired judgment access to our secrets."

Lia noted a hint of fear around the warden's eyes.

"You will not prosper." The old woman's expression was fierce. "They never do."

Lia's pulse quickened. "Then there have been others, like me, who wished to go on hearing?"

"Dead, every last one of them, or will be soon." The warden scowled. "Crazy as loons!"

"I don't believe you." Lia understood finally that what she had gained was more powerful than mere strength of body. She left the Mother Warden standing there, mouth agape, and walked back down the winding staircase and out into a golden twilight bursting with song.

The warden called after her, then summoned the guards, commanding them to stop her. Lia ducked down the long, orderly spice beds, avoiding pursuit through advice from cinnamon trees nodding in the breeze. There was no need to hurry. The beds of cardamom knew just when she should pause to let the guards pass by. The sage plants told her when it was safe to go on.

When the time was right, she would find her way out of the gardens, then down the mountainside, and from there—it was hard to say. The world was immense, full of intoxicating life, and she had just been made a most unexpected and welcome gift of it. And whatever happened, wherever she went, she would never be alone again.

You just can't keep a good fat man in the background, anymore than you can keep a writer like Jody Lynn Nye from creating a really unique hero. The character of Ben Barber first appeared in "What? And Give Up Show Business?", published in the anthology *Otherwere* from Ace Books in 1996.

Casting Against Type
by Jody Lynn Nye

"Quiet on the set!"

At the assistant director's cry, Ben Barber froze in place in the half-shadow behind the scenery flat. "Action! Roll film!" He stayed still, listening to the low murmur of voices and the hum of the hot spotlights, whose light he could see peeking through the cracks in the set.

At the cry of "Cut!", Ben began to move again, striding swiftly toward the center of the warehouse where the most lights were before the next take began. He was so happy to be there, he didn't want to miss a moment. If he was moving in the right direction, he should come up behind the director and the camera, with a full view of the action. He swung around the edge of the flat into a narrow, low-ceilinged passage that he just filled.

"Oh!"

A small figure, hurtling toward him, stopped short before bumping into his belly.

"I'm sorry," the young woman said, clutching a pile of notebooks and a cellular phone to her. She was very thin, with short, dark, reddish hair and dark-rimmed glasses that framed large, clear hazel eyes. She looked him up and down as if amazed. Ben had no illusions about what she must have been thinking. What did the PC types call him these days? "Gravitationally challenged"? A "person of size"? True, he tipped the scales at 400 pounds, but he was six feet three inches tall, and his weight was fairly well distributed on his frame. He preferred "big" or "fat". Shorter terms, in less need of insincere apology, and to hell with the professors. They didn't live in the real world anyway. In fact, he didn't think he was at all bad-looking, with his strong jaw, wide blue eyes, black hair and long lashes. He smiled down at the young woman, who regarded him warily.

"Can I help you?" she asked.

"Ben Barber," he said, putting out a hand. After a moment, she offered hers, which disappeared within his fingers. He shook it very gently. "I'm here to scope out the dressing room. For the elephant."

Her whole body relaxed. "Oh!" she said. "Yes, of course. Come with me. I'm Roxanne Walters, the continuity director." She turned a hand to direct him back the way he had come, and followed until there was room for them to walk side by side. "We're very excited to have him. We've heard so much about his talent. We're grateful the Ringman Circus is willing to lend him to us. He's…he's called Ben, too, isn't he?"

"Certainly is," Ben said. "He was named for me."

"That explains it," Roxanne said, leading him to one side of the warehouse that was being used for set construction.

In fact, Ben's excuse didn't really explain the elephant. Even if the woman worked in the make-believe business, she'd have a hard time understanding the truth. The elephant wasn't only named for Ben, he *was* Ben. At night during the full moon, he went through a metamorphosis that transformed him into the world's only were-elephant. It had seemed like a liability when it had first happened, but he had managed to find a significant silver lining inside the large gray cloud. Where he couldn't get film parts as a human, the door was wide open for a smart elephant. Ben didn't care, so long as he got screen credit somehow. "County Fair" was to be his second movie. He wasn't nervous at all, just excited.

"This part could only work out with something like Ben," Roxanne was saying. "The director wants him to be a real character in the movie. He's supposed to be playful and funny. If…er…Ben wasn't capable of following instructions so well, it just wouldn't work."

"I've seen the script," Ben said, waving a hand airily. "He can do all of that stuff. Just tell him what you want."

Roxanne stopped before a huge sliding door. "Here it is." She pushed at the door. It didn't budge. Ben just leaned against it a little bit, and it opened. Just needed a little weight behind it.

"Perfect," he said, surveying the large, clean room. There was only one other entrance, the door that led from the loading dock, and no windows at eye level, so he couldn't be spied on by anyone while he went through his transformation. He didn't want to be thought of as a freak. An odd statement, perhaps, from a guy who worked as a sideshow fat man, but circus folks were allowed their dignity by their management. That was why show people stuck so closely to one another's company; outsiders didn't understand.

"I've never heard of a nocturnal elephant before," Roxanne said, while Ben checked the latch on the inner door. He could raise that with his trunk, he was sure. If not, his buddy Ricky would be on hand to help.

"I know," Ben said. "It's got something to do with why he's so smart."

For the next few hours, he hung around the periphery of the set, quiet as any mouse who weighed 400 in his stocking feet, watching and trying to stay out of everyone's way. Roxanne introduced him to people whenever she went by. She pointed out the producer, and the director Terzo Padrone, whom Ben recognized from film industry magazines. Otherwise, Roxanne was pleasant to him but distant, not really seeing him. He was a tree or a piece of furniture, not a human being. She didn't have experience in interacting with someone of his physical stature. Ben wasn't surprised. Everyone else she knew was like her. All these film people were so little! Short and thin like pipecleaners. The only gal with some size he'd ever seen was that foxy woman on the TV lawyer show. Why, if she could break the mold, couldn't he? He had all he needed to make it in the movies. He was good-looking. He had talent. He had a thick skin, God knew. All that was left was to get that break. It hadn't happened yet, but Ben cherished the hope that it would. In the meantime, acting incognito was good enough.

Close to moonrise, Ricky backed the circus van up to the loading doors and, with great ceremony, pretended to be herding an invisible elephant inside. He was rigged out in his full uniform: a scarlet tunic with gold frogging, high billed cap, black pants and shiny boots. Ben grinned. All circus people were actors. Ricky was just taking the opportunity to show off.

The film people gathered, curious about the noises. This was Ben's cue. "I'd better get in there and help him," he said before slipping through the big door and closed it behind him.

"Hey, man," Ricky greeted him. "How's it going?"

"Great," Ben replied. "It's the best. You should see everything in there. They've got a whole fair dummied up: midway, rides, even a race track." Ricky latched the door and kept a lookout while Ben stripped out of his clothes and wrapped himself in a towel. "Wish I could be me out there," he said wistfully. "Why am I doing this?"

"Ten grand a day," answered Ricky. "For five days, I mean, nights."

Ben smiled. Even Stallone didn't get ten grand a day. Ringman's had negotiated that much because they wanted the same fee as the tame Hollywood kodiak grizzly commanded. If a lousy bear with only animal intelligence could command ten large, why not the world's only were-elephant? Ben glanced up at the window. The full moon was rising.

"Remember," he told Ricky as his mouth began to alter.

"Yeah, I know," the animal trainer replied with a grin. "No poking around you-know-where. I'll keep 'em away from your butt." Ricky gathered up Ben's clothes and stuffed them into a carry-all.

Ben watched impassively as his friend seemed to grow smaller and shorter, but it was Ben who was changing. The transformation took control of his body. He felt his legs thicken. His body grew too heavy to stand upright. He let himself drop forward onto his palms. His hands and feet disappeared into plate-sized gray feet with nails the size of teacups. His eyes spread apart, widening his field of view and making room for the trunk that grew from his face to the floor. He swung it from side to side. Every time it happened, he couldn't believe it really worked just like a born elephant's. He obligingly let out a trumpet that elicited excited murmurs from outside the door.

"Okay, pal," Ricky said, throwing open the door, "your public awaits."

Raising his trunk in a majestic curve like Jumbo's, Ben strutted out onto the set, into the midst of the tiny film people who clustered around him, oohing and aahing. Ricky slapped him on the shoulder and strutted toward the director, whom Ben pointed out with his trunk.

"Evening, sir," Ricky said to the goggle-eyed Padrone. "Your star is here."

The first night on the set was enormous fun. Ben's script called for him to perform simple stunts, like reaching over the petting zoo wall and stealing a man's hat as he went by, and picking up the end of a chain in time to trip the villain of the piece as he ran down the midway. As soon as Ben proved he could do those without any trouble, the director hauled over the writer—a plump, bespectacled, thirty-ish man—and had him beef up the part. Padrone demanded more, bigger, funnier! Anything they threw at him, Ben could do. By the time they stopped filming for the night, Ben was tired but happy. If only it could have happened to him as a man, he'd be in heaven.

He showed up on the set again the next day, hoping to be allowed to stay. All right, if the truth be told, he was kind of hoping to be discovered. But since that was unlikely, all he wanted to do was watch the movie being made. He found Roxanne on the side of the set, writing intently on her clipboard. He waited until she looked up and smiled down at her. She jumped, surprised, then swiftly recovered and offered him a professional smile.

"Oh, it's you. You were the one who brought the elephant."

"That's right," Ben said. "Can I stick around and watch?"

Roxanne frowned thoughtfully. She was kind of pretty, in spite of being a skinny waif who looked about fifteen years old. "Well, we'll have to ask the director."

"Sure, he can stay!" Padrone said expansively. "I gotta tell you, your elephant is marvelous. Why can't we have him here all the time?"

"He's only cooperative during the full moon," Ben replied.

"Cooperative! He's a genius!" exclaimed the director. "My God, he does everything to the split second, the very second! I wish my actors had his timing. And I think," Padrone added with a twinkle in his dark eyes, "he has a little sense of humor."

"Oh, he does," Ben agreed heartily.

On schedule, Ricky showed up with the van, and Ben went away to 'help' him bring out the elephant, whom the enthusiastic director received like an old friend. Ben's part was padded still more, even upstaging the kid actor who played the son of the hero.

By the third day no one looked twice when he showed up to watch. Unlike the night shoots, which were structured to move along at speed in order to make use of the temporary resource of the elephant, the director could take his time during the day. He put his actors through their paces again and again, sometimes taking a scene over and over. Ben, hanging around just behind the camera tracks, got a little bored seeing the same action for the twentieth time and looked for somewhere to sit down. The pipsqueaks regarded him nervously, as though he might sit on them, until he found a lighting trunk big enough to hold him.

All of the people who worked in the movies seemed so thin and frail-looking, even the ones who said they worked out or did karate or whatever the current fad martial art was. They held their hands as though they were afraid of getting them dirty. They sashayed around as though magazine photographers were following their every move. In a way, they had a point. You never knew what could happen. Magazine photographers *did* sneak onto the set, and an actor's whole life depended on image. They didn't want to be caught doing something stupid. In their defense, Ben acted as an unpaid bouncer. With his long experience in the sideshow, he was good at memorizing faces. When he saw someone who didn't belong on the set, he just used his bulk to intimidate them over to the side of the warehouse until the assistant producer or assistant director could sort them out.

The current intruder was a woman Ben recognized from the television news magazine *Hollywood Evening.* She looked up at him while he waited for the AD to detach herself from the group of cameramen she was talking to.

"So, are you somebody?" the reporter asked.

"No," Ben admitted. To no one's surprise, even his, as soon as the woman was given permission to stay, she walked away from Ben without a word. He wasn't there to her or any of the other trade reporters. He didn't care. He was allowed to stay as long as he liked. To him, *this* was the circus.

Some of the others who worked on the film were more real. The roustabouts, or grips as they were called here (like any stagestruck guy, Ben knew all the film terminology) were more accepting. After a couple of non-PC remarks that rolled off Ben but shocked the actors and crew, he struck up a kind of friendship with them, but it came with warnings.

"Remember," the representative of the union said, gesturing at the sets, the lights and the cameras, "you don't touch anything. Not a single thing. You're not in the union. You'll get in big, big trouble."

"Okay," agreed Ben good-naturedly. "I just want to get along."

He invited them to the circus, freely handing out passes that the ringmaster/manager had supplied. He thought it was good business, even though the higher-powered film types tended to behave badly.

Most of the time, the grips and the rest of the crew ignored Ben and went about their business. He didn't mind. Being on the set was like candy. He couldn't get enough of it. He would sit with eyes wide open, watching the grips put together a section of the set. Determined to be a professional even though he had no official status, he was always well-dressed and behaved in a friendly and polite manner to everyone. Roxanne, the continuity woman, lost her fear of him and started deliberately coming over to talk with him.

"You are really nice, you know," she said, sitting with him during a free moment while the director rearranged a scene. "I mean, for someone…I'm sorry," she said. "I am being really rude, aren't I?"

"Not at all," Ben replied gallantly. Roxanne's cheeks reddened under the dark glasses frames. She studied her feet.

"You've been a considerate visitor, and all of us appreciate that. You've seen the other kinds we have to deal with."

"Hey, I'm enjoying it. I've always wanted to be in the movies."

"You know, you ought to do voice-overs," Roxanne said, tilting her head to one side with a critical expression. "Your voice is good."

"I'd rather be in front of the camera," he said.

Her expression told him just what she thought of his chances, but all she said was, "Yes, you're pretty good-looking." You had to be really tactful in the movie business, Ben thought. She was nice, but she was an insider and he wasn't.

Sooner than he expected, the last night of the full moon came and went. When he arrived on the set the next afternoon, Padrone spotted him and rushed up looking hysterical.

"Ah, the fat man! I could not reason with your animal trainer. He takes Ben away. We have to have the elephant back tonight! We are not finished with him!"

"There's nothing I can do," Ben said sincerely. "You'll have to wait until next month. A...an Asian crew's got him until then."

"We'll double his fee!" Padrone exclaimed, clutching his hair.

"Sorry," Ben said, really regretting it, but the true curse of lycanthropy was that the transformation lasted no more than five days. He'd been lucky. Sometimes it was only three, depending on the ascension of the moon. "A contract's a contract. You wouldn't want anyone horning in on yours, would you?"

"No, no...*diabolo*! We can pick up those shots later if we have to."

"Can I still come back?" Ben asked, wondering if, as the bearer of bad news, he would be punished.

"Oh sure, sure," the director said expansively, even though he looked preoccupied. "We have had...so many noisier visitors. You are good and quiet."

"Mr. Padrone!" a panicky voice shouted from the other end of the lot. The director rushed away, his assistants in his wake.

Ben knew the director had been going to say was that he'd had *smaller* people who were a problem, and even if Ben was fat, he was careful. He didn't care. He was welcome on the set.

Not only the moon had finished her cycle. It was also time for the Ringman Circus to move on. It didn't go far, to Ben's delight, just to the next big town. Ben could drive the distance in an hour and a half. The crew greeted him like an old friend.

"You're here in the morning," Roxanne said, surprised.

"Got afternoon and evening show times all week," Ben explained. It was the deal he had struck with the ringmaster.

Since he wasn't staying up all night acting, he didn't need to sleep in the mornings. Satisfied with the circus's 50% cut of Ben's take, Williams had agreed he could keep the early part of the day as his own until the film crew left the area. He glanced up as Padrone called for the lunch break. "Would you like to go for a cup of coffee?"

"I'd love to," Roxanne answered warmly. Then she glanced around. "Would you like to go into town? I'm sorry. You understand?"

Ben was sad, but he did. She wanted to be far from the set so no one would see her with him. Still, a date was a date.

When she wasn't constrained by her peers looking over her shoulder, Roxanne was good company, telling him about growing up in Southern California with her parents and five brothers. She accepted only a cup of coffee for herself. Her eyes widened when she saw the huge pile of pastries Ben had ordered.

"Want one?" he offered.

"I don't think I should," Roxanne said, then daringly added, "I don't want to be offensive, but have you thought of what you should be doing for your health?"

"You mean a diet?" Ben asked. She blushed but nodded furiously, looking relieved he'd said the word for her.

"Yes, a diet."

"This *is* my diet," Ben explained. "I'm fat for a *living*. I have lost fifty pounds. I used to eat when I was depressed. Now, things are better."

"Are they?" Roxanne asked shyly. "I'm glad. I wish I could just eat pastries whenever I wanted."

"Why not now?" Ben said, pushing the plate toward her with a twinkle in his eyes. "Try it! No one's looking." She looked around to make sure, but took the sweet roll off the top of the pile.

"Elephant ears, huh?" she asked, laughing a little guiltily.

"Hey, you are what you eat," Ben said, grinned because he knew, in his case, it was true. Roxanne smiled back, even though she didn't understand the joke.

They returned after the lunch break, Roxanne immediately detaching herself to go check on the next scene to be filmed. The director waved at Ben over the actors' heads.

"Eh, Small Ben! Still no chance of getting your namesake up there?" Padrone asked.

"I'm really sorry, Mr. Padrone. He's as far away as the moon."

"Oh, poetry? So you're a writer, too?" With a friendly grimace, the director went back to work, and Ben left to return to Ringman's.

One of Ben's favorite parts of getting behind the scenes was watching them design the set, especially the special effects. Seeing it all up close was much better than watching the 'Making Of' specials on television that he loved. The way the crew made things was amazingly sophisticated in its detail. Pieces of wall meant to break away were multi-layered to looked like real splintering wood, not like cartoon cutouts. Effects like gunshots he knew about, knowing the explosions went off at the point of contact, not at the barrel of the gun. The effects he really admired involved stunts. He liked the stunt guys. Buddy Lane, the stunt coordinator for "County Fair," had been an acrobat in a rival circus for a while. He and Ben had some good talks about old times.

At the coordinator's suggestion, Ben arrived at the crack of dawn a week later to watch a stunt being set up on the race track, meant to be a climactic moment in the film. Most of the race had already been filmed up to this point, when the hero and villain would duke it out in a pair of souped-up stock cars as the villain's henchmen fired at the hero from the stands. Ben watched in awe as every part of the open-air set was measured to a fare-thee-well. A huge oil slick was laid out near the finish line, to be set ablaze by the punch of a button. The two lead race cars had been rigged to turn over when they struck one another. Flash explosions were set up at intervals and tested again and again to make sure they'd fire on cue. The stunt men were dressed in asbestos padding. There were asbestos dropcloths everywhere to wrap around them when they came staggering blindly out of the fire. In case of accidents, the fire marshall was on standby with a full crew manning a fire hose and extinguishers.

The set looked great. Standing in the middle of the track, Ben would never have guessed that the other side of the camera-side grandstands was nothing but two-by-twos and metal framework. It looked like a real fair, even to the suggestion of the midway booths off in the distance. On the other side, hundreds of extras were herded onto the benches. A bridge over the track joined the two parts. A camera and half a dozen lights and their crews were perched on top of it, waiting to catch the action from above. Ben spotted six other cameras set up at different places around the track. He was excited. This was a big moment.

"Now, look," Padrone shouted into the megaphone he carried. "We gonna try to do this in one take, right?" He got a murmur of agreement from the extras. Buddy and the assistant director came over to give the director a thumbs-up. Ben and the other non-essential crew drew back part-way behind the dummy grandstand to watch. "And…Action!"

Like turning on a switch, the set came to life. Onlookers in the stands cheered and screamed. The henchmen popped up here and there, firing blanks toward the hero's car. Everything happened so fast. The two cars sped past Ben, zigzagging back and forth the width of the track. They zoomed into the oil slick, which exploded into flame like a charm. Everything behaved as it was supposed to, parts shooting harmlessly off in all directions. All except for one tire.

It came bouncing out of the fire and slammed into the fake grandstand. Over the roar of the engines, the fire and the crowd, Ben heard a loud *ping*! as a single bolt shot up into the air like a champagne cork. He realized it was the one holding the flat to the next pylon. Ben stared as the flat started to topple down toward the high bridge holding the camera crew. No one else seemed to notice, all intent on the cars and the actors.

There was no time. Ben grabbed a fire cloth and jumped forward. There were no gloves to put on his hands, but he'd helped raise plenty of tents. Hanging on to the framework with the cloth to protect himself, Ben leaned backward, counting on his leverage and weight to haul it back.

"Hey, get away from that!" the grips yelled at him. "Hey, you! Lardbottom! Hands off!"

Ben could yell, too, when he needed to.

"Get some ropes and help me! The frame's coming apart!"

The action stopped at his shout, and the director dashed over to see what was wrong. The delay was long enough for the extras in the stands to scramble out from underneath the arch, as the grips threw their inadequate bulk alongside Ben's. He could see the pale faces of the crew up on the arch, hanging on as their support swayed underneath them. He was strong but wished he could summon up his elephant strength just for a moment to pull. But it was enough. Before his arms gave out, the grips had brought around the crane and hooked the framework long enough for the crews to scramble off with their precious equipment.

Flashing lights lit up Ben's silhouette on the flat, telling him a photographer was back there snapping away, getting pictures of the back of his head. Just his luck! "I'm ready for my close-up, Mr. DeMille," he growled.

"All right!" Buddy Lane shouted. "Everyone's clear!"

"Let 'er go!" the key grip yelled.

Ben released the section he was holding. It fell, tearing the one next to it, booming to the ground like a tree-trunk. The set builders looked at it and told the director, "Four hours." The special effects guys were blaming the car wrangler, who blamed the stunt man, who blamed the set designer. At least no one was yelling at Ben that he'd ruined the take. The actors were grateful, fluttering away to phone their agents, a few clustering around the magazine photographer getting their side of the story in. The director rushed over to shake Ben's hand.

"Thank you, Small Ben! Thank you! I never figured you for a hero!"

The union representative shoved his face into Ben's. "That's going to cost you a hefty fine. mister. This is a union set!"

"Cheaper than medical bills," Ben said, shrugging.

"There's that," said Padrone nervously.

"And lawsuits," Ben persisted. Padrone appealed to the producer, who had come running up.

"All right, I'll pay for it," the producer said to the union rep, then turned to Ben. "We owe you one, buddy. If there's anything we can do…?"

Ben looked at them, hope shining in his eyes. He opened his mouth to ask, "Could I do a walk-on?"

"A bit part?" Roxanne said, before he could speak. She smiled up at Ben. He was pleasantly surprised. Truth to tell, he wouldn't have picked her as the gutsy type, but she must have been to survive in this business. It was very daring of her, and Ben knew what such a suggestion might cost her in terms of her career, spending the producer's money like that. A bit player got a lot more money than an extra. But he was pleased. She'd stopped seeing his size and started seeing him as a fellow human being, knew what he dreamed.

"Why not? We can write him in," the producer said to the director.

"A speaking part?" Ben asked, astonished. To him, writing meant dialogue. From their expressions, he guessed that *wasn't* exactly what they had in mind. He tried not to let the disappointment show on his face. Anything would do. Any part. This was the movies.

A longer, silent conference between the two men, during which both of them summed him up from feet to face.

"Okay," the producer said at last. "He's got good features. And he can talk. My ears are still ringing from that Tarzan yell." Roxanne was beside Ben, squeezing his arm for joy. Ben was stunned. A speaking part! He would not only get to appear on film as himself, he'd have lines!

"Oh, yes," the producer said, looking back as he started away with the union rep and the writer to make arrangements, "and measure him for a chair. He's been hanging around here for so long, he's getting to be like family."

"It'll have to be special-ordered," said the assistant producer, eyeing Ben.

"Fine! Do it!"

The assistant smiled at Ben warily, afraid of saying the wrong thing. Ben didn't care what the guy was thinking. This was the happiest day of his life. An aide from costuming was waved over to measure him. Obligingly, he presented his backside for the tape measure. At last he belonged here. Who knew if this would lead to more parts? He was enjoying the moment. The production assistant muttered behind him.

"You say something?" Ben asked, glancing back over his shoulder.

"Oh no, sir!" squeaked the PA.

"Yes, yes," said the director as they walked away. "I can't wait until the elephant comes back next week." He waved his hands expansively. "Get him and Small Ben in the same shot—absolutely *filmic*!"

"Uh-oh," Ben mumbled to himself.

"Did you say something?" Roxanne asked.

"Nothing. I'd better just hope for some more of those special effects. You want to go for coffee after the shoot?"

Roxanne smiled up at him. "I'd love to."

Connie Wilkins says that her story "grew out of thirty-four (and counting) years of happy marriage and the realization that, however perfect the union, self-image counts." To which we say "Yea, verily!"

Meluse's Counsel
by Connie Wilkins

Raymond paused in deep shadow at the edge of the moonlit path. He might yet turn back; the old hound at his feet would be pretext enough for the evening walk, the stiffness of her joints eased by a gentle ramble.

Light flickered through twisting vines at the cottage windows. The witch might already sense his presence, but that mattered little. In spite of his weariness, the ache that drove him would not let him rest. He could not turn back.

He strode boldly into the moonlight and up the path. Watched or no, he would not skulk to the door of a cottage on his own lands.

The door swung open before he could knock.

"Lord Raymond." The strong, clear voice held an edge of mockery, for all the crone's apparent age and frailty.

"Meluse," he greeted her with the courteous hint of a bow. "I hope I see you well."

Firelight played across two angular faces. Black eyes looked into black eyes over arched noses, the resemblance more marked now that neither was young, though, indeed, Raymond could not remember Meluse as anything other than old.

Those same hawklike features were common throughout the district. Raymond, who labored hard as any peasant, wondered sometimes how his philandering great-grandsire had found the time.

"Well enough, my lord. And you?" Her eyes snapped with dark amusement. "If all went well I would never see you here. It is many a year since you felt the need to consult me."

"True enough," he said a bit ruefully, "but you must know that if you are in need of aught that I can supply, you have only to send word." He knew well the duty of a lord to his people, and observed it in its broadest spirit, though he had little wealth beyond the land and the loyalty of those people.

"Yes, yes," she said impatiently, "but you have not come to tell me that, nor yet to ask for herbs to ease your hound's old bones. Your lady wife can attend to that as well as I, and no doubt has done so."

She saw him tense, and suspected where the true problem lay, but then a smile lit his face with a vestige of youth and he shrugged lightly.

"So much for that excuse. You are right, of course, Alisoun has done wonders for Riffka, as she does in all things, though I fear neither poultice nor spell can serve much longer."

"Sit down, Raymond, and get to the point. Your problem is clearly with Lady Alisoun."

He took no offense at her lack of deference to him, but approved her genuine respect for his lady.

Meluse knew that she lived here in comfort and esteem by the sufferance of that lady, who was no fool and understood well the difference between herb-lore and true magic. She would not quibble over the use of either, for the well-being of those under her care, but neither would she brook their darker aspects. Except that once, when it had been her lord's life in the balance…

"It may be that I need nothing more than counsel," Raymond said. "Has my lady seemed troubled to you of late?"

Meluse considered. The lady's health, at any rate, had seemed unchanged at last viewing, her ample form moving with its accustomed brisk efficiency. "We work together in the village from time to time, when the common good requires it, but we are scarcely confidantes. I have seen Lady Alisoun only in passing since your son's wedding. She sends me a portion from the hunt, as always, and from the castle garden in season, but I am scarcely the one to whom she would open her heart." Her look told him what he knew, that he had always been that one, and should be still.

"There is, I fear, some trouble now, but…but I cannot begin to describe it." Or could not bring himself to try.

She waited, quelling impatience; men were not bred to easily show their hearts, or their pain. But at his next words her forbearance vanished in a snap.

"Have you a true love potion, as the villagers say?"

"What, exactly, do you have in mind, my lord?" The bite in her voice would have cut him if he had noted it through his own turmoil.

"Some spell, some draught, that renders one ravishingly desirable to the chosen other?"

Meluse's eyes narrowed, and her voice was perilously close to a hiss. "Do you believe I have such power?" An inner rage swelled, tempting her to give way to dangerous impulses. Did he wish to stray? She knew, none better, what men could be, but that this man, secure in the love of such a lady, should prove so base!

"Have you?" he asked simply, and her restraint snapped.

"Observe my power!" Smoke billowed from the fire as she rose. Raymond coughed, and when the smoke cleared, his mouth hung open still.

Flames had leapt from the hearth to her head; but no, it was a glory of fox-russet hair, flaring about a pointed, full-lipped face of unearthly beauty and allure. White fur robed her body, then slipped away, and her pearl-sheen flesh was the throbbing vision of men long deprived and boys in their first rush of manhood.

He felt a pang of recognition, a remembrance of his own stripling dreams, and wondered suddenly whether they had been something more than dreams.

The vision smiled, stepped toward him, swaying, inviting. He rose and backed away. It was not that he had any notion of how close he stood to destruction, but that another vision rose between them, an image swelling from his heart and mind, leaving room for no other.

Meluse saw it, too—Lady Alisoun's familiar form. The cloud of soft dark hair, the tender mouth, the blue indomitable eyes… Her nakedness was something of a shock, but her husband had every right to envision her so. If her face seemed smoother, her form substantially more slender, than in recent years, there was little fault in him for seeing her forever young.

"Enough!" Lord Raymond rasped. "Your point is made!" He coughed as the smoke swelled again, then ebbed. "My God, witch, do you often take such guise?"

"Very seldom," she said with some regret. "It suits my purpose to be crone, with rare exceptions." And, indeed, she was old and gray again.

Raymond drew breath to speak, but thought better of it. He was not sure he wished more knowledge of such matters, especially as they might touch on his own youth.

"All that is beside the point," she went on briskly. "Clearly you do not weary of your lady and lust after another, so what need have you of love spells?"

"Weary of…no! Never! It is closer to the reverse!"

Meluse sighed, exasperated. So much drama, such expenditure of energy, for what must be a simple misunderstanding. "You will not persuade me that she tires of you! You were never handsome, Raymond, but your years, even your scars, become you."

She toyed briefly with the thought of demonstrating his attraction most explicitly. That he had so recently rebuffed her mattered little; the siren guise had been a mere test; she had means he could not resist. But she discarded the notion out of loyalty to the lady.

"It is not that I doubt her love. How could I bear to think of it? Her spirit cleaves to mine as ever, but of late her flesh… Yet her every thought is to please me, and always she succeeds, perhaps too well."

There was a long pause, until she prompted, "And yet you feel the need of spells to attract her? Come, you must be frank if you wish my help. Far-reaching as my sight may be, it does not extend into the lord's bedchamber."

He flushed, but said lightly, "That is welcome reassurance." He sobered then and sat again before her. "I will try to explain, but it does not come easily." His voice lowered as he spoke, until she had to lean close to hear him. "The change in her came sometime near young Geoffrey's marriage. I thought it weariness at first, from all the work and planning, but that was two months gone. And matters grow, if anything, worse. She does all, and more, to give me pleasure, but I can no longer seem to please her. I try to hold back ever longer, but she drives me deliberately beyond endurance."

He shifted in the chair and stared down at his own tense hands. "I tried stratagems I had heard spoken of by soldiers on Crusade, but that was a mistake. I fear she thinks I acted from experience, not hearsay."

"I would not fret," Meluse said. "You can have no secrets on that score from the woman who nursed you through those weeks of fever and delirium."

"From either woman, I suppose," and he looked up with a glint of a smile.

"So you did know I was there."

"It was more that I always knew when Alisoun was not there, and gradually saw that she trusted only you to take her place. I never thanked you, but I do so now, with all my heart, not least for making her take time to rest."

"None but a witch could have done that," she agreed.

It was as well he never knew how close to death his wounds had brought him. They had festered for weeks as he struggled across Europe from the Holy Land, in feverish longing to see his young wife and home.

By the time he succeeded, he seemed already claimed by death. His spirit could be soothed by his true love's embrace, but his torn flesh could scarcely hold that spirit.

There had come a night when its tenuous hold seemed finally broken. After the priest had departed, the young wife had vowed to follow her lord past Death's gate and beyond, but it was the witch who had summoned the power to reach into that abyss and draw him back. She had been as awe-struck as the lady at the surge of dark strength within herself. The memory had become both bond and barrier between them. They never spoke of it, least of all to Raymond himself, and if he remembered aught he thought it but a dream.

Meluse shook off such shadowed thoughts. "In the present case, I think you have no need of me. Only tell her what is in your heart! I have a simple spell of eloquence, if you feel the need, that has worked many a wonder."

"No doubt," he said dryly, "it works only when the user trusts fully in its power?"

"And is best taken with a goodly amount of wine," she assented. The lord was no fool, either, in most matters.

"I have tried, Meluse," he said, in earnest now, "but she will not open her heart to me."

She was silent for a space. "Your son's new bride is very young and beautiful."

"Too young, I fear." He wondered at the direction of her thought. "She would have done well to stay for Alisoun's instruction, but Geoffrey was needed to hold the eastern keep, and would hear of no more separation. What…"

She abandoned subtlety. "Your lady may feel suddenly old and unattractive. A woman, unlike a man, must believe herself desirable to give herself up to desire."

"But surely…"

"Men are creatures of habit; she may think herself lucky that you have the habit of desiring her, and yet be unconvinced that she warrants your arousal."

"What can I do?"

"My first advice is still my best, but if you feel the need of something more…" She considered. "There is a spell, difficult and costly, that can restore a subtle look of youth and beauty, if you wish to go that far."

"Anything for her happiness, which is my own!" he said. "But as to the expense, what coin I had went for wedding pageantry, and there will be little more until next harvest, if then."

"Something can be arranged. Let us say this; I will waive the cost unless the spell fails to achieve your aims."

He frowned. "Surely you mean the reverse?"

"I know what I do! Leave all to me. I will visit Lady Alisoun tomorrow, on reasonable pretext. Perhaps to discuss the smith's wife, who is heavy with twins. You may look for some change in two or three days. The rest is up to you."

He asked for certain reassurances, then rose and thanked her, and bent to ease his old hound to her feet. He caught the witch's gaze on him, an appraising look, but thought he must have misread its carnal tone.

When Meluse left the castle next day, two things had changed. For one, there were ingredients the lady did not suspect in her morning herbal brew; for the other, it was no longer true that the witch's sight stopped short of the lord's own bedchamber.

The following night, as Lady Alisoun brushed her hair before her mirror, the mirror, in a sense, looked back at her. Her husband waited in the great bed, watching too, in eager hope of some noticeable change in her demeanor.

The lady's brush strokes slowed. A pleasant, dreamy lassitude flowed through her. The face in the mirror glowed with soft luminescence. She reached, with some reluctance, to snuff the candle, then paused and left it lit.

She raised her hand to the fastening of her robe. Slowly the garment slid to the floor, while she watched her body's reflection with languorous approval.

Raymond was taut with hope and longing. Letting the candle burn was, in itself, a hopeful sign. At last he could resist no longer and went to her, embracing her from behind, and she laughed to see the mirror image of his brown hands cupping her full white breasts.

The witch, with great reluctance, veiled her glass. There was a limit to how much the lady might forgive, perhaps already passed, and to watch more might cause Meluse's good intentions, shaky at best, to shatter utterly.

When, at dawn, she looked again, the lord and lady were entwined in such exhausted bliss that there could be no doubt the spell had worked.

Now would come the difficult part.

Alisoun stirred, stretched, yawned. She nuzzled against her husband's chest, gently kissed the old scars there, and swung herself upright. She stood before the mirror a moment, brush in hand; the small smile of remembered ecstasy faded and a slight frown took its place.

"Raymond…"

"Mmmm?"

"Do I look different to you? Younger, slimmer, than a week ago?"

He tried to shake off sleep. "You look different every time I see you, and yet the same. Your infinite variety amazes and enchants me."

She laughed and came to sit once more beside him. "Your eloquence amazes me, my lord. One might think you had swallowed one of old Meluse's potions."

He rubbed his eyes and hoped the gesture masked his face.

"Indeed," she added thoughtfully, "the witch was here just two days past." He felt her body stiffen. She searched his face, then turned away and bowed her head. Her voice, when at last it came, was filled with muffled pain and anger. "And is it worth whatever price you paid, this spell to give me back the look of youth?"

He would not lie. "There was no price, or rather, there need be payment only if the charm does not succeed. Strange, I know, but true."

"You need not trouble. I will see to her reward!"

For the first time Meluse was undivided in her hope for the lord's success. If he botched all now…

"Alisoun, my love…"

She shook his hand away and stood, "Do not fear. All shall be as you desire!" Her bitterness subsided into weariness. "If you wish me to put on the slender look of youth, so be it. I will see the spell renewed as necessary; you need but tell me when it begins to fade."

A chasm yawned before him; he edged along the narrow bridge of truth. "But only you can say, my love. The spell is for your eyes alone. I would not let my sight of you be altered, or clouded even by memory! How could I wish to erase a day, a minute, from your being?" He thought he spoke the truth, which was all that mattered. "Each moment together builds on all those before, each pleasure seems greater, or did, until…until I could no longer…please you." The slight catch in his voice did him more service than any flow of eloquence.

"No, no, it was not you!" She leaned into his embrace and rested her head against his shoulder. "It was all my own foolishness. Geoffrey's bride…is so young and slim and lovely…"

He knew her anger was gone, but not her sadness.

"She has the allure of promise, of potential, I suppose. I thought her too young, too insubstantial, but clearly Geoffrey has no such doubts."

"Quite clearly!" Her soft laugh was wistful. "He looks at her as you looked at me when we were newly wed."

"Have I ceased to look at you so? My eyes are not so old or tired as that! Or do you think I no longer truly see you? Oh, my love, however dear the memory of youth, I would not trade for the beauty I see now. It is this face…" he stroked her cheek, "these eyes, this mouth…" he kissed them in turn, "this body that stirs me." His hands stroked down the line of her throat to her breasts. "Surely you can see how I take pleasure in your fullness, and in stirring you to pleasure, too!"

He thought all was well, knew that desire rose in her as it did in him, but she laid a finger on his mouth to silence him and twisted out of his embrace.

"Just a moment, my love." She picked up her nightrobe from the floor. "I fear the witch has worked her spell too well and will not collect her fee." She moved to the mirror and gazed into it intently. For a brief moment, blue eyes bore into black, and told them clearly, "I will deal with you later!" It was not entirely a threat.

Then the robe covered the mirror, and Meluse turned away with a sound half sigh, half rueful chuckle. The lady was no fool.

If ever she lapsed again, though, into folly that drove her lord to seek the witch's counsel, the witch would not let such a man as that go easily a second time.

"A few years ago," writes Paula L. Fleming, "I joined a gym. Like a lot of big people, I felt embarrassed exercising in public. However, when I noticed that some of the instructors were large, too, I felt a lot more comfortable. Ruby Chandel is my vision of the ideal fitness instructor."

Polyformus Perfectus
by Paula L. Fleming

"Bipedals, jack it! Everyone else, jog!"

Ruby ran over to show a new Ritluyin how to jog to the beat. The four-count music was always hard for the tripedal folks at first. That was going to be one of her first projects at the Institute, to get aerobics music recorded in 6/8 time as well as 4/4.

"Okay gang, last eight! Let's work it!"

And her last class on Sigma XI was over. She swallowed a feeling of letdown. The new job would be great, developing fitness routines for other species and training instructors to teach them. Still, she packed up her music discs with some regret.

A woman in a clingy bizsuit glanced into the dance studio. She slipped her wiry form past the last of Ruby's students as they headed for the locker room. "Excuse me, I'm looking for the instructor. Is she still here?"

"Yes she is. I'm Ruby."

"Oh no, you can't be."

"I can't be?" Ruby put on her best Attitude. If this little girl thought Ruby Chandel didn't know her own name because she was black…Well, kiss the bottom of my big toe, honey. You should have left that attitude back in EarthZone, where someone might appreciate it.

"I'm looking for the instructor who's coming to work at the TGIF. That's the Trans-Galactic Institute for Fitness."

She sounded like she was going to spell it next.

"I know what the TGIF is." Ruby slipped into the grammar of the refugee camps. Aunt Belle used to smack her for speaking camp slang, and after six years of college her Unispeak was first cousin to the Queen's English. But it was fun to play with people's expectations. "Listen, Ruby ain't no common name, and unless I got me a twin, I the only Ruby running around Sigma XI in red spandex. I be your woman."

"Well, then there's been some kind of mistake."

"You telling me I be a mistake?"

The woman wouldn't meet Ruby's eyes. She started to speak quickly. "It must be the low gravity. I'm sure you're an excellent teacher…here, but we have Earth-normal gravity at the Institute. We need our instructors to be fit, and you're…well, you're quite *large*."

"'Quite *large*?' Don't be dumping that fly-by speak on me. I'm five-five and 200-some pounds of strength and sass. I ain't ever going to wear no Miss Universe crown, but that don't mean I can't teach. Besides, don't it feel like Earth-normal gravity in here to you?"

"Well…" The woman looked scared, as if vids of refugee riots were playing in her mind.

"Listen." Time to switch syntaxes. "The University built its science department on this moon so scientists could conduct experiments in a low-gravity environment. However, almost everyone who works here came from planets with Earth gravity, plus or minus a little bit. They need to work out in an Earth-grav gym to maintain bone mass and muscle tone. Therefore, I am highly experienced at teaching in such an environment."

The woman began to back up. "I'm sure you believe you're in good shape," she countered, "and the aliens don't know any better—they think you're a fit human—but you're not. I'm sorry, but I have to go. My flight just happened to be laying over here, and I thought I'd stop and say hello to a new employee, but—"

"Wait just a star-shooting second. But what?"

"But I'm not going to hire you after all. I'm sorry. Good bye."

"Not so fast." Ruby blocked her path and grabbed her wrist. "First of all, what's your name? I like to know who I'm dealing with."

"I'm Lara Jerecyzk, the Director of TGIF. Let go of my arm."

Ruby took a deep breath. *You can take a body out of EarthZone, but it's not so easy to take EarthZone out of a body*. She let go of Lara's arm but took a half step closer so her chin was nearly touching the shorter woman's nose. "Nice to meet you, Lara. Now let me make sure I understand this. I've got three years' experience teaching aerobics, strength, and stretch classes to all kinds of aliens. I have a B.A. in xenobiology and a Master's in sports physiology. I studied like a crazy woman to get my Xenofitness Certification. I have references that glow in the dark they're so strong. And you're saying I'm not qualified?"

"You didn't look like this," Lara waved her hand across Ruby's midsection, "in the video. The discs must have gotten mixed up. My secretary is just awful. I'm sorry."

She scuttled around Ruby and hurried from the gym. Ruby turned to the mirror that lined the room's front wall. "Well, how do you like that?" she said to her reflection. She felt the language of the camps well up inside her, and she gave it free vent. "She thinking there be too much of your glossy black hide for her Institute. But, girl, you still got a paid-for ticket. They ain't going to get rid of you easy."

Ruby liked spaceflight. The hyperjumps that made other passengers sick made her pleasantly giddy. She sipped champagne through a straw and giggled as the bubbles bounced around her stomach. Then a jolt slammed her head into the seatwebbing.

"Say what?" she asked the universe.

Another jolt hit. She put the plastic cup of champagne into the bulkhead cupboard, stuck out her tongue at the "remain seated" light, and unfastened her webbing. She yanked open her cabin door and stepped into the hall, just in time to get run down by a couple of crew members.

"Get back in your cabin!" one yelled as they pounded pell-mell past her.

She gave their backs the finger and headed the other way. The corridor remained empty until she reached a wider, carpeted hall. A Ship Captain's seven-pointed star capped the door at the end. The door was half-open, held so by a decapitated human body with Captain's stars on the shoulders. The head, neatly congealed at the neck, rolled toward her as another jolt shook the ship.

"How'd you get in here?" Lots of adult bodies moving, blocking her view, their faces exchanging anguished glances they thought she didn't understand. Aunt Belle snatching up her hand, pulling her away from Momma-in-four-pieces. The gravity slipping, Momma's arm lifting like it was gonna wave, her own feet slipping. They were gonna fly off to heaven together, she and Momma, except Aunt Belle's grip pulling her back, away, to the bunkroom, pushing her under the bedwebbing.

Ruby jerked her head back as if she could physically fling the memories from her brain. "Got enough problems now without living those long gone," she muttered, repeating what Aunt Belle had said so many times. She picked up the Captain's head and addressed it, "So I'm supposed to stay in my cabin until this happens to me? I don't think so." She drop-kicked it through the door and went looking for the control room.

As she got to the front part of the ship, she heard people yelling, not encouraging yelling, the kind that says *Hurray for our side!,* but more like screams of pain. A lot of them cut off in the middle, as though the screamers suddenly had something more important to do, like dying. Ruby proceeded more slowly, grateful she'd worn her old aerobics shoes for the trip. Their Tigeran rubber soles were out of style, but they were quiet.

The corridor turned a corner, spread out, and ended in a semi-circular balcony. A half dozen uniformed bodies, human and alien, lay haphazardly against the railing. Ruby crouched low and crept closer. The bodies were marked by the same neatly-sealed wounds as the Captain's neck. On either side of the balcony, corkscrew stairs descended to the control center. She pulled herself forward on her belly to lie amid the dead folks and peer through the railing, just in time to see a firing squad in action.

A couple dozen humanoid soldiers—Gratzu judging by their body armor—had the remaining crew lined up against the far bulkhead. Without ceremony, the Gratzu fired silent energy beams through their captives' chests. Donut-sized clumps of congealed flesh hit the bulkhead as the crew members screamed and collapsed.

Ruby squirmed back into the corridor and stood up. "Ick," she muttered. "Okay, girl, where do you go from here? One thing for sure, you aren't going anywhere without some help." She started jogging back toward the passenger cabins. When she reached the first one, she gave the door a quick knock and opened it. A Yelq'r body spilled out, its tentacles reflexively grasping at Ruby's ankles even though a neat hole had been drilled through its center.

"Now why'd they do that to you?" Yelq'r were about the most inoffensive creatures in this arm of the galaxy. Now granted, Gratzu were about the most offensive, but still... Hijacking a lumbering passenger liner carrying nothing but decades-old tech seemed pretty pointless.

"Unless one of the passengers is pretty special," Ruby told the dead but writhing Yelq'r.

Footsteps were marching this way. They sounded too disciplined, too confident, to belong to anyone fleeing the Gratzu. Ruby ducked into the cabin, pulled the Yelq'r onto her lap, and closed the door. Her breathing sounded like a steam engine in the small space. *Deep breaths, deep breaths*, she told herself, *just like you're cooling down after a workout*. The feet came closer, closer...and passed without pausing.

A tentacle dangled for an instant in front of Ruby's face, then quickly withdrew to the overhead luggage bin. Ruby stood up, letting the dead Yelq'r slide to the floor, and turned around. The single tote bag bulged to nearly bursting. One of the securing straps was undone. Ruby leaned forward and put her eye up to its drawstring-puckered hole. A big eye blinked back at her.

"You can come out. I won't hurt you."

The bag erupted in a mass of tentacles, and a Yelq'r slithered down on top of her. It clung to her as hard as it could with all sixteen of its limbs, making breathing difficult.

"Hey, hey, hey. Just relax. Ooze a little. Soak up some air. Feel the oxygen spread through your body. Let it dissolve all your fear and tension."

To Ruby's relief, the Yelq'r let go of her and plopped onto the seat before it oozed. Yelq'r ooze was clear and odorless, but it had the consistency of egg white.

"Doesn't that feel better? Now, let's put your friend into the bag so you can give," she checked its gender, "him a nice burial when you get home. I'm Ruby, by the way. What's your name?"

"I'm Qylt'r. You can call me Quilt."

"Quilt's better than the hash I'd make of your real name, huh?" Ruby lifted the deceased, while Quilt's tentacles levered him into the bag.

"What's happening out there?" Quilt asked.

"Gratzu soldiers have boarded the ship. They've killed most, if not all, the crew and apparently they're killing passengers, too. Any idea why they killed your friend here?"

Quilt considerately pulled a blanket from the side compartment and spread it over the seat. Ruby sat down and pulled the webbing over her, just in case there was another jolt. Quilt looped her limbs over various protuberances so she dangled eye-to-eye with her.

"Not really," she said quietly. "I was under the seat taking a nap. Hyperjumping makes me sleepy. The door opened, and someone asked my mate if he was Doctor Black Cloud. They had to repeat the question several times before Rulq'r understood; their Unispeak was really bad. When he finally told them he wasn't Doctor Black Cloud, they shot him."

Quilt oozed again. Ruby pulled part of the blanket over her lap to catch the drippings. "Doctor Black Cloud. I know him. Liked to come in real early to run around the track. I was always after him to add weights to his workout for upper body development, but he always had some lame excuse. But that's no reason for the Gratzu to be looking for him, and they're sure going to a lot of trouble here. We should get out of their way. Are you ready to find a lifepod?"

"I'd rather crawl back in the bag."

"Quilt, what if the Gratzu blow up the ship when they're done with it? Your mate wouldn't want you to stay here. Now here's a blanket. Dry off so you don't leave a trail, and we'll find a way out of here."

Ruby wished she'd paid more attention to the holographic ship's tour offered to passengers before takeoff. She only remembered that the passenger cabins, a few hundred of them, were in the middle decks and the lifepods were at the top and bottom of the ship. Which way to go?

"Let's go up. It's better exercise," Ruby suggested out of habit.

Quilt put a tentacle through the bag's handles and coiled it tightly on her back, then used about nine limbs, give or take a few, to follow Ruby. The other tentacles restlessly explored the walls and ceilings, opening and closing cabin doors as the pair moved cautiously down the hall. The cabins on this corridor were either empty—and looked as though they'd been that way for the trip—or held recently deceased occupants. The whole scene was eerie and depressing, and Ruby wanted to sing to banish the heebie-jeebies that were creeping up on her. But of course they had to be quiet.

They found a recess in the wall with a ladder leading to the deck above them, just as a Gratzu started climbing down. Ruby ducked back into the hall and looked for someplace to hide, but there wasn't anything close enough. *Time to find out if kickboxing is just good exercise or if it actually works as self-defense.* However, with the speed that sixteen limbs gave her, Quilt dashed forward, snagged one of the soldier's legs, and whisked herself back into the corridor. The soldier's body armor clanged loudly against the deck. Ruby jumped on him, snatched his sidearm from its holster, and turned his head into something she didn't want to look at. Another soldier poked his face through, and she did the same thing to his head.

When she was satisfied they were alone, Ruby turned to Quilt and saw the Yelq'r had her tentacles wrapped tightly all around her body. She looked like a ball of spaghetti. "That was really brave of you, Quilt," Ruby said softly.

Quilt oozed a little and loosened her protective coil enough to peek out. "No, just not as scary as dying."

"Yeah, well, that too."

The next deck was another passenger area. The Gratzu had been messier here than below. The cabin doors toward the front of the ship were ajar, some propped open by bodies. However, the few cabins between the hatch and the ship's rear looked undisturbed.

"Watch my back." Ruby opened the nearest one. A familiar face glanced up from a holodisplay.

"If you've come to hassle me about that job, I'll call security!" Lara Jerecyzk said, putting a finger on the emergency button.

Ruby threw her head back and laughed. Then she doubled over and kept laughing. She had to clasp her arms over her belly to ease its hurt, she laughed so much. Tears ran down her cheeks and around the seam between her chins. Rads, that bugged her! She wiped them off.

"Yeah, baby," she said finally. "Yeah, I killed a couple Gratzu just so I could beg you for a job. But you're right about one thing, I don't want you hitting no button." She found the camp slang slipping back onto her tongue and left it there. Aiming the gun at Lara's hand, she released the woman's seatwebbing and said, "And you don't want to hit that button neither. Now come on out real easy, and no one getting hurt."

Lara looked like she wanted to kick Ruby's butt, but she eased out of the cabin.

"Quilt, please explain the situation to this lady. I got to find out what's so raddly fascinating she don't have a clue what's going on around here." Ruby ducked into the cabin and watched the holodisplay for a couple of minutes.

When she came out shaking her head, Quilt had assembled the occupants of the other two cabins. They'd been wondering why the Captain hadn't made an announcement about the jolts they'd felt and why they hadn't felt any more hyperjumps. They were packed and ready to move.

The group made quick introductions. The Tigeran man was a school teacher named Mee-York, pronounced like a cat in heat. With longish necks on spotty, furry, four-legged bodies, Tigerans always looked to Ruby like a jaguar and a giraffe had done something unnatural.

The eight-foot-tall Amoo woman was a pro wrestler who went by the handle Destructo-Babe, D-B for short. Ruby recognized the name but not the face, but then all Amoo looked alike to her, like trees with the biomechanics of pogo-sticks. Made for spectacular wrestling matches. The Amoo in her class back on Sigma XI had told her they recognized each other through smell and, at a distance, by subtle differences in the unique, complicated patterns on their tunics. Well, there was only one here so it didn't matter.

Quilt mentioned that she was a systems engineer, Ruby introduced herself as a xenofitness instructor, and Lara said, "I'm the Director of the TGIF Institute, that's the Trans-Galactic Institute for Fitness, and I guess I'm in charge here."

"Say what?" Ruby turned to her with Attitude on full blast. "And who told you that?"

"Well, I mean, if you think about it, I have more leadership experience than everyone else and," she added with a giggle, "I'm the only one besides you with opposable thumbs."

"Which you were twiddling while you watched the EuroEarth spring fashion holoshow and the ship was hijacked. Don't you know ninety-nine-point-nine percent of the folks in the galaxy can't wear those clothes? I should have left you alone. Look," she addressed the group, "how about we scoot out of here and then discuss who our leader should be?"

"Works for me," said Destructo-Babe. The others, except for Lara, nodded.

"Oh yeah, one more thing. Any of you know where Doctor Black Cloud's berth is?"

They shook their heads. "Is he human?" Lara asked. Ruby ignored her.

"Right then, let's go."

D-B boinged down the hall, clacking her giant lobster claws in Lara's face on the way. Lara didn't look scared like she should have, just repulsed. Mee-York padded after the Amoo, sniffing the air and extending quivering whiskers, and Quilt followed him. Lara took her time getting her bags. The woman actually paused for a second to watch a trio of EuroEarth models stalk the screen. Eventually she strolled after the others.

When Ruby pulled herself up to the next deck, grateful she hadn't slacked off on her chin-ups, Mee-York, D-B and Quilt stood over a couple of bloody pulps clad in Gratzu body armor and Amoo footprints. Quilt had several tentacles wrapped around her eyes while several more still grasped the soldiers' ankles. "Don't forget to ooze, Quilt," Ruby told her softly.

This was a big improvement; just as quiet as the guns but not as creepily bloodless. This whole scene had been feeling like some kind of hologame or a bad dream, and Ruby liked life nice and solid.

This corridor looked different; the floor here was corrugated metal instead of soundproof tile, and the bulkheads were unpainted. Mee-York moved the most quietly, so he explored while the others stood guard. Lara picked a gun off one of the dead Gratzu. Ruby hoped she could shoot straight.

The excited twitching of Mee-York's tail signaled that he'd found something. He stood on his hind legs, leaned a paw against a pressure-plate, and crept through the door that slid open. After a moment he came back. "It's the lifepod control room. You get to the bays through here. Looks like the Gratzu came by earlier, but it's not guarded now."

They hurried into the control room. The two crew members who had run past Ruby earlier lay dead on the floor, their dislodged flesh in tidy clumps by their heads. Lights on wall panels glowed and blinked, showing that the systems here were active. "All right, let's hightail it out of here." Ruby followed the sign pointing to the launching bays. "That's not an ethnic reference," she added as an aside to Mee-York.

The bays were empty. All of them.

"What the—!" She issued a stream of obscenities that would have made her Momma mad, and her Grandmomma proud.

Quilt was a blur of movement into the control room. When the others caught up with her, they found her hanging from a ceiling beam by one limb while the others tapped delicately at the control panels. Displays lit up with scrolling data. "There," she said after less than a minute, "the lifepods were never on board."

"What? They have to be on board. It's the law!"

"It is the law, but it's also very profitable to sell them on the black market."

"Well shoot me dead! That explains why the Gratzu aren't guarding this place. There's nothing here to guard."

Ruby suddenly felt the way a too intense workout made her feel, all deflated and kind of weary and jumpy at the same time. She sat down on the floor and rested her head on her hands between her knees. The others gathered around and joined her in silent thought, except Lara. She found a reflective surface on one of the panels and pulled a makeup kit from one of her bags. *Oh, why not*, thought Ruby, *it's as useful as anything else we've done.*

Then Quilt spoke up. "I have an idea. The Gratzu are looking for Doctor Black Cloud, right? If we could find him, maybe we could negotiate. I don't really mean turn him over to the Gratzu, but if it's just knowledge they want, or documents..."

Ruby felt her energy return. "Yeah!" she said. "That's a great idea! But we have to hurry."

"No!" Lara looked up from her facial engineering. Everyone looked at her. "I mean, well, it's just that what chance do we have? You know, with the Gratzu all over the place and everything. We should just stay here, you know? Where they probably won't come back?"

"If they don't find what they want, they'll blow up the whole ship just for fun," Ruby countered.

D-B nodded agreement and clacked her claws together for emphasis. "We should do everything we can, not just sit here hoping the Gratzu play nice. They're not nice."

"I agree," Mee-York chipped in.

Lara snapped shut her compact, raised her Gratzu gun and pointed it at them. "I think it would be safer if you all just stay right here."

"Whoa! Wait a minute, girl. Just what's your angle on this?"

"I'm the Director of the Trans-Galactic Institute for Fitness."

"If that's supposed to explain something, then lawyers make sense. Go on."

"It's perfectly simple. They're looking for Doctor Black Cloud. Doctor Black Cloud is dead because I killed him. I stashed his work in my compact, and it's not leaving until I get where I'm going."

"Are you just a very sick individual, or should I ask why you did this?"

"To make a lot of money. TGIF underwrote Doctor Black Cloud's work. It was an ex-per-i-ment."

Dump it all if she didn't sound like she was going to start spelling again.

"See, there's a protein that promotes weight loss in all carbon-based life forms with multi-stage digestion. In Sigma XI's low gravity, scientists were able to produce extra-large crystals of this protein. Engineers can use the big crystals as models to come up with a process for producing the drug in mass quantities while maintaining its quality. And investors, like me, will make a killing. Isn't it exciting?" Bimbo-ese seemed to be a dialect Lara could turn on and off.

"You're saying this isn't to do with military or industrial tech? It's all about a diet drug?"

"Well, sure! Everyone wants to be thin. It's too bad you couldn't be a part of it. Your experience with aliens would have made you a good sales rep."

"Yeah, I'm crying so hard I'm out of tears."

"Our agents told us the Gratzu would make a move. They've been interested in getting out of pirating and into real business for awhile now."

"They're going about it wrong," Ruby muttered.

"But they won't have a chance to blow up the ship." Lara glanced at the unitime display on the wall. "Fortunately I sold out my TGIF partners. They funded the research, but I can make brighter stardust working with the EuroEarth Consortium. They should be arriving…" lights flashed on several panels, "right about now to 'kidnap' me. Best of all, TGIF will think the Gratzu did it! I've always said, 'Life works out perfectly for the perfect.'"

Machinery whirred in one of the lifepod bays. "That's my ride," Lara said. She giggled and pointed the gun at Destructo-Babe. "You first, you huge, disgusting *mutant*."

Four tentacles whipped around Lara's wrists and ankles, holding her tight and pulling the gun down. Mee-York was in her face with his claws, blinding her with her own blood. When she did blink her vision clear, she was looking into the muzzle of Ruby's gun. D-B had bounded from the control room and, judging from the screams coming from the docking bays, was scaring the designer jeans off the EuroEarth Consortium thugs.

"Looks like *our* ride is here," Ruby said. "You and your buddies can stay here and tough it out with the Gratzu. We," she picked up Lara's makeup bag, "are going to give Doctor Black Cloud's property to his heirs and report a murder."

"Traitor! I was going to spare you. I thought we were two of a kind, but you've thrown in with the animals. There'll be a price to pay! You just wait. When civilization falls and the beasts take over, you just remember the role you played…"

Ruby tuned her out because D-B had come back, holding a couple of people off the ground by their collars with each claw. One of the captives kicked her and stubbed his toe. Mee-York found some extra cable in one of the storage bins which worked well to tie them up. Then the Amoo, the Yelq'r, the Tigeran, and the human boarded the EuroEarth shuttle, figured out where its mapping button was—rads! why did it have to be in a different place in every model?—and zipped past the Gratzu and EuroEarth ships busy fighting each other.

Ruby cracked open a beer and sipped. "I guess 'life works out perfectly for perfect people,'" she said, doing a fair imitation of Lara's smug tone, and giggled. The hyperdrive had kicked in, and the beer bubbles were doing a dance in her stomach.

"Aw rads!" She set her beer down.

The others, except for Quilt who was napping under a seat, looked at her in concern.

"I thought I understood what happened back there, but there's one thing I don't understand. Why does someone who hates non-humans go to work for a xenofitness company in the first place? It doesn't make sense."

"No, it doesn't," Mee-York agreed, "except that there seems to be a lot of money in it."

"So," D-B turned to her, "what are you going to do about it?"

"What am I going to do about what?"

"If TGIF isn't what it should be, then why don't you start a business that is?"

"Start a business? How am I going to start a business?"

A tentacle wandered from under her seat and waved to get her attention. "My mate had a lot of life insurance. I'll invest in you," Quilt said. "Rulq'r would like that."

"I'll do commercials for you. I've been wanting to move into acting anyway," D-B added.

"And I'll help you present your curricula so they look good to planetary authorities. Paperwork is half my job now anyway," finished Mee-York.

"Just don't be correcting my Unispeak," Ruby warned him. "We in business, not school."

"Never," he replied solemnly, "as long as you don't tell me to take up jogging."

"I won't be needing to. You going to want working out. Wait until you see the circuit training routine I done developed for folks with claws. It got climbing and jumping, and…"

Mee-York and the others rolled their eyes, but they were laughing. She kept talking, using the tough language of tough times to hold back overwhelming elation and gratitude. It would never do to get too happy. That's something else Aunt Belle always said: "Don't ever lose your cool; it may be all you've got."

No, I've got a lot more than that, Aunt Belle. I have what my Momma would have wanted for me.

She shut up and let the tears come. They trickled down her face and followed the crease between her chins. Rads, she hated that! Her friends fell silent, too, respecting her mood.

"I forgot to say thank you," she said when she had her voice again. The camp dialect had left with the tears. "So thank you. It sounds like I have a job teaching fitness to the galaxy after all, and I have wonderful friends." Ruby raised her beer. "To all of us perfect people, and to our new enterprise—Polyformus Perfectus!"

"Don't pick on my Latin either," she warned Mee-York.

She finished the beer and wiped her face. "Now let's kick some TGIF, diet-drug, human-rule, EarthZone butt!"

"It is amazing," says Bradley H. Sinor, "where one's mind will go when someone you care about is in pain." In this case, it was while sitting in his father's hospital room under circumstances similar to those of the next story's main character. "I would like to think," he continues, "my dad would like this story." I have a hunch he would.

Eleven To Seven
by Bradley H. Sinor

The drug pump ticked steadily away like an old hand-wound pocket watch. Sam Larsen looked up from his newspaper, eyed the dispenser, and then checked his watch.

It had been just under ten minutes since the light on the dispenser had shifted to red. When it shifted to green, in less than a minute, that would mean another dose of Demerol was available.

Mark Larsen, Sam's seventy-five year old father, stirred in the hospital bed.

Sam drew a deep breath. He wanted to do something, anything, to alleviate his father's pain. But all he, or any of the rest of the family, could do was sit there and hit the pain medication button every ten minutes. The drug helped, there was no doubt about that, only Sam felt like there ought to be something more that he could do.

The family had been there for two days. No, it was closer to three, he realized. Thankfully Debbie, Sam's wife, and his cousin Karen had managed to convince his mother to go home around 9:30. Otherwise the stubborn older woman would have remained at her husband's bedside twenty-four hours a day.

"Mom, you need the rest. Go home. I'll stay with him," Sam had told his mother. "And don't try and say that *I* should go home and rest; you need it worse than I do. You may be stubborn and hard-headed, but remember, I get it from both you and Dad. So no matter what, I'll win."

She had laughed and hugged him. "I want you to know," she said, "that you are picking on your old, decrepit mother. Is that any way for a loyal son to act?"

"Mom, you are neither old nor decrepit, and I've heard that line from you since I was two or three years old. Don't you think it's time that you got some new material?"

He'd promised them he would stay only a couple more hours. Right now, this was where he needed to be, for himself as much as for his father's needing him. The older man had been sleeping on and off since early morning, but rarely for more than an hour or two at a time.

It had been early Friday morning, just after six, when they had followed his parents' car on a round-about route to Northwest Memorial Hospital.

"It will be all right," Debbie said.

Sam desperately hoped so. After a lot of effort to save it, the doctor had advised amputation of the lower part of Mark Larsen's leg as the only remaining course. A history of bad circulation, infection and several strokes had made it inevitable.

"It was either this, or the next thing would have been gangrene and that would have killed him," Sam's mother had explained. "The doctor told us everything and then left it up to your Dad. He thought it over for twenty-four hours. It was his decision to make."

The operation had gone well; only about forty-five minutes and they had him in recovery. Another half-hour and he was awake and on the way to a room.

Sam rested his elbow on the chair's arm. At least these were more comfortable than those hard plastic-and-metal things in the surgical waiting room. Whoever had designed *those* didn't seem to understand the concept of comfort.

The wall behind the hospital bed was crisscrossed with shadows. Familiar shapes—bed railings, chairs, a dresser—

were all twisted and formed into other, outsized shapes by the glow coming from the small safety light built into the wall near the floor.

For a long time Sam just sat there, watching the shadows, listening to the pump sound, half-hearing the innumerable hospital sounds that drifted in through the partially-closed door. And, with a precision edge honed by exhaustion, he never missed the scheduled time for the drug button.

"You know, you're not doing him any good if you run yourself into the ground." A short, fat, red-haired woman stood on the other side of the bed. She wore a blue surgical scrub uniform, a laminated ID badge clipped to one pocket. It took Sam several seconds to focus his eyes enough to read her name: Kara Allison, LPN.

"How many times a week do you end up having to give that kind of advice?"

"Maybe five or six at the most." She began to check his father's pulse, first at his wrist and then in the left foot. Sam watched her ever-so-gently hold a stethoscope against the sleeping man's chest.

"Not checking the blood pressure?" Sam asked.

"No need to wake him up right now. I think he's going to sleep pretty well for the rest of the night. Everything else looks pretty good, considering what he's been through." She picked up the medical chart from a nearby table and began to make notes in it.

"I'm glad to hear that. It's been a rough couple of days." Sam nodded toward her ID badge. "Is it pronounced Care-a?"

"That's right."

Sam stared at her for a long time. She seemed to blend into the darkness, all but her eyes. They seemed to pull in what little light there was in the room, reflecting it back in a silver haze.

"I haven't seen you here before," he said. "Have you been working the eleven to seven shift long?"

"Sometimes it seems too long," she sighed. "But I work where I have to, where I'm needed. At least it's a job."

They say that sometimes the human mind can make great intuitive leaps if it's put under the right stress, the right set of pressures. At that moment Sam's did, and all traces of exhaustion fell away from him.

"I think we've met before, haven't we?" he asked.

"Really? This isn't going to be a pickup line now, is it? You know that, in spite of what you saw in all those old Roger Corman drive-in movies, all nurses aren't horny and easy."

"No, it's definitely not a pickup line. I wouldn't try to pick you up."

"Really?" Kara said, sounding slightly offended. "That's what they all say. At least you have the class not to try and secretly slip your wedding ring off."

Sam ran his finger along the edge of his wedding ring, the grooves that made up the Hopi design in it sharp and prominent.

"No, I really don't think that it would be a good idea to try and seriously put any moves on Death."

Kara made a final notation on the chart and returned it to the bedside table. Sam thought he heard a soft sensuous chuckle.

"Death? Me? I have to wonder, Sam, if you've been helping yourself to some of your father's medication. I imagine, in the right amounts, it might be fun. You should have at least offered to share. Who knows, it might have gotten you somewhere."

"No, I doubt that. No drugs. Just a feeling that I have seen you before. At fires, at wrecks, that sort of thing. The faces are different, but that glow in your eyes—it's always the same."

Kara pushed a loose hair back behind her left ear. "You're something pretty special, Mr. Larsen. I've heard a lot of fantasies and been the subject of my share of propositions, but this is an entirely new one."

"So I'm wrong, am I?"

"What do you think?"

"Maybe, maybe not. If I am, then you can just put this down to the raving of a patient's exhausted son," Sam said.

Only he knew he was right. The feeling in his gut had hardened into a certainty with each passing moment. Sam stood up and walked around the bed to face Kara with only the standard, hospital-issue wheeled table between them.

"Now, if I were who you think I am, why do you think I would be here?"

"Don't try to talk to me like I'm an idiot," Sam said gently. "You also don't have to worry, if I'm wrong, about me maybe trying to do something physical."

"That's a relief," she said. "Then let's talk about this. I've got a few minutes. If I am Death, and I'm not claiming that, am I here for him?" She gestured toward the bed.

"That's what I think."

"Or maybe am I here for you? You smoke too much, work too hard, are stressed out to the max and haven't really relaxed since you were around eight years old."

Sam stared at her. A cold breeze wrapped itself around his gut. Every word she had said was dead-on accurate; Debbie had been nagging him about those same things for years. "So how do you know all this about me?"

"Well, I could be, as you suspect, Death itself and, therefore, know everything. Or on the other hand, I could just be extremely observant and able to make some good guesses. You know, the way Sherlock Holmes did."

"If it's me that you've come for, I won't resist. That's fine. But if you're here for him, then I guess we may have to tangle about it," he said.

There was a long silence between them, wrapped in the echoing of a gurney being pushed past the door.

"No, son."

Mark Larsen had raised himself up on his elbow, the light playing over his pale face.

"Dad, relax. You need to rest. Try to go back to sleep. Leave this to me," Sam heard a slight tremor in his own voice as he spoke.

"No. I've been awake for awhile and heard what you've been saying. I know how crazy it sounds, but if you're right, then there isn't a damn thing that either one of us can do about it."

"Dad, I can't let you go like this. Not if there's a chance to change things. You always said a man takes care of his family. I saw you do that quietly every day I was growing up. You never said a lot, you just did it. Now it's my turn."

The older man smiled. "Sam, you've got a lot more ahead of you than I could possibly have ahead of me. If she's come for me, then it's best that you let me go. You think I wouldn't want to spend another fifty years with your mother, provided she could put up with me?"

"But at least this way the pain will be stopped," he continued. "It's been ten years since I wasn't in some kind of pain. There are times it's hurt so much that I've found myself praying to die."

"I know, Dad, I know. It's driven me crazy seeing you like that and wishing I could do something about it."

"I'm proud of you for what you're trying to do." Sam smiled. It helped to hear those words. He knew his father had always been proud of him, but Mark was the kind of man who rarely said things about how he felt. Sam reached over and took Mark's hand, squeezing it tightly. For the first time in a long time, he felt the old strength in his father's hand.

"Kara," he said to the redhead. "You're just going to have to take me as well, if you want him."

She stared at them both, her silver eyes lighting up the room.

"You've got a hell of a son there, Mr. Larsen," she said as she leaned forward and kissed Mark on the cheek. "I suspect he takes after his old man. Listen, I think you two guys have got a lot of talking to do, so I better be getting along." Before either man could speak, Kara turned and headed for the door.

"See you around sometime, fellas," she said sensually.

Kara Allison stood in the hospital snack bar and studied the soda machine. Four of the seven offerings glowed red, i.e., empty. The remaining selections were none too appealing. Well, what did she expect, Kara reminded herself, the wine list at the Ritz Carlton, especially at 2 a.m.?

With a sigh she began to search through her pocket for some change. What she retrieved was a yo-yo, a number of pieces of scrap paper, and a crumpled-up chewing gum package. Wrapped up inside the latter were two quarters and a buffalo head nickel.

This wasn't the first time she'd been recognized. It wouldn't be the last. Only, in this case, being recognized was the whole reason she was there in the first place.

There were other things she did, besides her established duties. Other things that affected people for good or ill.

Oh, she'd be back for Mark Larsen in the not-very-distant future. His son would join her for a walk eventually, as well. But for now they had a chance, a chance to really talk. That was important.

Kara smiled, shoving the quarters into the machine. For less than a heart beat she allowed herself to morph into what most people would have considered her traditional form. A skeleton hand pushed the button for Diet Pepsi—caffeine-free, of course.

"I haven't traveled quite to the edge of the galaxy," says Celeste Allen, "but I've gotten as far as Mongolia—which certainly qualifies as the end of the earth." She further says that the setting and some of the characters that follow evolved over some nine years of amusing herself and a friend with storytelling.

Last Chance Gravity Fill Station by Celeste Allen

"You're going where!?" Two grizzled spacers gawped at me, amazed.

I fought down the glow that showed in my face every time I said the name. "Chengdu Station."

One of the graybeards leaned forward. "Pardon my asking, son, but…what in tarnation for?"

Not the response I'd hoped for. Nevertheless, it was all I could do to keep my chest from swelling when I answered, "You're looking at her new station master."

The gale of laughter which greeted me left me feeling just a tad prickly. Sure, Chengdu Station was situated in the hind end of nowhere, but she was mine.

I'd spent the better part of ten years working my way up through the paper storm to become assistant station master of the regional capital. Unfortunately, since no ranking management close to home showed any signs of relocating, retiring or dying, the only way to be promoted from there was to look to the borderlands for an opening. This warded off most prospective new station masters right away. With the less than enthusiastic stampede to the border, in under a month after putting in my request, WHAM, I'd found myself packing for Chengdu Station, the last bastion of civilization before the hinterlands. And though doing the "wild west" thing had never figured into my game plan, hey: Noburo "Flexibility" Rao, that's me.

The only immediate transport to "Last Chance", as Chengdu Station was colloquially known, was a local. It checked in at every mail stop between Earth and the farthest reaches to pick up or drop off veteran spacers, wide-eyed colonists, military types "secretly" en route to intelligence postings, and a small contingent of ETs heading home after the annual Interspecies Technology Conference.

Over the past six weeks I'd done a fair job of pegging my traveling companions: nailing who might be trouble, who might be a solid information source, who would fall on the right side of the law in an altercation. Now with just four days to go, I'd sat down for a beer with these two coots who looked like maybe they could give me a little scoop on the borderlands.

By the time they stopped laughing, Geezer Number One was wiping tears away. "Boy, don't you know Last Chance is Val Dupre's station?"

My blank look must have given my answer, hopefully without giving away the irritation roiling in my chest. "I don't know this Val Dupre, but Sol Alliance has clear jurisdiction…"

"You don't know Val Dupre?" Geezer Number Two ogled in astonishment. "Of the Baton Rouge Dupres?"

"Ah." My concerns vanished. "I recently met Ambassador Dupre. He…"

"Well, you ain't met his little girl." Number One's hoary head jerked a nod. "Ambassador Dupre disowned her ten year ago."

"Disowned?"

"After she made off with his company's flagship. Went renegade and changed names…hers and the ship's both." Number Two whistled a laugh through gapped teeth. "They call her 'Valkyrie' now."

"And she christened the ship *The Belligerent*."

Valkyrie Dupre I hadn't heard of, but *The Belligerent*…

Sure, unruly aliens, pilfering shuttle pilots, demanding colonists, transient spacers, these I was more than equipped to handle, but nobody back at the home office had ever mentioned pirates. I did a little quick mental reshuffling. I hadn't actually taken possession of the station. Other options would surely come up. Perhaps it wasn't too late to…

What was I thinking! The prize lay before me: my own station. I leveled an unwavering stare on the geezers. "*Belligerent* or no, Chengdu is *not* Val Dupre's station."

"You don't know what took out the last station master, do you, young'un?"

I'd read about the poor woman's disposition. "Family issues."

"Family!" Number Two's jowls billowed with his sputtering laugh. "That fool woman tried to levy a tax on *The Belligerent.* Val Dupre scared her to Theta Tau is what happened."

"And you think Chengdu Station is yours!"

After a few minutes' more ribbing, I sidled away from the old farts to gather my thoughts and plan a strategy. Yet for the remainder of the voyage, I couldn't escape the geezers' half-pitying, half-sneering glances. On the up side, I no longer needed to ply them for information. Every time I walked into the dining area, they flanked me and regaled me with sniggering tales of *The Belligerent* and her lawless crew and captain.

If half their stories were true, my tenure at Chengdu Station could prove to be very trying indeed.

By the time we docked, I'd already checked my incoming correspondence, reviewed the manifests of each ship in port, and memorized the layout of every corridor in the station.

The nickname "Last Chance" derived from the fact that Chengdu was the farthest full gravity facility from the heart of Sol Alliance territory. Everything beyond this station was free-float or "make your own g"—a pricey proposition at best. To "commemorate" the station's unique status, the entrance from the low-g docking arena to the main station boasted a man-sized sign in eight languages: "LAST CHANCE GRAVITY FILL STATION" and its equivalently inaccurate description in the other seven languages.

When the hatch hissed open onto the sharp metallic tang of oils and graphite and canned air, I strode out to the cool damp of condensation rising off the ships, and just this once I stood before the quirky sign, grinning like a fool. I bathed in the clanging, sparking, revving of dock life, the white arcs of welding torches and utility lights. One toe-hold on and I already knew Chengdu Station was "my lady".

A jostle from behind reminded me that I had more to do than gaze on the—admittedly—less than perfect splendor of my prize. So, ever a believer in taking the bull by the proverbial horns, I turned aside and made a beeline for *The Belligerent's* berth.

The ship was mammoth, a converted liner capable of hauling more metric tonnage than, frankly, the law allowed. But I was betting what the law allowed was of no concern to Valkyrie Dupre. I'd found no photo ID or background information about her on record, a common enough practice among criminals and the children of the elite. So as I traversed the perimeter of the ship, I asked after her of the first person I saw—a small, dark, heavily-muscled man with an Angkar Penal Mine tattoo on his neck.

He put down the sputtering soldering gun in his hand, eyed me a moment, then jutted his pointed chin toward *The Belligerent's* open hold, where an extraordinary number of cargo crates were unloading. "By the control booth," he mumbled.

My gaze followed the line of his chin down the dock, up the side of the ship, across the top of an eight-meter stack of crates, and to the crane. There I saw the woman herself.

She was…well…large. I'm no lightweight; my father was a sumo wrestler, my mother a sous chef. I've got big genes. But Valkyrie Dupre was a woman of tremendous proportions. She couldn't have stood less than six feet tall and sported a girth to match. Clearly she had taken her new name to heart, framing her face with two waist-length platinum braids and keeping a weapon strapped to her thigh. At any rate, she did stop shy of the Viking helmet and brass brassiere. And although she had none of the "jolly fat man" about her, she looked appealingly content, operating the crane and directing the stevedores.

She glanced down at my approach and called to her crew, "Take ten." Then she nodded to me. "Welcome to Last Chance Station. I'm Val Dupre. And you would be the young Mr. Rao."

I stopped short.

"No, I'm not clairvoyant, my boy, but my spies are everywhere." She scooped a be-ringed hand toward a stack of crates. "Come, join me." And she pirouetted off the crane and landed nimbly atop the tallest crate, sliding down to sit so the heels of her swinging feet knocked against the universal triple-triangle biohazard symbol.

Not to be outdone, I took advantage of the low-g and clambered up the side of the crates to stand above her on the boxes. Not my best entrance, but I wondered if that was her plan. "Captain Dupre…"

"Sit, please." She patted the spot next to her, and I noticed that, as pirates go, she looked a mere youngster. Certainly no older than I and with laugh-creased seafoam eyes and a full mouth which looked hard-pressed to keep from grinning. "Sit and talk to me, lad."

"Captain Dupre," I squatted down beside her, "you flatter me; I can't imagine you're any older than I."

"Oh, but while you've been behind a desk all your adult life, I've been…well…busy out here."

"About that…"

"Yes, I know all about you. Top of your graduating class, made assistant station master in under ten years—of Nairobi Station, no less. Quite impressive. They say you ran the place while the old man took all the credit. You're no common *schlep*. Nevertheless, we grow up fast here on the border, Master Rao." Was that an intentional dig or just the formal use of title? "So indulge me to see you as my junior."

Her *junior*? At least she didn't say "inferior", although she might as well have. Smiling eyes be damned; the law was going to be laid down here and now. "Allow me to be direct, Captain. I'm given to understand that you are both the source and the controller of all illegal activities here on Chengdu Station." I glanced down at the crates we rested atop and wondered what cargo they held. "I intend to shut down your operations by whatever means necessary, and prosecute any subsequent offenses to the full extent of the law."

Valkyrie's cat smile lacked only the tell-tale tail feathers. "How long did it take you to memorize that speech, lad?"

I sucked my teeth. "You've been warned." I sprung to my feet, climbing down the crates. No graceful exit here either.

"Don't leave in a huff, Master Rao," she called. "I like a person who's straightforward. No skulking or wheedling or backstabbing. I think we could be great friends."

"I'm afraid that's unlikely, Captain Dupre. I *will* investigate you, and I *will* prosecute you."

"Do your damnedest!" And she waved, grinning and still swinging her feet like a child.

For the next week I immersed myself in the requisite duties of a new station master: glad-handing, schmoozing and ingratiating myself to anyone on station who currently had influence, previously had influence, or might potentially have influence in the future, i.e., everyone from grandmas to toddlers.

Daily I strolled through the serpentine corridors of Chengdu Station, meeting and greeting, everywhere feeling the fine grit beneath my boots as the neon-bright lights illuminated dusty storefronts. Minutely faded green-and-white striped awnings hovered over imitation street-side cafes, the aromas of roasting nuts and disinfectant wafting out, mingling with strains of *Aida* and the shriek of machinery. She was a painted lady who'd seen her prime, was my station. But I'd be hanged before I'd let some high-born pirate run her into the ground.

After assuring every law-abiding resident of Chengdu Station that their lives and livelihoods would continue in unhampered prosperity, I settled into reviewing old ordinances, changing routines that hadn't worked for years, enforcing new mandates, and scouring the records for evidence of any crimes I could springboard from in my pursuit of Val Dupre and *The Belligerent.*

Even before I'd gone to meet her, I'd figured Valkyrie Dupre would require more than a little civilized threatening (although I hadn't expected to be patronized). And I'd already decided our next showdown would occur in my office the following week. Now I was letting her sweat a while and try to figure out what I was thinking.

Unfortunately, what I was thinking was that any administrator worth his file cabinets should have been thrilled to get a posting like this. No record of short shipments, shady dealings, not even a bar fight reported in over four years. Chengdu Station read like the model facility. So why was I feeling edgier with each new pristine report? Either the brawling Barbary Coast image I'd gotten of Last Chance Station was sadly askew, or Val Dupre was a master criminal and had the slickest fixers this end of the Milky Way cooking my records.

It was time to arrange that meeting.

Valkyrie Dupre was a woman remarkably difficult to locate when once I'd decided to contact her. *The Belligerent* sat in dock, not scheduled to disembark for another three days, but according to dock security, Dupre hadn't shown her face since the ship's unloading.

After leaving word for her at every local bar and amusement, I finally decided to personally visit her official residence, a suite of rooms over the only source of "fine dining" on station. The restaurant was run by the resident ET, a cold-blood who'd seen one too many antique Maurice Chevalier videos.

I'd dined gratis at *Frenchy's* my first night on station. I liked his rich, exotic cuisine, his vaguely eccentric art nouveau decor, and mostly his jovial come-all attitude. Beyond that, I saw him as a potential friend, and I didn't want our relationship to take an unpleasant turn. When your job entails constantly evaluating people's usefulness, friends are a rare find.

"Noburo!" Frenchy stretched his arms wide as if to embrace me when I strode into the restaurant. "So good to see you again. But we do not serve until the lunch."

I shook his tough hand before he could kiss me on either cheek. "Sorry to say, Frenchy, I'm here on business, not pleasure." Then I asked about Val Dupre.

When he told me she hadn't been home since before *The Belligerent's* last run, I asked, "Captain Dupre couldn't have slipped in and out through the back door without telling you?"

Frenchy hissed out a chuckle. "There is no slipping in and out with Mademoiselle Dupre. She is the model tenant: clean, prompt with the payment, quiet. Oh, the occasional party, but never overly boisterous, and no shenanigans of any kind!"

His combination ET/faux-French accent swallowed the middle two syllables of "shenanigans" so completely, it took me a moment to decipher what he'd said. "Then," I said, "it's possible she has…another residence?"

"Oh!" Frenchy gasped with an audible click of his mandibles. "I will hear none of this kind of talk about Mademoiselle Dupre." He snapped his vest and motioned toward the door. "Please, Monsieur Rao, before I must become displeased, you will leave now."

I sighed, shrugged, dredged up my most winsomely sincere look. "No, Frenchy. As I said, this is business. I'm afraid I won't leave now."

I could see his collar plume battling to inflate as Frenchy pulled himself so straight his long chin nearly grazed his midsection.

"It's not you I don't trust." I patted his cool, pebbly shoulder. "But I will need you to let me into Captain Dupre's apartment…if I'm to continue trusting you."

We ascended to the second story, Frenchy's muttered multi-species curses preceding me. He unlocked the door and stood aside. "I trust you will not disturb Mademoiselle's possessions."

"You can stand here and watch me." I pressed the access panel, and the door slid open…

Onto a perfectly normal three-room suite. No posh decadence, no indulgent extravagance. The only thing that struck me as odd was the enormous open space between the living/dining room and the kitchenette.

Frenchy, clearly following my gaze, said, "Mademoiselle is the dancer *extraordinaire.* Sometimes when she orders the dinner in, I have the orchestra play her favorite songs just so I might see her dancing when I bring her meal up to her."

Although I would be hard pressed to call Frenchy's five-piece band an orchestra, a history of dance certainly explained Dupre's nimble acrobatics on the crates the day we'd met. "You like Val Dupre, huh?" was all I said as I moved further into the apartment.

His small jewel-like eyes sparkled. "Mademoiselle is a treasure. When I arrived at Chengdu Station, she loaned the money to open my restaurant. She is not a bad person, Noburo."

"Huh."

Frenchy followed me as I poked my head through the doors of a quietly understated bedroom and a sparsely furnished office. One seamless meter-and-half slab of malachite composed the tidy desktop. A queen-sized ergonomic chair, suited to fit one queen-sized pirate, was sidled up behind it, but no evidence of anything potentially incriminating lay about. Just as I turned to close the door, I caught the faintest whiff of something not quite perfume. And as I closed the door, it came to me: graphite and oil.

"Please don't lie to me, Frenchy. You know where she is."

"*Non*!" Then after a moment, "Perhaps I could…attempt to get a message to her."

This to go with the thirty other messages I'd sent out for her? "I'll be back for dinner tonight. Perhaps that message could get to her by then?"

"I will try."

If this turned into trouble, I didn't want Frenchy in the middle of it, but he was my only lead so far. I patted his shoulder again. "Thanks…*mon ami*."

Frenchy's boasted "dinner and a show" twice a month, and tonight's show was an ET act from the far edge of the sector: a traditional Travenian dance and music troupe, whatever that entailed. Purely out of curiosity I'd hoped to catch the show, but as I entered the restaurant and saw Frenchy's beetled brow, I wondered if I might just be catching something more.

Even with this afternoon's encounter heavy in the air between us, Frenchy nevertheless greeted me cordially as I passed under the Arc de Triomphe entryway.

"You made contact with Captain Dupre?" I asked as my nose was tickled by scents of coriander and basil wafting out of the kitchen.

"*Oui,* Monsieur Rao. She will see you tonight."

"Tonight?" She'd set the stage again.

"But of course." Frenchy's hissing laugh was nearly lost in the chatter of the restaurant patrons. "Mademoiselle would never miss a dance troupe. She has the special wines and foods imported for every event."

I shook my head. "At least she enjoys life."

"Enjoys? *Mon ami*, she exults!" Then Frenchy turned eyes on me, which were, I'm sure in his species, ardent. "Leave her be, Noburo. She will cause you no harm."

"I just need to talk to her, Frenchy." We'd see what happened after that. I moved into the low-lit restaurant, where Val Dupre waited at a table in the rear. Tonight her platinum braids coiled atop her head like a coronet, held in place by a menagerie of jade hair picks.

"Master Rao!" She extended a hand when she saw me. "You're just in time. The show promises to be exceptional tonight."

"Captain Dupre, I've left messages for you all over Chengdu Station. Now, I require an official interview…"

"Official." Dupre waved a hand. "Please, my boy, we can come to an agreement without doing anything *official*."

I took two steps closer so I pressed my not-inconsequential bulk against the table as I leaned toward her. "The only agreement we can come to is for you to agree to come to my office first thing in the morning."

"Now how would it look for me to be seen going to your office, lad? Be serious."

"I'll have security escort you if necessary. In fact, maybe I'll just have them come now."

"Not before the show!" Her alarm looked genuine.

I reached for my security pager, and Valkyrie Dupre seemed to droop, as if the joke had lost its humor. "Master…Mr. Rao, have you seen any evidence of vice here on Chengdu Station? Gambling, prostitution, illegal substances…litter?"

I opened my mouth, couldn't find an answer.

"If this station was the den of iniquity it's made out to be, don't you think you'd have seen some sign of that by now?"

"What are you saying, Captain Dupre?"

"You haven't found anything on me. And you've exhausted every conceivable information source. I know because I've kept tabs on you."

"A truly adept criminal…"

"Look around, man!" Her gesture swept more than just the room. "It's a ruse. The whole sinister Last Chance Station persona. It's a front I've created to keep my hyper-controlling family out of my hair."

"*The Belligerent...*"

"Has never gone on a raid. We were boarded by privateers twelve years ago, and Daddy thought he'd lost the ship. When he found out I was alive and, worse, he'd have to return the insurance money for the ship, he was livid. Told me he didn't care what I did or where I went as long as it was out of the insurance adjustor's reach. So I gladly gave him his out."

"But those geezers on the transport said..."

"Herbert and Friedrich?" The grin returned. "They're my 'bards'. I pay them to travel around and tell stories. Good, aren't they? And if their stories paint me, my crew, my home in...less than flattering colors, well..." She shrugged. "It keeps the traffic down."

I stood, gaping, a long time before Val said, "This place may have been your first chance to have the life of your own choosing, but it was my last. Now will you sit down and enjoy the show? We can talk about my 'operations' afterwards. Deal, Mr. Rao?"

Finally I closed my mouth and pulled out a chair. "My friends call me Noburo."

And she has ever since.

Selina Rosen says it occurred to her, being a big girl herself, that there was a certain security in carrying a little extra weight. The idea first ended up in a stand-up comedy routine she does.

Nuclear Winter
by Selina Rosen

During the Middle Ages, people used to put on a few extra pounds to help them make it through the long, hard winter months. Fat people lived; skinny people died. It wasn't too hard to figure out.

This is why fat women were so highly regarded during the medieval era. See, even without the aid of modern science, men easily figured out that a fat woman was better than no woman at all, and certainly a dead woman caused all sorts of problems. Not to mention being a real drag at parties.

I'm not saying I've always been happy with my weight. That would be an out and out lie, as well as a sign of total ingratitude. After all, my parents, teachers and peers had worked very hard to make sure I knew that there was something wrong with me, and I wouldn't want them to think I hadn't been listening.

The constant teasing was bad enough, but almost worse was "The Lecture."

No school day, vacation, trip to the grandparents' or summer camp would have been complete without hearing it at least once. The faces associated with it are different, but "The Lecture" was always the same and is engraved indelibly on my brain.

"Jean," (that's me) "Jean," they'd say. "You have such a pretty face. You would be beautiful if you'd just lose a little weight."

Then of course there was the lecture they kept for special occasions, like Thanksgiving and family Christmases. You know, the times when the main event is eating, and you'd just like to—just this once—be left alone to enjoy the day.

"Jean," they'd say, "I don't care what you look like, but what about your health? You're a wonderful person, Jean, and we'd all like to have you around for a very long time."

Then there was the one reserved just for my mother.

"Jean, you'll never find a decent man looking like that."

So, armed with their words of 'encouragement,' I rode off on an exercise bike to wage war against the fat gods. I fought the battle of the bulge with a celery stick in one hand and taste-free dressing in the other. I wrestled my appetite with Jenny Craig, Weight Watchers and—God help me—hypnotherapy.

I'd lose ten pounds and put it back on; lose twenty and gain thirty. I felt frustrated, sick and ugly. I was lonely, unhappy and ashamed.

I'd look at pictures of emaciated models in the latest styles and cringe. Was that really what people wanted me to look like? Did anyone really think I'd look better if I looked as if I had just been released from a concentration camp?

Naturally, none of those clothes would fit me. I was lucky to find anything at all, and finding something the least bit attractive was impossible. Skinny women no doubt did this because they knew there were men who liked large women, and they didn't want to encourage that.

I thought my nightmare would never end.

Then it happened. Whomp! Overnight my whole life changed, and your life could change, too, with these few simple…

Sorry, couldn't help myself.

Anyway, I had this vision. It came to me as I watched a newscast, and suddenly I knew what I had to do. Until that moment, my life had been consumed with torturing myself. That and trying desperately to find a man who wouldn't tell me how lucky I was to have him the first time I complained that he was treating me badly. And I'd been floating from one dead-end job to another without pride or purpose.

But the vision changed everything. I got a good job, bought a house, and started to prepare. I didn't worry about my weight anymore; I cherished it. No longer did I waste my time chasing men who only wanted to use me. I had better things to do.

I bought a computer and started my own web site. In the beginning, I only got a few hits, but in less than a year we had almost a hundred members. Seems I wasn't the only one who saw the writing on the wall. Through the Web, we bridged miles and shared ideas on how to survive the coming ordeal. We made plans.

I made friends I never saw and who liked me just the way I was. I began to wish I'd found the Net years earlier. It's amazing how open and giving people can be when they can't see what you look like.

I didn't horde my information. It was never my plan to play God, choosing who should live and who should die. I wasn't selfish or vindictive. I didn't want anyone to die who didn't have to. I wanted to help as many people as possible, give them a chance to prepare. Toward the end, I would stand on street corners and hand out fliers.

I have to admit that it was sort of nice to be called something besides "fat", although I'm not sure "crazy" was a whole lot better. A couple of times I was even "lucky" enough to hear a muttered "fat, crazy bitch". Police told me to move on. Jesus freaks cursed me. Mostly, people just laughed.

Well, look who's laughing now. And the nice thing about having gone through all that crap is that now I don't have to feel guilty that I knew and didn't tell them. I told them and they didn't listen. I told them and they did nothing and now they're dead and it's not my fault.

See, I told them about the bombs. With all the wacko Third World dictators playing with the atom, it was only a matter of time till someone—let's call them Group A—blew someone—Group B—up. Then Group B retaliated, and Group A bombed Group B again. Then someone else—

Group C—jumped in just because they hadn't gotten to blow anyone up yet. Before they could totally irradiate the planet, we'd have nuclear winter. It's what the scientists had said for years.

When you're going into a long, hard winter, you had better put on a few extra pounds. People in the Middle Ages knew that, but these stupid, "health-conscious," twenty-first century twits didn't have a clue.

I tried to tell them; they just wouldn't listen. Kept telling me I was "unhealthy". Kept screaming thin was in.

Now here I sit eating the last of my MREs — Meals Ready to Eat — and my hoarded Godiva chocolate in my fortified basement, all the skinny people are dead, and it turns out that fat *is* where it's at.

My friends and I have kept in touch over the last five years by CB. Once a week we call a different person on the list. This way we know basically how everyone's doing.

Poor Stanley was at ground zero in New York. Cindy and Mike both succumbed to radiation sickness. A couple of the thinner members of our group couldn't handle the isolation, and they went nuts and killed themselves. At least that's what we figure happened, based on their last transmissions and the subsequent lack of communication. See, thin people aren't cut out for isolation. They aren't used to being excluded from the loop. Fat people…well, some of us have spent our whole life isolated.

When we rebuild the world, it will be different. People of size will be the norm. Skinny people will be seen as perverse. We'll make attractive clothes in only large sizes, chairs that are sturdy and wide enough, and bathroom stalls big enough for a real person to pull their pants down in. Fat-free will be available by prescription only.

I had to ration my food—after all, five years is a long time—so I lost a little weight. But, hey! The snow is melting and the sun is out. Think I'll poke my head out and go looking for some food.

The character of Fat Moriah in this next story is based on a modern card sharp Patrice Sarath encountered on a casino cruise. According to Patrice, "the lessons in three-card monte left an indelible impression."

The Djinn Game
by Patrice E. Sarath

When night fell on Jubai, the bazaar woke, throwing off its dowdy daytime guise and stepping into finery. Its thousands of glass lanterns, their light reflecting off the greasy water of the harbor, dazzled with their brilliance, and merrymakers thronged the market square eager for excitement.

As always, a crowd gathered in front of Fat Moriah's card table. Keeping one eye out for the guard and the other on the likeliest marks, the big woman shuffled the ancient pack of cards with nimble fingers beringed with intricate jewelry. The cards whuffled and thumped as she fanned them out, made a bridge between her palms, and divided the deck one-handed.

"Tell a fortune, Fat Moriah!" cried a reveler, a weaselly wharf dweller who survived as a thief's accomplice. The card sharp shook her tousled curls and chuckled slyly, unable to resist a dig.

"Oh, I think we all know where *you're* going to end up, Tanco," she cracked, and the crowd laughed heartily. Moriah made the deck disappear and reappear on the table, her namesake queen of spades face up. She allowed the cards to linger for an eyeblink, then swept them up again. "Fortunes, my friend, are made, not told. And the fortune you made yesterday…" she displayed the swan of coins, "will be told by the watch tomorrow."

The crowd cheered and catcalled as the deck thumped down with a flourish and the top card fell to the table face up. The jack of swords. Tanco made a face.

At the back of the crowd, Moriah saw the usual suspects take advantage of the audience's concentration to lift a few wallets. The wharf rat would be paid more than his normal pittance for his work tonight. Fat Moriah passed her hand over the cards, and the deck disappeared once more. "But in the end, Tanco, we come back to the beginning, where all fortunes are the same, rich or poor."

She split the deck one-handed to reveal the hanging man, and the crowd cheered in mordant appreciation. None of this was making her any money, however, so Moriah briskly bent three cards and scattered them face down on her table. She scanned the crowd and winked at a rawboned farm boy in uniform.

"Find the dark lady, young lord?" Moriah flattered, grinning invitingly. The chest of the upcountry boy swelled; he bet extravagantly. She flipped up a card to reveal the queen of spades, made sure her mark had his eye on it, turned it over and began moving the cards with breathtaking speed. The boy's eyes darted back and forth as he followed the card through its travels on the table. He bit his lip with concentration; even the tips of his ears flushed.

At length her hands came to rest. She beamed up at the young soldier. The crowd cried out their picks ("Left!" "Right!" "Middle!") and he hesitated, need warring with fear in his expression. Finally, his hand darted out and he turned over the middle card.

A deuce. The crowd "aahed" with mock sympathy; some outright laughed. The soldier's face reddened. He reached out to sweep over the remaining cards, but Fat Moriah was faster, gathering them up just out of his reach.

"Game's over, sir," she told him lightly, and the boy let out a curse, obviously one just learned in the barracks.

"You filthy…!" he cried out, his voice climbing. "I want my money back. The devil was in those cards!"

The crowd grew quiet; accusing Fat Moriah of fixing cards was unwise. But the big woman never argued with the self-righteous. She looked away as if dismissing him and shuffled the cards once more, the bent ones disappearing into the deck. The boy reached out and pushed her. Moriah took a step backward and locked eyes with him, no longer laughing.

"Go home, boy," she said, openly contemptuous. "Come back when you can take on Fat Moriah."

For a moment all hung in balance, and then a shrill whistle signaled the approach of the guard. The young soldier's friends hastily dragged him off, and the hole left by their departure filled in with new onlookers. The soldier's voice rose sharply above the buzz of the crowd as he was marched off. "The devil was in those cards! It was the middle one all along! She cheated!"

Fat Moriah scooped up the cards with a flourish, smiling cheerfully at the large man who had taken the boy's place. Then her smile faltered. Moriah stared into his intense eyes, obsidian-black in a pale-bronze face. Lamplight gleamed off his bald head and winked from the jewel set in one large ear. He wore loose trousers, his broad chest bare to the chill night air. A djinn.

In the face of true magic, the crowd prudently dispersed, pushing at each other with barely controlled panic.

"I propose another game," the djinn intoned. "For higher stakes."

"Name them," she said, her voice steady. Fat Moriah did not frighten easily or for long, but when he smiled, exposing large, even teeth, she swallowed hard.

"Servitude," he replied, lingering over the word. "If I win, you are mine. And if you win…"

Promise suffused the unfinished sentence, and she flushed. "What would I do with you for a servant?" she managed to scoff.

His teeth gleamed in the torchlight from the market stalls, less a smile than a threat. He leaned over the table and whispered in her ear, his deep voice soft as a lover's kiss. "What would you *not* do?"

He stepped back and raised an arm, shouting a harsh word. Instantly a whirlwind rose up from the cobblestones, pulling together detritus from the alleys and the booths, and spun off madly down the square. Caught by his storm, distant onlookers screamed and fled. Moriah's hair flapped wildly in her face and the wind scattered her cards like autumn leaves. Panicked, she jumped up, but he called the storm to an abrupt halt and, with a snap of his fingers, summoned the cards helter-skelter backward into his hand.

Gallantly he offered her the tidy deck. "If you win," he said, "that power is yours."

"No offense, my lord djinn, but why me?" she asked. "I don't think a fine magician as yourself can gain anything from a poor card shar…entertainer like me."

"You are the best card player in the city. I only play the best."

She of all people knew flattery when she heard it. For an instant Moriah's practiced smile revealed a truer expression, wry and charming, that would have astonished any wharf-dweller who saw it. Then she got herself under control.

"And if I say no?" she asked.

His smile turned urbane. "Then life goes on in Jubai. The card sharp takes up her spot in the market and shuffles her deck, and all the while her hands slow and her eyes and spirit dim."

Moriah winced involuntarily at the hopeless future he presented her. The bazaar was not kind to the weak, she knew. She thought of the small lockbox hidden in her hovel, its trove of coins suddenly pitifully inadequate. It would never be enough, she saw now, for her to escape the cruelty of Jubai. She was her own worst mark for believing it.

She looked up and met the djinn's black gaze, wondering suddenly at the source of her despair. *What thoughts have you put in my head, djinn?* she asked silently. No matter. It would be a cruel thing indeed if she were to turn down his offer and wonder, always wonder, if her bleak fate had been his doing or her own.

"My terms," she said at length. He inclined his head. "If I win, you become the devil in my cards, to do my bidding and become my accomplice."

For a barely perceptible moment, his slanted brows rose in surprise. Then once again he nodded graciously.

"As you wish, *noble lady*," he said, taunting her with her own patter. With a snap of his fingers, the djinn summoned a sumptuous hassock from nowhere and sat down. Briskly he shuffled and thumped the deck on the table. She tapped it fatalistically, and he swept up the cards and began to deal.

It was an unfamiliar game. He dealt out ten cards each, setting the remainder of the deck between them, a jack of coins face up. He explained the rules succinctly; each player's goal was to end up with a hand of two sets of three of a kind and either one set of four of a kind or a straight.

She could use the jack. But Fat Moriah quickly surmised that picking from the discard pile too soon would reveal which cards she needed. She drew from the deck. A deuce. Nothing. Moriah discarded and settled down to play for her life. If I am to win, she thought, there must be more than one game being played here.

For a while they played in silence, the only sound the slapping of the cards. A slight breeze from the harbor swirled around them, tugging at Moriah's curly mane. Though the wind had an edge to it, she could see it had no effect on the djinn's naked torso.

"Are you not cold?" she asked with sweet solicitousness. He grunted, scowling at the cards in his hand, another creature now the game had begun.

"I find it refreshing," he said tersely.

"Because I would think after coming from…there, it would be uncomfortable," she went on.

He said nothing, discarding a seven of wands.

"What is it like?" she asked, drawing.

He looked at her over his fanned cards. "What?"

"What is it like? It is your home, after all. I'm just curious."

"I know what you're doing," the djinn said. "It will not work. Play in silence or suffer the consequences."

"I am not doing anything," she protested, fearing her words were all too true.

"You wish to distract me. You think your inane prattle will make me lose my concentration. As I said, you will fail. Your only hope..." he leered, "is to win." He let his gaze linger over her. Moriah reddened and the djinn smiled cruelly, aware that she was snared by the promise of lust even though she had to know better. If she lost, there would be no romp of passion with this demon.

If? How many mortals won a duel of wits with a devil?

How many devils had played Moriah? she thought stoutly.

"As you wish, my lord," she said obediently. A moment later, she hid her smile behind her cards. He caught her expression and scowled.

They played without speaking until finally he snapped, "Well? What is it?"

Moriah jumped. "What is what?" she asked.

"Why are you smiling? Answer quickly! It's almost as bad as..." he caught himself before admitting the rest.

"Are you sure? Because I know you said that my talking distracted you and I didn't want..."

"I am not distracted by your talking!" the djinn shouted. "Do as I command! Tell me why you are smiling!"

Moriah, whose expression at that point was one of open-jawed astonishment, looked innocently bewildered.

"I...I'm smiling?"

The djinn rose from his hassock, his body swelling like a sail before the wind. His muscles bulged, his eyes glowed red, a stench of sulfur emanated from his body. Moriah shrank back. "Answer me!" he thundered, his voice so hollow and distorted it sounded as if it came from the earth's bowels. Moriah held her hands over her ears. The air in the bazaar roared around her head and she squinted up at the djinn, now enormous in his fury.

Moriah spoke fast. "My lord, I do not mean to anger you!" she cried, her puny voice barely heard over the raging elements around her. "If I do not please you, it is not because of any malice on my part. Surely you understand that, in my position, I do not wish to displease one who will undoubtedly have a great effect on the comfort in which I spend the rest of my life. I ask for your forgiveness and beg of you to excuse my dull wit that I cannot give you the answer you require." She bowed her head, not even sure he heard any or all of her speech.

After a long moment the storm abated, and soon Moriah could hear the blood pounding in her temples. She dared to look up, and saw the djinn, still swollen in his rage, eyeing her contemplatively. Gradually he diminished until he held his former shape and size. Only his eyes still glowed. He regarded Moriah with cruel pity.

"Poor frail creature," he rumbled, and he reached out and cupped her chin in one large hand. "So frightened. But I can be lenient as well as terrible; let me give you a taste of what you crave."

He leaned forward and brought his warm lips to hers. Moriah braced herself, but it did not prepare her for the blast of sulfur that invaded her mouth. Gagging, she twisted to get away. After a moment he allowed her to escape, and she bent over and took in great, whooping breaths, struggling for air. The djinn watched, his amused eyes black as before.

"Now," he urged when she was able to breathe again. "Tell me…why were you smiling?"

"I was only thinking," she said hoarsely, "about the mischief we could make together, with you as the devil in my cards." She wiped her mouth with the ends of her shawl. He mulled that over for a moment, his wicked chuckle almost human.

"We could, couldn't we?" He grinned. "What did you have in mind?"

But Moriah smiled shakily in return, tossing her unruly curls. "Oh no, my lord, you have to lose to find that out."

His lips tightened, and for a moment she was afraid she had tried his temper again. But the djinn relaxed and inclined his bald head elegantly.

"I concede the point, though not the game," he said, and laid out his hand.

Three eights, three queens, four sixes. Moriah's stomach lurched. She folded her cards and laid them face down on the table.

Woman and djinn looked at one another.

"I confess," he said at last, "to a certain boredom with this outcome." He shrugged. "You will have to amuse me for a time."

Moriah raked up the cards and handed him the deck. "Well then, best two out of three," she said to his puzzled expression. "Here's your chance to lose."

He looked as if he were about to object, then leaned forward and began to shuffle. "You are brazen," he said, half-admiringly. "You have more fire than most lords, streetwoman."

"I am not a streetwoman," she said, irritated despite her best intentions. The edge in her voice was clear. The djinn raised his brow sardonically even as he put up his hands to signify surrender. Moriah rose to her feet, only partly acting.

"Do not patronize me, *djinn*," she said, her voice shaking with rage. "Just because you see before you a woman of no property does not mean she sells her body to survive. I live by my wits and the cleverness of my hands, and I answer to no man—or devil—for my life."

He folded his arms over his chest, leaning back as he regarded her in her fury. "I do not mean to anger you," he replied at last with a smug smile. "If I do not please you, it is not because of any malice on my part. Surely you understand that I do not wish to displease one who will undoubtedly have a great effect on the comfort in which I spend the rest of my life."

Moriah glared, but in the face of his parody, her mouth twitched in a grudging smile. He could see her struggle to hold back her amusement, and his grin widened. For a moment, they exchanged knowing looks, then, with a start, Moriah came to her senses.

"You would do well to remember that," she snapped, and he conceded with a graceful nod and began to deal.

Reprieved, she thought, as she gathered up her cards. She had been lucky, and that, more than anything, sharpened her sense of survival. *I've been playing like a mark*, she told herself scornfully. Relying on luck that way…it had to stop. She could not afford to lose a second time. She was a card sharp; she did not play for the enjoyment of it.

But he does, a little voice whispered in her brain. She kept her expression bland as she sorted her hand. The djinn was a dedicated amateur, nothing more. *And he cannot read minds*, she thought. Her experiment in testing his temper had proved that. Her extra deck, conveniently concealed by her long sleeves, burned against her wrist.

This time, Moriah adopted a more reckless strategy for game two, drawing and discarding seemingly at random. It unnerved the djinn, she could tell, when for the fourth time in a row, she drew one of his discards and tossed down another she had picked previously.

The djinn moved restlessly on his hassock. "Why…" he began, then almost bit his tongue to keep from continuing.

"What, my lord?" she asked obediently.

"Nothing," he snapped. He waved a hand curtly. "Just play." With an obvious effort, the djinn changed the subject. "So, if you win, what amusements do you have to keep me from boredom?" he asked, sorting his hand.

"As I said, there is but one way to find that out."

"Very clever," he said approvingly. "But really, did I forget to tell you? I never lose."

"Then you are in for a treat," Moriah replied, adjusting her hand. She needed only one more card and decided for the sake of appearances to draw it from the deck on the table. With all her will, she kept her expression bland. "But there are plenty of people on the waterfront who can tell you what it's like."

"Oh that's right; you had a winning streak, too, didn't you?" The djinn grinned, drawing and discarding. "But that's all over now, isn't it?"

Time slowed as she picked up his discard.

"Oh, not yet," she managed finally, and presented her hand, looking him straight in the eye but hardly daring to breathe. If he suspected anything, now would be the time he would speak. The djinn stared darkly at her for a moment, then threw his cards in a petty fit. They skidded off the table onto the ground. The blood pounding in her ears, Moriah drew herself up. *He doesn't know. He doesn't know*!

"Those are my cards," she said primly. The djinn made a nasty face and snapped his fingers. The cards flew back onto the table. Moriah scooped them together and shuffled, and he cut them in grim silence.

Fog rolled in off the waterfront, a drifting curtain that muffled sight and sound. Water lapped against the docks, the sound seeming to originate almost at their feet in the distorted air. A ship's mournful horn bleated the hour from somewhere in the mouth of the harbor.

Moriah shivered, her curly hair plastered to her head and moisture dripping from her temples. "Bone fog," she murmured, drawing her threadbare scarf tighter around her shoulders. The djinn eyed her over his cards. "The fog is so cold and wet, it cuts to the bone," she explained. "And some people call it that because it is the kind of fog that settles around old graves." The djinn grunted, unimpressed. He gestured sharply, and a warm shawl draped itself over Moriah's shoulders. Startled, she drew it over her head, not sure what to make of his kindness but grateful for it nonetheless. "Thank…thank you," she said uncertainly.

"I would think you would all welcome death to rid yourselves of such uncomfortable lives," he said acidly. "Bone fog, indeed! If you are born in squalor, you suffer, sicken and die. If you are born in privilege, you go out of your way to find suffering, disease and death. I see no difference in your little lives, no great variety that would justify your meaningless existences."

"Of course, djinn such as you live - *exist* - in such grandeur," Moriah replied sweetly. "I can imagine all the infinite variety of flame and yet more flame. I wonder that you could even drag yourself away to come and play a game of cards."

The djinn grew thunderous. With all her self-control, Moriah continued to fuss over her cards, trying to keep from looking up. She knew if she saw his eyes glowing, it would break her.

"You see us as nothing but demons," he growled. "Though our existence follows a different course from your own pitiful lives, you can neither understand nor appreciate the vast realm in which we live." He stopped and smiled maliciously. "Though you will learn. Oh yes, you will learn."

Moriah collapsed her hand. "But I don't understand why you came to *me*," she protested, leaning forward earnestly. "If your life, if it can be called that, is so fulfilling, why come here and torment me?"

He cocked his head. "It is a diversion," he admitted. "Usually we do our wickedness at the bidding of our master. At other times, we are let free to do our own will. Where would you people be, otherwise, if mischief did not now and again come into your lives?"

"We make our own, thank you," she said.

He laughed. "But admit it, you are enjoying this. Look at you. You have something to fight for now, and you are playing better than you ever have against those miserable cretins in the bazaar."

She stared down at her cards, torn between fury and laughter. So her soul was worth only how well she played to protect it. A duel of wits? In a way, she had to agree, though not for the reasons the djinn might think. With great deliberation she drew, then folded her cards, laying them face down on the table under her hand. The djinn's eyebrow rose.

"We both know," she said, keeping her hand where it was, "that this is the deciding hand. The game ends, and one of us enters servitude tonight. But who?"

He snorted. "Delaying tactics, Moriah? Surely you can do better than that."

For answer, she flipped a card, turning up a king of flame-red hearts.

The djinn cast his eyes skyward. "Do go on," he said with elaborate politeness. With measured cadence she turned three more kings and three sevens. Now only three cards lay face down.

The djinn stared. "Turn them all over! Now!" he shouted.

For answer she flipped another card, her eyes intent upon his. A queen of hearts.

And flipped another. A queen of diamonds.

He grabbed her wrist. For a moment all was still in the glow of his magical light.

"Shall I turn it over?" she asked. "Or do you wish to call off our wager?"

His grip tightened, and his eyes flickered between black and flame. "No. You will not play me the way you play those poor fools in the marketplace. I warn you, Moriah, do not try to bluff me. It will only make your fate worse."

She held his gaze with her own stonelike one and slowly took her hand away.

He looked at the card as if he had never seen one before, need warring with fear. His hand reached out, darted back, reached out again. He turned it over.

The queen of spades.

For a moment all was silent, and then his scream shattered the air. She cowered beneath its onslaught. The djinn continued howling even as he collapsed in on himself and disappeared with a pop of displaced air. The hassock thumped to the ground.

She got to her feet, swaying with weariness. As she gathered up her cards, one began to wiggle, then slide as she put her hand on it. Moriah gave a tired shriek and darted backward. The card fell to the ground.

"Watch out!" a tiny voice cried. Moriah reached down and turned it over. From the beribboned finery of the jack of hearts, the djinn glared out at her, his bald pate shining amid the roses and flowers of the jack's costume. She brought the card up to her face.

"This isn't over yet, Moriah," he said viciously, his voice as high-pitched as a lapdog's. "I don't know how you won, but I promise you, when I find out, you'll live to regret it."

She laughed. It felt good. "I won, *djinn*, because I don't play cards for amusement, as you do. I play for keeps."

The fury in his eyes belied his gay clothes. "Let me go."

She shook her head. "And give up the devil in my cards? I don't think so. You agreed to the terms, now you must abide by them. And look on the bright side; it's not the eternal flames of hell, but at least you won't be bored."

The djinn tried to summon a great fit of rage, but Moriah only put him face down on the table. His anger turned into squeals of shock. "I can't see! Turn me over!"

Ignoring his complaints, she threw her second deck into the gutter, kicking debris over the evidence. It would not do for the djinn to find out how she had helped her luck along.

The sound of slamming shutters caught her attention. The marketplace was waking, the merchants preparing their stalls. Fat Moriah tucked the cards inside her bodice, muffling the djinn's protests. She tapped her chest smartly, ignoring the miniature *oof!* let out by the jack.

"Hush," she said *sotto voce.* "It's time to go."

An awed crowd began to gather, drawn by the sight of the djinn's abandoned hassock, the scattered cards, and the bleary-eyed card player whom no one had ever seen in the market at that hour before.

Moriah felt at peace. Now she had the devil in her cards she had asked for, and she was ready for bigger marks than the poor fools looking for entertainment in the marketplace. No more scrabbling for crumbs. No more keeping an eye out for the guard.

With an easy smile that belied her exhaustion, Moriah turned to go. The crowd parted, and she made her way to her little hovel on the edge of the market. She could feel their eyes on her and knew that, come nightfall, the stories would be flying about the marketplace thicker than moths around lamplight. All to the good, she thought; her new reputation could only enhance her take.

Fat Moriah's smile widened. Come, she told herself. Let the games begin.

Barbara Krasnoff once lived in a small apartment across the street from where a group of women gathered every evening it wasn't too wet or too cold. "They were," she tells us, "the kind of Brooklynites about whom jokes are made—loud, nosy, opinionated, in cheap housecoats and stiff bleached hair—but they were comfortable with themselves and their world." She began to wonder whether there was more to these women than met the eye, and the result follows.

Stoop Ladies
By Barbara Krasnoff

This is the way the world ends, Lisha reads. *Not with a bang but a whimper.* She lifts her eyes from T.S. Eliot's poem to a puffed-up pigeon grooming itself on the windowsill. "That's me," she tells the pigeon. "They fired me, and all I could do was whimper." A typical Brooklyn bird, it doesn't seem particularly interested.

A high cackle bounces into the room from across the street. The pigeon flaps anxiously away while Lisha peers outside.

The ladies have gathered.

Every summer evening, after the dishes are done and their men placed safely in front of the television set, they sit in the small yard next to the stoop, some on folding chairs and others on the concrete steps. The youngest in her fifties, the oldest past eighty, they watch the passersby and talk of schools and children, of changes in the neighborhood, of the new theater on the corner and the cops who ticket double-parked cars.

On her way home from the subway every evening, Lisha usually nods to the ladies as she goes home to chicken-and-rice or a pizza from the restaurant on the corner. Although they nod back, and even wave their hands in invitation, she can't bring herself to actually cross and join the crowd of elderly, gossiping women. It's bad enough, she tells herself, that she has to work so hard to be accepted by the beautiful, thin executives at her office or the well-dressed middle-aged men at the bars, who look past her without even focusing. She's not going to associate herself with a group of obvious losers, blue-haired women past their prime. That would be admitting defeat. Admitting that her life is over after never having happened.

Although, Lisha sometimes concedes to herself, the few times she actually let the voices draw her from her solitude, the ladies made her welcome. And it was pleasant, standing around with people who actually talked to her as if she was important and asked for her sympathy and advice on stolen cars, misbehaving computers, children going astray…

Her beeper buzzes at her; she pulls it quickly from her belt and checks the message. *No luck so far*, it reads. *Will try to talk to Sam. Stay cool. Ginnie.*

The hell with it. Lisha turns on the TV and flips through the channels for a few moments, finally settling for a sitcom in which a man tries to avoid an oversexed, overweight, badly dressed secretary. But the chatter from outside pushes past the canned laughter and demands her attention. Lisha sighs, leaves the bedroom and goes into her tiny kitchen. I'll make myself a snack, she tells herself, but halfway through a lettuce and tomato sandwich she changes her mind, pulls the half-full garbage bag out of its plastic can, ties the ends, and takes it out her front door and down the steps.

On the bottom landing she passes Mrs. Golini's door. Living one on top of the other, both she and her landlady have maintained a respectful distance. They smile hello and exchange holiday gifts at Christmas, and ignore each other's existence the rest of the year.

Outside, a slight breeze eases the summer humidity. Lisha drops her garbage in one of the cans at the side of the stairs and glances surreptitiously across the street. Six of the ladies are out tonight. Lisha glances up at her windows where the blue light of the television reflects off her shades. The loneliness of the evening is nearly overwhelming. Slowly, almost without thinking, Lisha turns her back on her building and crosses the street. "Hi," she says tentatively.

The women smile at her. "We were wondering when you'd come over again," says Mrs. O'Neill, sitting comfortably in her wheelchair. The wheelchair is more for convenience than necessity; after breaking her hip two years ago, she decided that it was more comfortable than her folding chair and told the hospital authorities it had been stolen. As usual, she wears an old, threadbare pink sweater over a long flowered housedress; her chubby bare feet are pushed into an old pair of slippers.

"We even took penny bets on it," grins Jackie, a part-time beautician who works in the hair salon around the corner. She rests one hip against the railing, a cigarette dangling loosely from her wide, sardonic mouth. "I won."

Lisha smiles back. The night is pleasant and cool; a few cicadas vibrate in a neighboring tree.

"Come sit," one of the women— a thin, dry lady named Norma—says, patting the step beside her.

Lisha shakes her head. "That's okay," she replies. "I prefer to stand."

Mary, a pleasant bleached blonde who can sometimes be heard yelling down the block for her teenage son, nods at her. She is, as usual, sitting next to Mrs. O'Neill on a small cloth director's chair. "How are you, Lisha?" she asks in a voice tinged with the Irish accents of her childhood.

Lisha shrugs. "Fine," she says. In her loose green tee shirt, sweat pants and old sneakers, she feels a little underdressed next to Mary's careful polyester fashion.

"Have you found a new job yet?" asks Mrs. O'Neill.

"Why is she looking for a job?" demands another woman whom Lisha doesn't know, a withered form in a bright pink jogging suit, who sits comfortably crocheting in an old blue folding chair.

"That's my older sister Myra," explains Mrs. O'Neill, not bothering to look at her sibling. "She's staying with me for a couple of days while her house is painted." She sniffs. "Of course, if it were me, I'd want to supervise their every move. You never know what painters are up to."

Myra doesn't seem bothered by her sister's apparent contempt. "My husband Joe is perfectly capable of watching the painters," she says. "No reason why I need to put up with the mess and smell if he's willing to." She looks back at Lisha, inquiring.

"They laid me off," Lisha tells her.

There is a general murmur of sympathy. "That's too bad," says Mary. "You were there a long time, too, weren't you?"

"Seventeen years. They said they had to cut back on the payroll in my division."

"I hear a 'but' in there," says Myra, a knowing tone in her voice.

Lisha shrugs. "Sam, my boss, hired an 'assistant' for me about two months ago—young woman, right out of college—and somehow she's being kept on while I'm being let go. He said it was because they had to eliminate some of the higher-salaried workers." She pauses. This is where her listeners usually change the subject or offer vague reassurances.

"But you don't think that's the whole story," Mary prompts. The others look on expectantly, their faces friendly, sympathetic. Lisha feels something rise to her throat.

"No," she finally says. "The company is one of the major PR organizations around for technical corporations. When we started out, we were small, taking whatever clients we could get, but now we've got offices on both coasts and handle a lot of the biggest companies around. We had a meeting last month, and Sam told us that we were going on to the 'next plateau of success'—he talks that way—and that we were going to have to refine our image in order to pick up more Fortune 500 firms." She takes a breath. "I think that a size 16 PR representative doesn't quite fit into that image."

There is a moment of silence.

Mrs. O'Neill finally snorts, something between a laugh and a sneeze. "Well, never mind," she says, and launches into a long explanation of how the oldest son of a distant relative was fired, found another job through some kind of vaguely illegal connection, and was eventually rehired into a higher level of his former company. Lisha soon loses the gist of it, but the sound of the narrative and the murmurs of the listeners are strangely soothing in the fading light. It's as if all of them are caught in some old-time photograph that will never change: just the ladies, and the street, and the summer evening.

Mrs. O'Neill finishes her story. "You don't think that something like that could happen to you?" she asks. Lisha, startled into awareness by the question, shrugs.

"No. A friend of mine said that she's going to ask around, see if there's anything she can find out that might get me back in, but we both know that it's pretty useless. And in today's market, not too many other firms will have openings either. I'll probably have to look into relocating."

"You know," calls out Bev, whose considerable girth is comfortably draped in a loud muumuu, and who has been busily filing her nails, "it's too bad that companies like yours consider a few pounds to be some kind of crime against humanity. When I worked for that Greek travel agency, they were grateful to have somebody as good as I was."

"I remember that agency." Jackie says. "Went out of business. didn't they? Something about the Department of Immigration?"

Bev scowls and returns her attention to her nails. Mrs. O'Neill cackles and turns to Norma. "What do you think?" she asks. "Is this a wine occasion?"

For a moment, the ladies are quiet. Lisha looks from one to the other, but they all seem otherwise occupied, pulling at stray threads or lighting cigarettes. Norma finally shrugs. "Why not? It's been too long since we treated ourselves."

Jackie clears her throat. "I have a box of wine that I picked up today," she says. "I'll just go and get it." There is a general murmur of approval. Jackie stretches slowly and ambles down the block to her house.

Rusting metal squeaks as Mrs. O'Neill pulls herself awkwardly from her wheelchair. "These bugs are driving me crazy," she announces. "I'm going to get that bad-smelling candle my son sent me. He said that it would keep the mosquitoes away." She shuffles slowly back to the door that leads to her ground-floor apartment.

A car bounces along the street, its suspension badly in need of repair. "I hope he breaks an axle," Bev says, irritated. "That's what he gets for going so fast. On a block with children, too."

"Do you have any children, Lisha?" asks Myra. Lisha shakes her head. "But she still could," says Mary. "Couldn't you?"

Lisha hates conversations like this. "I could, I guess. It's not very likely though. I mean, I'm nearly forty-seven. It's not as though I've got much longer to go."

"No." The listening women nod noncommittally.

"Don't worry," Mary tells her. "The menopause isn't so bad. At worst, it's a pain in the butt for a year or so. Then you don't have to worry about it again. And there are other things you can do then. New things."

Lisha nods again but looks away. It's fine for her, a middle-class woman with a house and a 13-year-old son. I've got nothing. Nobody. Unless you count a mother who still sends me articles on diets, and friends who try to set me up with geeks.

Just cut the crap, she reminds herself sternly. Your friends mean well. And what does Mary have that you want so much? A divorce, a mortgage, and an adolescent? So stop pitying yourself and get on with it.

"Here we go, ladies." Jackie ambles back up with a large cardboard box labeled *Chablis*. She places it on one of the steps. Mary gets up and goes into the house, returning a couple of minutes later with a package of paper cups in one hand and a large bag of popcorn in the other.

Jackie takes the paper cups and starts filling them and handing them around. Mary offers Lisha the popcorn bag. "Open this, would you?"

"So," asks Myra, "what was the name of that company of yours?"

"Caesar Communications," says Lisha through her teeth, trying to pull the stubborn plastic apart.

"Interesting name," says Mrs. O'Neill, slowly lowering herself back into her wheelchair. She is holding a small candle in a jelly jar, which she balances on the armrest. "In the city?"

"Yes," Lisha mutters. The bag finally splits open. "Mid-town." She takes a handful of popcorn and gives the bag to Mrs. O'Neill.

"It's too bad that you need to move. But you should find something."

Lisha accepts a cup and sips cautiously. Not as bad as she expected.

A small gray cat ambles out from under one of the parked cars on the street and stops, regarding the group of people with a surprising lack of fear. Lisha, who is still standing outside the area railing—and who likes cats—kneels slowly down, trying not to alarm the animal, and holds out the hand with the popcorn. Above her, the conversation goes comfortably on.

The cat stops and stares at her for a few moments. It then ventures carefully forward, bright green eyes flickering warily from her face to the food.

"Do cats eat popcorn?" Jackie asks above her.

"My sister had a cat once would eat lettuce," Bev says. There is the quiet flick of a lighter and a faint acrid smell—the candle?—tickles her nose slightly.

"You had a cat once, didn't you?" asks Mary. Lisha nods carefully, trying not to alarm the animal. "Yes," she says.

The cat doesn't seem to mind her voice; it continues to edge closer. "Darwin. He died about four years ago."

"Why didn't you get another?" Norma asks.

"Mrs. Golini doesn't like cats. She told me once that she couldn't ask me to get rid of the one I had, but after Darwin died, she didn't want any more in the house."

"Pity," Mary comments.

Lisha nods. "Come on, cat," she whispers as the animal slowly edges up to her hand. "Come on. I won't hurt you."

It stares up at her, down at the popcorn.

"It would be a pity if you left the neighborhood," says Mary. "Just when we were starting to really get acquainted. We would miss you at our little gatherings. We'd like you to sit with us regularly."

"We would, indeed," says Jackie.

"We would," echoes Myra.

"It would be a blessing if your company decided to keep you on," says Norma.

"A real blessing," Bev agrees.

"A blessing," Mrs. O'Neill whispers and then hums, a strange, singsong murmur that Lisha can't quite catch. Her attention turns back to the animal.

It stretches out its neck, carefully sniffs at her fingertips. "That's it, cat," says Lisha as, having finally decided that her offering is acceptable, it begins nibbling at the popcorn. Lisha, charmed, places her cup on the ground, reaches over, and gently scratches the animal's soft head. For a few seconds, there is nothing in Lisha's world but the quiet purring of the cat trembling against her fingers.

A sudden hiss from behind her. Startled, Lisha looks up. A small gray wisp of smoke curls up from the extinguished flame. "Oh, dear," said Mrs. O'Neill. "Now look what I've done. Spilled my wine. And right on the candle, too."

"Don't worry about it," Jackie says. "Plenty more where that came from."

The cat quickly turns and scoots off. Lisha reaches for her cup and stands with some difficulty, feeling unexercised muscles protest. She takes another sip of wine.

"I'll bet you miss having a cat," Mary says.

Lisha smiles. "Yes, a bit. Things are a lot cleaner now without the cat litter and furballs, but I do miss having a pet around. They seem to know exactly when you need somebody to caress."

"I'm allergic to animals," Bev complains. "Cats make me break out in hives."

"I've told you that you should get a bird," Mrs. O'Neill tells her.

"Birds are dirty," Bev grouses.

"Only if you don't clean their cages," Lisha tells her. "I had a parakeet when I was a kid. It was nice. I trained it to ride on my shoulder."

Suddenly, her beeper chimes at her. "Better check that," Mrs. O'Neill says.

Lisha pulls it off her belt and checks the screen. *Clients in revolt. Expect a call. Demand a hefty raise. You owe me dinner. Ginnie.*

Lisha looks up wordlessly. "Good news?" Mrs. O'Neill asks, accepting another cup of wine from Jackie. "Maybe that Sam found he needs you after all?"

Lisha stares at her. But the woman just brushes some popcorn crumbs off her housedress and smiles.

"Good," Mary says. "It would be a pity for Lisha to have to leave just when we were really getting to know her."

"You know," says Jackie, "that cat really took to you. Maybe you should adopt it."

"If you do, get it fixed," Norma says. "Too many wild cats around here."

Lisha looks at her neighbors. "Mrs. Golini won't let me have any pets," she says slowly.

"Maybe," Mrs. O'Neill says, "we can change her mind."

Take Sharon Lee's and Steve Miller's Liaden Universe. Add a bit of "popular wisdom" and a deep debt to "Mr. Peter Sellers and the cast of the wonderfully demented motion picture, 'What's New, Pussycat' for the image of the operatic Valkyrie leading the charge against the Forces of Darkness". The result is this fitting finale to our volume.

Naratha's Shadow
by Sharon Lee and Steve Miller

For every terror, a joy. For every sorrow, a pleasure. For every death, a life. This is Naratha's Law.

—from Creation Myths and Unmakings, A Study of Beginning and End.

"Take it away!" The Healer's voice was shrill.

The Scout leapt forward, slamming the lid of the stasis box down and triggering the seal in one smooth motion.

"Away it is," she said soothingly, as if she spoke to a child instead of a woman old in her art.

"Away it is *not*!" Master Healer Inomi snapped. Her face was pale. The Scout could hardly blame her. Even with the lid closed and the seal engaged, she could feel the emanation from her prize puzzle—a grating, sticky malevolence centered over and just above the eyes, like the beginnings of a ferocious headache. If the effect was that strong for her, who tested only moderately empathic as the Scouts rated such things, what must it feel like to the Healer, whose gift allowed her to experience another's emotions as her own?

The Scout bowed. "Master Healer, forgive me. Necessity exists. This…*object*, whatever it may be, has engaged my closest study for…"

"Take. It. Away." The Healer's voice shook, and her hand, when she raised it to point at the door. "Drop it into a black hole. Throw it into a sun. Introduce it into a nova. But, for the gods' sweet love, *take it away*!"

The solution to her puzzle would not be found by driving a Master Healer mad. The Scout bent, grabbed the strap and swung the box onto her back. The grating nastiness over her eyes intensified, and for a moment the room blurred out of focus. She blinked, her sight cleared, and she was moving, quick and silent, back bent under the weight of the thing, across the room and out the door. She passed down a hallway peculiarly empty of Healers, apprentices and patrons, and stepped out into the mid-day glare of Solcintra.

Even then, she did not moderate her pace, but strode on until she came to the groundcar she had requisitioned from Headquarters. Biting her lip, feeling her own face wet with sweat, she worked the cargo compartment's latch one-handed, dumped her burden unceremoniously inside and slammed the hatch home.

She walked away some little distance, wobbling, and came to rest on a street-side bench. Even at this distance, she could feel it—the thing in the box, whatever it was—though the headache was bearable now. She'd had the selfsame headache for the six relumma since she'd made her find, and was no closer to solving its riddle.

The Scout leaned back on the bench. "Montet sig'Norba," she told herself loudly, "you're a fool."

Well, and who but a fool walked away from the luxury and soft life of Liad to explore the dangerous galaxy as a Scout? Scouts very rarely lived out the full term of nature's allotted span—even those fortunate enough to never encounter a strange, impulse-powered, triple-heavy *some*thing in the back end of nowhere and tempt the fates doubly by taking it aboard.

Montet rested her head against the bench's high back. She'd achieved precious little glory as a Scout, glory arising as it did from the discovery of odd or lost or hidden knowledge.

Which surely the *some*thing must carry, whatever its original makers had intended it to incept or avert.

Yet, six relumma after what should have been the greatest find of her career, Montet sig'Norba was still unable to ascertain exactly what the something was.

"It may have been crafted to drive Healers to distraction," she murmured, closing her eyes briefly against the ever-present infelicity in her head.

There was a certain charm to Master Healer Inomi's instruction to drop the box into a black hole and have done, but gods curse it, the thing was an artifact! It had to do something!

Didn't it?

Montet sighed. She had performed the routine tests and then tests not quite so routine, branching out, with the help of an interested if slightly demented lab tech, into the bizarre. The tests stopped short of destruction; the tests, let it be known, had not so much as scratched the smooth black surface of the thing. Neither had they been any use in identifying the substance from which it was constructed. As to what it did or did not do…

Montet had combed, scoured and sieved the Scouts' not-inconsiderable technical archives. She'd plumbed the depths of archeology, scaled the heights of astronomy, and read more history than she would have thought possible, looking for a description, an allusion, a hint. All in vain.

Meanwhile, the thing ate through stasis boxes like a mouse through cheese. The headaches and disorienting effects were noticeably less when the thing was moved to a new box. Gradually, the effects worsened until even the demented lab tech—no empath, he—complained of his head aching and his sight jittering. At which time it was only prudent to remove the thing to another box and start the cycle again.

It was this observation of the working of the thing's…aura that had led her to investigate its possibilities as a carrier of disease. Her studies were, of course, inconclusive. If it carried disease, it was of a kind unknown to the Scouts' medical laboratory and to its library of case histories.

There are, however, other illnesses to which sentient beings may succumb. Which line of reasoning had immediately preceded her trip to Solcintra Healer Hall, stasis box in tow, to request an interview with Master Healer Inomi.

"And much profit you reaped from that adventure," Montet muttered, opening her eyes and straightening on the bench. Throw it into a sun, indeed!

For an instant, the headache flared, fragmenting her vision into a dazzle of too-bright color. Montet gasped, and that quickly the pain subsided, retreating to its familiar, wearisome ache.

She stood, fishing the car key out of her pocket. *Now what?* she asked herself. She'd exhausted all possible lines of research. No, check that. She'd exhausted all orderly and reasonable lines of research. There did remain one more place to look.

The Library of Legend was the largest of the several libraries maintained by the Liaden Scouts. The largest and the most ambiguous. Montet had never liked the place, even as a student Scout. Her antipathy had not escaped the notice of her teachers, who had found it wise to assign her long and tedious tracings of kernel-tales and seed-stories, so that she might become adequately acquainted with the Library's content.

Much as she had disliked those assignments, they achieved the desired goal. By the time she was pronounced ready to attempt her Solo, Montet was an agile and discerning researcher of legend, with an uncanny eye for the single true line buried in a page of obfuscation. After she passed her Solo, she opted for field duty, to the clear disappointment of at least one of her instructors, and forgot the Library of Legends in the freedom of the stars.

However, skills once learned are difficult to unlearn, especially for those who have survived Scout training. It took Montet all of three days to find the first hint of what her dubious treasure might be. A twelve-day after, she had the kernel-tale. Then it was cross-checking—triangulating, as it were—trying to match allegory to orbit, myth to historical fact. Detail work of the most demanding kind, requiring every nit of a Scout's attention for long hours at a time. Montet did not stint the task—that had never been her way—and the details absorbed her day after day, early to late.

Which would account for her forgetting to move the thing, whatever it was, from its old stasis-box into a new one.

"This is an alert! Situation Class One. Guards and emergency personnel to the main laboratory, caution extreme. Montet sig'Norba to the main laboratory. Repeat. This is an alert…"

Montet was already moving down the long aisle of the Legend Library, buckling her utility belt as she ran. The intercom repeated its message and began the third pass. Montet slapped the override button for the lift and jumped inside before the door was fully open.

Gods, the main lab. She'd left *it*, whatever it was, in the lab lock-box, which had become her custom when she and the tech had been doing their earnest best to crack the thing open and learn its inner workings. It should have been…safe…in the lab.

The lift doors opened and she was running down a hall full of security and catastrophe uniforms. She wove through the moving bodies of her comrades, not slackening speed, took a sharp right into the lab's hallway, twisted and dodged through an unexpectedly dense knot of people just standing there, got clear and stumbled, hands over her eyes.

"Aiee!"

The headache was a knife buried to the hilt in her forehead. Her knees hit the floor, the jar snapping her teeth shut on her tongue, but that pain was lost inside the greater agony in her head. She sobbed, fumbling for the simple mind-relaxing exercise that was the first thing taught anyone who aspired to be a Scout. She crouched there for a lifetime, finding the pattern and losing it, beginning again with forced, frantic patience. Finally, she found the concentration necessary, ran the sequence from beginning to end, felt the agony recede—sufficiently.

Shaking, she pushed herself to her feet and faced the open door of the lab.

It was then she remembered the stasis box and the madcap young tech's inclination toward explosives. "Gods, gods, gods…" She staggered, straightened and walked—knees rubbery, vision white at the edges—walked down the hall, through the open door.

The main room was trim as always, beakers and culture-plates washed and racked by size; tweezers, blades, droppers and other hand tools of a lab tech's trade hung neatly above each workbench. Montet went down the silent, orderly aisles, past the last workbench, where someone had started a flame on the burner and decanted some liquid into a beaker before discovering that everything was not quite as it should be and slipping out to call Security.

Montet paused to turn the flame down. Her head ached horribly, and her stomach was turning queasy. All praise to the gods of study, who had conspired to make her miss the mid-day meal.

The door to the secondary workroom was closed and refused to open to her palmprint. Montet reached into her utility belt, pulled out a flat thin square. The edges were firm enough to grip, the center viscous. Carefully, she pressed the jellified center over the lockplate's sensor and waited.

For a moment—two—nothing happened, then there was a soft *click* and a space showed between the edge of the door and the frame. Montet stepped aside, lay the spent jelly on the workbench behind her, got her fingers in the slender space and pushed. The door eased back, silent on well-maintained tracks. When the gap was wide enough, she slipped inside.

The room was dim, the air cool to the point of discomfort. Montet squinted, fighting her own chancy vision and the murkiness around her.

There: a dark blot, near the center of the room, which could only be a stasis box. Montet moved forward, through air that seemed to thicken with each step. Automatically her hand quested along her utility belt, locating the pin-light by touch. She slipped it out of its loop, touched the trigger—and swore.

The stasis box lay on its side in the beam, lid hanging open. Empty.

Montet swallowed another curse. In the silence, some-one moaned.

Beam before her, she went toward the sound and found the charmingly demented lab tech huddled on the floor next to the further wall, his arms folded over his head. She started toward him, checked and swung the beam wide.

The thing, whatever it was, was barely a dozen steps away, banked by many small boxes of the kind used to contain the explosive trimplix. The detonation of a single container of trimplix could hole a spaceship, and here were twelves of twelves of them stacked every-which-way against the thing.

"Kill it," the tech moaned behind her. "Trigger the trimplix. Make it *stop*."

Carefully, Montet put her light on the floor. Carefully, she went out to the main room, drew a fresh stasis box from stores and carried it back into the dimness. The tech had not moved, except perhaps to draw closer round himself.

It was nerve-wracking work to set the boxes of trimplix gently aside until she could get in close enough to grab the thing and heave it into the box. It hit bottom with a thump, and she slammed the lid down as if it were a live thing and likely to come bounding back out at her.

That done, she leaned over, gagging, then forced herself up and went over to the intercom to sound the all-clear.

Panopele settled her feet in the cool, dewy grass; filled her lungs with sweet midnight air; felt the power coalesce and burn in her belly, waking the twins, Joy and Terror. Again she drank the sweet, dark air, lungs expanding painfully, then raised her face to the firmament, opened her mouth—and sang.

Amplified by Naratha's Will, the song rose to the star-lanes: questing, questioning, challenging. Transported by the song, the essence of Panopele, Voice of Naratha, rose likewise to the star-lanes: broadening, blossoming, listening.

Attended by four of the elder novices, feet comforted by the cool grass, strong toes holding tight to the soil of Aelysia, the body of Panopele sang the Cycle down. Two of the attendant novices wept to hear her; two of the novices danced. The body of Panopele breathed and sang, sang and breathed. And sang.

Out among the star-lanes, enormous and aquiver with every note of the song, Panopele listened and heard no discord. Expanding even further, she opened what might be called her eyes, looked out along the scintillant fields of life and saw—a blot.

Faint it was—vastly distant from the planet where her body stood and sang, toes comfortably gripping the soil—and unmistakable in its menace. Panopele strained to see, to hear more clearly, hearing—or imagining she heard—the faintest note of discord, the barest whisper of malice.

Far below and laboring, her body sang on, voice sweeping out in pure waves of passion. The two novices who danced spun like mad things, sweat soaking their robes. The two who wept fell to their knees and struck their heads against the earth.

Panopele strained, stretching toward the edge of the song, the limit of Naratha's Will. The blot shimmered, growing, the malice of its answering song all at once plain.

Far below, the body of Panopele gasped, interrupting the song. The scintillance of the star-lanes paled into a blur; there was a rush of sound, un-song-like, and Panopele was joltingly aware of cold feet, laboring lungs, the drumbeat of her heart. Her throat hurt and she was thirsty.

A warm cloak was draped across her shoulders, clasped across her throat. Warm hands pressed her down into a chair. In her left ear the novice Fanor murmured, "I have water, Voice. Will you drink?"

Drink she would, and drink she did, the cool water a joy.

"Blessings on you," she rasped and lay her left hand over his heart in Naratha's full benediction. Fanor was one of the two who wept in the song.

"Voice." He looked away, as he always did, embarrassed by her notice.

"Will you rest here, Voice? Or return to the temple?" That was Lietta, who danced and was doubtless herself in need of rest.

Truth told, rest was what Panopele wanted. She was weary, drained as the song sometimes drained one, and dismayed in her heart. She wanted to sleep, here and now, among the dewy evening. To sleep, and awake believing that the blot she had detected was no more than a woman's fallible imagining.

The Voice of Naratha is not allowed the luxury of self-deceit. And the blot had been growing larger.

Weary, Panopele placed her hands on the carven arms of the chair and pushed herself onto her feet. "Let us return," she said to those who served her.

Lietta bowed and picked up the chair. Fanor bent to gather the remaining water jugs. Panopele stopped him with a gesture.

"One approaches," she told him. "You are swiftest. Run ahead and be ready to offer welcome."

One glance he dared, full into her eyes, then passed the jug he held to Dari and ran away across the starlit grass.

"So." Panopele motioned and Zan stepped forward to offer an arm, her face still wet with tears.

"My willing support, Voice," she said as ritual demanded, though her own voice was soft and troubled.

"Blessings on you," Panopele replied, and proceeded across the grass in Fanor's wake, leaning heavily upon the arm of her escort.

There was, of course, nothing resembling a spaceport on-world, and the only reason the place had escaped Interdiction, in Montet's opinion, was that no Scout had yet penetrated this far into the benighted outback of the galaxy. That the gentle agrarian planet below her could not possibly contain the technology necessary to unravel the puzzle of the thing sealed and seething in its stasis box, failed to delight her. Even the knowledge that she had deciphered legend with such skill that she had actually raised a planet at the coordinates she had half-intuited did not warm her.

Frowning, omnipresent ache centered over her eyes, Montet brought the Scout ship down. Her orbital scans had identified two large clusters of life and industry—cities, perhaps—and a third, smaller cluster, which nonetheless put forth more energy than either of its larger cousins.

Likely, it was a manufactory of some kind, Montet thought, and home of such technology as the planet might muster. She made it her first target, by no means inclined to believe it her last. She came to ground in a gold and green field a short distance from her target. She tended her utility belt while the hull cooled, then rolled out into a crisp, clear morning.

The target was just ahead, on the far side of a slight rise. Montet swung into a walk, the grass parting silently before her. She drew a deep lungful of fragrant air, verifying her scan's description of an atmosphere slightly lower in oxygen than Liad's. Checking her stride, she bounced, verifying the scan's assertion of a gravity field somewhat lighter than that generated by the homeworld.

Topping the rise, she looked down at the target, which was not a manufactory at all, but only a large building and various outbuildings clustered companionably together. To her right, fields were laid out. To her left, the grassland continued until it met a line of silvery trees, brilliant in the brilliant day. And of the source of the energy reported by her scans, there was no sign whatsoever.

Montet sighed gustily. *Legend.*

She went down the hill. Eventually, she came upon a path, which she followed until it abandoned her on the threshold of the larger building. Here she hesitated, every Scout nerve a-tingle, for this *should* be a Forbidden World, socially and technologically unprepared for the knowledge-stress that came riding in on the leather-clad shoulders of a Scout. She had no *business* walking up to the front door of the local hospital, library, temple or who-knew-what, no matter how desperate her difficulty. There was no one here who was the equal—who was the master—of the thing in her ship's hold. How could there be? She hovered on the edge of doing damage past counting. Better to return to her ship quickly, rise to orbit and get about setting the warning beacons.

And yet…the legends, she thought, and then all indecision was swept away, for the plain white wall she faced showed a crack, then a doorway, framing a man. His pale robe was rumpled, wet and stained with grass. His hair was dark and braided below his shoulders; the skin of his face and his hands were brown. His feet, beneath the stained, wet hem, were bare.

He was taller than she, and strongly built. She could not guess his age, beyond placing him in that nebulous region called "adult". He spoke; his voice was soft, his tone respectful. The language was tantalizingly close to a tongue she knew.

"God's day to you," she said, speaking slowly and plainly in that language. She showed her empty hands at waist level, palm up. "Has the house any comfort for a stranger?"

Surprise showed at the edges of the man's face. His hands rose, tracing a stylized pattern in the air at the height of his heart. "May Naratha's song fill your heart," he said, spacing his words as she had hers. It was not quite, Montet heard, the tongue she knew, but 'twould suffice.

"Naratha foretold your coming," the man continued. "The Voice will speak with you." He paused, hands moving through another pattern. "Of comfort, I cannot promise, stranger. I hear a dark chanting upon the air."

Well he might hear just that, Montet thought grimly, especially if he were a Healer-analog. Carefully, she inclined her head to the doorkeeper. "Gladly will I speak with the Voice of Naratha," she said.

The man turned and perforce she followed him, inside and across a wide, stone-floored hall to another plain white wall. He lay his hand against the wall and once again a door appeared. He stood aside, hands shaping the air. "The Voice awaits you." Montet squared her shoulders and walked forward.

The room, like the hall, was brightly lit, the shine of light along the white walls and floor adding to the misery of her headache. Deliberately, she used the Scout's mental relaxation drill and felt the headache inch, grudgingly, back. Montet sighed and blinked the room into focus.

"Be welcome into the House of Naratha." The voice was deep, resonant and achingly melodic, the words spaced so that they were instantly intelligible.

Montet turned, finding the speaker standing near a niche in the left-most wall.

The lady was tall and on a scale to dwarf the sturdy doorkeeper. A woman of abundance, shoulders proud and face serene. Her robe was divided vertically in half—one side white, one side black. Her hair was black, showing gray like stars in the vast deepness of space. Her face was like a moon, glowing; her eyes were black and insightful. She raised a hand and sketched a sign before her, the motion given meaning by the weight of her palm against the air.

"I am the Voice of Naratha. Say your name, Seeker."

Instinctively, Montet bowed. One *would* bow to such a lady as this—and one would not dare lie. "I am Montet sig'Norba," she said, hearing her own voice thin and reedy in comparison with the other's rich tones.

"Come forward, Montet sig'Norba."

Forward she went, until she stood her own short arm's reach from the Voice. She looked up and met the gaze of far-seeing black eyes.

"Yes," the Voice said after a long pause. "You bear the wounds we have been taught to look for."

Montet blinked. "Wounds?"

"Here," said the Voice and lay her massive palm against Montet's forehead, directly on the spot centered just above her eyes, where the pain had lived for six long relumma. The Voice's palm was warm and soft. Montet closed her eyes as heat spread up and over her scalp, soothing and—she opened her eyes in consternation.

The headache was gone.

The Voice was a Healer, then. Though the Healers on Liad had not been able to ease her pain.

"You have that which belongs to Naratha," the Voice said, removing her hand. "You may take me to it."

Montet bowed once more. "Lady, that which I carry is…" she grappled briefly with the idiom of the language she spoke, hoping it approximated the Voice's nearly enough for sense, and not too nearly for insult. "What I carry is…accursed of God. It vibrates evil and seeks destruction—even unto its own destruction. It is…I brought it before a…priestess of my own kind and its vibrations all but overcame her skill."

The Voice snorted. "A minor priestess, I judge. Still, she did well if you come to me at her word."

"Lady, her word was to make all haste to fling the monster into a sun."

"No!" The single syllable resonated deep in Montet's chest, informing, for a moment, the very rhythm of her heartbeat.

"No," repeated the Voice, more quietly. "To follow such a course would be to grant its every desire. To the despair of all things living."

"What *is* it?" Montet heard herself blurt.

The Voice bowed her head. "It is the Shadow of Naratha. For every great good throws a shadow which is, in its nature, great evil."

Raising her head, she took a breath and began, softly, to chant. "Of all who fought, it was Naratha who prevailed against the Enemy. Prevailed and drove the Enemy into the back beyond of space, from whence it has never again ventured. The shadows of Naratha's triumph, as terrible as the Enemy's defeat was glorious, roam the firmament still, destroying, for that is what they do." The Voice paused. The chant vibrated against the pure white walls for a moment, then stopped.

This, Montet thought, was the language of legend—hyperbole. Yet the woman before her did not seem a fanatic living in a smoky dream of reality. This woman was alive, intelligent—and infinitely sorrowful.

"Voices were trained," the Voice was now calmly factual, "to counteract the vibration of evil. We were chosen to sing, to hold against—and equalize—what slighter, less substantial folk cannot encompass. We were many, once. Now I am one. Naratha grant that the equation is exact."

Montet stared. She was a Liaden and accustomed to the demands of Balance. But this— "You will die? But, by your own saying, it wants just that!"

The Voice smiled. "I will not die, nor will it want destruction when the song is through." She tipped her massive head, hair rippling, black-and-gray, across her proud shoulders. "Those who travel between the stars see many wonders. I am the last Voice of Naratha. I exact a price, star-stranger."

Balance, clear enough. Montet bowed her head. "Say on."

"You will stand with me while I sing this monster down. You will watch and you will remember. Perhaps you have devices that record sight and sound. If you do, use them. When it is done, first bring the news to Lietta, First Novice, she who would have been Voice. Say to her that you are under geas to study in our library. When you have studied, I require you to return to the stars to discover what has happened…to the rest of us." She paused.

"You will bring what you find to this outpost. You will also initiate your fellow star-travelers into the mysteries of Naratha's Discord." The wonderful voice faltered and Montet bent her head.

"In the event," she said, softly, "that the equation is not entirely precise." She straightened. "I accept your Balance."

"So." said the Voice. "Take me now to that which is mine."

The Voice stood, humming, while Montet dragged the stasis box out, unsealed it and flipped open the lid. At a sign from the other woman, she tipped the box sideways, and the thing, whatever it was, rolled out onto the grass, buzzing angrily.

"I hear you, Discord," the Voice murmured, and raised her hand to sign.

Montet dropped back, triggering the three recorders with a touch to her utility belt.

The Voice began to sing. A phrase only, though the beauty of it pierced Montet, heart and soul.

The phrase ended and the space where it had hung was filled with the familiar malice of the black thing's song.

Serene, the Voice heard the answer out, then sang again, passion flowing forth like flame.

Again the thing answered, snarling in the space between Montet's ears. She gasped and looked to the Voice, but her face was as smooth and untroubled as glass.

Once more, the woman raised her voice, and it seemed to Montet that the air was richer, the grassland breeze fresher, than it had been a moment before.

This time, the thing did not allow her to finish but vibrated in earnest. Montet shrieked at the agony in her joints and fell to her knees, staring up at the Voice who sang on, weaving around and through the malice: stretching, reshaping, *reprogramming*, Montet thought just before her vision grayed and she could see no longer.

She could hear, though, even after the pain had flattened her face down in the grass. The song went on, never faltering, never heeding the heat that Montet felt rising from the brittling grass. Never straining, despite the taint in the once clean air.

The Voice hit a note—high, true and sweet. Montet's vision cleared. The Voice stood, legs braced, face turned toward the sky, her mighty throat corded with effort. The note continued, impossibly pure, soaring, passionate, irrefutable. There was only that note, that truth, and nothing more—in all the galaxy.

Montet took a breath and discovered that her lungs no longer burned. She moved an arm and discovered that she could rise.

The Voice sang on, and the day was brilliant, perfect, beyond perfect, into godlike, and the Voice herself was beauty incarnate, singing, singing, fading, becoming one with the sunlight, the grassland and the breeze.

Abruptly, there was silence, and Montet stood alone in the grasslands near her ship, hard by an empty stasis box.

Of the Voice of Naratha—of Naratha's Shadow—there was no sign at all.

About The Editor

Lee Martindale has been called a "warrior-bard", an apt description for a lady who "walks between the worlds" of size issues activism, science fiction, fantasy and filk.

Lee, who describes herself as "fat, 50 and fabulous", became involved in size acceptance in the early '80s when she used her bathroom scales for target practice and wrote the anti-diet song "Fat Lady Blues". In the mid-'80s, she began writing a column on "living a full-figured life in a small-minded world" for her local Mensa newsletter, which led to forming a local special interest group, then a national SIG. In 1992, she "took it to the streets" as the Founding Publisher/Editor of *Rump Parliament Magazine*, a nationally-recognized publication devoted to size issues activism.

Considered by many to be one of the leaders of the Size Rights Movement, Lee's work to include "weight or size" in existing civil rights laws frequently takes her in front of audiences of all kinds as a spirited voice for an end to weight discrimination. In 1996, a workshop she conducted for the Texas Convention of the National Organization for Women led to unanimous passage of a resolution calling for anti-discrimination law. Among other accomplishments: bringing International No Diet Day to the U.S. in 1993 and serving as the U.S. Coordinator for its first five years, and being called "not a nice person" by a certain tearfully ubiquitous weight loss guru.

Her career as a fantasy writer began in 1992 with the sale of "Yearbride" to the *Snows of Darkover* anthology edited by Marion Zimmer Bradley. Since then, she's sold stories to two volumes of *Sword and Sorceress, Pulp Eternity Magazine, XOddity, Zone 9,* and *MZB's Fantasy Magazine*. Two of them, "Neighborhood Watch" in *MZBFM*

#40 and "The Folly of Assumption" in *Pulp Eternity Magazine*, feature fat and feisty heroines, and the former was named to *Tangent Magazine's* "1998 Recommended Reading List".

A lifelong musician and songwriter, the move to filk was inevitable. In 1997, she collaborated with longtime friend R.L. West, Jr. and her husband George on *The Ladies of Trade Town*, a collection of thirteen original pieces honoring science fiction, fantasy, horror and bardcraft.

In her spare time, Lee is a member of the Society for Creative Anachronism, where she is Lady Llereth Wyddffa an Myrddin, an early Celtic bard, merchant and voice herald. She also enjoys attending SF&F cons, where she's earned a reputation as a popular and hardworking guest. She and George live in Plano, Texas.

For more information about *Rump Parliament Magazine*, the RP Catalog of size-positive slogan merchandise or *The Ladies of Trade Town*, visit

http://web2.airmail.net/lmartin

or write to:

Rump Parliament
PO Box 865137
Plano, TX 75086-5137

About The Authors

Celeste Allen, a native of Pittsburgh, PA, credits a "lucrative educational background of a bachelor's degree in Creative Writing with a minor in Ancient Civilizations" for her "work as a secretary, freelance writer and editor, occasional English teacher and missionary". She currently resides in the United Kingdom.

Martha A. Compton is a native East Texan currently residing in Dallas. She is employed in a state government land survey office and recently earned accreditation as a Registered Professional Land Surveyor. After hours, she is a watercolorist, occasional writer/traveler/dreamer/seeker/mischief-maker, connoisseur of margaritas (shaken and served on the rocks), member of the Society for Creative Anachronism and collector of antique maps. She has appeared in *Rump Parliament Magazine* as a writer, cover artist and photographer.

Marian Crane spends her days working as a designer and chief production assistant (sometimes referred to as "den momma") at one of the nation's biggest commercial art studios. Her own creative time is shared by silversmithing, computer graphics, her award- winning textile art and—oh, yes—writing.

Lisa Deason's short fiction has appeared in multiple volumes of *Sword and Sorceress* and *Marion Zimmer Bradley's Fantasy Magazine*. She is an active member of SFWA and, like Everybody Else, is working on a novel.

Paula L. Fleming pays the bills by working part-time as a management consultant. Other distractions from writing include the care and feeding of two big dogs, two cats and one husband. Her stories have appeared in *Tales of the Unanticipated*, as well as other print and electronic magazines.

Ralph Gamelli has some two-dozen small-press credits, including *Dead of Night, Vampire Dan's Story Emporium* and *Burning Sky*. This is his first appearance in an anthology. When not writing, Mr. Gamelli can be found "sweating in the gym, on the tennis court, or in front of the stock page."

Jon Hansen is an expatriate Southerner living in the Midwest. Since 1996 his short fiction and poetry has appeared in a variety of places, including *Marion Zimmer Bradley's Fantasy Magazine, Millennium SF, Dark Regions* and *Star*Line.* He also has made sales to *Aboriginal Science Fiction, Flesh and Blood* and *Pulp Eternity*. He currently lives in Cedar Falls, IA with his wife (whom he credits as being a "sensible influence") and three cats.

Carol Y. Huber was born in Boston, spent part of her youth in Chicago, and the rest in Plano, Texas where she currently resides. **Mike C. Baker** is a computer programmer, SCA participant and Bard who came to Dallas, Texas from Oklahoma. His previous publishing credits include wargame scenarios and numerous articles in *Rump Parliament Magazine*.

Barbara Krasnoff was born and raised in Brooklyn. She currently resides in Bay Ridge with her partner, Jim, several computers and endless piles of books. Since 1981 she has earned her living as an editor and writer for various computer publications. Her first fiction sale, "Signs of Life", was published in *Amazing Stories* and an anthology called *Memories and Visions: Women's Fantasy and Science Fiction.*

Sharon Lee and Steve Miller are the authors of the Liaden Universe novels *Conflict of Honors, Agent of Change, Carpe Diem* and *Plan B*, as well as recent short fiction in *Absolute Magnitude* and *Catfantastic V*. Steve was the founding curator of the University of Maryland Baltimore County Science Fiction Research Collection, and Sharon serves as Executive Director of the Science Fiction and Fantasy Writers of America. Born in Baltimore, they moved to Maine about ten years ago and live in an aging ranch style house with four cats and a large cast of characters.

Catherine Lundoff says that writing fiction changed her life and how she think about myself. Her short fiction sales include stories to *XOddity, Pulp Eternity, Cherished Blood, Taste of Midnight, Year's Best Lesbian Erotica 1999*, and *Electric: Best Lesbian Erotic Fiction.* She lives in Minneapolis with her "wonderful, supportive girlfriend and annoying kitties".

Cynthia McQuillin is well known in the SF&F community as a singer-songwriter, writer and frequent Guest of Honor at conventions all over the country. She's also a long-time size acceptance activist: a regular contributor to *Rump Parliament Magazine*, spokesmodel for the groundbreaking photobook *Women En Large* by Laurie Edison and Debbie Notkin, and creator of the stunning *This Heavy Heart*, a powerful collection of songs in the key of self-acceptance and self-esteem.

Jody Lynn Nye has authored twenty published science fiction and fantasy books, including the *Taylor's Ark, Mythology* and *Dreamland* series, as well as over fifty short stories, including one in each of Esther Friesner's three *Chicks* anthologies.

Teresa Noelle Roberts started writing "before I entered kindergarten" and has never stopped. Her poetry and fiction have appeared in numerous anthologies and literary magazines, including *Bellowing Ark, The Christian Science Monitor* ("a bit of a fluke", she says), *Cries of the Spirit* and anthologies from Crossing Press and Circlet Press.

Selina Rosen and "a few other masochists" run a small-press publishing house called Yard Dog Press, which "prints only truly odd stories and books". Her short stories have appeared in various magazines and anthologies, including *Sword and Sorceress 16*. *Queen of Denial*, her first novel, was published in May '99 by Meisha Merlin Publishing. *Chains of Freedom*, the first book of a trilogy, is due out from them in 2001.

Joette Rozanski trained as an accountant and a paralegal before discovering computers, the small press, and her current position as publications specialist for a non-profit organization. She spends her evenings writing fantasy and science fiction, her favorite genres.

Patrice Sarath has been a newspaper reporter, magazine editor, business and technology writer and, less glamorously, stablegirl and short order cook. She lives in Austin, Texas with her husband and two children.

Elizabeth Ann Scarborough is the author of twenty-three published novels, with four more in the works, and thirty-odd (very odd) short stories. Her novel of nursing in Viet Nam, *Healer's War*, won the 1989 Nebula Award.

Not too long ago, **Bradley H. Sinor** ran into a friend he hadn't seen for several years. The friend asked if Brad was still writing, to which Brad's wife Sue replied, "There's still a pulse. So he's still writing." His short fiction has appeared in the *Merovingen Nights* series, *Time Of The Vampires, On Crusade: More Tales Of The Knights Templar, Lord of the Fantastic: Stories In Tribute To Roger Zelazny, Horrors!: 365 Scary Stories*, and *Merlin.*

Laura J. Underwood has authored thirty-four short stories in the fantasy genre. Her work has appeared regularly in *Marion Zimmer Bradley's Fantasy Magazine, Adventures In Sword & Sorcery*, several volumes of *Sword and Sorceress*, as well as *Catfantastic, Vampire Dan's Story Emporium*, and *Bonetree.* Residing in East Tennessee, she is an avid hiker of the Great Smokey Mountains, a fair harper and a former fencing champion.

K.D. Wentworth got her start in the L. Ron Hubbard Writers of the Future Contest in 1988 and has since sold short fiction to such markets as *Aboriginal SF, Magazine of Fantasy & Science Fiction, Hitchcock's Mystery Magazine, Return to the Twilight Zone, Did You Say Chicks?!* and *Realms of Fantasy*. Two of her stories were Nebula Nominees: "Burning Bright" (*Aboriginal SF*, 1997) and "Tall One" (*F&SF*, 1998). She has also published four novels, the most recent being *Black/On/Black* from Baen. She resides in Tulsa, OK with her husband, numerous finches, a 126-lb. Akita, and a job as an elementary school teacher.

Connie Wilkins lives in western Massachusetts, where she co-owns two stores supplying the non-essential necessities of student life. Her stories have appeared in *Marion Zimmer Bradley's Fantasy Magazine* and the DAW anthology *Prom Night*, among others.

Gene Wolfe is the author of such works as *Operation Ares, The Fifth Head of Cerberus, Peace, The Devil In A Forest, The Book Of the New Sun*, and the recently-published *On Blue's Waters*, first book of the new *Book Of the Short Sun* trilogy. His work has won two Nebulas, three World Fantasy Awards, the British Science Fiction Award, the British Fantasy Award and, most recently, the Premio Italia for *The Urth of the New Sun.* His short fiction collections include *Storeys From The Old Hotel, Endangered Species*, and the newly-published *Strange Travelers.*

Come check out our web site for details on these Meisha Merlin authors!

http://www.MeishaMerlin.com

Kevin J. Anderson
Edo van Belkom
Janet Berliner
Storm Constantine
Diane Duane
Sylvia Engdahl
Jim Grimsley
George Guthridge
Keith Hartman
Beth Hilgartner
P. C. Hodgell
Tanya Huff
Janet Kagan
Caitlin R. Kiernan
Lee Killough
George R. R. Martin
Lee Martindale
Jack McDevitt
Sharon Lee & Steve Miller
James A. Moore
Adam Niswander
Andre Norton
Jody Lynn Nye
Selina Rosen
Kristine Kathryn Rusch
Michael Scott
S. P. Somtow
Allen Steele
Freda Warrington

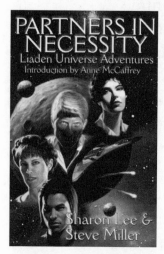

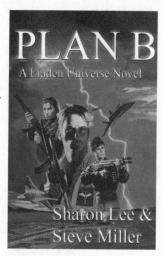